A KISS IN THE SHADOWS

Marie Patrick

Crimson Romance
New York   London   Toronto   Sydney   New Delhi

CRIMSON
ROMANCE
Crimson Romance
An Imprint of Simon & Schuster, Inc.
1230 Avenue of the Americas
New York, NY 10020

For information about special discounts for bulk purchases, please contact Simon & Schuster Special Sales at 1-866-506-1949 or business@ simonandschuster.com.

The Simon & Schuster Speakers Bureau can bring authors to your live event. For more information or to book an event contact the Simon & Schuster Speakers Bureau at 1-866-248-3049 or visit our website at www. simonspeakers.com.

ISBN: 978-1-4405-9493-9
ISBN: 978-1-4405-9491-5 (ebook)

*To my beta readers, Jan Walkosz and Paige Wood,
thank you so much for taking the time to read through my
manuscript and for giving me your valuable insight.
I appreciate you both more than you know.*

*To Jess Verdi, editor extraordinaire, for helping me
make this the best story it could possibly be.*

*To Lexi and Ann, my critique partners, for holding my hand
and encouraging me every step of the way.*

*And lastly, to my husband for being my hero, for always
supporting this passion of mine, for... everything!*

Chapter 1

New Mexico 1885

Stephanie Raelene Buchanan, Stevie Rae to those who knew and loved her, slouched in her chair in the corner of Hagan's Saloon and watched the room darken as Brock MacDermott opened the batwing doors, his broad shoulders blocking the sunlight. A hush settled over the occupants as all eyes turned toward him. Even the piano player missed a few keystrokes in his rendition of "Camptown Races," which didn't seem to make much difference.

"Brock, honey!" A woman straightened against the long mahogany bar running the length of the room, feathers fluttering from a twist in her flaming red hair. She pulled the strap of her maroon and black gown back up her shoulder, patting the attached silk flower for good measure, then directed her attention to the man behind the bar. "Winston, whiskey for Mr. MacDermott."

No smile graced Brock's face as he took careful measure of each and every person in the room. Stevie Rae held her breath as his gray glare fell upon her then released it when his gaze drifted on to the next person. Seemingly satisfied, he sauntered into the saloon as if he hadn't a care in the world and yet, she knew better. He had a loose-hipped gait, but she could see the tension in him—his eyes darted from one side of the room to the other. Did he expect trouble? Here in Little River? In Hagan's Saloon?

Well, of course, he does. He probably expects trouble everywhere he goes.

"Pepper," he said, acknowledging the woman now rushing across the floor, a glass of whiskey in one hand, the bottle in the other. He pulled his hat from his head, revealing a wealth of dark hair with just a touch of gray at the temples. He removed his dark brown duster and laid it across an empty chair, then took a seat at a small table with a long, drawn-out sigh. Pepper placed his glass as well as the bottle in front of him. "Thanks."

Stevie Rae continued to watch from beneath the brim of her hat, fascinated by everything about him—the way he moved, the dark stubble on his face, and the tightness of the black shirt stretched across his wide chest. He was more handsome than she'd remembered him to be and his voice…well, his voice was something straight out of heaven.

She shook herself and clamped her lips together tighter to ignore the heat bubbling in her stomach.

He took a drink, tipping the glass back until all the liquid was gone, his Adam's apple bobbing as he swallowed. He slid the glass onto the table, then ran his fingers through his hair before pouring himself another shot of Pepper's whiskey.

She didn't know him personally, had never met him, but she'd seen him before and knew *of* him. From Denver, Colorado, to Albuquerque, New Mexico, and all places in between, everyone knew of the bounty hunter Brock MacDermott. His reputation, at least. No one could claim to know the man behind the reputation. Speculation abounded. Some said he was a former military man. Others said he'd been a lawman in Texas. Or it could have been Colorado. Maybe Arizona.

No one in Little River seemed to know. He'd shown up one day a little over a year ago, bringing three outlaws to Sheriff Hardy, and had been back a few times since, but he never stayed long… only long enough to collect his money, send a couple of telegrams, have a drink, and perhaps a little tumble with one of Ruby's girls, before he left again.

Rumor had it he always got his man…except for one…the same man Stevie Rae hunted. Zeb Logan. Thief. Cattle rustler. Bank robber. Murderer. No, cold-blooded murderer. Thinking about the man who had changed her life made her heart hurt all over again.

Stevie Rae took a sip of the whiskey in front of her and turned her attention back to Brock MacDermott. She hadn't seen him in over six months, not until earlier today when she saw him ride into town with Hank "The Gun" Simms tied to the saddle of the horse behind him just moments after she had arrived in town empty-handed once again. Zeb Logan proved to be elusive prey, though she'd searched for him throughout the mountains and valleys of northern New Mexico—heading out several times in the four months since he'd killed her father.

She decided then and there she'd offer to ride along with him in his pursuit of Logan. Two heads were bound to be better than one when it came to the outlaw. She didn't even want the bounty on the man. She just wanted her revenge for the senseless killing of her father. Now, all she had to do was work up the nerve.

She took a deep breath, mentally preparing what she would say, but a flash of color and the glint of metal grabbed her attention as Tripp Simms pushed through the batwing doors, his pistol pointed directly at Brock. She recognized him immediately from the poster hanging in the sheriff's office.

"Ya got no cause to be lockin' up my brother, MacDermott!" His words were slurred, as if he'd found false courage in a bottle of whiskey. The gun shook in his hand, but his eyes were focused and intent upon the bounty hunter.

"You don't want to be doing this, Simms." Brock didn't move, didn't look away from the man ready to take his life. "Put your gun back in the holster and walk away. We'll forget this ever happened."

"The hell I will!" Tripp pulled the trigger. The shot went wild and glass tinkled to the floor as the bullet shattered the mirror behind the bar.

Before she could draw her father's army-issue Colt revolver, Brock jumped from his seat, his chair clattering to the floor behind him. In one smooth motion, his pistol cleared leather and a bullet left the chamber with a poof of smoke and a sharp report that made her ears ring. The dark-haired man coming through the batwing doors didn't have time to clutch at the blood staining his filthy shirt before he crumpled to the floor, the revolver still in his hand. No one had time to scream. Or dive for cover. Or anything else. It was over before it had begun.

Lane Coswell, the faro dealer, tugged down the edges of his silver brocade vest and inspected the damage to the man on the floor. He whistled low and turned his attention to Brock. "Mighty fancy shootin' there, MacDermott. He's dead."

Brock said nothing as he slipped his Peacemaker back into its holster and approached the body. He crouched down and inspected the dead man just as the faro dealer had. "Ah, hell, Tripp, why'd you have to do that?" he asked, his voice harsh, his disappointment and regret clear. He turned to Pepper. "Sorry about the mess, Pepper. I'll notify both Sheriff Hardy and the undertaker, but you might want to cover him up until Digger gets here."

He adjusted his hat on his head and grabbed his coat, then without another word, left the saloon.

Stevie Rae finished her whiskey in one swallow, tugged at the waistband of her trousers, and adjusted her hat, making sure her eyes were shielded from the midday sun before she followed him. Once outside, she pulled the edges of her cream-colored duster closer together against the sudden chill the day had taken despite the steady stream of sunlight.

It wasn't that long ago when she'd trodden this same sidewalk, her hand firmly in her father's as they picked up supplies from Garrity's General Store, then later, her hand tucked into the crook of Lucas's elbow as they made plans for their future.

How quickly it all had changed.

In the space of a heartbeat, whatever plans she had made for her future were gone. Her father was now buried beside her mother in Little River's cemetery. Lucas had broken their engagement and left town, unable and unwilling to understand her determination to see justice done.

And Logan? The man responsible for all the changes in her life? The man whose image was burned into her brain?

He remained free. But he wouldn't be for long. She promised herself he wouldn't. She'd ridden out several times in search of him—once with Sheriff Hardy's posse and the rest alone—but each time she returned without him.

Stevie Rae inhaled deeply and let the memories dissipate with her exhale. Her gaze drifted from Brock MacDermott's wide shoulders, broad back, and perfectly rounded backside to the dress on display in the window of Mrs. Manville's dress shop.

It was still there—the dress she had been saving up to buy for her wedding to Lucas. No one had purchased it yet. She had the money now. The crisp bills folded neatly in her pocket from the sale of the last things she could sell, including her father's horse, were more than enough to pay for the dress, but why should she bother? Lucas was gone. There would be no wedding.

And if she were truthful, when would she ever have opportunity to wear a dress like that? Besides, the money was needed to buy supplies so she could head out again.

She shook her head, freeing herself of her thoughts, but continued to stare at the dress, hope springing eternal in her heart. From the corner of her eye, she watched Brock step into the undertaker's place of business.

MacDermott wasn't inside the building long. He paused outside the door for a moment, hands resting on his hips, staring at…well, she didn't know what he stared at, but he sure was intent upon it, whatever it was. After a moment longer, he stepped off the sidewalk and into the street.

"Mr. MacDermott," she called out as she, too, stepped into the street. He stopped and turned. Stevie took a deep breath to calm the pounding of her heart in her chest and swallowed. Her mouth suddenly dry as dust, she approached him. Her voice still came out hoarse. "Can I talk to you?" This close to him, she realized he was taller than she first thought and broader, yet she detected an inherent kindness in his face. "I saw what happened."

The dark slash of his eyebrow rose over one eye, seeming to disappear beneath the hat pulled low on his forehead. "And?"

"Tripp Simms drew on you. It was a righteous kill. I can tell Sheriff Hardy," she said in a rush. She shifted her weight from one leg to the other, then licked her dry lips. "I saw you bring in his brother earlier."

"Is that so?"

Weariness settled on his face in the fine lines that radiated from the corners of his clear gray eyes and in the firm set of his mouth. She understood that weariness. She lived with it each and every day, like an unwelcome guest who refused to leave.

"Thanks for your kind offer, but I don't need your help." He turned and strode away, heading toward the sheriff's office, his long legs eating up the distance and churning up dust in the dirt road.

Stevie Rae raced after him, jumping up to the wooden sidewalk beside him. "I wasn't done."

"But I was," he said simply, then entered the sheriff's office, leaving her standing in stunned silence, her mouth open. She took a deep breath and debated her options. She could rush inside and make a nuisance of herself—she was pretty good at that—or she could wait for him here. Deciding that it wouldn't help her cause to interrupt the man now, she folded her arms across her chest and took a seat in the rocking chair on the sidewalk to wait.

The people of Little River nodded toward her as they went about their business. Some smiled at her and truly meant it when they wished her a good afternoon. Some didn't mean it at all and after saying hello, turned to their companions, no doubt to whisper in hushed tones about the death of her father. Or about Lucas, the man who had proclaimed to love her, breaking their engagement and leaving town. Even her best friend had abandoned her. Edie Sinclair wouldn't look at her now, let alone talk to her. Like Lucas, Edie didn't agree with the path Stevie Rae had chosen to take.

Uncomfortable beneath the scrutiny, she lowered the brim of her beat-up hat even more, swallowed over the lump growing in her throat, and tried to let their comments and remarks flow off her back. They couldn't understand what drove her now. No one could. Except, maybe, Brock MacDermott.

She rose from her seat, unwilling to face any more well-meaning and not-so-well-meaning townspeople, and tramped to the door. It swung open just as she reached for the doorknob. Brock stepped over the threshold, followed closely by Sheriff Hardy.

The sheriff acknowledged her presence with a quick nod in her direction before he adjusted the gun belt slung low on his hips, stepped off the sidewalk, and headed toward Hagan's Saloon. He met up with Henry Barstow, the undertaker, who had earned the unfortunate nickname of Digger many years ago, on the other side of the street.

"Mr. MacDermott, I still need to talk to you." She stepped in front of him, for the moment barring his passage. He could easily slide around her or simply push her out of the way, but she didn't think he would.

"You again." He didn't seem angry, just annoyed by her persistence. "All right. You have two minutes."

Now that she had his attention, she didn't quite know where to start. She licked her dry lips again and blurted out, "We are after the same man, Mr. MacDermott. I thought, maybe, we could do it together. Two heads are better than one in the hunt for Zeb Logan."

He didn't look at her. His gaze went to the street, to the people walking along the sidewalk on the other side, his impatience clear as he folded his arms across his chest. "Look, kid, I'm a busy man. I don't have time for this."

"I may look young, but I assure you, I'm no kid."

His gaze swung back to her and focused, his eyes sharp shards of granite as they took in her appearance from the crown of her hat to the boots on her feet and back again. His lips tightened a bit more before he drew in his breath. "Yes, I can see that now, but that doesn't change the facts. Zeb Logan is a vicious criminal—"

"You're not telling me something I don't already know." She'd never be rid of the image of Logan shooting her father while she remained hidden in the root cellar, peeking through the floorboards of their little cabin, unable to move. It had been a senseless killing, with no rhyme or reason except that Logan had seemed to get a certain sick satisfaction from it.

"Sorry, kid. I can't help you."

"Why not? We could be a help to each other."

A muscle jumped in his cheek as his jaw clenched. After a moment, he drew air through his nose and released it slowly through his mouth. "I work alone. By myself. Singular. That means no company, no one traveling beside me. I can't be worrying about someone else, especially a girl, when I'm after someone as violent as Logan."

"You wouldn't have to worry about me. I can take care of myself."

He took a step back, his eyes peering deeply into hers. A long sigh whispered between his lips. Stevie Rae watched him as carefully as he watched her. He was wavering, mulling it over, but perhaps it was all wishful thinking. "Go home, kid. Go back to your mama and daddy. Bounty hunting isn't for the likes of you."

"I can't go home, Mr. MacDermott. I haven't got one anymore. Mr. Rendell at the bank took it." The words brought not only a lump to her throat, but the sharp sting of tears to her eyes. She blinked quickly, hoping he wouldn't see, and berated herself for her lack of control.

Understanding dawned. She could see it in the subtle flickering of his eyes, but he still shook his head. "I'm sorry, but my answer is still the same. I work alone, and bounty hunting is no business for a girl."

He moved past her, stepping into the street, heading back toward the saloon with his loose-hipped gait. Stevie Rae swiped at her tear-filled eyes and drew air into her lungs. Anger surged through her. She had lost this battle, but she wasn't ready to give up. She'd find Zeb Logan, with or without Brock MacDermott's help.

I ain't down yet. Not by a long shot.

Stevie Rae adjusted the collar of her coat and brought the dirty bandanna around her neck up to cover her mouth as a bitterly frigid wind swept down from the mountain and swirled between the buildings lining Little River's main street, whipping the grains of sand into stinging pellets that needled the face and hands and anything that wasn't covered. Shadows deepened as the sun disappeared behind quickly moving black clouds and the smell of rain hung heavy. She glanced toward the east and Hagan's Saloon. MacDermott was in there, having another drink, probably getting warm and cozy with Rosie or one of Pepper's other girls while she stood out here in the freezing wind.

It wasn't in her nature to give up, but she could fall back and regroup, at least until morning. She doubted MacDermott would be leaving Little River before the sun rose. If he followed his pattern from other visits, he'd be here two or three days.

Stevie Rae headed south, but not to the little cabin on the mountainside that had been her home for the past two years. Instead, she turned the corner at the barbershop and continued until Martha Prichard's rooming house came into view. Right before Martha's house was the one she'd grown up in. Someone else lived in it now, loved in it. She blinked back the sting of tears and forced herself to look straight ahead.

Lights glowed in Martha's windows, a welcome sight to someone who had been sleeping on the ground and eating jerky for weeks. Stevie Rae trudged toward that golden glow—her haven since Mr. Rendell at the bank had hung his eviction notice on the door to her father's cabin two months ago—knowing Martha would have a hot meal, a warm bed, and a loving embrace for her. Martha had been trying to take care of her since her mother passed on twelve years ago, honoring the dying wish of a dear friend. Stevie Rae hadn't made it easy.

She climbed the stairs to the front door, weary and heartsore, and reached for the bellpull. Before her hand could twist the knob, she turned to scan her surroundings, a habit she'd picked up recently, and noticed the clumps of dirt left on the wooden planks by her boots. As tired as she was, she wouldn't drag dirt into Martha's clean house and across the beautiful rugs that had come from as far away as New York. She hopped down to the street just as the promised rain came down, not in a gentle mist, but in a deluge as if the clouds above simply split apart. The street around her darkened as if night had fallen though it was still late afternoon. Now, not only was she cold, dirty, and tired, she was wet, too.

She cast her gaze heavenward as she headed toward the kitchen at the back of the house and sighed. "Let me guess. You don't like what I'm doing, either, do you?"

Removing her wet, muddy boots, she placed them side by side beneath the chair on the back porch then knocked, remembering to remove her hat before the kitchen door flung open. Martha stood on the threshold, drying her hands on a dish towel, and peered into the darkness the sudden rain had brought.

"Stevie Rae?"

"Yes, ma'am."

"Land sakes, child! Why didn't you come to the front door?" Martha pulled her inside.

"Come in before you catch your death," she said, then mumbled something about common sense and turnips, but Stevie Rae didn't quite catch it.

She stilled the sudden twitching at the corners of her mouth and remained where she was, unwilling to move any farther into the kitchen, although the heat from the oven felt wonderful as it started to steal the chill from her bones. "I didn't want to be draggin' mud into your house and gettin' everything wet."

An eyebrow rose over one of the woman's warm brown eyes and her hands rested on her ample hips. Color highlighted her cheeks. "Your language is atrocious, young lady, as is your attire. And just look at that rats' nest you call hair." Martha *tsked* several times while she shook her head, then, despite Stevie Rae's current wet, filthy state, pulled her into the warm embrace she'd been craving since she rode into town this morning. "Just because you've decided to hunt for a madman doesn't mean you can't be a lady like your mother taught you."

The absurdity of the statement struck Stevie Rae but she resisted the urge to laugh. Dressed for ease of riding in men's clothing that hadn't seen the benefit of soap and water in weeks, her hair knotted and gnarled after being tucked up beneath her hat for days on end, she hardly looked like the lady her mother had so wanted her to be. She could try once more to let Martha know she was only doing this until Zeb Logan died for his crimes, but the statement would be ignored, as it had been before. Instead, she murmured, "Yes, ma'am. I'm sorry."

"That's better. I bet you're hungry."

"Yes, ma'am. Starved."

"Before you eat, though, I think a nice hot bath is just what the doctor ordered. Come along." She grabbed Stevie Rae's hand and pulled her through the kitchen then down a long hallway toward the bathroom.

Stevie Rae had no choice but to follow. And truthfully, she didn't mind. Having deprived herself of such a luxury for a while, she would adore a long soak in steaming hot water, the smell of honeysuckle soap heavy in the vapor. Washing up in the various cold-water creeks each morning had had to suffice for far too long.

More than an hour later, after she bathed, dragged a comb through her mass of tangled blond hair, donned clean clothes she'd rummaged from her saddlebag, and eaten her fill of Martha's Yankee pot roast, Stevie Rae leaned back in her seat as Martha poured her another cup of coffee and slid into the seat across from her. "Dan stopped by while you were soaking away weeks of dirt," she said, the affection she held for the sheriff clear in the tone of her voice. "He told me Brock MacDermott came into town today. You still planning on asking to go with him when he rides out again?"

"Yes, ma'am." She didn't mention she'd already spoken to the man and he denied her request. It didn't matter. As frightening as it was, she'd continue to ride out alone, although that just seemed to be like asking for trouble, especially since she couldn't hit anything she aimed at with her father's Colt. Thankfully, she had the shotgun. Even if she didn't hit her mark, the buckshot could do quite a bit of damage.

Martha sighed and her forehead wrinkled with worry. "I so wish you weren't bent on this course, Stevie Rae. I promised your sainted mother I'd keep you safe."

Stevie Rae said nothing. She took a sip of coffee and studied the woman who had been more of a mother to her than her own had been. Raelene Buchanan had been sickly for as long as she could remember and Martha—dear, sweet Martha—had done the best she could to take care of Stevie Rae when Raelene couldn't. Even when her father, Steven, had given up his medical practice, sold the little house in town, and mortgaged everything to buy

Poor Man's Dream, the gold mine that never produced, Martha had tried to keep Stevie Rae close. And she'd succeeded.

"I thought we agreed not to talk about this. You know—"

"Yes, I know. If it's the last thing you do, you're going to see Zeb Logan die for what he did," Martha said, repeating the phrase as well as the promise she knew by heart. "I just…there has to be a better way." She reached out and grabbed Stevie Rae's hand. "Let the law do it, honey. Men like Dan and Brock MacDermott. They're used to dealing with vicious men. You're not. This isn't a job for you."

Stevie Rae snatched her hand away and shot up from her seat. She glared at the woman, tears of frustration welling in her eyes. There were words building in her chest, words she so wanted to say, and yet not one could squeeze past the lump in her throat.

"Now, don't get in a lather and go running off like you always do. You know I'm right." The older woman heaved a sigh, one of disappointment and heartache. "If your mother…"

Finally, she found her voice. "It's not fair bringing Mama into this argument. She would do the same as me."

"Would she?" Martha shook her head. "I don't think so. Not the Raelene Buchanan I knew. You know I loved her like a sister, but your mother would never do what you're doing. She placed great importance on being a lady, no matter what the circumstances."

"Being a lady does not mean being helpless."

Martha continued as if she hadn't been interrupted. "No, it does not, but she wasn't as strong as you, Stevie Rae, didn't have your stubbornness. She liked being pampered and coddled. Indulged. And your father—"

Stevie Rae swiped at the tears in her eyes with the heels of her hands and swallowed the words in her throat as well as the lump. She took a deep breath and gazed at the woman who always offered comfort when she needed it most…except now. "I love you, Martha, but I can't let you say anything more about Mama and Daddy. I can't listen to it. I'm going to bed. I'll be gone in the morning."

The woman gave a regal nod of her head and drew in her breath, letting it leave her in a sigh. She folded her hands on the tabletop as a frown settled on her face. The warmth glowing in her light brown eyes never dulled though.

"Good night, Martha. And thank you."

"For what?"

"Everything, but mostly for loving me." Despite her heartache, she leaned over and gave Martha a kiss on the cheek before heading up to the attic and the small, comfortable space she'd created for herself beneath the eaves. The mattress on the floor as well as the cocoon of thick blankets beckoned. Exhausted, weary down to her bones, Stevie Rae didn't change out of the clean clothes she'd donned after her bath. She just crawled beneath the covers, drawing the heavy blankets up to her chin. The wind howled just outside the building and rain pounded on the roof. The sounds acted like a lullaby and sang her to sleep.

• • •

Dan Hardy tucked the report into a folder and shoved it in the drawer of his desk. From another drawer he pulled out a bottle of whiskey and two glasses, then grinned at Brock. "Now that that's done, you up for a game of chess? I haven't touched the board since your last visit." He gestured to the small table in the corner, the chess pieces, carved from ivory, glowing dully in the lamplight. "As I recall, I had your queen on the run."

"Sure." Brock rose from his seat beside the desk and ambled over to the chessboard. He wasn't in the mood for a game of chess—his mind was on other things—but he settled in the chair anyway. Dan was a good man and a good sheriff. A warm friendship had developed between them, and truthfully, a game of chess, especially at this hour of the night, might be exactly what he needed. The sheriff joined him at the table, poured whiskey into both glasses, and handed him one. "To your health," he said as he raised his glass high and took a drink, finishing the two fingers of finely distilled liquor in one swallow. Brock did the same, the whiskey burning its way to settle in a warm pool in his stomach.

While Dan studied the chessboard laid out before him, Brock's gaze swept over the Wanted posters tacked to the wall. One was missing from the last time he was here. Hank "The Gun" Simms, the man he'd brought in earlier today. Wanted for cattle rustling, the outlaw was now safely locked behind the steel bars in Dan's jail, lying on his bunk. His gaze slid to the other posters then stopped. Zeb Logan's ugly mug and black eyes stared back at him. Instantly, the hair on his arms rose as a cold chill skittered up his back.

Hatred, pure and simple, simmered in his gut as he continued to stare, willing the ink on the paper to give up the depicted one's secrets even though he knew that would never happen. "A couple of months ago, someone told me Logan had a hideout in the Sangre de Cristos." He gestured toward the outlaw's ugly face. "Any truth to that?"

Dan followed his line of sight then shrugged. "If there's a hideout, I've never found it, but then, I've never looked for it, either. I've never, not once, laid my eyes on the man, Brock. Couldn't tell you if that picture is accurate or if Logan has horns coming out the sides of his head." His gaze swung back to Brock then the chessboard. His fingers settled on his knight, and he started to move it forward then changed his mind. A long sigh escaped him as he studied the board then moved that same knight again. "You might want to talk to Stevie Rae Buchanan though."

"Stevie Rae?"

The sheriff nodded, poured them both another drink, then fished half a cigar from his shirt pocket. "You should go up to

Poor Man's Dream and take a look around," he said as he lit the cigar and waved away the blue-gray smoke in front of his face.

"Poor Man's Dream?"

"Gold mine. Steven Buchanan's gold mine." Hardy raised his glass, saluted Brock, then swallowed the fiery brew in one gulp. He wiped his mouth with the back of his hand. "Or was. Doc Buchanan's dead. After he dug the bullets out of Logan's leg and shoulder, Logan killed him."

Brock stiffened, every muscle in his body taut and thrumming, and he almost shot out of his chair. "Logan was here? When?"

Dan shook his head and scrubbed his hand over his face, his gaze focused on the black and white squares of the chessboard and the pieces still available for play. "Couple of months ago."

"Why the hell didn't you tell me when I first rode into town?"

The man shrugged. "Thought you knew."

Anger surged through him. A couple of months ago. Hell. If he *had* known…

He forced himself to take a deep breath then another, tamping down the inclination to throttle the man in front of him and race up to Poor Man's Dream right now. But what would he see in the dark with the rain coming down as if the sky were pissing after a night of drinking? He glanced at the clock on the wall ticking away the minutes. Morning was just a few hours away. He could wait. In the meantime, he'd find out what he could from Hardy. "How do you know all this?"

"Buchanan's daughter, Stevie Rae." Dan leaned back in his chair. The expression on his face revealed nothing, but intelligence and knowledge gleamed from his dark brown eyes. "She saw the whole thing. Rode with me when I took out a posse after she reported her father's death, but we never found Logan. She's been looking ever since. Against my wishes, I might add."

Was Stevie Rae the woman who had approached him in the street, asking if she could ride with him? She must have been—the deep blue of her eyes had flashed with the sadness and anger of one who knew the pain of losing someone to violence. He felt a twinge of contrition for his rudeness, but he meant what he said. He rode alone. Still, he should make certain.

He shook his head to clear it. "You believe her?"

"Of course. I have no reason not to. I've known that girl all her life. She's many things, but a liar isn't one of them."

"Tell me everything."

Sheriff Hardy stretched out his long legs and crossed his ankles, the pieces on the chessboard forgotten for the moment. Smoke rose to the ceiling as he stuck the cigar's wet end between his lips. He inhaled then exhaled quickly, taking his time, squinting his eyes as he studied the curling wisps of vapor in front of his face.

The slowness, the deliberate bid for time, stretched Brock's patience to its limit. After a moment or two, when he could no longer tolerate the growing silence, Brock opened his mouth, but never had the opportunity to say a word.

"Talk to Stevie Rae." Dan didn't remove the cigar from between his lips when he finally started talking. He simply spoke around it. "But in the meantime, I'll tell you what I know."

Chapter 2

As Brock traveled the road leading out of town, he drew in a deep breath, trying to relieve some of his tension, but it didn't help. Tired didn't begin to describe the weariness, the sadness, that lived deep within his bones. One thing and one thing only kept him in the saddle and on the trail of Zeb Logan. Revenge. Simple. Sweet. All-consuming. And if he could bring in other lawbreakers while he was searching, all the better.

But his heart ached…constantly.

Too much sorrow.

Too much death, by Logan's hand as well as his own.

His thoughts flew to Kieran, as they did so often.

The oldest of the MacDermott boys, the most peace-loving of the bunch, Kieran had been an excellent marksman, with both pistols and long-range rifles. He could shoot the ace out of the middle of a playing card with deadly accuracy, and he won medals every year at the county fair from the time he was ten years old.

His years of practice hadn't helped him when Logan came at him with guns blazing—surprise on his side as he burst through the door of Whispering Pines—and shot Kieran dead-center in the heart. Brock hadn't had time to even react as Logan turned, the bore of the revolver still smoking, and shot Mary and Matthew, both in the head, the echo of the blasts deafening in the front parlor of the ranch house. Then he trained his weapon on Desi Lyn, Kieran's two-year-old daughter. Without a thought, Brock had thrown himself over his niece just as Logan pulled the trigger three more times in quick succession. The bullets found their mark—two in his back and one in his shoulder—and Brock's world had gone dark while Desi Lyn screamed beneath his sheltering body.

He remembered opening his eyes and seeing the colors of a gaily embroidered pillowcase on the bed where he lay on his stomach. Pain had held him captive, but he had forced himself to turn his head. His brother Teague sat beside him in a rocking chair, keeping vigil, one arm in a sling, the other holding Desi Lyn, her pretty little face blotched with red spots from the tears she had cried. Brock had cried his own tears when Teague told him about his brother Eamon, who lay in the next room, recovering from his own wounds—Tell Logan, Zeb's brother, had nearly killed him.

It had taken a long time to heal. Months before he felt like himself, and the only thing that helped him was the promise he'd made to himself, his brothers, and his niece. He would find Zeb Logan, no matter how long it took or what the pursuit did to him.

And the chase did affect him. He'd become bitter. And solitary. Whiskey did nothing to diminish the pain of losing Kieran, except leave him with a sour stomach and a pounding head. Nor had time dulled the loss of his brother's wife, Mary, or their son, Matthew. Their sweet faces haunted him when he closed his eyes. Hell, even with his eyes wide open, he could see them. Eighteen months after their passing, guilt for his part in their deaths continued to eat at him, day by day.

He added one more name to his list of those who died around him…or because of him. Tripp Simms. He hadn't planned to kill Tripp, hadn't even known the man was in the vicinity of Little River when he captured Hank until the man walked into the saloon. He should have known, though. Hank and Tripp were as close as he and his brothers had been.

And now he had another reason to feel guilt. He'd been downright rude to someone who had suffered just as he had. He shouldn't have been so dismissive of the young woman who had approached him on the street, offering to ride with him until Zeb Logan no longer caused anyone else heartache. Remorse for his rudeness trickled through him, but the truth was, he worked alone. He didn't want to be responsible for someone else while he was on the trail of a dangerous criminal. He needed no reminder of what could happen. Those images and memories, like the physical scars from the bullet wounds on his shoulder and back, were with him all the time, never letting him forget the part he played.

Brock nudged Resolute with his knees and tugged on the reins, turning his mount up the rutted mountain path Sheriff Hardy had told him about. A wide stream rippled alongside the trail, flowing swiftly from the rain last night. Sunlight dappled the dark dirt beneath Resolute's hooves. Birds chirped and flitted from Ponderosa pine to aspen to cottonwood.

Halfway up the mountain, he saw a clearing and a gaping hole hewn into the mountainside—Poor Man's Dream, he assumed. To the left, a cabin with a steep roof, a sight familiar in this part of New Mexico. The steepness assisted in keeping the snow from staying on the roof and causing the roof to collapse. Two rocking chairs kept company on the front porch.

A golden palomino stood in front of the structure, her reins loosely wrapped around the porch railing. Beside the palomino, a mule waited, weighed down with a bulging soft-sided valise, a worn leather satchel, bedroll, and assorted burlap sacks.

Brock took in his surroundings, his gaze passing over the entrance to the gold mine. Buchanan must have had a wry sense of humor, naming his gold mine such a thing.

Dismounting, he tied Resolute's reins to a nearby tree.

"What are you doing here?"

Brock turned and faced the voice coming from the doorway of the small cabin. It was her, the young woman who had approached him on the street, the one he'd so rudely dismissed.

"Miss Buchanan?"

She didn't answer, just stood there staring at him, her mouth set in a grim line.

He eyed the Winchester shotgun in her hand. He didn't know if she could use the weapon, but why should he take the chance of finding out? Even if she wasn't a crack shot, she wouldn't miss him…some of the buckshot would surely catch a body part he might need later. "Are you Stevie Rae Buchanan?" he asked again, just to be certain.

She wasn't wearing the beat-up hat now, which made it so much easier to see her features harden. She squinted in his direction, but before she did, her eyes seemed to grow darker and glitter with dangerous intent. The finger caressing the trigger of the gun tightened just a bit. If the situation weren't so serious, he'd laugh because he'd managed, just by showing up, to make her angry.

Her chest rose and fell beneath the threadbare shirt and light duster she wore. Dark trousers fit her like a second skin, showing off her long, shapely legs and slim waist. "I'm her." Those eyes of hers narrowed as she stepped out of the doorway and drew closer to him, her boots loud on the wooden planks before she jumped to the dirt. "I asked what you were doing here."

Sunlight glinted off her dark blond hair, showing various shades from spun gold to dark honey. He could plainly see the smudges of dirt on her face and the color of her eyes, which were nearly sapphire, but brighter. He let out his breath in a sigh. At least her finger wasn't teasing the trigger of the shotgun anymore.

"Dan Hardy told me about you. About what happened." He watched her as she drew closer, saw the stiffness come over her as if she drew into herself. One look at her told him how much she suffered from her tragedy, and the last thing he wanted to do was make her relive the torment of losing her father. Yet he needed to know what she knew. "I wanted to ask you a few questions about…that night."

"And why should I help you?" The expression on her face betrayed nothing, but her tone spoke of grief and anger. He knew that grief, that anger. Both emotions sustained him when he didn't think he could face another day. He supposed those emotions sustained her as well. "You weren't exactly friendly when I approached you in town."

What could he say? He'd been an arrogant ass, but in his own defense, he had been just a little busy. He'd killed Tripp Simms only moments before. He tipped his hat now. "I'd like to apologize for that. I'm not usually… I didn't know who you were, didn't—"

She cut him off. "Save it, MacDermott. I ain't got time for your excuses. I'm busy."

"I understand," he said but didn't move to climb back on his horse. Instead, they stood only a few feet apart. A stalemate, as it were, like the chess pieces he and Sheriff Hardy had moved about the board last night. She had information he needed and he would be a horse's ass if he didn't try one more time to glean it from her.

"You're not going to leave, are you?"

He said nothing, but his gaze never left her face. He took in the fine lines around her mouth as her lips pressed together in annoyance, but his gaze kept roaming back to her eyes. They were beautiful. Such a fine color…and so shiny with the tears he believed she kept at bay. A moment passed. Then two. Resolute's tail swatted flies, hitting him in the back as it did so. He didn't move. Hell, he hardly dared to breathe.

"Fine. I'll tell you what I know." She threw her shoulders back, then turned and stomped toward the sagging front porch. "You might as well come in and have a cup of coffee."

Stevie Rae didn't wait for him. She hopped up on the porch and entered the house. Brock wasted no time in following her— she could change her mind if he didn't move quickly and he didn't want that.

He noticed the paper nailed to the door, announcing that the property would be auctioned off for non-payment of the mortgage as he removed his hat and ducked beneath the door frame. Despite the ramshackle appearance of the cabin's outside, the inside was remarkably cozy, clean, and bigger than he expected. She gestured to a chair then swept past him and grabbed another cup and the coffeepot. She filled his cup and refreshed her own. "Hope you like it black. I ain't got—" She winced and began again. "I'm sorry, but there's no milk or sugar."

Brock waited until she took her seat then dropped his hat on the table and slid into the chair opposite her. His eyes once more roamed her face as he waited for her to speak. She wasn't nearly as young as he'd originally thought. When she approached him in the street with her hat pulled low on her head, he assumed she'd been sixteen or seventeen, but now he knew he'd been mistaken. Or perhaps it was the weariness on her face that made her appear older—twenty-four or twenty-five, just a few years younger than himself. He took a sip of his coffee, which was surprisingly good, and continued watching her. She opened her mouth several times, but no words came forth. She swallowed, then drew a deep breath as she pushed out of her chair and began to pace the small confines of the cabin.

"This is harder than I thought." Her voice came out in a little whisper. "I haven't spoken of that night since…that night."

"Take your time." Brock wanted to comfort her somehow— soothe away some of her hurt—and yet he had the distinct feeling this woman would rather face a sack full of rattlesnakes than allow him to offer sympathy.

She nodded before slumping into the chair once more. Another deep breath moved her chest beneath the threadbare shirt he assumed was once blue, but now was so faded, he couldn't be sure. "A little more than four months ago, Zeb Logan came to this cabin and changed my life. He had a bullet in his leg and one in his shoulder. Daddy saw him ride up, but he didn't like the looks of him so he made me hide in the root cellar." She gestured to the trapdoor in the floor, partially hidden by a small throw rug that hid some of the bloodstains as well. "They didn't speak while Daddy fixed him up." She spoke matter-of-factly with hardly a hitch in her breath, but he could see the tears shimmering in her eyes.

The recollection pained her. He commiserated. He knew how painful it was to bring up hurtful memories. He fought that particular demon all the time, and against his will, his heart ached for her. "Once he was patched up, he killed my father. Just shot him where he stood, the bloody bandages still in Daddy's hand. Then Logan laughed and rummaged through my father's pockets like he had the right." She swallowed and an unusual sound issued from her throat, a sorrowful mix of anger, hurt, and regret. "I...I couldn't do anything. I was trapped in the root cellar, Daddy's..."

Again, she paused, the long column of her throat moving as she swallowed hard. Her eyes glittered and her lips tightened. "I saw everything but couldn't do anything. He stood right there and killed my father." Her voice was hoarse, but filled with anger. "I didn't even know who he was until I went to fetch Sheriff Hardy and saw Logan's Wanted poster hanging on the wall. Recognized him right away. Wanted to kill him right away, too, but I didn't know where he'd gone after he...after what he did to my father."

She must feel guilty for remaining hidden, even though it seemed like she hadn't had a choice. Did rage carry her and keep her from falling into a million little pieces like it did him? "You've been looking for him ever since."

She lowered her head, her shimmering blond locks falling into her face, but she never admitted or denied his statement. When she glanced up at him again, it was with steely determination.

Brock took a deep breath and tried not to let her heartbreak affect him. "What are you doing up here now? I thought you said the bank..."

"I couldn't leave town without this." She drew a pocket watch from her pocket, the gold glinting as it rocked back and forth on the small watch fob. He saw engraving on the back but couldn't read it before she pressed a button, opening the cover to reveal the clock face and a picture of a woman. "My mother," she said as she showed him.

"She's lovely. Where is she now? Will you be going to her?"

"She's gone, Mr. MacDermott. She died twelve years ago."

"I'm sorry."

She waved away his sentiment like it didn't matter, but he could see the truth written clearly on her features. Stevie Rae's mother might have passed twelve years ago, but time hadn't lessened the sorrow.

"I heard Logan might have a hideout somewhere in the mountains."

His statement drew her attention and she sat up straighter. "I hadn't heard that. You wouldn't happen to know where, would you?"

Brock shook his head and almost chuckled as fresh hope eased the tenseness of her features. "If I knew, we wouldn't be sitting here right now. Logan would be in jail."

She said nothing for the longest time then finally, "I know these mountains. If he has a hideout, I could find it."

Brock pushed the tin cup toward her and rose to his feet. "Thank you for your time and the coffee. I know this was hard for you, and I truly am sorry for your loss. For all your losses."

"That's it?" Stevie Rae rose as well, her body stiff, her eyes flashing.

"What do you mean?"

"I tell you everything and then you leave? What about me? I thought—" Anger sharpened her tone.

"You thought what?"

"I thought…you wanted my help. I…" Her words trailed off and he knew what she thought—that he would take her up on her offer to ride with him to bring Logan in.

Such sorrow radiated from her, he almost had a change of heart, but common sense and his own set of rules prevailed. He worked alone and needed to keep it that way. "I did. You answered my questions. Told me what I needed to know."

She drew a deep breath, her tall, lithe body tense with anger, then moved away from him to grab the coffeepot and dump the remains over the coals in the little Ben Franklin stove, her movements stiff. The red coals hissed and popped, sending steam into the air.

"I'm sorry." The words sounded hollow and useless to his own ears.

"Go to hell." She didn't turn to look at him as she said the words, simply wiped out the coffeepot with a rag then tossed the metal container into the sink with a bang. She stood with her back to him, her hands clenching the edge of the porcelain.

Brock grabbed his hat and jammed it on his head. He glanced at her and his mouth opened, but another apology would be useless. She didn't want to hear it, and he supposed he wouldn't want to hear it either. He closed his mouth and strode to the door, but lingered for a moment. For reasons he couldn't explain, he didn't want to leave her this way. Yet, if he didn't, he might change his mind and allow her to accompany him. He couldn't do that. Zeb Logan was a dangerous man, and Brock couldn't be responsible for another human being.

He had failed before. The memory haunted him.

With a sigh, he slipped through the doorway without a word and sauntered across the dirt yard to where Resolute waited. Untying the reins and grabbing the pommel, Brock pulled himself into the saddle. Tension bristled along his spine, and the fine hairs at the back of his neck rose. He turned slightly to see Stevie Rae standing in the doorway, the coffeepot and two tin cups in her hands, her lips pressed tightly together. Her hat, once more on her head, shadowed her face but couldn't hide the murder in her eyes. He nodded once, then nudged Resolute with his knees and rode off.

. . .

Stevie Rae drew in a deep, ragged breath as Brock MacDermott rode away. Hurt simmered within her, filling her heart. When he first rode into the little yard in front of the cabin, she thought he'd changed his mind and they'd hunt Logan together. She shouldn't have allowed herself that small seed of hope, for now the sorrow, which had become her constant companion over the past four months, doubled, the pain almost paralyzing her.

She drew a deep breath and glanced south, catching glimpses of MacDermott between the trees. He sat tall in the saddle, his broad back straight as his hands gently held the reins. Anger washed over her, a much better friend than the sorrow, and one she knew well.

"This ain't over, MacDermott!" Stevie Rae snarled.

Jumping to the dirt yard, Stevie Rae stuffed the coffeepot and tin cups into one of the sacks Whiskey Pete carried on his back, then hopped up onto the porch once more. Tears shimmered in her eyes despite her best efforts to keep them tamped down, blurring everything as she took one last look at the cozy confines of the cabin and slowly closed the door.

She wouldn't be coming back here, not for a long time. If ever. She'd been happy here, but now, a touch of evil seemed to permeate her home. She couldn't stay very long without that malevolence seeping into her bones and making her sick to her stomach.

Attaching Whiskey Pete's reins to the back of Willow's saddle, Stevie climbed onto the worn leather, fitted her feet into the stirrups, and nudged the horse's side. She'd say good-bye to Martha and Sheriff Hardy before continuing her hunt, but she would not turn around and look at the little cabin. Keeping her eyes straight ahead, she rode toward town.

Chapter 3

"Hello the camp."

Brock recognized her voice right away and let out his breath, the tension in his body easing. He uncocked his pistol but kept the pearl-handled revolver in his hand. One moment more, if she hadn't called out, he'd have snuck behind the big boulder and gotten the drop on her. He didn't like being followed, and he knew he had been almost as soon as he left Little River. He just hadn't realized it had been Stevie Rae. He should have known, though, should have realized when he left her at the cabin she wouldn't be far behind, though he had told her unequivocally he worked alone. "Come."

She approached from the direction of the stream running beside his campsite, leading the pretty palomino and the mule by the reins, the last rays of the fading sun illuminating her figure, wisps of flyaway blond hair visible beneath the brim of her hat. Those soulful blue eyes of hers pinned him, and something in his chest, around the region of his heart, seemed to soften. He slid the pistol into its holster and placed his hands on his hips.

"You again." He shook his head and resisted the urge to chuckle. "I will say this for you, kid...you are persistent."

She said nothing as she tied the horse's reins to a low-hanging branch beside his mount then did the same for the mule.

"Thought I told you I work alone."

"You did."

"Then what part of 'I work alone' didn't you understand?"

She didn't answer his question. Instead, she said, "I know all about you, Mr. MacDermott."

Startled by her statement, he lifted his head a bit and studied her from beneath the brim of his hat, his hands on his hips. "No, you don't, kid. No one does." He couldn't hide the plaintive note

Chasing after a wanted killer was not what a woman should be doing. She was young—and beautiful. She should be dancing and socializing, flirting with young men like other women her age. Or married with a passel of children hanging on her skirts. She should be dressed like a lady instead of in the tight-fitting buckskin trousers and faded shirt she wore, wearing fancy hats instead of the beat-up one perched on her head, her blond hair curled into bouncing ringlets.

And for a split second in time, with the scent of honeysuckle and pine all around him, he saw her that way, her arms around him as they danced a waltz, the bell of her skirts brushing against his legs as they swirled around the dance floor. He even felt the softness of her velvet gown beneath his fingers, the softness of *her* as he held her close.

Startled by the image in his head, he blinked and finally tore his gaze away from her. *Where in the hell did that come from?*

"I was just about to make something for supper." He needed a distraction, any distraction, and food was as good as any other.

"Let me." She turned away from him then, her long ponytail curling down her back, and strode to the pack mule. Untying one of the sacks from the mule's back, she proceeded to pull out two cast-iron skillets, several tins, two little sacks, and a small white paper package tied with string. "I'll prove to you that taking me along won't be a hardship."

Brock said nothing as he leaned against one of the boulders that made up his campsite and watched as she set to work, her movements methodical and efficient. She untied the white string holding the paper package together and began to cut up chunks of smoked beef into one of the skillets with a knife she pulled from her pocket. Opening one of the tin cans, she dumped the vegetables on top of the beef and placed the pan on the coals.

Stevie Rae remained silent as she worked. He stayed silent, too, as he watched, fascinated by the economy of her movements.

A lock of honey blond hair slipped from beneath her hat and dangled in her face, wavering in the breeze. Brock had a sudden impulse to tuck that errant tress behind her ear, but he forced himself to remain against the rock.

Into the other skillet, she dumped a tin can of sliced apples in a brown syrup, added what he thought was oatmeal and several other ingredients, and mixed it well before placing the lid on top and resting the pan on the hot coals of the fire. His gaze remained on her as she placed some of the coals on top of the skillet's lid using a pair of tongs she'd pulled from the sack, before she turned her attention back to the other pan, the contents of which had started to bubble merrily. And she made a fresh pot of coffee, too, dumping the last of the bitter stuff he made.

After a while, the smell of food tickled the emptiness in his belly, tempting him to move closer to the fire.

"It's ready."

He didn't waste any time. Darkness shrouded the campsite, the glow of the fire the only light. He sat next to her and they shared the beef stew from the same skillet. He'd been prepared to eat a tin of cold beans, but this was too good to interrupt with talking, although, in truth, he never spoke much anyway. And the apple concoction? Her version of apple cobbler left his mouth filled with the tart sweetness and just a taste of cinnamon.

In fact, the meal filled the hole in his stomach quite nicely. Perhaps having her along wouldn't be the worst thing that could happen.

• • •

As Stevie Rae cleaned the skillets and put them away, she smiled a little to herself. The first part of her plan had gone wonderfully, although for a moment or two, when she first approached him, she thought he'd shoot first and ask questions later.

She removed the bedroll from Whiskey Pete's back, untied the strings holding it together, then smoothed the heavy blankets on the ground near the fire before settling on top of them with a sigh. Sitting with her legs crossed, she removed her hat and pulled the leather strap holding her hair back. She finger-combed the long, curling mass into some semblance of order—all under his intent stare.

What is he thinking?

Finally, his gaze left her and he placed several more logs on the fire. She couldn't quite take her eyes from him as he stretched out on his own bedroll, his back propped up against his saddle. When she first saw him, she thought he was handsome. Now, as he sat across from her, the firelight dancing on his stern features, she revised her opinion. Yes, he was quite possibly the most handsome man she'd ever seen, bar none—not even Lucas matched the granite set of his features nor his piercing eyes—but there was more to him than just good looks.

She asked herself what drove him. What made him ride from town to town in search of one man?

He didn't speak as he pulled a pipe and pouch of tobacco from his saddlebag and tamped the tobacco into the bowl. Taking a small stick from the fire, the end burning brightly, he touched the flame to the tobacco and puffed the pipe alight. The aroma of the fine blend mixed with the pervasive scent of the pine trees and the wood smoke of the fire brought a memory she didn't want. Her father had smoked a pipe. It had been a constant part of Steven Buchanan, clenched between his teeth more often than not. The aroma of the tobacco permeated everything he owned. Even when money was tight, he always made sure he had a pouch of tobacco. She still had the meerschaum pipe wrapped in a square of burlap tucked it into her saddlebag along with his pocket watch, the only things left of the man who had loved her unconditionally.

She cleared her throat, swallowing against the sudden, unbidden lump rising there. "You don't talk much, do you?"

"Got nothing to say." Smoke wreathed his head and his teeth clamped harder on the stem of the pipe.

She ignored his terse reply and asked, "Why do you hunt Zeb Logan? What did he do to you?"

"That's my business, don't you think?"

"I told you what he did to me." Though her tone was flat, she couldn't help the hopefulness that had snuck into it.

He stared at her, the firelight reflecting on his face, and his eyes, those sharp shards of granite, glittered. With pain? With sadness? After a few minutes of silence, he removed the pipe from his mouth and said, "Let's just say he needs to be brought to justice."

"So that's it? You have nothing personal at stake here? You just want to collect the bounty and nothing more?"

The pipe stem went back in mouth, his jaw tightening as he clamped the stem between his teeth once more. He fished a silver flask from his saddlebag, started to unscrew the top, but changed his mind and put it back. Through it all, his intent stare never left her face. Finally, after what seemed like hours instead of minutes, when Stevie Rae began to squirm under the scrutiny of that glare, he said, "Look, kid, it's none of your business if I'm here to collect a bounty or why I want him. Just be thankful I'm letting you tag along."

She said nothing, but she could have-- the words were just sitting on the tip of her tongue. She should be thankful? Heck, she didn't need him. She could just as easily find Logan on her own. Yet, she hadn't been able to for the past four months, four long months. Then again, Stevie pondered, Brock hadn't been able to find the man in more time than that.

"I suggest you get some sleep. Tomorrow will be a long day."

Stevie Rae removed her boots and crawled between the blankets, not because he suggested it, but because she was tired.

Brock dumped the ashes from his pipe into the hot coals of the fire and tucked the pipe into his saddlebag. She didn't say good night, simply turned on her side and closed her eyes, but she heard him settle down into his own bedroll on the other side of the fire and she let out an easy breath for the first time in months.

Chapter 4

Have I lost my ever-loving mind?

Not for the first time, the question chased through Brock's brain.

He hadn't slept…at least, he hadn't slept for very long or very well. The nightmare, the one that had haunted him for eighteen long months, but which had blessedly been absent for the better part of a week, chose this night to disturb him once again. This time, though, instead of seeing his sister-in-law's face, he saw Stevie Rae's, her marvelous blue eyes wide open but unseeing, just as Mary's had been.

He'd woken with a start and a curse on his lips and hadn't been able to go back to sleep—didn't want to go back to sleep and chance seeing that awful image once again. He cracked open one eye and studied Stevie Rae wrapped in blankets, sleeping on the other side of the campfire, which had long since dwindled to glowing coals.

What had possessed him to say she could accompany him? What about her made him break his rules? She had valid reasons for wanting to go after Logan, and granted, she was a heck of a cook, but letting her accompany him was a bad idea all around. Hunting a man as dangerous and unpredictable as Zeb Logan wasn't a job for a woman, especially not *that* woman, and the last thing he needed or wanted was to be responsible for another person's safety. He had failed once. And once was more than enough.

He rolled onto his back. The moon, big and beautiful, seemed to hang suspended over the edge of the earth to the west. To the east, the faint glimmer of daylight marked the coming of a new day.

He had perhaps another thirty minutes or so before dawn broke. Better to leave her now rather than later.

Decision made, he moved with the silence of a cat, slipped out of his bedroll, and pulled on his boots after shaking them out to make sure nothing had crawled into them while he slept, then quickly rolled up his blankets and attached them to the saddle that had served as his pillow for the night. He grabbed the coffeepot from the rocks surrounding the fire pit, dumped the dregs of the coffee, then tucked the pot between the blankets of his bedroll. With an economy of motion, he lifted the saddle, placed it on the horse's back, adjusted the cinches, and glanced behind him.

Stevie Rae hadn't awakened to catch him in the act of leaving.

The blankets covered her up to her neck, leaving her head exposed, her silky blond hair shimmering in the glow of fading moonlight. She slept peacefully, her face, the little bit he could see through the heavy fall of her hair, serene and lovely.

He whispered an apology as he untied Resolute's reins and led the horse away from the camp, knowing the thick carpet of pine needles on the ground would muffle any sound.

Brock MacDermott had never considered himself a coward, but as he settled himself in the saddle, the truth emerged—perhaps he was becoming one. Why else would he have snuck out of camp without waking her? He'd faced scores of dangerous men—men who would kill rather than look at him—and never once had he been afraid. But he just couldn't face Stevie Rae Buchanan. He didn't want to see tears fill her eyes when he told her he'd changed his mind. Did that make him a coward? Possibly.

• • •

The twittering of birds woke Stevie Rae from a sound sleep, the best one she'd had in months. She opened her eyes and stared at the canopy of tree limbs over her head, then stretched, ready to find Zeb Logan and end his miserable life.

Aside from the birdsong, the camp was eerily quiet. She rolled to her side and scanned her surroundings.

Damn!

He'd left her.

As she sprang to her feet, the blankets tumbled to the ground, and the chill of morning touched her through her clothing. She whirled around in the direction of the horses and heaved a sigh of relief. Willow and Whiskey Pete were still there, reins tied to the low branch, but his horse was gone. In fact, looking around, there was no proof MacDermott had been there at all. Even the fire had died to nothing but ash.

"Son of a…biscuit eater!" The birds scattered and Whiskey Pete brayed at the sound of her voice. "If he thinks I'm giving up, he's mistaken."

She glanced around the empty camp one more time, torn between the desire to cry and the desire to punch MacDermott in the belly. The longing to do him bodily harm won out. She took a deep breath through gritted teeth, shook out her boots, then stuffed her feet into them and gathered up the blankets of her bedroll, securing the heavy quilts to Whiskey Pete's back. Within minutes, without the benefit of coffee, without even bothering to wash her face, brush her teeth, or empty her full bladder, she climbed into Willow's saddle and nudged his sides with her knees. She'd find MacDermott and give him a piece of her mind and then…then she'd find Zeb Logan without his help.

Not knowing which direction he'd taken—he could have headed back to Little River, but that was unlikely—she headed toward the stream and turned north. It's the way she would have gone and made complete sense to her. Whether or not *he* had that sense remained to be seen. Willow's hooves splashing up water, Whiskey Pete's plaintive braying disrupting the peace of the morning, she rode deeper into the Sangre de Cristo Mountains.

Stevie Rae had always loved these mountains, especially this time of year. Though April had brought warmer weather, patches of snow still remained on the ground. Tender shoots of green burst through the covering of white—new grass and flowers growing beneath the snow. In another few weeks, the landscape would be teeming with color as those flowers bloomed, and yet, at this moment, she hardly noticed. And she cared even less. Her thoughts were focused on one thing—well, two things—first finding MacDermott so she could give him a piece of her mind, then finding Logan.

A rustling in the trees drew her attention and she tugged on the reins, bringing her horse to a halt. Was it the wind stirring the sweeping branches of the pine trees? Or something else? Her mouth went dry and she shivered beneath the duster she wore as she studied her surroundings.

There were bears here. And mountain lions, too. Once, long ago, when she assisted her father as he practiced medicine, Stevie Rae had seen what a mountain lion could do to a man, if he survived the attack. She'd never forgotten, nor did she ever want to see that again.

Every muscle in her body tense, her eyes focused on her surroundings, she reached for the shotgun resting in its fitted slot on the saddle.

Willow shifted nervously beneath her. Did she smell something? Sense something in the air? She glanced at Whiskey Pete behind her, but the mule seemed unconcerned. His ears twitched, but that was all. Her gaze returned to the forest of trees, the path ahead of her, and the possibility something lurked within the shadows of the branches.

How long she stayed in this position, muscles taut and slightly trembling, shotgun resting in her arms, she had no idea. Time didn't seem to matter as she heard the distinct yowl of a puma on the prowl. She only hoped he wasn't on the prowl for her.

Or for MacDermott. Both of them—as well as their traveling companions—would make a tasty meal.

Another snarl startled her and she tensed even more, but willed herself to stay still. She squeezed her knees against Willow's body, signaling the horse to stay still as well. No sense in drawing attention to themselves. Movement would just make them an easier target for the big cat.

In the mountains, sound traveled and became deceptive and she couldn't tell from which direction the cougar hunted, but his yowls seemed to be moving farther away from her. Stevie Rae let out her breath in a huff. She wouldn't be the predator's breakfast, at least not yet, but her unease stayed with her. Moving the rifle onto her lap, she urged Willow forward.

Ah, Stevie Rae, what in blue blazes do you think you're doing sitting out here in the wilderness, easy pickings for bears and mountain lions? How stupid can you be to chase after a man who doesn't want you around to find another man who doesn't want to be found? The thoughts rambled through her head, followed by uncertainty and doubt. *Maybe MacDermott is right. Maybe I should just go home, try to get on with my life, and let the law bring Logan in.*

Her vision blurred as unwanted tears filled her eyes and a ragged breath caught in her throat. Once again, she tightened her knees and brought Willow to a halt, struck by indecision and an overwhelming sense of…despondency. She could go back to Little River, but why? She no longer had a home there. With both her father and Lucas gone, she had no future and no one to love her except Martha and Dan. And until she settled the score with Logan, she'd have no life at all.

She slid the shotgun into its fitted slot and stared unseeing at the horizon in front of her as the tears she fought so hard to repress seeped from her eyes to wet her face. Her throat constricted to the point that she could hardly breathe. Searing pain seized her heart as she tried to draw a breath. She dismounted, afraid she'd lose her balance and fall if she didn't and staggered to the stream burbling merrily down the mountain. She fell to the ground on her hands and knees at the brook's edge, tossed her hat to the side, and plunged her entire head into the cold liquid, screaming her frustration and despair into the swiftly flowing water, until there were no words left, no air in her lungs. Pulling her head from the stream, she sputtered and gasped from the frigid bite of the water, then sat back on her heels, her hair dripping onto her duster to wet it as well as her shirt beneath. She gazed upward through the drops of water clinging to her lashes. Big, puffy clouds dotted the dazzling blue sky.

"What should I do, Daddy?" she asked, her throat raw.

No response came from the heavens, no voice telling her what she should do, just the birds chirping from the trees, but clarity rocked her to her core just the same. The pain receded and her indecision cleared into one thought. *Never give up.* And yet, fear still jangled her nerves.

Stevie Rae drew a deep breath, then another, and slowly rose to her feet. She swiped at the water on her face, relieved that tears no longer blurred her vision as she grabbed her hat and plopped it on her head. Her heart no longer hurt, at least not with the clenching pain of moments ago. Instead, the resolve she'd come to depend on filled her once more.

She stumbled back to Willow, exhausted from the turmoil that had claimed her. She rubbed the horse's nose, then climbed into the saddle, nudged the horse with her knees, and continued onward.

By the time Stevie Rae smelled the acrid scent of a campfire and saw the wisps of gray smoke rising upward between the trees, her hair was dry and her emotions were in full control. Except for the anger, the sweet blessed anger that sustained her when nothing else did. She tugged lightly on Willow's reins and turned in that direction, Whiskey Pete bringing up the rear, and for once, silent. She saw the flames of his fire first—and then she saw *him*, dropping an armload of wood beside the ring of rocks making up the fire pit.

She rode into his camp without announcing her presence. "Did you think it would be that easy to get rid of me?"

"You again." Resignation, not anger, colored his voice as he glanced in her direction. His eyes lingered on her for a moment before he carefully placed a small log on the fire, allowing it to catch flame, then rose to his full height.

Stevie Rae slid from the saddle and advanced on him, stopping less than a foot from his broad chest. Her hands clenched at her sides and her heart thundered in her chest. The desire she'd felt earlier to do him bodily harm made her breath catch in her throat, but she denied herself the pleasure of punching him in the belly. "Did you think I wouldn't find you? Just because you backtracked and went in circles to throw me off your trail? I was still able to hunt you down, MacDermott." Anger simmered a little bit hotter. "Was it more important to lose me than find Logan?" Her entire body shook as she uttered the words through barely parted lips, her eyes never leaving his face. "Well, no need to worry on that account. I won't be bothering you anymore. I no longer need your assistance…and I wouldn't ride with you if you were the last man on earth."

Having said her piece, she turned and stalked back the way she'd come, grabbed the pommel of Willow's saddle, and nearly vaulted into her seat. She glared at him, the heat of her anger keeping her warm despite the chill in his eyes. "Stay out of my way, MacDermott. I may shoot you by mistake, but then again, maybe it wouldn't be a mistake."

She nudged Willow's sides and rode off, Whiskey Pete making his displeasure known with his high-pitched *hee-haw* as he followed behind.

I don't need him. I can do this on my own. The words careened around her mind as she followed the bend of the stream, but they were a lie. She did need him. The realization made her shoulders slump in defeat.

There was only one thing she could do…apologize and beg him to let her tag along. That glimmer of insight alone made her grit her teeth. Apologies had never come easily to her, neither had admitting she needed help, but the plain truth, if she were honest, was that she didn't want to do this alone. Hadn't her scare earlier in the day shown her that?

Stevie Rae slowed Willow to a walk and turned in the saddle to look behind her while she debated her choices. Admit defeat? Or continue hunting Logan alone? Neither option appealed to her. She hated feeling so vulnerable. Weak and afraid.

She took a deep breath, then another as she studied the trail…

And spotted Brock, coming up the path behind her. She couldn't see his face, but she didn't need to. He rode fast, Resolute's hooves pounding the dirt beneath him. "Stevie! Wait!"

Stevie Rae had no desire to wait for him, but she didn't dig her heels into Willow's sides either. She kept to a steady pace.

He caught up with her in mere moments, then slowed Resolute to a walk beside her and made a grab for Willow's reins. Stevie Rae slapped at his gloved hand. He pulled back, then moved his horse closer to hers, and reached for the reins once more. Again, she slapped his hand away, in no mood to listen to anything he had to say, although the fact he'd come after her cooled her anger…a little.

Frustration gleamed from his granite-colored eyes as he reached for Willow's reins one more time. "Stop," he bellowed, his voice raw with aggravation. Whiskey Pete *hee-haw*ed in response.

"Why should I?"

"Because we need to talk."

Stevie Rae stared straight ahead, unwilling to look at him. "So talk, although why I should listen to a word you say is beyond my comprehension."

"Damn it, kid." Exasperation filled his voice, making it gruffer and overloud in the silence of the forest. He blew out his breath between his lips in a huff, then dropped Willow's reins to grab her hand. Warmth and comfort flowed through her from his strong fingers, despite their gloves and her anger. His tone gentled. "Please."

Stevie Rae turned her head in his direction to study him and noticed, not for the first time, how his jaw tended to clench and make a muscle jump just beneath the skin. His expression was dark and set as if carved in stone, but it was his clear gray eyes, warm and glowing, that made her tug on Willow's reins and bring the horse to a halt. She didn't dismount. Instead, she continued to stare at him and waited for whatever it was he wanted to say.

"I shouldn't have left, but it was for your own good. Hunting Zeb Logan is a foolish thing to do."

"Why? Because I'm a woman?"

He didn't respond to her question. Instead, he drew another deep breath, his broad chest rising and falling. Strands of dark hair peeked from the open space at the base of his throat where he'd left the buttons of his shirt collar undone. "You need to go home, Stevie."

"I told you before, I have no home. *He* took it all away from me."

"I understand."

She shook her head, and her hands tightened on Willow's reins. "No, I don't think you do. My life changed completely the night Logan killed my father, and not for the better. He needs to pay for that." She didn't mention how Lucas Boyle had broken their engagement when she told him she planned to find Logan, nor how it felt when Mr. Rendell came up to the cabin and posted his sign on the door, letting all know the property had been seized for non-payment of the mortgage. Pride kept those emotions locked in the recesses of her heart. Maybe it was false pride, but it was all she had.

She swallowed over the lump growing in her throat. "I'm going to find that man if it's the last thing I do."

His voice lowered, the deep, rich timbre barely a whisper. "It may well be the last thing you do, Stevie. I can't—I won't have that on my conscience."

"I'm not asking you to."

"I don't want to be responsible for your safety," he said, as if he hadn't even heard her. The muscle in his jaw seemed to tic faster, and a flicker of sadness shadowed his eyes when he mentioned being responsible, but it was gone so quickly, she wasn't sure she'd seen it at all.

"Look, MacDermott, I never asked you to be responsible for me. I can take care of myself. I simply wanted to ride with you. That's all." She continued to watch him, her gaze taking in the stubble of whiskers on his handsome face, the small scar near his left eyebrow, the bump on the bridge of his nose that told her it had been broken, maybe more than once. "But that just seems to be too much to ask, doesn't it?"

The question must have upset him, if the sudden tensing of his body was any indication. The iciness that came into his eyes might have scared someone else, but not her. He inhaled deeply, his frigid glare intent upon her as his breath whistled between his lips. "You're not going to veer from this path you've settled on, are you?"

She wondered if he'd been dropped on his head a time or two when he was a baby, because he just couldn't seem to get it through his thick noggin that she was determined to find Logan and nothing he said or did would change her mind. "No."

"Damn." Again, his icy gaze settled on her. Stevie met his glare straight-on. She didn't blink or avert her eyes. His lips tightened into a thin line until he finally shook his head. "All right. You win. Against my better judgment, you can ride with me."

Despite the fact she had won this battle, his patronizing tone stung her and she responded in kind. "Don't do me any favors, MacDermott."

"Good God, kid! You are the most stubborn—"

She cut him off. "Yes, I am. That and more. It would be best if you remembered it."

Chapter 5

Two days later, with an uneasy alliance still developing between them, they rode into a small clearing to find a dilapidated, crumbling cabin, if the structure perched upon short stilts could be called a cabin. A shelter from the elements, but nothing more. The roof had partially collapsed to expose the interior to everything Mother Nature could unleash—rain, snow, wind. The windows at one time had glass but they didn't now. Small shards, still stuck in the window frames, glittered in the late afternoon sun. Trash—old newspapers and empty whiskey bottles—littered the area. A shirt, threadbare and worn, hung from the branch of a tree, beside a washtub resting on a tree stump, rusted and abandoned like everything else Stevie Rae saw.

Beside her, Brock sighed and gently tugged at the reins, bringing his mount to a halt in front of the structure. "If this is Logan's hideout, he hasn't been here in a long time," he said, disappointment clear in his voice.

"Did you think it would be that easy, MacDermott?" Stevie Rae asked as she slid from the saddle and let the reins dangle to the ground. "There's more than one abandoned cabin up here in the mountains. The Sangre de Cristos are filled with broken dreams as well as broken buildings."

She didn't pause as she pushed against the partially open warped door, making it scrape against the equally warped floorboards to produce a sound that sent shivers skittering up her spine. Despite the eerie sound, she entered the lopsided, crumbling abode. The inside was worse than the outside, a state of utter chaos in the form of old clothes strewn about, molding mattresses, battered pots and pans, rotten food—the wooden frame reeked with the smell of desperation. And beneath the pungent aroma of despair, she smelled evil. The same smell that had permeated the cabin she'd shared with her father after Logan killed him.

"Look at this." Dark brown stained the floorboards as if someone had lain right there and bled until he died. Brock came up behind her, his huge frame blocking out the light coming in from the doorway. "Someone died here."

He hunkered down and rubbed his fingers over the stain, but the blood, if it was blood, had long since dried. His features had hardened to granite when he looked up at her. "I believe so, but long ago. Several weeks at least. Predators must have dragged the body away."

Stevie Rae stared at the stain on the floor, unable to draw her gaze from the evidence that someone had lost their life right here. With effort, she forced her eyes to focus on something else, and there, on the wall, was a handprint of the left hand. In blood. And the little finger was missing.

She couldn't seem to draw enough air into her lungs. The back of her throat burned with the acid rising from her gut. "Logan was here." She swallowed hard and tried once more to breathe. "This wasn't his hideout, but he was here."

"How do you know?"

"He left that." She pointed to the handprint.

"How do you know Logan left it? I don't recall ever seeing anything like that before."

"It's the same as the one I scrubbed off the wall in my cabin. He killed whoever lived here, then went on his merry way as if he hadn't a care in the world." Tears stung the back of her eyes and her stomach lurched. "I can't stay in here." She scrambled for the doorway and blessed freedom from both the cabin and the malevolence that settled in the pit of her stomach. She filled her lungs with fresh air, but it didn't help. The taste of metal and the bacon she'd consumed for breakfast filled her mouth.

Without warning, she leaned over and vomited.

Brock came up behind her and rested his hand on her back. When the nausea passed and there was nothing left in her stomach, he handed her the faded red handkerchief he usually wore around his neck. "It's all right."

No, it wasn't. And she doubted it would ever be again.

Stevie Rae grabbed the piece of fabric and wiped her mouth… and kept wiping until the awful taste was gone. She took a step away from him, then turned to face him. Concern for her well-being etched his face, but nothing else. No disappointment. No censure for losing her breakfast in a most undignified manner. Self-doubt filled her, fighting against the stubbornness and rage that had carried her. "Why am I doing this? What possessed me to think I can hunt and capture such a horrible man? I can't fight that. I can't fight *him*."

"You're right. This isn't something you should be doing. A smart woman would go home."

It wasn't his words, but something in his intent gaze, in the tone of his voice, filled her with resolve, made her stiffen her spine, and allowed her to breathe. "I have no home, MacDermott."

His mouth spread into a lazy grin as he grabbed her upper arms and stared into her eyes. "Then stay and help me find him, Stevie. No one deserves to go what you went through. What I went through."

She returned his intent gaze. Sorrow dwelled within the clear gray of his eyes. What had he gone through? Did Logan kill someone he loved? Was that why he pursued a madman to hell and back?

She wiped her mouth one last time and whispered, "Yes."

He pulled a silver flask from his pocket and unscrewed the cap. "Here, rinse your mouth, then take a drink. It'll help."

Stevie took the flask and sniffed at the opening. The smell of whiskey assailed her nose before she tipped the container toward her lips. Taking a small amount, she swished the liquid fire around her mouth as instructed and spit—her mother would have had an apoplexy if she had seen that—then took another drink and swallowed. She coughed against the raw burn in her throat as the heat of the whiskey traveled all the way to her empty stomach, flaring outward, chasing away the chill that seemed to permeate her.

"Better?"

"Yes." She handed him the flask, noticing that her hand no longer trembled. "Thank you."

Brock screwed the cap on the fancy flask and tucked it back where it belonged. "Anytime, kid." His lips spread into a generous grin. "What do you say we make camp early? Rest up a bit? Things will look better with a new day."

"Yes, of course." Her gaze took in the desolate cabin and the desperation infusing the structure. "But not here."

• • •

They found three other cabins like the first one, minus the splotch of dried blood on the floor. And the handprint on the wall. All were abandoned.

"This is hopeless." Frustration changed the tone of Brock's voice, making it sharp. "I don't even know where the hell we are." He drew air into his lungs to relieve whatever tension he felt, as if forcing himself to stay calm and focused. "Where's the next town?"

Stevie Rae pointed toward a valley between the mountain ridges. "There's a small settlement not far from here. We could be there before nightfall."

"What's there?" he asked as they continued riding forward.

"A general store, a few homes." She gave a long, drawn-out sigh. "The Silver Spur Saloon. The town doesn't even have a name, Brock. At least it didn't the last time I was there." She shrugged, as frustrated as he. And tired. Oh, so tired—of chasing a man who didn't want to be caught, of finding abandoned homes, the general air of depression surrounding each sapping her strength. She wondered when she had last laughed. Or smiled, for that matter. Still, it wasn't in her nature to give up, no matter how hard the task might be. After a few days of continuous riding, from sunup to sundown, she felt his aggravation as deeply as he did and shifted in the saddle, trying to find a more comfortable position for her sore bottom.

"What about the law? Is there a sheriff? A marshal?"

She shook her head and glanced down at her hands holding Willow's reins. Despite the soft kid gloves, a blister had developed between her fingers. And she dearly longed for a hot bath and a hot meal, not necessarily in that order. "There's no law. At least there wasn't. Why?"

His body stiffened in the saddle, his muscles taut. He released his horse's reins and stretched his hands, wiggling his fingers—she assumed to relieve the cramping after holding the straps of leather so tightly for so long. "What about a telegraph? Is there someone who can send a telegram for me?"

"There's a station where the stagecoaches change their horses and people can get a bite to eat and stretch their legs." She took off her hat and wiped the sweat from her brow, then placed it back on her head. "It's not too far. Bill Ransom runs it. He might have a telegraph machine, but I can't be certain. It's been a long time since I've been there."

"At this point, I'll take whatever I can get. Lead the way."

Stevie Rae nudged Willow's sides and moved ahead of him on the small path, leading them down a slippery slope covered in dried pine needles and fallen leaves. They didn't speak, which wasn't unusual. After a week riding beside each other and sharing a campfire at night, she didn't know any more about him than when they'd started this journey. Brock MacDermott didn't share very much, but then, neither did she. The only thing about him she could say with certainty was that she admired the breadth of his shoulders and the easy way he sat a saddle when she rode behind him. And she liked his smile, though seeing that was a rare thing, indeed, but oh so wonderful when he bestowed it upon her.

The settlement had changed in the thirteen years since Stevie Rae had been there with her father when he went on his rounds to treat the sick. The Silver Spur still stood, as did the station where Bill Ransom had exchanged horses, but she got the distinct feeling Bill wasn't there anymore. A proud man, he would never have allowed the station to fall into such disrepair. The corral still held a few horses, but an air of ennui and abandonment oozed from every slat of wood used to erect the buildings around her.

The general store was shuttered, heavy boards nailed over the windows. The sign swung in the breeze, suspended over the raised wooden sidewalk by one hook. The barbershop, where one could get a hot bath as well as a shave, had closed its doors as well. If there was a telegraph machine here, she doubted it would be usable or that anyone was left to operate it.

A few of the homes looked lived in, if one could call it living, and she saw a curtain draw back from a window in one of the houses they passed, then quickly swing back into place. No one strolled the dirt road winding its way between buildings, though Stevie Rae could hear bits of conversation behind closed doors— whispers about who they were and why they were here, followed quickly by admonishments to hush and get away from the window.

The train at Raton Pass must have taken away the stagecoach business, leaving this nameless settlement to die a slow, painful death. But it was more than that. There was fear here. Stevie Rae could feel its insidiousness creeping into her bones. Despite the warmth of the day, she shivered against the cold chill skittering up her back.

Brock must have felt it, too.

"Stay close to me," Brock said, his words barely audible.

Stevie Rae glanced in his direction, noticed how stiffly he held himself, and moved Willow a little closer to his horse.

A woman strolled out onto the second story porch of the Silver Spur. She rested her hands on the wooden railing and watched their passage. Strands of flame-red hair caught the breeze and worked themselves loose from the haphazard knot piled on top of her head. She wore pantalets that might have once been white, but now were dingy yellow, a corset, and a loose robe. One of the ruffles at the edge of her pantalets had torn loose from the garment and hung down her skinny leg, emphasizing the gaping hole in her stocking. She looked tired and worn out, a woman who had no hope of a better life and knew it. She didn't nod in their direction, but rather narrowed her eyes as she watched their progress. After a moment, she went inside, closing the door.

Stevie Rae stared at the spot where the woman had been and came to a quick decision. She led Willow toward the saloon and slid from the saddle, her boots kicking up a whirlwind of dust as they met the hard, dry street. She swung the horse's reins around the post in front of the building.

"Stevie! You can't go in there," Brock hissed, as if knowing raising his voice would not be wise.

"Who says? You?" She didn't wait for his answer. Instead, she stepped up onto the raised sidewalk and slipped through the batwing doors. After the fading light of day, the candlelit darkness inside the saloon temporarily blinded her. She stood motionless in the doorway as the conversation in the room silenced. The shiver of fear that had skittered up her back before returned twofold as she became the object of everyone's attention—because she was a stranger? Because she was a woman? Or both?

The answer didn't matter. Neither reason boded well, and her plan to boldly announce she was looking for Zeb Logan died a quick death. She willed herself to remain calm and fight the sudden churning in her belly.

There were six men inside, not counting the bartender, who stood behind the bar, resting his big, beefy hands on the polished mahogany. Three men occupied a table closest to her—whiskey bottles in front of them. Two others stood at the bar, holding shot glasses, gun belts slung low around hips, the holsters tied down around their thighs in the fashion of professional gunfighters. She didn't miss the slight movement as one of those men reached down to rest his hand upon the handle of his revolver. He made no other move, but his gaze settled on her and stayed. Weariness and suspicion gleamed from his eyes.

Stevie Rae didn't blink as her focus shifted to the last man, who sat alone at a corner table, his hat drawn low, hiding his face. He glanced up and she sucked in her breath as recognition hit her with all the subtlety of a wooden plank across the back of her head.

In fact, she recognized them all. The Wanted posters hanging in Sheriff Hardy's office had depicted each and every one of them with detailed accuracy. Hal Beech and his brother, Tom, wanted for bank robbery. Deacon Roberts, Sweet Jimmy Aldrich, and Jesse Murphy, members of the gang that stole cattle from unsuspecting ranchers. And the man in the corner, once more hiding his face from her scrutiny? Carl Windom. Wanted for murder.

This unnamed, dying settlement had become a haven for men wanted by the law.

And here she stood in the middle of them.

Her heart hammered in her chest so hard, she thought it might burst, but the churning in her belly was so much worse. She shouldn't have come in here. She should have listened to Brock, but now it was too late. She couldn't turn tail and run. She had no choice but to play it through, no matter how foolish and dangerous. If she didn't, she might not make it out of the saloon alive.

She nearly jumped out of her skin when an eighth man came out of the backroom and settled himself at the piano in the corner. She shouldn't have been surprised, but she was, when Texas Jim Roberts started playing a classical piece full of angst and heartache. Not something she would have expected from a murderer.

Pretending bravery she didn't feel, Stevie Rae strutted across the floor toward the bartender as the man studied her, his bushy black eyebrows drawn into a frown, lips pressed together into a thin line. "Ain't seen you before."

"Just passing through," she said, staring the man down as she dug a few coins from her pocket and laid them on the bar. "Got thirsty. I'll take a bottle of whiskey."

As she stood at the bar, the batwing doors swung open, filling the interior with a flash of dying sunlight then shadow as Brock entered the saloon. All gazes shifted toward him, including hers. The music, so loud just moments before, died. If anyone recognized him, they'd both be dead. Tension became a tangible thing, the uneasiness growing within the confines of the room. She heard the audible *click* of the hammer being drawn on someone's pistol, then nothing but silence.

For the longest time, no one moved, no one said a word—until Brock opened his mouth. "We gotta go." His voice sounded overly loud—and angry—as his gaze swept over the men in the saloon. If he recognized the outlaws, he didn't give himself away, though his stance remained alert and wary. His focus shifted back to her. Their eyes met and held. "Told ya we ain't got no time for a drink."

Her lungs burning, her body quivering, Stevie Rae released her breath in a rush, then ordered, "Whiskey for the house." Her voice stayed calm, belying the inner turmoil rumbling inside her like an earthquake she'd once felt. She grabbed the bottle and glass the bartender offered and sauntered over to a table as the music started once more. Placing the bottle on the rickety table, she kicked the chair back with her foot, then slumped into it, willing her body to relax and her heart to stop its frantic pounding. Her gaze rose to Brock. She gave one slight nod of her head. He returned her nod with one of his own, then strolled over to her table as if he hadn't a care in the world, his boot heels heavy on the wooden planks under his feet. He said nothing as he slid into a chair, but the rage flashing in his eyes frightened her, almost as much as the group of wanted men staring at them.

"You and I will discuss this later." His voice lowered to barely a whisper, but within that whisper, was anger. "If we make it out of here alive."

She opened her mouth to respond, but never had the chance as the bartender bellowed, "Annie, quit yer lollygagging and get yer ass down here!"

Her gaze swung to the staircase to her left, the one she hadn't even noticed, and saw the woman who'd been standing on the balcony earlier. She'd changed into a dress that seemed to be held together by a minimum of thread and sheer force of will, the once-vibrant color of red faded to pink. As with her pantalets, a piece of black lace at the edge of her skirt had pulled away and hung below the hem, resembling the intricate spinning of a spiderweb. She looked so much younger than Stevie Rae originally thought as she watched the woman step across the floor and approach the bar. Annie cringed, as if expecting a slap as she retrieved several bottles of whiskey from the bartender.

She made short work of passing out the booze to the saloon's patrons, handily sidestepping the hands reaching out for her.

Annie slowed her pace and her eyes narrowed as she approached their table. She drew in a deep breath, then a warm smile transformed the harsh lines of her face. "I remember you." The barmaid slid a glass onto the surface in front of Brock though her intent stare never left Stevie Rae. "You came up here with your father when you were just a kid. He took care of me real good when I was sick." A bruise near the woman's eye, faded with time and a heavy dose of powder, drew Stevie Rae's attention. "How is Doc?"

"He's dead."

The woman took a step back and brought her hand to her chest. "Oh, I'm so sorry. He was a good man. What happened?"

"Zeb Logan killed him," she said, trying to keep her tone even. "You seen him?"

The woman moved closer, her eyes flitting over the outlaws around her. She lowered her voice. "He was here about a week ago, but I haven't seen him since."

"Do you know where he went?"

Annie shook her head. "Don't care where he went." Her fingers came up and gently touched the bruise on her face. "Just glad he's gone."

Stevie Rae dug into her pocket and pulled out a small roll of crisp bills. "Here, take this and get out of town."

The woman looked at the money, the sadness in her eyes almost overwhelming. "I ain't got no place to go."

"Yes, you do. Martha Prichard in Little River will take you in, help you get on your feet. Tell her Stevie Rae sent you."

Wariness flickered in her eyes as if compassion was not something she expected. Or that it came with a price. "Why are you being so kind?"

Stevie Rae shrugged. "I have no reason to be unkind, Annie. Take the money. It's a chance to get away from this and start a new life." She pressed the cash into the woman's hand.

After a moment, the bills disappeared into the bodice of Annie's dress. She didn't say thank you, but she didn't have to. The tears shimmering in her eyes showed more than enough gratitude. She drew in a deep breath, then swiped at those tears. "He headed south. Taos, I think." Her voice cracked just a bit before she cleared her throat and sashayed back to the bar.

Stevie Rae poured herself a glass of whiskey, took a sip, and tried to relax despite sitting in a saloon among outlaws. It was easier than she thought. Aside from the occasional glance in their direction, the patrons left them alone.

Now she only had to contend with Brock.

The murderous gleam in his eyes never dimmed.

Chapter 6

"What the hell did you think you were doing?" Brock grabbed her arm, his fingers digging into the soft skin, and yanked her toward Willow. She'd scared the hell out of him—a deeply unsettling feeling. After their drink, which had done nothing to alleviate his anger, leaving the saloon turned out to be relatively easy. No one tried to stop them. No one even looked at them, all patrons happily finishing off the whiskey Stevie Rae had purchased for them. "You could have gotten us both killed."

"But I didn't." Her chin rose as she rubbed her arm where his fingers had pressed into her skin. The stubborn expression she wore, the one he'd become used to, riled him even more.

"Sheer luck," he hissed as he helped her into her saddle. "Let's get out of here."

Darkness had descended, but the full moon shed an eerie light. A few lanterns glowed in the windows of the buildings on either side of the saloon and across the street as well. A curtain fluttered as shadows moved behind the glass. They were still being watched, by whom he could only guess.

Townspeople? Or more outlaws?

He had no desire to find out. His one thought was to get out of town while they still drew breath, then report what he'd found to Sheriff Hardy so a posse could arrest every single one of those outlaws.

He climbed into Resolute's saddle, clicked his tongue against the roof of his dry mouth, and led the way south, back the way they'd come, away from the possibility he'd feel the pain of a bullet between his shoulder blades at any moment.

An hour later, he still seethed. Shoulders stiff, stomach still churning with anxiety, his fingers cramping around the reins gripped in his hands, Brock peered through the trees and spotted a likely campsite for the night. He glanced behind him to make sure Stevie Rae still followed when all he really wanted to do was leave her on the mountainside—or shake her until she finally found some sense.

Stevie Rae Buchanan was trouble looking for a home. Impetuous. Reckless. Hasty. And foolish, too, not thinking before she acted, a trait that would be the death of him. Of them. Didn't she realize how dangerous a cornered outlaw could be? Or that she could get herself killed?

It was the last thought that made his stomach clench even more. He tugged Resolute's reins lightly and headed deeper into a copse of trees and came to a stop. He slid from the saddle, his feet landing atop a pile of pine needles, silencing any sound. "We'll camp here."

"Fine." Stevie Rae rode up beside him and dismounted as well.

He grabbed her, pulling her closer, his fingers once again digging into the soft skin of her upper arm, but a little gentler this time. He tipped back her hat so he could see directly into her eyes, which widened with surprise in the moonlight. "Remember what I said about being responsible for someone else, Stevie?"

Stevie Rae nodded as her eyes narrowed. She made no move to free herself from his grasp. "I remember." She never blinked or tried to turn away, and once again, Brock was struck by the depths of her conviction, her pride, her tenacity, but most of all, her lack of trepidation. Most women—and some men—would have quailed before his anger. Not her. She stood absolutely still, her gaze holding his captive. "I also remember telling you that I hadn't asked that of you. I can take care of myself."

He took a deep breath, willing himself to gain control, to tamp down his irritation and yes, his fear, but he failed. "And walking into a saloon full of outlaws is your idea of taking care of yourself? What were you thinking?"

She didn't answer his question but asked one of her own. "Are you finished yelling at me?"

"I'm not yelling, but I'm a long way from finished." He released her then, dropping his hands to his sides and taking a step back. "I oughta take you over my knee and tan your hide for that little stunt!"

Her slender frame tensed. "Are you man enough to do it?"

He said nothing as he stared at her, but his thoughts ran rampant. Hell yes, he was the man to do it. That and more. Staring into her eyes, seeing the defiance written clearly on her face, he was torn between making good on his threat...or crushing her enticing lips beneath his own.

Startled by the path his thoughts had taken, his breath hissed through his teeth. "Don't tempt me, kid."

Eyes flashing, daring him, she straightened to her full height. "Try it! I guarantee it'll be the last thing you do."

He took another step back, his hands balling into fists at his side, then took another and another until he was on the other side of the camp. Despite his anger, he'd never raised his hand to a woman. He wasn't about to start now.

He said not another word as he turned and headed into the woods.

By the time he came back to the camp, his anger was under control, but barely. He dropped the armload of wood beside the small fire she had already started. She'd seen to the horses—both had been divested of their saddles—and now all three animals munched contentedly on the oats filling the feedbags tied around their heads, but there was no coffee brewing, no dinner cooking over the flames. It was just as well. He wasn't certain if hunger gnawed at his belly or if his stomach still churned from the events of the past few hours, but in any case, he didn't think he could eat.

Stevie Rae's bedroll was neatly laid out and she was already beneath the heavy quilts, her boots off to the side, the gun belt draped over them. She didn't acknowledge his presence, and that was just as well, too.

He glanced at her still figure as he added more logs to the flames, then grabbed his own bedroll and spread it out on the ground on the other side of the fire—as far away from her as possible. He placed his saddle at the top of the bedroll, then slipped between the blankets and rested his head against the worn leather. He stared at the stars over his head, willing them to calm him.

Sleep took a long time coming, and he felt like he had just barely closed his eyes when a muffled sound startled him. His eyes flew open and his hand slowly reached for the pistol that was never far from his side. He studied the stars above, his ears attuned for the sound that had woken him from his fitful sleep. Had they been followed? Was one—or more—of the men from the outlaw stronghold waiting in the darkness to strike a deadly blow?

A wolf howled in the distance, followed by a chorus of responses. Resolute shifted, his hooves shuffling against the carpet of dried pine needles beneath him. Beside him, Stevie Rae's palomino huffed lightly and the mule that carried her supplies became a hulking shadow in the moonlight. None of the animals seemed concerned by the noise that had awoken him.

Still, Brock strained to hear and identify what had startled him from sleep…until he heard it again.

"Stevie Rae?" He turned his head in her direction and peered into the darkness beyond the flickering flames of the dying fire.

"Hmm?"

"Are you all right?"

A hoarse one-word answer came from her direction. "Yes."

"What's wrong?"

She sniffed, and her voice seemed as if it was dragged from her throat. "Nothing."

Another strangled sound met his ears. She lied. She wasn't all right.

"Are you crying?"

"No."

But she *was* crying, and his heart just couldn't take it. She turned to face him. Her eyes glistened in the moonlight streaming through the trees, and he clearly saw the tracks tears had made on her cheeks.

He shouldn't, but he couldn't seem to help himself. Moving his blankets aside, he beckoned. "Come here."

She didn't move. Instead, she turned her head away from him. "No."

Stubborn!

He made a snap decision, be it right or wrong. Despite his anger, for he was still angry with her, he rose from his bedroll, dragged the heavy blankets across the campsite, and settled in beside her. Stevie Rae needed no more encouragement than his arms wrapped around her. She turned and leaned against him, resting her head on his chest.

"I'm sorry."

"About what?"

"For being so...stupid. And stubborn. I know I could have gotten us killed. I just..." Her voice came out muffled, yet so tight, as she tried to stop the flow of tears. "I miss him so much."

"I know."

"I want Zeb Logan dead."

"I know that, too, and he will be. I promise you. Once we bring him in and he stands trial, we'll both watch him swing."

She hiccupped against his chest. Brock tightened his embrace and casually stroked her hair, running the fine, silken strands through his fingers. It was softer than he could have imagined. *She* was softer than he imagined as she drew closer to him and nestled against him.

The scent of honeysuckle assailed his nose. Damn, he'd just made the biggest mistake of his life. He hadn't held a woman for anything other than sex—and even that was infrequent—in a long time. He'd forgotten what it felt like to have someone else's warmth *this* close, to feel *needed* by someone. And she needed him. For all her bravado, Stevie Rae was still a woman mourning those she'd lost and he wondered if anyone had offered her comfort.

After her breathing settled to normal and he was certain she no longer cried, Brock continued to hold her in his arms.

He grinned, despite the realization that holding her was his second biggest mistake, not the first. The first was allowing her to come along with him.

• • •

Stevie Rae woke with a start, the heaviness of an arm wrapped around her stomach, holding her tight. Warmth traveled up her back where she nestled against Brock's solid chest and taut stomach. Her face heated with embarrassment as she remembered how she came to be in his arms.

Oh, what he must think of her!

All the stubbornness that had carried her since the day her father was killed seemed to have disappeared in one fell swoop, leaving her a shaking, trembling mess. She hadn't been able to stop the tears or tamp down the sadness filling her as she had on every other occasion.

Carefully, so as not to awaken him, Stevie Rae slipped out of his arms.

She studied him. In sleep, he looked younger, the fine lines radiating from his eyes not as deep. Dark hair tumbled across his brow now, and she fought the impulse to push the black locks from his forehead.

Who was this man? One moment, he was threatening to "tan her hide"; the next, he held her in his strong arms and offered comfort despite his anger with her.

She shook out her well-worn boots—one never knew if a snake would curl up inside the leather—and tugged them on her feet, then picked up her gun belt as she watched him.

This devil had a soft side, one he tried to hide. She would have never known. Nor suspected. For the first time in far too long, Stevie Rae smiled and followed through on her earlier impulse. With trembling fingers, she smoothed his hair away from his forehead. He sighed in his sleep, and she pulled her hand away quickly.

Rising to her feet, she moved about the camp, purpose in every step. She hunkered down beside the fire pit and stirred the embers, then tossed a few more logs on the glowing coals. Smoke rose to the sky as the dried wood popped and crackled before bursting into flame. By the time she came back from her bath—and she would be taking a bath, albeit in a cold stream and not a brass tub filled with hot, steaming water—she could make coffee and something for breakfast.

From her saddlebags, she pulled soap, a towel, and clean clothes, then, checking once more to make sure Brock still slept, headed toward the stream, following the brook a little ways from the camp, where it narrowed and deepened. Morning sun shimmered on the water as she dropped her gun belt atop the towel, then sat on the bank and pulled off the boots she'd just put on. Thick wool socks came next and she wiggled her toes. She stood to remove her trail-stained trousers, sweat-stained shirt, and undergarments.

The coolness of the mountain air skimmed her flesh as she stepped into the water. Goose bumps pebbled her skin in an instant, and she squelched the squeal rising in her throat as the cold liquid climbed up her calves then hit her thighs. For as long as she lived, she'd never get used to freezing baths, but at the moment, there was no help for it. If she wanted to be clean—and she so desperately did—she'd have to endure.

Taking a deep breath and mentally preparing herself, Stevie Rae plunged into the water. The shock stole her breath and she bobbed to the surface, gasping and sputtering and flinging her wet hair away from her face.

After a hurried wash, her hair tied in a ponytail, still damp and wetting the back of her shirt, gun belt once more securely fastened and riding low on her hips, Stevie sauntered into camp to find Brock awake. He hunkered down beside the fire, setting the coffeepot on a metal rack over the flames. Steam rose from the tin cup in his hand. She could smell the bitter brew, and despite knowing how bad it would taste, her mouth watered and her empty stomach growled.

He glanced at her, the clear gray of his eyes visible beneath the brim of his hat. No smile graced his mouth. In fact, his lips were pressed together in a thin line. "I thought you'd finally gotten some sense and went home."

"Hardly." She quirked an eyebrow at him but said nothing more as she set about making breakfast. He never listened. How many times had she told him she no longer had a home? How many times did she have to say she wasn't giving up until Zeb Logan was dead? Did he not understand? Wasn't he just as driven to find Logan? And why did he seem angry this morning? Because he'd offered her comfort and she'd seen his softer side? Or was it something else? Was he as aware of her as she was of him?

Stevie Rae shook herself from her musings as bacon sizzled in one skillet and biscuits browned in the other. From the corner of her eye, she watched him put his bedroll away then pull clean clothes out of his saddlebag and saunter away from camp. He returned shortly, his hair wet, clad in clean clothes, his gun belt clasped loosely around his hips, the holster tied down around his thigh. He sat beside the fire and, in silence as was his nature, ate several strips of bacon and three of the biscuits, then finished the bitter coffee. His eyes flitted her way several times and she thought he might speak but he never did.

Brock MacDermott gave new meaning to the description of the strong, silent type.

Stevie Rae released a sigh, flipped the last piece of crisp bacon into her mouth, and crunched it to nothing, though she barely tasted it. She caught him staring at her again and felt a flutter deep in her belly beneath the intensity of his glare. That hadn't happened before. "What?"

After a moment, he shook his head. "Anytime you're ready."

Stevie Rae gave a slight nod, then made quick work of cleaning the skillets and putting them away.

Smoke rose from the fire as he dumped the last of the coffee on the flames, then pushed dirt over the remaining hot coals and put the coffeepot away.

There was something different in his eyes now as they lingered on her, something she couldn't define, which made her tingle all the way to her toes. She returned his unflinching stare, then swallowed hard, trying to ignore the fluttering in her belly. "We need supplies. I used the last of the bacon for breakfast and we're getting low on coffee."

He said nothing, just nodded as he climbed into Resolute's saddle and clicked his tongue. Stevie Rae attached Whiskey Pete's reins to Willow's saddle, then hoisted herself onto Willow's back and followed.

Chapter 7

Flames danced along the bark of the wood Brock laid carefully on the fire, casting shadows on the boulders surrounding the spot he'd chosen to make camp. Stevie needed to hear a voice, a human voice, and not just her own. If she had to endure another long day of riding, the only sounds the steady *clip-clop* of the horses' hooves, the birds flitting from tree to tree, and the gentle breeze rustling through pine boughs, she'd jump out of her skin. Tomorrow, they'd make Taos to pick up supplies. Maybe then her desire for conversation would be satisfied.

She glanced at Brock as she placed the just-cleaned iron skillet into the burlap sack tied to Whiskey Pete's back. He spread out his bedroll, then removed his gun belt and boots, setting them within reach.

He was so different from her father. Steven Buchanan could talk a blue streak, jumping from subject to subject. Lucas, too, could discourse on any topic, and there were many lively, spirited debates between both men when they used to sit in the rocking chairs on the porch of the little cabin.

Brock MacDermott was the opposite. He didn't speak unless it was to give direction or to berate her for something. He didn't talk just to hear himself talk.

"You would have liked my father."

She jumped, startled. The silent man spoke!

Smoke curled around his head, rising up toward the starry sky. "He was a lawman. Stepped off the ship from Ireland, dragging my mother and us boys with him, and became a policeman in Boston before we knew what happened. Back in Ireland, he'd been a constable."

A long sigh escaped him before he stuck his pipe in his mouth and spoke around the stem. "We never stayed in one place very long. Mam, God rest her soul, said Shamus MacDermott had happy feet. We followed him from city to city—New York, Philadelphia, Cleveland, Chicago, St. Louis."

Brock crossed his legs at the ankles and made himself more comfortable. "After all that moving around, we finally settled in Paradise Falls, Colorado. Da was sheriff up until the day he died. My beautiful and courageous mam, Siobhan MacDermott, died shortly thereafter. Said she didn't want to live without him. One day, her heart just stopped. You remind me a lot of my mother. She was a stubborn one, to be sure."

He grinned suddenly, and Stevie Rae's world turned upside down. Oh, what that man's smile did to her!

Stevie Rae removed her gun belt and boots, then grabbed a brush from her saddlebag and settled on her own bedroll to tease the tangles from her hair as she listened, enjoying the deep timbre of his voice and the faint, musical Irish accent that somehow reappeared the more he spoke of his father. Her stomach full from the meal she'd prepared, weary from a long day spent in the saddle looking for a man who didn't want to be found, she let his words drift over her like a gentle rain to ease her fatigue.

"There were four of us boys. Kieran, the oldest and the wisest of us, who swore once he found himself a home, he'd never leave. Myself, the second born, and if I can believe the tales my mother told, possessing the same pair of happy feet as my da." He glanced at her and his eyes seemed to soften in the glow of firelight. "I liked to 'explore.' A lot. Mam said I was the one who put every single gray hair on her head." He puffed on his pipe, smoke wreathing his head. Stevie Rae inhaled the fragrant tobacco as she pulled the brush through her hair. Her gaze never left him, and a thrill coursed through her when he gifted her with another one of his rare smiles.

"Teague, the prankster, and Eamon, the youngest and the most good-hearted of us all. We were rambunctious as hell. How my mother managed I'll never know, but she did. She never raised her voice." He chuckled. "She never had to. All it took was one look from her, and we knew there would be the devil to pay if we didn't straighten up and behave."

"Where are they now? Your brothers, I mean?"

He stiffened, the muscles in his body tightening, as if he'd said too much and regretted it. For bringing up memories better left buried? He made a production of filling his pipe with more tobacco, then lit it once more. As he inhaled and exhaled, he dug the silver flask from his pocket, unscrewed the cap, and took a deep drink of the whiskey it contained. His throat moved as he swallowed, Adam's apple bobbing until he'd drunk his fill, then he screwed the cap back on and tucked the flask back in his pocket.

Stevie Rae took a long, slow breath and wondered if she'd asked the wrong question. "Brock?"

He stared into the fire for a long time before he finally spoke. "Teague is sheriff in Paradise Falls, Colorado. He took over when my father died. He'll never leave." A long sigh escaped him and his voice grew hoarse, his words stilted. "I don't have a clue where Eamon is. I haven't seen him…in a very long time. He's a U.S. Marshal. A good one."

"You all went into the law."

"Except Kieran. He stayed in Paradise Falls, too. He married a widow and became a rancher, raising fine horses as well as a beautiful family. He's gone now. His family, too, except for little Desi Lyn. Teague is raising her."

"What happened? Is Kieran and his family gone because of Logan? Did he kill them?"

He didn't say anything, and for a while, Stevie Rae didn't think he would speak at all. He removed the pipe from between his teeth and tapped the bowl against one of the rocks ringing the fire pit, spilling the ashes onto the glowing coals. He didn't put it away, simply held it in his hands. He opened his mouth, then closed it, then opened it again, and finally, when the words starting flowing, his voice was tight.

"Teague had captured Jeff Logan, Zeb's youngest brother, rustling Kieran's horses and had him in his jail. He telegraphed me, saying he needed help... I was sheriff in Pueblo at the time, but I went to Paradise Falls as soon as I got the telegram. Jeff might have been in jail, but his brothers weren't, and Teague thought he might need help just in case the Logan Gang decided to break Jeff out, which Jeff threatened more than once." He drew in a deep breath. By the light of the fire, she saw his jaw clench and a muscle jump in his cheek. The urge to go to him, to caress his face and ease some of his pain, nearly overwhelmed her, but she couldn't do it. She doubted he would accept that from her although he had offered her the same.

"You've heard of the James-Younger gang? And the Stockton Gang? Well, the Logan Gang was meaner, more daring. They were involved in everything from robbing trains, stagecoaches, and banks to rustling cattle and horses, leaving murder and mayhem in their wake." He drew a ragged breath.

"Teague telegraphed Eamon, too, which was a good thing because the Logan Gang came out in full force, just as Jeff had promised. There were nine of them that day, riding into Paradise Falls, shooting anything that moved. And things that didn't. There was a standoff at the jail, bullets flying in every direction. By the time it was over, Jefferson Logan was still in jail and six of the Logan Gang were dead, but so were several of the townspeople. Only Zeb and his brother, Tell, managed to get away because they hadn't gone to town. They came to Whispering Pines, my brother's ranch. I was waiting for Eamon. We were going to get Kieran's family to safety, but...it didn't happen the way it was supposed to."

His voice grew more husky as he stared at the flames in the fire pit. "Not only did that bastard kill Kieran, Mary, and Matthew, my nephew, but he shot me several times as well. His brother, Tell, nearly killed Eamon." He fiddled with the pipe in his hand, smoothing his fingers over the bowl. When he finally continued speaking, his voice was raw and full of guilt. "It was my fault. I was charged with keeping them safe and out of harm's way. I was responsible and I failed." He glanced up at her, and she saw the moisture shining in his eyes until he blinked. She wasn't sure if they were tears or just her imagination. It didn't matter. Her heart went out to him just the same, and if he couldn't shed tears for his loss, she certainly could.

She swallowed over the lump in her throat and swiped at her eyes with the back of her hand. "I'm sorry, Brock."

He grunted, but said nothing more, going back to the silent man she'd come to know, perhaps embarrassed he'd shared as much as he had. He didn't look at her as he put his pipe away, then stretched out on his side, his face turned toward the darkness of the woods beyond the firelight.

Stevie Rae released a long breath and stared at his back. She wasn't sure if she liked the talkative man or the silent one better, but she was glad he had shared a little bit about himself and shed some light onto what drove him. She'd had the impression he wasn't interested in the bounty Zeb Logan's capture would bring in and she was right. His mission—vengeance, plain and simple— was the same as her own. Almost.

It wasn't the money and never had been.

It was the fulfillment of the promise.

She finished brushing her hair, pulled the heavy mass into a ponytail at the back of her head, and rose to her feet. She tucked her brush into her saddlebag, but her eyes never left him. After a moment or two of indecision, she dragged her bedroll to the other side of the fire and dropped it next to his. He didn't stir as she lay down beside him and, without saying a word, held him close, offering him the same solace he had given her.

• • •

Stevie Rae took a deep breath and stared at the scenery as Taos Pueblos, just north of Taos proper, came into view. The sun dipped toward the horizon, casting everything in beautiful, blazing golden tones that reflected on the ancient buildings erected long before Spanish settlers arrived. A prettier town she had never seen, and despite Brock's silence, she had enjoyed the ride as they left the coolness of the mountain pines for the sun-drenched open plains.

She smiled to herself as she watched his broad back, the second smile to grace her lips in a long time. It didn't surprise her that Brock didn't mention all he had confessed the night before, nor did he acknowledge the fact that they'd slept side by side. At some point during the night, he had turned and held her. That's how they'd awoken earlier, their arms around each other, his thigh nestled between hers, her head tucked beneath his chin. She thought it amusing how he'd scrambled out of the twisted blankets of their bedrolls, his face rosy with embarrassment beneath the growth of whiskers. After a stammered apology, he hadn't said another word.

And he remained silent for the duration of their ride until they came to a hotel in the heart of the plaza. He slid from his saddle, tiny puffs of dust rising upward from the road to coat his already dusty boots. After wrapping Resolute's reins around the post in front of the building, he reached up to help her. "Grab your saddlebags. We'll stay here."

The sign above the etched glass double doors read "The Hacienda" in flowing script. A small bell tinkled as he opened the door, then ushered her through.

The woman behind the registration desk looked up from the ledger in front of her and smiled, her dark brown eyes glistening with undisguised pleasure.

"Señor Brock! So nice to see you again. Manuel will be pleased, as will Mama." She put down her pen, came around the desk, and walked toward him, her delicate hands outstretched to clasp his. She wore a lovely multicolored skirt and white blouse that showed off her dusky skin to perfection. Strands of gray threaded through her sleek black hair, which was simply pulled away from her face with silver combs to hang down her back in a silken fall—all of which had the power to make Stevie Rae feel dowdy and dirty in comparison.

"And you, Elicia? Are you pleased I'm here?"

She laughed as she rose on tiptoe to kiss his cheek. "Of course. I am always happy to see an old friend."

Stevie Rae watched the exchange and couldn't help noticing the warm, easy way in which Brock had greeted the woman. Fondness colored his tone, and again, he flashed that wonderful smile that made her insides flutter.

The woman stepped away from him and smiled in Stevie Rae's direction. "You have brought a friend."

Brock grabbed Stevie Rae's hand and brought her forward. "Elicia de la Cruz, please meet Stevie Rae Buchanan."

"A pleasure," Elicia said, as welcoming as she was beautiful. "You must join us for dinner in our private apartment."

"Thank you." Stevie Rae let go of her hand and resisted the urge to sweep the dust from her dirty attire. "We would be honored."

"I'm going to take care of the horses, then check in with the sheriff." Brock nodded in her direction. "I'll be back. Elicia will take good care of you."

"Of course. Come, we will get you settled. I have a lovely room with a view of the courtyard for you." The petite woman gestured toward the stairs leading up to the second floor before she scooted behind the desk and grabbed keys from the slotted cubby. She handed one to Brock, but kept the other. "Come."

Stevie Rae followed her up the stairs. She turned once to look at Brock, but he was already gone, the door slowly closing behind his passage.

Elicia hadn't lied. The room was lovely. A big four-poster bed, covered in a beautiful, multicolored quilt with plump, inviting pillows leaning against the headboard, took up most of the room, but French doors leading outside to a small balcony made the space appear larger. In the corner, set at an angle, sat a small bureau with the customary pitcher and basin on its surface. A looking glass took up space beside the bureau. She noticed the rim of a brass tub peeking from behind an ornate screen in another corner and sighed. A hot bath would be heaven right about now, but there were other matters to attend to, such as her appearance. She glanced at her dirty clothes and dusty boots. "Is there a place I can purchase some clothes close by?"

"Oh yes," Elicia answered in her accented English, "the Emporium isn't far. You can get anything you like there. Tell Rosa I sent you."

"Thank you. I'll be back shortly."

"And I will have a hot bath waiting for you." The woman grinned, handed her the key, and slipped out the door.

Stevie Rae tossed her saddlebags on the floor next to the bed, tucked the key into her pocket, then left the room. In no time at all, she was strolling down the street, peering into the windows of the small shops lining both sides. Seeing how lovely Elicia de la Cruz looked in her simple skirt and blouse, she regretted not stopping at Mrs. Manville's before she left Little River and buying that dress. It was too late now, but still, she'd like to look presentable when she joined Elicia and her family for dinner.

A dress in the window caught her eye immediately. Prettier than the one that had been on display in Mrs. Manville's, the midnight blue velvet seemed almost black in the light of the fading sun. She pressed her nose to the glass for a better look, admiring the intricate lace around the low collar and cuffs, the row of tiny buttons along the bodice, the flaring sweep of the skirt.

Peeling herself away from the window, she glanced up to see "The Emporium" written on the sign above.

She opened the door and stepped into the shop. The delicate scent of roses mixed with the masculine aroma of tobacco invited her in.

The Emporium had everything a person could desire—from frilly ribbons and bolts of fabric and little bins filled with buttons to beautiful dishes on display for the ladies. On the other side of the big room, men's suits and boots and small wooden boxes labeled with different blends of tobacco were neatly arranged. There was also a fine assortment of pipes and cigars.

"May I help you?"

Stevie Rae looked to the left and noticed a woman coming through a curtained doorway. She wore a tape measure around her neck and a pincushion tied around her wrist. Sleek black hair was pulled back on the sides of her head and held in place with ivory combs…and she wore the same exact dress in the window, except hers was hunter green, the lace trim black. When she smiled, she resembled Elicia. In fact, they looked enough alike they could be sisters. She held out her hand as she approached. To her credit, she accepted Stevie Rae's dusty, trail-worn clothes without expression. "I am Rosa. What can I do for you today?"

Stevie Rae stepped away from the door. "Elicia sent me. I'm looking for—"

"A dress. The blue one in the window." Rosa nodded with a knowing smile.

She laughed, surprising herself. Yes, she had admired the dress, but practicality was second nature and a dress such as the one in the window had no place in the task she'd set for herself. And yet, curiously, she now wanted that dress more than anything. "Yes, how did you know?"

The woman shrugged. "I just knew. The coloring would be perfect for you. It will bring out your beautiful eyes. Make them sparkle."

Stevie Rae laughed again and it felt so good. She hadn't really laughed in a long time. Nor had she ever owned anything that made her eyes sparkle. "I'll take it."

"Very good." The woman strolled to the window and made short work of removing the garment from the metal dress stand. "Try it on." She pointed to the doorway she'd come through a few minutes ago.

Stevie Rae took the dress, careful not to let it touch her clothes, and slipped through the curtains covering the door. She found herself in a small workroom filled with more bolts of fabric, frilly lace, colorful ribbons, and several dressmakers' dummies. A sewing machine, one of the newest models, sat upon a specially made cabinet, the chair before it strewn with more fabric and ribbons. In the corner were another chair and a large, standing mirror.

Quickly, Stevie Rae removed her clothes and tried on the dress. She studied herself in the mirror, admiring the fit and color, which did do something for her eyes. Rosa had been right. Her eyes seemed bluer and twinkled with just a touch of mischief. She removed the dress, donned her dirty trousers and threadbare shirt, and entered the main room of the shop.

Rosa looked up from a book of patterns on the counter and smiled. "Yes?"

Stevie Rae nodded as she approached the woman, the dress slung over her arms, but away from her body. "Yes."

"Good." She took the velvet creation and moved to the long counter toward the back of the room where a roll of brown paper resided on a brass rod. "I'll just wrap this up."

While Rosa packaged the dress, Stevie Rae wandered over to the men's fashions and unfolded a pair of black trousers from the shelf. She shook them out and held them against her legs. "I'll take these as well."

"And ruin my reputation?" Rosa stopped in the process of tying a bow in the strings holding the paper around the dress together and shook her head. "I will not sell you men's clothes. You are *muy bonita*, señorita, and should not dress like a man." She took the trousers from Stevie Rae's hands and moved away from the counter, stopping before several items hanging from a metal rack. She turned once, studied Stevie Rae with a critical eye, and pulled a split skirt of butter-colored soft suede from the hanger. "Here, try these. They are comfortable as well as practical, and you will still look like a lady." Rosa pulled a pristine white blouse from the same rack and handed both items to her.

A blush rose to heat her face before she disappeared into the workroom once more to try on the offered clothing.

Fifteen minutes later, she handed the garments to Rosa, pleased with the fit and feel of the split skirt and simple blouse. "Thank you. I will take these." As Rosa pulled a length of brown paper from the spool, Stevie Rae glanced at the garments beneath the glass counter and spotted several pairs of lace- and ribbon-trimmed drawers. "I'll take a couple of pairs of those as well."

The woman smiled as she pulled the frilly undergarments from the pile beneath the counter, quickly wrapped the clothing in plain brown paper, then rang up the charges. Stevie Rae dug several folded bills from her pocket, paid for her purchases, and left the shop with a definite bounce in her step. She strolled down the street toward the square, peeking in windows, then breezed through the etched glass doors of the Hacienda.

Elicia looked up from the ledger as the little bell over the door chimed, and came around the desk to greet her. "Rosa was able to help you, yes?"

"Yes." Stevie Rae held up the paper-wrapped packages and grinned. "She was most helpful."

"Excellent! I knew she would be." She ushered Stevie Rae up the stairs but remained on the landing. "Your bath has been prepared, and when you are ready, I will have your clothes laundered. Dinner will be at seven."

"Thank you."

Once in her room, Stevie Rae stuffed the paper-wrapped dress in her saddlebag to save for a special occasion, and opened the package with the new blouse, split skirt, and several pairs of frilly drawers. She folded them neatly on the bed, intending to wear her new clothes to dinner. The ornate screen hiding the brass tub had been moved, and as promised, the tub had been filled with hot water. Steam rose up from the surface to dissipate in the air. Stevie Rae dug a small sliver of honeysuckle-scented soap out of her saddlebag, unwrapped the paper protecting it, and dropped it into the steaming water. She inhaled as the hot water released the fragrance then quickly removed her clothes, leaving them in a pile on the floor, and climbed into the bath for a long, leisurely soak.

Chapter 8

After Brock put the horses up at the livery down the street, and sent several telegrams, he stepped into the dim confines of Sheriff Heriot's office. The room was empty. No sheriff, no deputies, no one occupying the jail cells, waiting for their time before the circuit judge who passed through Taos once a month or so.

Brock's glance immediately went to the Wanted posters tacked to one wall, and there he was front and center—Logan— surrounded by others who were not quite as dangerous or deadly. Black eyes stared back at him. Though he himself still searched, it was disappointing that no one else had managed to bring that vile criminal to justice.

Yet.

"Thought that was you, MacDermott." Sheriff Heriot entered the office through the same door Brock came through a moment before, flinging his hat toward the hat stand in the corner of the room. The hat, a fancy thing with a silver and turquoise band around the base of the crown, twirled on a hook then settled into place.

"Saw you from across the street. Lena still makes the best chicken and biscuits I ever had." He patted his full stomach, then extended his hand.

"Tim," Brock returned the greeting, shook the man's hand, then gestured toward the empty cells. "I see business is bad."

The older man grinned. "It's been nice and quiet around here since Brody Pierce got put away. I still got drunkenness on Saturday night when the cowhands come in from the ranches to spend their hard-earned money, but every other day of the week, Taos seems like a little bit of heaven." He gestured to a chair beside the desk. "Sit. Sit."

Brock removed his hat and tossed it across the room, aiming for the hat rack where Tim's hat already nestled. As the sheriff's hat had done, it twirled on the hook and came to rest. He grinned as he took his seat.

"Where ya stayin'?"

"The Hacienda."

The man nodded in approval. "You tell Manuel to treat you right."

"He always does."

"Drink? You look a might parched. Imagine you been riding hard since I last saw you."

At his nod, Tim pulled a bottle and two glasses from the drawer, then poured the single malt whiskey. He slid a glass across the desktop toward Brock, then raised his own and gestured to the posters on the wall. "To getting that bastard."

The whiskey burned his throat as Brock swallowed.

"Saw you ride in a little while ago. Who're you riding with?"

Brock took a deep breath, not surprised by the question, and finished the liquor in his glass. Nothing much happened in this town without Tim Heriot knowing about it. He relaxed back in his chair and studied the man he'd met a little over three years ago when Heriot had chased Black Jack Callahan all the way to Pueblo just to arrest him. They'd become friends almost immediately, recognizing in each other the drive and perseverance it took to keep their respective towns peaceful. Aside from a few more gray hairs in his impressive handlebar mustache, and fewer hairs on his head, Heriot hadn't changed much.

"Her name is Stevie Rae Buchanan," he replied but didn't elaborate.

The sheriff nodded, as if the simple statement answered all his questions. "Not like you to ride with someone." He poured more whiskey into their empty glasses, then leaned back in his chair and rested his feet on the desktop, crossing his legs at the ankle. "So what brings you to my little piece of paradise, as if I didn't know?"

Brock glanced toward the Wanted posters, his gaze resting on the face of the man who haunted his nightmares. "You seen him? I heard he was heading this way."

"Nah." The sheriff shook his head. "He's a smart man. He don't wanna come here."

"You'd shoot first." Brock grinned, knowing the man's penchant for letting his pistol do his talking. "And ask questions later, right?"

"Damn right. Ain't got the time nor the patience for that son of a bitch, knowing what he's done." He rubbed his head, threading his fingers through the few strands of hair left there, and squinted his eyes, as if both actions could help him remember. "I did hear of a murder not too long ago up in Raton and another over to Little River. Can't be certain it was him, but sure sounded like his handiwork." A long sigh ruffled through the heavy mustache on his upper lip, and sadness filled his dark brown eyes. "He didn't leave no one to tell."

"That's not true." Brock cleared his throat and finished off the whiskey in his glass. "The girl I'm riding with saw the whole thing. It was her father who was murdered up in Little River. From what she told me, her father removed bullets from Logan's leg and shoulder and got killed for his trouble."

A dubious expression flickered over the man's face for a moment before he scrubbed his big hand over his features, effectively erasing whatever he felt. Brock never wanted to face the man over a card table—he'd lose for certain. "That don't sound like Logan. He don't usually leave witnesses. At least, not as far as I know."

"She was hiding in the root cellar. He didn't know she was there. If he had, she'd probably be dead, too." As soon as he said the words aloud, his gut twisted. Stevie Rae had been very lucky. *He* had been very lucky. He never would have met her if Logan followed his usual pattern of leaving no one alive. And for reasons he couldn't explain, despite the circumstances, he was glad he was coming to know her. In the course of their journey, he'd come to care about her.

Feelings of protectiveness and responsibility flared in his gut. He sat up straighter in his chair, knowing how dangerous those emotions could be. Why had he allowed them to grow? And when? He scratched at the growth of new whiskers on his face, determined to tuck those feelings deep within his heart, where he tucked every other emotion he'd had since…since the Logans had wreaked havoc on his family, but she made it harder than it had ever been before. Watching her brush her long, silky hair did something to his insides, made him want her as he'd never wanted anyone else.

As well as coming to care for her, he had come to admire her, too. She never complained, no matter how long they rode in any given day, or how sore her behind might have been from spending all those hours in the saddle. Others, he knew, would have. Hell, others had. They would have given up the chase, but not her. Yes, she was trouble looking for a place to land, but he couldn't fault her perseverance.

"MacDermott?"

Startled, Brock snapped to attention. "What?"

"Where'd you go? I lost you for a moment there." Amusement twinkled in his eyes, and a knowing grin flashed across his face.

Brock shook his head. He knew exactly where his thoughts had gone—to her, as they did more and more often of late—but he wasn't about to admit that to Tim. "I gotta go. I'm not gonna find Logan if I'm sitting here, jawing with you." He rose from his seat and reached across the desk to shake the sheriff's hand. "Keep your wits about you, Tim." He grinned. "And keep your pistol holstered."

"You do the same." The man stood, his hand coming to rest on the mentioned revolver. "Anytime you're ready to give up the hunt, you could come be my deputy. It's a sweet deal."

Brock smirked. "I'll consider the offer."

He plopped his hat on his head, then left the office, closing the door behind him. The sun had set, but the sky was hazy in twilight. The street still teemed with people going about their business. He reached up to scratch at the whiskers on his face once again, then strolled down the street toward the barbershop, where he knew he could get a hot bath and a shave.

An hour later, freshly shaved and clean, his body still warm from his soak in one of Luis's special brass tubs, Brock strolled through the etched glass doors of the Hacienda. A young man, one he didn't recognize, stood behind the desk.

"Ah, Señor Brock, so nice to see you again."

Brock stiffened, his muscles tightening beneath his skin, until he got a closer look at the clerk. Recognition came swiftly and he relaxed. "Estevan?"

"Sí."

"What happened to you? The last time I saw you, you were just a little boy."

"Señor Brock, you tease me. We saw each other just last year. I was no little boy." Estevan de la Cruz grinned, showing off perfect white teeth and dimples in his cheeks. He must drive all the young girls wild with that smile. "Mama and Papa are holding dinner for you. Come, I will take you to them."

Brock held up his saddlebags. "Let me put these away first, but don't wait for me. I know my way."

Estevan nodded and left the room with all the vitality of a sixteen-year-old on the verge of manhood. Manuel and Elicia must be very proud of their oldest child. He'd grown into a charming, polite young man.

Brock let himself into his room at the top of the stairs, dropped his saddlebags onto a rocking chair in the corner, and left.

Conversation didn't stop as he entered the dining room of the de la Cruzes' private apartments on the third floor of the hotel a few moments later. They were all there—Manuel, Elicia, and their children: Serafina, Estevan, Matias, Luciana…

And her. Stevie Rae glanced at him, nodded in his direction, then picked up her glass of wine. She took a sip, her straightforward gaze on him until Serafina drew her attention.

Before he had a chance to greet those around the table, Sofia de la Cruz, Manuel's mother, came into the room from the kitchen, pushing against the swinging door with her elbow, a tureen nestled between her hands.

"Señor Brock!" The woman's dark brown eyes lit up with pleasure. "Sit. Sit." She gestured to a chair with a quick nod of her head, then lapsed into rapid-fire Spanish, but he only managed to catch a word or two—*guapo*, which meant "handsome," and *bueno*, which meant "good." Sofia kissed his cheek before she set the tureen in the middle of the table beside a stack of freshly made tortillas and bowls of salsa. The spicy aroma of *posole*, a hearty soup made with pork, hominy, and beans, rose up to tickle his empty stomach. As Sofia filled their bowls, Brock's glance slid over to Stevie Rae. She lifted the spoon to her mouth, and her eyes closed in pure bliss as she savored the pork concoction.

She looks different tonight.

The thought zipped through his brain as he continued watching her, unable to take his eyes from her.

He was used to seeing her in her tight-fitting trousers and threadbare shirt, but tonight, the pristine white of her blouse showed off the tan she had acquired riding with him. Her hat was gone, and his gaze rested on a thick, straight sheaf of honey blond hair falling over her shoulders. She glanced up. Their gazes met… and held. A blush colored her cheeks before she turned away.

It wasn't her dress that was different.

Stevie Rae was different.

She was animated as she spoke with those around the table, gregarious. Her eyes, brilliant blue, sparkled with undisguised pleasure, and her mouth spread into a smile he would spend every last dollar he had to see again and again. She laughed at something Serafina said. He'd never heard her laugh before. The sound touched him deep within his heart, and for reasons he couldn't explain, he felt happier than he'd been in a long time. He barely tasted the *posole*. He had eaten because the hunger gnawing at his belly had insisted, but that hunger was quickly replaced by another kind of yearning…for her, and a longing for a real life— one that did not involve chasing criminals and dealing with the lowest of human beings.

He glanced around the table at the people he'd come to cherish and the desire grew. *This* was what he wanted—had always wanted. A wife who looked at him with undeniable love as Elicia now looked at Manuel. Beautiful children. A warm, comfortable home. He would have had that life if the Logans hadn't changed everything, if he hadn't traded in his silver star in the pursuit of those murderers.

His gaze drifted to Stevie Rae once again. She watched him, her lovely eyes wide and filled with curiosity and warmth and perhaps a touch of sadness. Had she wanted the same things?

"How goes your search?" The question came from Manuel and pulled him out of his thoughts. As he snapped to attention, he noticed the children had cleared the table of the dirty dishes, except for a plate filled with sopapillas and a silver coffee service. Only the adults remained in the dining room.

"Zeb Logan seems to always be one step ahead of me," he replied, frustration making his voice tight and low. He heard the children washing dishes in the kitchen and lowered his voice even more. "The *bastardo* frustrates me no end."

"We will find him," Stevie Rae said and his gaze darted to her.

"Yes, you will." Elicia passed around the platter of sopapillas. "Keep your faith. He won't always be one step ahead of you."

"Perhaps it is time you gave up this search, *guapo*." Sofia pinned him with her dark brown eyes as she poured coffee into his cup. "Perhaps it is time for you to let the past be in the past. Forgive your enemies. Revenge is not always sweet."

He stared at Sofia and swallowed the words in his throat. There were so many things he could have said to the woman in response. Forgive Logan? He didn't think he could. And he didn't want to. Kieran and his family had been good people—honest, loving, hardworking. The townspeople the Logans had killed were good people as well. He owed it to those who had lost their lives to bring the man to justice. There was nothing else he could do. And he wouldn't rest until he succeeded. "Could you, Mama? Could you forgive your enemies?"

She thought hard, her brown eyes snapping as her gaze remained on him. After a moment, she bowed her head. "Perhaps not, but I would try."

Brock rose from his seat, his stomach now clenched, the soup sitting in the pit of his belly like a rock, the coffee and sopapillas no longer enticing, and gave her a kiss on the cheek, then walked around the table until he stood beside Stevie Rae. "I'll take you to your room unless you'd like to stay."

She turned toward him and took his outstretched hand, slipping her fingers easily within his grasp as she stood. "Thank you all for a lovely dinner," Stevie Rae said before the door closed behind them and they left the private apartments on the third floor. Her hand remained in his as they went downstairs to the second floor, the warmth of her fingers easing some of his frustration. "They're lovely people."

He didn't speak for some time, trying to get Sofia's words out of his head—and his heart. "Yes, they are."

"Mama Sofia doesn't understand, but if it makes you feel any better, I will never forgive Logan for what he did, either. I can't."

She took a deep breath, released his fingers, then rested her hand on his arm. "I won't. There is no forgiveness for what he's done."

Brock drew in his breath. She understood, which amazed him and eased some of his heartache. His stomach began to relax, the hard knot of tension melting away with her words. She didn't think him wrong for pursuing Logan, didn't think he should let the past remain in the past. The plain simple truth was that Logan had committed numerous crimes—he needed to be held responsible for all the sorrow he'd caused.

They came to her door and she turned toward him, her steady gaze holding him captive. Her eyes sparkled in the lamplight and all the colors of her hair—from honey to burnished gold—gleamed in the light shining on her head. Her lips parted and her small pink tongue darted out to lick them before her impish grin teased him once again.

Her smile had enticed him throughout the evening, her lips tempting him to take just a taste, and he couldn't wait another moment. He dipped his head, lightly touching her mouth with his. She made a small noise, somewhere between a startled squeak and a husky groan before she responded.

Brock enjoyed kissing and had from the moment he started practicing with a neighbor girl in Paradise Falls when he was thirteen. There was nothing in the world like the first touch of someone's lips beneath his own, but this...*this* was different. Her mouth was soft and pliable, moving beneath his in a heady mix of innocence and knowledge. The honeysuckle scent she wore filled his head as her hands reached up and entwined around his neck, her fingers lightly brushing against the hair curling at the collar of his shirt.

And he couldn't get enough. He had to have more. Now. He captured her mouth with his own, deepening the pressure, pulling her long, lithe body tight against him as his tongue swept into her mouth.

His heart hammered in his chest. She tasted like heaven, her response even sweeter than he could have imagined.

And yet, he shouldn't be doing this—shouldn't be touching her at all. He had rules—rules he was breaking for her one by one. He pulled away, a blush warming his face. He needed air with no flowered scent to entice him. Without a word, he left—before he lost whatever sanity he still possessed.

• • •

Stevie Rae watched his departure with wonder and amusement mixed with a touch of disappointment, certain the coloring on her face matched his own. She let herself into her room and leaned against the door, the wooden panels stiff and unyielding against her back.

She had been kissed before—she *had* been engaged and Lucas had been a demonstrative man, showing the world she was his, but this...*this* wasn't like anything she had experienced previously. There had been no possessiveness, no domination as when Lucas kissed her. She hadn't lost part of herself in the touch of his lips. Kissing Brock MacDermott had been an equal sharing of excitement and anticipation, longing and desire.

Stevie Rae drew a deep breath and, weak-kneed, stepped away from the door. The exhilaration and expectation of something more didn't leave her. Indeed, as she changed out of her clothes and slid into bed in her chemise and drawers, she wondered how she'd be able to sleep.

Chapter 9

Dressed in her favorite trousers and too-large shirt, both laundered and pressed by Elicia's staff, Stevie Rae entered the dining room in the hotel for some much-needed coffee. She stifled a yawn as she took a seat in the nearly deserted room. Only three other people—a man, a woman, and a young girl—were there, sitting at a table beneath a shimmering chandelier. They did not speak as they ate, concentrating instead on the plates of scrambled eggs, link sausages, and potatoes in front of them.

The aroma of freshly brewed coffee drifted to her nose and Stevie Rae inhaled, her mouth beginning to water as she made herself comfortable and grabbed the menu. There was nothing she liked better than a good cup of coffee. She knew from dinner last night that she would not be disappointed.

A grandfather clock in the corner chimed the hour of eight. As if on cue, Elicia swept out of the kitchen, coffeepot in hand, and refilled the cup of the gentleman at the other table. She smiled, promising to bring the young girl another glass of milk before she made her way to Stevie Rae's table.

"Good morning, *mi amiga*," she said as she nodded toward the cup on the table.

Stevie Rae turned the cup over. "Good morning." Her voice came out hoarse and froggy and she cleared her throat.

"You did not sleep well," Elicia commented as she poured the coffee, filling Stevie Rae's cup nearly to the brim. "Was the bed not comfortable?"

"The bed was fine."

"Then it is something else that has made dark circles beneath your eyes." Her gaze never left Stevie's face, her dark brown eyes warm with compassion and concern. "This quest you are on—finding this Zeb Logan—hurts your heart."

Stevie Rae studied the woman and slowly nodded. It wasn't only finding Logan that hurt her, it was the memories of what he had done and the new nightmares she'd had last night after her kiss with Brock. In her dreams, she relived every moment of her father's murder. And more. Logan's face haunted her, his cruel smile somehow more menacing, his acts of terror so much more horrible as he came after Brock, a bloody knife in his hand. She'd awoken from that particular nightmare bathed in perspiration, a gasp on her lips, barely able to breathe.

With effort, she brought her attention back to Elicia, firmly pushing the remnants of her nightmares away. "Yes."

"What did this man do to you?"

"He killed my father."

Sympathy radiated from Elicia's beautiful face. "And no matter how much it hurts your heart, you will find him, yes?"

"Yes."

"Ah, you and Señor Brock are very much alike. You are both determined, yes? Both unwilling, as Mama says, to forgive."

Stevie Rae's muscles tightened, her nerves raw. She drew in her breath, prepared to argue, but she never had the chance as the downward pull of Elicia's mouth reversed. "I hope finding this man will heal your heart," she said, her voice filled with sincerity. She gestured to the menu. "I'll be back to take your order in a moment. Will Señor Brock be joining you?"

"I don't know. I have not seen him since dinner last night."

The woman nodded, then scurried toward the kitchen, leaving Stevie Rae alone...with her own thoughts, a dangerous prospect. She studied the menu, but the choices held no interest. Indeed, the thought of food made her stomach clench, but she had to eat, if for no other reason than to keep up her strength. Chasing a man who didn't want to be caught was an exhausting, frustrating experience no matter how determined she was.

"Good morning. May I join you?"

Stevie Rae looked up from the menu, her heart picking up an extra beat at just the sound of Brock's voice. Warmth infused her, settling in her belly and tying her tongue in knots. She swallowed against the sudden dryness in her throat and nodded toward the empty chair across from her.

A sheepish grin curved his lips as he perched his hat on one of the spindles at the top of the chair beside him and slid into the seat.

Was it possible he'd grown more handsome in the course of a few hours? His hair had been slicked back this morning, combed through with water as he never used pomade. Strands of silver were threaded into the blackness at his temples but didn't detract from his attractiveness. Not one bit. His eyes, those sharp shards of granite, roamed over her face, which grew hot beneath his perusal. For once, his jaw wasn't clenched, and the smile stretching his lips made her heart flutter in her chest.

"I thought we'd stay here for a few days. Get our bearings and rest a bit. Plan our next move." His eyes flashed like quicksilver and again, a surge of warmth sizzled through her veins, warming her from the inside out. "Is that all right with you?"

"Yes, that's fine." She stirred sugar into her coffee and a sigh of contentment slipped through her lips as she prepared to take her first sip. "It would be so much easier to know where he's going rather than where he's been."

"One step ahead, but then, he's always been one step ahead of me. Not for long, though. I will find him." Determination hardened his features, then disappeared quickly as Serafina approached the table, coffeepot in hand, shy smile curving her lips. Brock turned his cup right side up without a word and smiled at the girl as she poured.

"Mama said I should take your order."

As he leaned back in the chair, his broad shoulders blocked the wooden spindles on the chair's back. He nodded toward her, those mesmerizing eyes of his gleaming. A lazy smile hovered on his lips. In an instant, those ever-present butterflies in her stomach took flight to leave a strange, but not unwelcome, warm fluttering. And once again, she couldn't help thinking he was one of the most ruggedly beautiful men she'd ever met.

"What will you have?"

It was on the tip of her tongue to say "you," but she kept the surprising word to herself and instead ordered a stack of hotcakes. His grin widened when he turned to Serafina and asked for *huevos rancheros*.

The girl nodded and rushed off, moving quickly between tables, which were beginning to fill up for the breakfast rush. Stevie watched him as his gaze took in the other patrons, then settled on her.

He didn't speak but that was fine. She'd gotten used to his long silences, though she still preferred to hear what he thought. He'd spoken only once about his brothers and his parents and she could see glimpses of him as a young boy, roughhousing with Kieran, Teague, and Eamon, laughing as the four of them found mischief and adventure. She wished she'd known him then, when he was young, when his eyes glistened with humor and not pain.

Her thoughts were interrupted by the arrival of their meal.

Brock remained silent only until Serafina was out of earshot. "Heriot said he hadn't seen Logan, and I trust the man, but there's always the possibility Logan slipped in and out of Taos without being seen by the law. In fact, I'm certain he wouldn't be seen. He wouldn't want to be." He dug into his eggs. After chewing and swallowing, he said, "I'm going to ask around."

"I'll go with you."

He paused in the middle of bringing a forkful of seasoned rice to his lips. Stevie almost laughed at his expression.

"Where I'll be going is no place for a lady."

Stevie did laugh then. "I'm well acquainted with painted ladies, Brock. Remember, I used to travel with my father when he saw patients. That included soiled doves."

"I really don't think—"

"Trust me. I've seen people in all walks of life. The good—" She cut a small section of fluffy hotcakes and drizzled syrup over it. "And the bad. Speaking to a scarlet woman or visiting a brothel will not shock my sensibilities. I've been to a bordello before." She grinned as the heat of a blush warmed her face. "And at this point in my life, I really don't care what people say."

"As you wish. Be ready by two o'clock." His gaze drifted over her features, warming her even more. Stevie Rae stilled, the fork with the hotcakes coming to a stop halfway to her mouth. She hardly dared to breathe until he smiled, then dug into his huevos rancheros once more.

• • •

Brock MacDermott was not a man used to waiting. This came as no surprise to Stevie Rae as she stood on the second floor landing and watched him pace to the window, hat in hand, peer into the street through the etched glass, then strut back to the fireplace over and over again, his body rigid with tension.

"I'm ready," she said as she came up behind him, hooked her hand into the crook of his arm, and allowed him to lead her outside. "Do you know where we're going?"

A flush stained his face as he glanced at her, a crooked grin spreading his lips ever so slightly, and she knew, without a doubt, he knew exactly where to go.

Many towns had a section or a street where painted ladies plied their trade. Even Little River had a house of ill repute. She remembered being fascinated with the women who lived there and the men who visited them.

Taos was no different. The houses on Dona Luz looked like any other. Nothing special adorned the solid structures to proclaim them for what they were. Occasionally, one caught a glimpse of a scantily clad woman through sheer draperies or a gentleman leaving the abode, a bounce to his step, but that was all.

Brock led the way up the walk of the first house and opened the door, then ushered her through. Stevie Rae stopped short in the parlor. Her mouth dropped open of its own accord at the scantily glad girls lounging on various pieces of broken or much-repaired furniture. She had lied to Brock. While it was true she'd been to a brothel, she'd only been to Ruby's and only as far as the kitchen, where Ruby herself plied her with milk and cookies while her father tended to the women of the house.

This was a whole new world and she tried not to stare, but it was next to impossible, although she was able to close her mouth. She had never seen so much exposed flesh in her life. She caught a glimpse of a nipple, which had most assuredly been rouged, before the woman adjusted the strap of her chemise. Another woman, a redhead with gleaming green eyes, reclined on a crimson sofa. She crooked her finger at her and winked just before she spread her knees, showing off her thighs—her bare thighs—beneath her slightly worn petticoat. A wicked grin twisted her lips as she hiked the undergarment higher, revealing more of her pale skin, an open invitation in her expression—one definitely not meant for Brock as the woman didn't so much as look his way.

The lace edge of the petticoat traveled another inch higher as the woman's gaze held her spellbound. Stevie Rae drew in a startled breath.

She's not wearing anything under her petticoat!

She swallowed hard and averted her eyes, her face aflame. She wasn't so uneducated she didn't know what the woman was suggesting and she almost bolted. Maybe she *should* have stayed behind while Brock visited the cathouses and asked his questions.

"I shouldn't be here," she whispered, beyond mortification, her gaze searching his face.

"If you're uncomfortable, you can wait for me outside," he said, his voice light, his eyes warm as he moved a little closer to her. His expression did not scream "*I told you so*." Instead, his features conveyed his concern for her discomfort. He wouldn't think less of her if she waited for him on the street.

Before she could make her escape, an older woman approached from the back of the house, smoothing her faded blond hair away from her face as she came closer. She, at least, wore more clothing than the others. Indeed, she seemed almost prim and proper in her stylish plaid skirt and jacket. Stevie Rae stopped, unable to move as she found herself on the receiving end of a thorough inspection beneath the madam's shrewd, calculating eyes. The woman waved her hand, setting the thin gold bracelets around her wrist to tinkling. The girls roused themselves amid grumbles and giggles and left the room.

When they had gone, the woman grinned. "I ain't looking fer a new girl, but yer quite a looker." The frank appraisal of her person continued, from the tips of her boots to the top of her head.

Stevie Rae felt sullied and somehow less of a human being under the woman's heartless, almost cruel, evaluation and she couldn't help wondering how many other girls had gone through this kind of inspection and felt the same sense of degradation she did.

"Little older than I usually take. Take off yer hat, girl, let me see what I'm buying," the woman ordered and then, without a by your leave, reached out in a vain attempt to grab the hat.

Brock moved so quickly, Stevie Rae didn't have time to react. Neither did the madam. He grabbed the woman's wrist in a tight grip and pulled her forward. "That's enough." His voice lowered to dangerous levels as he pinned the woman with a hot, intense glare. "She is not for sale."

The woman nodded, fear flickering in her dark eyes as Brock released her. "Well, then, if she ain't fer sale, what are ye here fer?" One thin brow cocked over her eye as she rubbed the circulation back into her hand. "Ye one of them girls?"

Stevie Rae shook her head and stepped behind Brock, her entire body shaking with indignation, her face not just warm, but burning. "I beg your pardon. We're here to—"

Before she could finish her sentence, Brock pulled the folded Wanted poster from his shirt pocket and opened it, nearly shoving it in the woman's face. "Have you seen this man?"

The woman hardly looked at the poster. "Ain't seen him," she said, anger making her voice a little shrill.

"Look again." There was steel in Brock's voice and the gleam in his gray eyes warned of consequences.

Spots of color now adorned the madam's pale, white cheeks and her body stiffened. "I tol' ye, I ain't seen him. Now get out!"

Stevie Rae couldn't leave the house fast enough. She turned so quickly, she nearly lost her balance, but then she righted herself and raced for the door. Once outside in the warm sunshine, she gulped fresh air and held on to the door frame to quell the tremors rippling through her.

Brock joined her a few moments later, his eyes as dark as granite. He said not a word as he reached out and grasped her chin gently between thumb and forefinger, raising her face just a bit so their gazes met. "Are you all right?"

Stevie Rae took a deep breath and let it slip out between her lips. "What just happened?"

A sad smile crossed his lips. "She assumed I wanted to sell you. That's how a lot of girls end up in places like that."

"How horrible." Stevie Rae couldn't help the shiver that raced through her. "Why?"

"Too many reasons to list, Stevie Rae."

He continued to hold her chin, his eyes peering deeply into hers, the warmth in them easing her jangled nerves.

"You don't have to do this, you know." He released her, his hand traveling down to settle on her shoulder. "You can go back to the hotel."

"No, I'm all right. I promise." She straightened, feeling the warmth of his palm through the thin fabric of her shirt, the concern in his eyes touching her. Pulling air into her lungs, she took a step away from him and adjusted her hat on her head. "Let's just do it and get it over with."

The second house they stopped in was nearly the same as the first, just populated by different girls, although the experience didn't leave her shaken. The madam hadn't given her the once-over, nor made any notion that she was interested in buying her, for which Stevie Rae was grateful, but again, no one claimed to have seen Zeb Logan. The scenario repeated itself in the third house. Stevie Rae could see as well as feel Brock's frustration. It matched her own. Tension built in his shoulders, making them seem broader, and the smile he had gifted her with earlier was nowhere to be seen as they entered a fourth home along Dona Luz.

"Can I help you?" A young woman, maybe sixteen at the most, greeted them. Her fresh-scrubbed face screamed innocence and yet, there was knowledge in her dark brown eyes. And she was fully dressed in a simple skirt and blouse, much to Stevie Rae's relief. As a doctor's daughter and a former medical student, she was no stranger to the human body; however, she really didn't need to ever see a rouged nipple or pale thighs again. Three times in a single afternoon had been more than enough, thank you.

"We're looking for the owner of this house." Brock removed his hat and held it in his hands. He stood beside Stevie Rae, so close she could see the rigid set of his jaw and the muscle twitching beneath his whisker-shadowed skin. So close, she could smell the soap he'd used to wash earlier in the morning.

"Miss Angie isn't in right now. I'm Dottie." She grinned as she opened the door a little wider. Though this might have been a house of ill repute, Dottie seemed well cared for. "You can wait if you want. Miss Angie should be back any minute."

Stevie Rae drew in a deep breath, the tension in her body slowly receding. This house seemed to be cleaner, the girls a little more refined. And a little happier, she noticed as Dottie led the way from the foyer into a warm, comfortable parlor. A number of girls were there, but none of them were lounging about in corsets and pantalets, arms, legs, and bosoms exposed. Indeed, all of them were dressed like Dottie, in clean skirts and shirts, all fresh faced and so incredibly young. Several of the girls were reading quietly. A sweet-faced young woman with a mane of glorious blond hair arranged flowers in a vase while yet another practiced scales on the piano.

"My name is Brock MacDermott." He pulled the poster from his pocket for the fourth time and unfolded the paper. "I'm looking for this man. Has he been here?"

Dottie took the paper and studied the picture, her dark brows furrowing. She shook her head slowly, then turned to the other young ladies in the room. "Girls, come take a look at this. These nice people are looking for this man."

Almost as one, the residents of Angie's house rose from their places and crowded around Dottie. Each perused the poster of Zeb Logan, but none admitted to seeing him. Stevie Rae thought they were telling the truth. For some reason, these young ladies seemed honest to her though she wasn't sure why.

"I'm sorry we couldn't help you," Dottie said as she handed the poster back to Brock. "But you might want to talk to Lily Boudreau. She used to be here with us until one of her favorite customers left her money in his will. She opened her own house on the other side of town by the river. Nice house, too. Real high-class girls." The girl's eyes held a wistful gleam and a long sigh escaped her as she fiddled with one of the buttons on her blouse, making Stevie think the girl would much rather be at Lily's house than here. A higher class of clientele, perhaps? A higher percentage of the profits for the girls? Whatever the reason, the girl wished she was someplace other than where she was.

"Thank you, Dottie. You've been most kind." Brock dug into his pocket and pulled out a crisp bill. The girl's face lit up, her dark brown eyes shining. "For your time."

"Thank you," she murmured and raised her gaze from the money to Brock's face. Stevie Rae watched, fascinated, as the young woman changed, in an instant, from charming innocent schoolgirl to a woman experienced in the arts of pleasing a man. The grin on her fresh scrubbed face disappeared, replaced with a sultry smile meant to draw attention. A slender hand reached up and twisted a curl of dark chestnut hair lying over her shoulder and she fluttered her thick lashes as she stared at Brock, the invitation clear.

Much to Stevie Rae's amusement, a blush rose to Brock's face as he stammered a quick thank-you and made a hasty exit. She almost laughed as she followed him outside, closing the door behind her. She could have teased him about his reaction to Dottie's open invitation, but chose to let it pass. "Are we going to Lily's house?"

"I think we should," Brock said but wouldn't look at her. The blush still colored his face as he stared into the street. "We could stop and get the horses at the livery unless you'd like to wait for me at the hotel." He finally turned to face her and Stevie Rae stifled the laughter bubbling up from her chest. Brock MacDermott, fearless hunter of dangerous criminals, had been frightened by a sweet-faced, though experienced, soiled dove.

"No, I'll come with you." *If only to protect you from painted ladies and their come-hither glances.* "It's been an interesting afternoon to say the least."

He did not respond as she slipped her hand into the crook of his arm and they started down the street toward the main thoroughfare. A low, two-wheeled, closed carriage waited at the corner, the driver polishing the brass fittings while he waited for a fare. Brock glanced at her and nodded toward the carriage. Stevie Rae gave a slight shrug of her shoulders. "Why not?"

The grin flashing across his face stole her breath and she couldn't help admiring the way he moved as he stepped away from her to approach the driver. "Are you for hire?"

The man rose from his stooped position, wiped his hands on the piece of flannel, then tucked the rag into his pocket. "If ya got the coin, I'll take ya anywhere ya want ta go." He bowed slightly, his mouth stretched into a grin. "The name's Cushing."

Without waiting for an invitation or for the transaction to be completed, Stevie Rae climbed into the seat and sat back against the cushions. She just didn't feel like getting on horseback so quickly after spending so many days in the saddle. Brock chuckled, then gave directions to Cushing. The carriage dipped a moment later as Brock took his seat, then dipped again as the driver scrambled to his perch.

Neither one of them spoke during the ride, which didn't surprise her. What did surprise her was that he slipped his fingers between hers and held her hand. She still didn't speak, afraid of ruining the moment, but she did stare at their clasped hands in wonder as warmth flooded her. Once again, he had managed to touch her heart with his small gesture.

A short time later, Lily Boudreau's house came into view. Partially hidden by tall trees and trimmed bushes, it was not at all what Stevie Rae expected. Built of wood rather than adobe, the house had three stories, all painted white except for black shutters and a bright red front door. A proper porch ran the length of the house with groupings of wicker chairs and small tables.

The carriage rolled to a halt in the drive. Brock climbed out of the conveyance, then reached inside and entwined his fingers with hers to help her down as well.

Cushing spoke from his perch. "Ya want me ta wait?"

"Yes, please. We shouldn't be long."

The man shrugged as he pulled half a cigar from his pocket and stuck it in his mouth. "Don't matter ta me. Take as long as ya want," he said, his fingers fishing in the same pocket until he produced a match, struck it against the sole of his shoe, and brought the flame to the stub of twisted tobacco.

"Are you ready?" Brock asked as he turned to her. His gaze held such warmth, heat pooled in her belly. At this moment, with his eyes meeting hers, with their hands clasped and the closeness of his body to hers, she was more than ready for another taste of his lips, even though she knew that wasn't what he meant. She swallowed hard and pushed away her heady thoughts. This was not the time nor the place, but soon, she would follow through on her desire to kiss him.

"Yes," she whispered and allowed him to lead her up the porch steps. Brock twisted the bellpull. A buzzer sounded within the house.

The door swung open a few moments later to reveal a young woman dressed in a starched uniform, a frilly mobcap atop her light hair. "May I help you?"

"We'd like to see Miss Boudreau." Brock swiped his hat from his head and held it in his big hands, his fingers worrying the brim.

"Do you have an appointment?"

"No, ma'am, but we'd like to see her just the same. It's a matter of some urgency."

The woman nodded and, moving aside, opened the door wider. "Please come in. I will tell Miss Boudreau you are here. Make yourselves comfortable." She gestured toward the chairs and sofas in the parlor, then crossed the room and climbed a long staircase.

No girls crowded the large, airy parlor, but she heard giggling and quiet conversation coming from the second floor. Stevie Rae moved farther into the room, brushed the dust from her split skirt, and sat on the edge of one of the leather chairs. Brock laid his hat on the table between them, then lowered himself to the matching chair next to her with a long sigh, his hands dangling between his spread knees.

Lily Boudreau's house was nothing like the houses on Dona Luz and she realized why the girl at the last bordello had wanted to be here. The color scheme was subdued and charming, like a real home. No crimson or gold filled the tasteful parlor, but rather pastel shades of greens and blues and even soft pink. Sheer lace draperies in the wide windows fluttered and flowed gracefully from ceiling to floor, letting in plenty of natural light that highlighted the nature paintings adorning the walls. Tasteful divans and comfortable leather chairs were grouped throughout the room, interspersed with small round tables covered in lacy cloths. Fresh flowers in crystal vases placed on those tables lent their aroma to the surroundings.

Lily's patron must have left her a lot of money. She'd certainly made the most of it. The house, or what Stevie Rae saw of it, could rival the governor's mansion or a railroad baron's manor in elegance.

A grandfather clock chimed the hour, then chimed again fifteen minutes later. Brock rose to his feet and began to pace. Stevie Rae watched him, which was quickly becoming her favorite pastime.

A slight noise drew his attention. He stopped moving and looked toward the stairs where the maid had disappeared. Stevie Rae stood and stared at the stairs as well, her breath stuck in her throat as Lily Boudreau paused on the landing. She was, in a word, stunning. And regal. Dressed in a gown of pale blue with white lace, her creamy white shoulders exposed, she descended the carpeted stairs, her hand sliding along the polished banister, as if she were a queen being presented to her loyal subjects. A huge diamond on a thin gold chain dangled between her breasts, drawing the eye.

Not a line marred her smooth cheeks, not a strand of gray spoiled the darkness of her sable hair. She could have been twenty or forty or even sixty, but no one would guess her age by looking at her.

She stepped off the stairs and practically glided toward Brock, her hand outstretched, her eyes only on him…as if Stevie Rae were invisible, which was fine. The last thing she wanted or needed was another madam giving her the once-over, inspecting her for her worth.

"I am Lily Boudreau. You wished to see me, handsome?" Lily asked, her voice as smoky and smooth as fine whiskey.

Without hesitation or introduction, Brock unfolded the poster and held it up. "Have you seen this man?"

Something flickered in Lily's bright green eyes, though she only glanced at the picture. Was it fear? Disgust? The coy smile she had given him disappeared and her lips tightened as she shook her head. "Not recently."

"How recent is 'not recently'?"

"Three months and two days." Her lips tightened even more and Stevie Rae was able to define the look in her eyes. It wasn't fear or self-preservation. It was hate. Pure, unadulterated loathing. "I could check my books, if you'd like, but I remember his visit like it was yesterday, and I can tell you, Zeb Logan is not welcome here, not after that night. I run a nice house, mister, and I treat my girls well. So does my clientele."

"What happened?" Stevie Rae asked.

The woman's shoulders slumped before she stiffened, every muscle taut beneath the pale blue gown she wore as she nearly staggered to one of the leather chairs and slowly lowered herself to the butter soft cushion. Brock followed and took the seat next to her. He reached for Lily's hand, wrapping her long, slim fingers within the warmth of his own. When she looked at him, Stevie Rae saw the tears in her brilliant green eyes.

"As you've seen, we're very secluded out here, which is what my clients want but that had never been a problem before…that night." She took a deep breath and her voice grew hoarse. "It was a Sunday. My girls were at a private party on the other side of town, so it was just Patrice and me. We were enjoying the peace and quiet." She disentangled her fingers from Brock's and reached into the sleeve of her gown to retrieve an embroidered linen handkerchief. She dabbed at her eyes, then touched the square of linen to her nose delicately before resting her hands in her lap. "Neither one of us heard him ride up before he came crashing through the door. I'd never seen him before but it seemed like Patrice knew him. And she was scared. So scared."

She pulled air into her lungs and stared at the hands folded in her lap. "She started talking fast, trying to…appease him, I guess. But it didn't work. He kept asking her where it was and Patrice kept denying she had anything." She glanced at Brock again and such pain radiated from her face, Stevie Rae gasped. The urge to comfort this woman rose in her and yet, she couldn't move. "I didn't know what they were talking about, and I didn't care. I just wanted him out of my house before he hurt her. I care about my girls, Mister…what did you say your name was?"

"I didn't, but it's Brock MacDermott. Please continue."

She gave a slight nod. "I tried to help her. To stop him from whatever he intended, but I was no match for his strength. He hit me." She touched her jaw with the tips of her fingers. Though the bruise was long gone, the memory was obviously still vivid. "I hit my head on the banister when I fell and everything went black. When I finally came to, he was gone. So was the money box and the house was quiet. Too quiet. I picked myself up off the floor and went looking for Patrice, but she…" She inhaled deeply and dabbed at her eyes once again. "I found her in the dining room. She'd been beaten so badly, I hardly recognized her."

Tears pricked Stevie Rae's eyes as she imagined what Patrice had gone through at the mercy of a madman, but she learned something she hadn't known before. Zeb Logan wasn't only proficient with his pistols. He was equally as dangerous with his fists—at least toward women.

"Is Patrice still here? I'd like to talk to her."

The woman shook her head and reached up to fiddle with the necklace hanging between her breasts, as if it were a talisman bringing her strength and comfort. Finally, she whispered, her voice full of pain and regret, "She died from her injuries a day later."

"I'm so sorry, Miss Boudreau."

She dabbed at her eyes and drew in a breath, her pain clearly evident on her pale face. "I am, too. Patrice was a good woman and a good friend."

Brock rose from his seat. "I know this was hard for you, but I appreciate what you've told me." He once more grasped her hand, his eyes peering into hers. "I know it doesn't help Patrice, but please know I will see Zeb Logan hang."

Lily remained in the chair but she raised her gaze to his, the brightness of her eyes shadowed by sadness, the lashes spiky from her tears. "Why do you want him?"

"Patrice wasn't the only person he hurt. He has a lot to pay for and I'll make sure he does."

The woman nodded. "Thank you."

Brock pressed her hands one more time, then reached for his hat and jammed it on his head, clearly uncomfortable with the gratitude radiating from Lily Boudreau's tear-filled eyes. He left the room quickly, the door closing with a soft *snick* behind him.

Stevie Rae swallowed against the constriction in her throat as she laid a comforting hand over Lily's. "Thank you for your time,

Miss Boudreau." She gave the woman a warm smile. "Rest assured, we will find him and he'll never bother you or your girls again."

The woman said nothing but there was appreciation in her eyes. Deeply touched, but unwilling to give in to the swirl of emotions whipping through her, Stevie Rae gave the woman's hand another quick squeeze then fled the house.

Brock waited for her on the porch, his back toward her, hands on his hips, his gaze focused on the river flowing gently to his right. His shoulders moved as he drew air into his lungs.

Stevie Rae came up behind him, her heart pounding, her vision blurred from the tears pricking her eyes. "Brock?"

He didn't speak as he turned to face her, weariness written clearly on his features, but it was the sadness in his eyes that nearly became her undoing. Stevie Rae tamped down the sudden urge to wrap her arms around him and just hold him. She took a step closer and raised her head until her gaze met his. "We will find him, Brock."

"I know. I just…it's…how many other people will he hurt before we do? How many other girls will be beaten? How many others will die?"

She touched him then, rested her hand on his arm, the muscles beneath his shirt bowstring tight. "It isn't your fault."

"Yes, it is. If I had captured the bastard when I had the chance, when he killed Kieran, this would be over, but…"

She shook her head and tried to ease the guilt from him. "From what you've told me, it wasn't possible at the time. You were shot."

"Doesn't matter," he muttered before his lips tightened into a thin line and the muscle in his jaw began to spasm. Stevie Rae drew in a deep breath. No matter what she said, no matter how many arguments she could give him, he'd never believe her. She also knew there would be no more conversation just by the expression on his face. He moved away from her, his gait stiff, and stepped off the porch, heading toward Cushing and the waiting carriage without a word.

Chapter 10

"Stevie!"

"In here." Stevie Rae looked up from the letter she'd been writing to Martha in the small sun parlor off the main room of the hotel as Brock rushed into the lobby. Instantly, her body stiffened as she stuck the pen into the inkwell and rose to her feet. She'd been waiting for this—an end to this idyllic respite. Though they'd only been at the Hacienda for three days, she'd seen how uncomfortable Brock had become, even though it had been his suggestion they stay.

Was it being within the embrace of a warm, loving family? She hadn't missed the expression of longing in his gray eyes when he was with the de la Cruzes, nor had she missed how the de la Cruz children seemed to gravitate toward him.

Was it the fact that out of all the people he had talked to, no one claimed to have seen Logan except for Lily Boudreau and that had been months ago? Brock had spoken to Sheriff Heriot, relating all that the madam had told them, but Heriot had been unaware. Lily hadn't reported what had happened, which, according to Brock, had made Heriot so very angry, for more than one reason—a murder had occurred in his town and he hadn't known and by Lily remaining silent, another opportunity to find Logan and end his madness had come and gone.

Or was it something else?

Perhaps the kiss they'd shared had made him uncomfortable. She could still feel, days later, the pressure of his mouth on hers, still taste him and see the look on his face when he pulled away—a mixture of fear and pleasure, and perhaps a touch of regret. She herself had no regret. Truthfully, she had wanted to kiss him for quite some time, longed to feel the touch of his lips on hers. And wanted to again, though she had been a coward and hadn't acted on her desires.

He rushed into the small room. "We have to go."

She studied his face, pale and tight with anger, and realized there was a fourth reason for his unease. Logan. While they were resting at the Hacienda, Logan was free to dole out his particular brand of mayhem. She approached him, her palms already damp, her heart pounding in her chest.

"Where?"

"Española."

Stevie Rae nodded. She was familiar with the town, though she had never visited. "What happened?"

"Tim Heriot received a telegram from the sheriff in Española. A family has been murdered." He drew in his breath, visibly shaken. If possible, his face became even paler and sweat made his forehead gleam beneath the brim of his hat. "I can't be sure it's Logan—at this point, no one can, but…"

Stevie Rae nodded, her stomach already tightening. "I can be ready in a few moments."

"I'll get the horses and meet you out front."

He was gone as quickly as he'd come, his movements relaying all the anxiety and fear he felt.

Sadness overwhelmed her as she sealed the letter to Martha, dropped it on the desk in the lobby for posting, and headed upstairs to gather her belongings. A short time later, no more than fifteen minutes, Stevie Rae left her room and strode down the corridor, her saddlebags slung over her shoulder, gun belt once more riding low on her hips. She stopped on the second floor landing, her breath wheezing in her lungs as pain assailed her heart.

More people dead by the hand of a madman. Could she and Brock have prevented this? Instead of staying at the Hacienda, they could have ridden to Española, but how could they have known? The last they'd heard, Logan had been heading to Taos…

and they had followed. Had Annie at the saloon lied to them? Offering them one direction when Logan, himself, had gone in another?

She swallowed over the lump in her throat, took a deep breath, and headed down to the lobby. Elicia waited by the etched glass doors, her hands clutching at the white apron tied around her waist, anxiety clearly written on her features. She pulled Stevie Rae into a warm embrace and whispered, "Be safe, *mi amiga.*"

When she pulled away, there were tears in the woman's eyes. Stevie Rae ignored them as best she could.

It surprised her how quickly she'd grown fond of the de la Cruzes, but fondness had no place within her now. She had a criminal to bring to justice.

Stevie Rae nodded once, then slipped through the door without a word.

Brock waited outside with the horses, his hands gripping the reins of both Willow and Resolute. Whiskey Pete's reins were tied to Willow's saddle, his back laden with just a few supplies. Brock said not a word but his jaw was clenched, the muscle in his cheek ticking like mad.

Stevie Rae attached her bags to Willow's saddle, then climbed into her seat. She tugged on the gloves that would protect her hands, adjusted her hat on her head, accepted Willow's reins from Brock, then waited for him to mount up before she nudged the horse's sides and rode out of Taos.

Despite the warmth of the late afternoon and the hot breeze that swirled the dust in the street, a chill snuck into her bones.

• • •

Taos was nearly an hour behind them when Brock noticed Stevie moving Willow closer to him. "Someone is following us." Her voice was low and Brock clearly heard her fear.

"I know. Has been since we left Taos." He didn't turn his head to look behind him, though every muscle in his body tensed and his stomach churned with anxiety. "Follow me." Despite the sudden burst of fear rippling through him, he tried to keep his voice calm for her sake as well as his own. Who had followed them? Was it Logan? The man knew he was being hunted. Perhaps, after killing the family in Española, he'd doubled back to Taos. It wouldn't have surprised Brock—Logan, though a criminal through and through, could never be called stupid—but the logistics were all wrong. Unless the man had a touch of magic, it wasn't possible to be in two places at one time.

Taking a deep breath to calm his unease, Brock guided them off the path they'd been following beside the Rio Grande and into a small copse of trees, then slid from his saddle beside an outcropping of jagged rock. Reaching out to Stevie Rae, he helped her down from Willow's back. Her eyes were wide and filled with apprehension and she looked like she wanted to run. "Stay behind me."

A flash of color—red and black—appeared between the trees, then more color as slowly the horse and rider became clear. Brock recognized the hat the uninvited guest wore as well as the horse he rode and the tension in his body eased.

Sam Whitaker. A fellow bounty hunter, friend, and all around good man.

He heard the sound of Stevie Rae's pistol clearing leather and the distinctive *click* of a hammer pulling back. He whirled around to face her in time to notice the paleness of her skin, the determination on her face, the fear glittering in her eyes...and the muzzle of the gun wavering wildly in her shaking hand as her finger rested on the trigger, but she had yet to raise the pistol. The bore pointed toward the ground.

"Don't shoot—" Before he could finish his sentence, the loud report of the Colt revolver echoed in his ears. The recoil made the pistol fly upward and instead of harmlessly sinking into the ground, the bullet expelled from the gun put a hole in the loose material of his trousers…right between his legs. An inch higher, and he would be missing…a very important part of himself.

Fear—and yes, anger—gripped him. Heat surged through his body, tensing his muscles as he snatched the gun from her shaking hands, tucking the Colt into the waistband of his trousers, the muzzle hot against his skin through the fabric of his shirt. "Holy hell, Stevie! What are you doing?"

"Protecting us," she whispered as she took a step away, her body trembling almost as much as the pistol had, her expression one of horror.

"By shooting me?" he barked as he studied the hole in his trousers, then poked his finger through singed material. "Shit! If you were trying to kill him, you missed by a mile." His gaze rose from the hole in his pants to her face and the tears shimmering in her eyes.

It had been an accident. She hadn't meant to pull the trigger.

Or had she?

"You wear this fancy rig—" His fingers grazed the gun belt slung low around her hips. "But you don't know how to shoot, do you?"

She took another step back, her gaze intent on his before she finally shook her head. There was an apology in her eyes—but not in the sudden grin she flashed at him. "I wouldn't have missed you with my shotgun."

Brock grunted instead of letting loose the relieved laugh that bubbled up from his chest, his anger disappearing in the impishness of her smile. Despite the fact she shot him, Stevie Rae Buchanan amazed him in so many ways. "I'll keep that in mind."

"Hell, MacDermott, you tryin' to kill me?"

Brock stepped away from Stevie Rae and studied the man who had been following them as he approached, leading his horse by the reins. A wide grin spread the thick mustache on the man's upper lip, letting Brock know there were no hard feelings. There never was with Sam Whitaker.

"Wasn't me," he said as he held out his hand to shake and nodded in Stevie Rae's direction. "She's a little nervous." He patted the pistol tucked into his waistband, assuring himself there would be no more random shots taken. At least for tonight. "Taking your life in your hands sneaking up on a man like that, Sam. What were you thinking?"

Sam shrugged as his gaze fell to the hole in Brock's trousers then back up to his face, amusement dancing in his light brown eyes, the mustache on his lip twitching. "Wasn't thinkin'. Saw you leave Taos. Thought I'd ride along with you for a while, if you don't mind."

"Don't mind at all. We're heading to Española."

"Española? Why Española?"

"There's been a murder. Could be Zeb Logan's handiwork."

The man nodded, well acquainted with the Logan family, the acts of horror they committed either together or alone, and Brock's determination to see their reign of terror ended. "Who's your shooter?"

Brock chuckled, but Stevie Rae bristled and blushed as he pulled her from behind the boulder. "Stevie Rae, this is my good friend, Sam Whitaker. Sam, Stevie Rae Buchanan."

Sam grinned at her, then held out his hand. "Pleased to meet you...I think."

"I'm sorry," she whispered as she shook his hand, her mortification complete as the blush staining her cheeks deepened. "But you shouldn't have been following us."

"You're right, ma'am. My own damn fault if'n you'd a shot me." His merry brown eyes darted to the hole in Brock's trousers once again then back to her face. "Like you did him." He laughed then, finding humor at Brock's expense, and perhaps a bit relieved he wasn't the one with a bullet hole somewhere on his person.

Brock didn't take offense—he'd known Sam too long to take the man's laughter seriously. Instead, he took a deep breath and studied Stevie Rae's face. The blush on her cheeks seemed to have taken up permanent residence and she looked…absolutely stunning.

"We'll camp right here and begin shooting lessons as soon as possible." He took another breath, his gaze riveted to her face. "I don't want to end up dead because you can't hit the broad side of a barn."

Stevie Rae said nothing, although her eyes darted to the bullet hole. She nodded slightly before she moved away to see to the horses, then grabbed the coffeepot and headed toward the river.

Camp was set up in no time at all and a fire blazed in the hastily made fire pit although the sun had yet to sink into the horizon. As Sam headed down to the river to catch some fish, Brock stepped behind one of the boulders sheltering their camp to change out of his ruined trousers. He tied his pants around the trunk of a tree several yards away then approached Stevie Rae as she crouched down beside the fire and placed a coffeepot on the metal rack above the flames.

He held her gun in his hands. "Are you ready?"

"As I'll ever be." She rose to her feet, body stiff, hand trembling as she reached for the pistol and wrapped her long, slim fingers around the handle. She didn't say a word, but doubt and uncertainty danced in her eyes before she walked away and positioned herself about twenty yards away from the target. Brock followed and stood slightly behind her and to the right. "Aim for the pants. That shouldn't be too difficult seeing as how you've already put one hole in them."

She harrumphed, then raised her arm, extending the pistol, and squeezed the trigger. The echo of the first shot had barely died before a second and third followed. She missed. All three shots, by several yards. He wondered if she took aim or if she closed her eyes every time she pulled the trigger.

"This isn't working. I can't do this." Her voice became tight.

"Try to relax, Stevie. This isn't a race. Or a game."

"I know it's not a game, MacDermott."

He ignored her sharp words and simply grinned. She had gone back to calling him MacDermott, letting him know not only by the use of his last name, but by her tenor, she was frustrated. He understood. "Let me help you."

He stepped up behind her, removed her battered hat, and placed it on the boulder they'd hidden behind earlier, then wrapped his arms around her, pulling her body against his. She stiffened within his embrace but only for a moment.

Too late, he realized it was a mistake to hold her this close.

Actually, it wasn't a mistake.

It was torture…sweet agony of the most pleasurable kind, as the memory of their kiss flared in his head. She was soft in all the places a woman should be soft, especially her rounded bottom, which he had been admiring for quite some time. He suppressed a groan as he pulled her closer still, that delectable behind pressing more firmly against his most vulnerable parts, the parts he'd come close to losing earlier in the day. The heat from her body warmed him, making it difficult to concentrate on the task at hand—teaching her to shoot, without killing him in the process.

He expelled a long sigh, ruffling the strands of honey blond hair next to her ear. That was torture, too, as the scent of honeysuckle rose to his nose. "Relax, Stevie. Let the pistol become an extension of your arm." With his arms around her, he helped her aim at the ruined trousers. "Pull back on the trigger gently."

She did…and again missed entirely, the bullet flying past the target to lodge in another tree several yards away. Her entire body slumped with disappointment. "I can't do this."

"Yes, you can. It takes practice. No one is born knowing how to shoot although some seem to take to it easier than others. Let's try again. Take a deep breath and let it out slowly. Line up the sight on the pistol with your target. When you're ready, squeeze the trigger. Gently."

Again, Stevie Rae did as instructed. The bullet whistled past the tree, nowhere near the intended target. Standing so close to her, feeling the tension in her body, Brock felt her disappointment as keenly as she did.

"Sam?" Brock turned slightly to see Sam approaching from the left, several gutted fish lined up on a hastily made spear. "You wanna try?"

The man shook his head though his perpetual grin remained in place. "Oh no, not me. I ain't getting near that girl. She's dangerous!" He squatted down beside the fire and carefully perched the makeshift spear on two rocks high above the flames.

"It's useless, Brock. I'll never hit the target." Defeat colored her voice and she tried to move away from him.

He tightened his arms around her, unwilling to let her go. Not yet at least. He enjoyed holding her and feeling her softness, smelling her delightful scent of honeysuckle. "Yes, you will. Where's your grit and gumption? The stubbornness you take such pride in? Where's your 'don't help me, I can do it myself' attitude?"

She turned her head slightly to look at him. He saw it then—in her face, in the tightness of her utterly kissable lips—the fortitude that had carried her this far, the tenacity that held her upright when most others would fall. Her eyes glittered, the blueness of them touching him deep in his soul. Her gaze held him captive for the longest time before she turned away and raised the gun.

"That's my girl," he whispered in her ear. As a reward, she shivered ever so slightly and sucked in her breath, her back moving against his stomach.

"I'm not your girl," she hissed.

He grinned. He'd made her angry again and wondered which words made her so. His questions about her determination? Or the fact that he'd called her his girl? In the long run, it didn't matter, as long as she learned to shoot, for his own safety if nothing else. "Concentrate. Imagine yourself as the bullet. Imagine me still wearing those trousers. Close your eyes and breathe deeply. When you open your eyes, squeeze the trigger gently, like you're caressing a baby's cheek."

Stevie Rae grew very still within his arms. She inhaled as instructed, then pulled the trigger as she exhaled. The bullet sank into solid wood with a *thunk*, leaving another hole in Brock's trousers, right beside the original. She released her breath in a sigh. "I did it!"

"Good. Now reload and do it again."

With the ease of someone who had practiced loading and unloading a six-shooter, Stevie Rae did as she was told. When she was done, she spun the cylinder.

"Where'd you learn to do that?"

She grinned at him. "Papa taught me. He thought I should know how to protect myself."

"He taught you how to load and unload, but didn't teach you to shoot?"

"He tried." She gave him a grin that told him the lessons hadn't gone well, then presented her back to him. Brock stepped closer and wrapped his arms around her again, though it had nothing to do with helping her aim and more to do with just liking the feel of her in his arms.

"Remember to breathe."

After five shots hit the target, two off to the right, the other three dead center in the crotch—she only missed once—she holstered the firearm, then turned in his arms, her eyes glistening with excitement and accomplishment, her mouth parted…and oh so inviting.

Brock did the only thing he could do under the circumstances. He tilted her head back and kissed her, his mouth taking possession of her soft, pliable lips. The scent of honeysuckle filled his senses as much as her taste, intoxicating him. He wanted more. Much more. He pulled her tighter against him, feeling the soft lushness of her body against his entire length. A shiver rippled through her as her arms wrapped around him, her fingers sliding through the hair at the back of his neck. Blood surged through his veins—hot. Insistent. Arousing.

Sam cleared his throat from the other side of the camp. "If yer done playin' kissy-face, the fish is ready."

He didn't want to let her go, but he had no choice. Stevie Rae stiffened in his embrace, then pulled away, her face flushed with embarrassment but her eyes darkened and glittered with excitement and, perhaps, passion. She opened her mouth, then closed it without saying a word before she gave a slight nod and hightailed it down to the river.

• • •

Hours later, the campfire burned brightly, the flames dancing along logs. Dinner, which consisted solely of the fish Sam had managed to catch, had been consumed, the tin plates and forks cleaned and put away. Stars twinkled in the heavens and anticipation curled in Brock's belly. He leaned against his saddle, filled his pipe…and waited. He wasn't disappointed as Stevie Rae pulled a horsehair brush from her saddlebag.

She settled on her bedroll, her legs crossed, and started brushing through her long hair, a nightly ritual he'd come to enjoy, though he'd never admit it.

Sam poured himself another cup of coffee and settled on his own bedroll on the other side of the fire, his eyes on Stevie Rae, admiration twinkling in their depths as she pulled the brush through her long, shimmering tresses.

Jealousy, an emotion new and unfamiliar to him, made Brock's stomach clench. As much as he liked Sam, he didn't like the way he watched Stevie brush her hair. That was his pleasure and his alone. He was about to say something to draw the man's attention away when the man grinned at him and spoke, but not to him. He directed his question to her.

"What's a nice girl like you doing with a bas—uh—hard head like MacDermott?" he asked, his grin stretching his impressive handlebar mustache. "Gotta tell you, I ain't never seen MacDermott ride with anyone for more than two days at the most. He prefers his own company." He chuckled, the sound grating in Brock's ears. "Sure as shit, never seen him try to teach anyone to shoot, neither. You done pretty good, girl, once you got the hang of it."

She stopped pulling the bristles through her hair and rested the brush in her lap. Her eyes glimmered in the firelight. "He's the only one I trust to help me find Zeb Logan."

Sam cut off a plug of chewing tobacco from the supply he kept in a small pouch and shoved it between his cheek and gum. "Why do you want to find Logan?"

"He killed my father."

"I am sorry about that. Logan ain't a nice man."

"No, he's not." A long sigh escaped her as she plied the stiff bristles of the brush to her long, thick hair once more. "My father was a very kind, gentle man, Sam. There was no reason for what Logan did to him, especially after he removed the bullets from Logan's leg and shoulder."

"Your father was a doctor?"

"Yes…before he…gave it up."

"Why'd he give it up?"

Brock stilled and waited for her answer, hoping to catch a glimpse of her life before tragedy drove her on the course she was on now. He'd known Steven Buchanan was a man of medicine, but he didn't know why he'd given up practicing.

Stevie Rae shrugged and for a moment, she looked so sad, he wanted nothing more than to enfold her in his arms and kiss her again. Repeatedly. Until she forgot the pain in her heart, until she was breathless and hungering for his touch as much as he yearned for hers. He restrained himself and remained on his side of the fire, though his heart pounded fiercely in his chest.

He had already broken too many rules for her. He couldn't afford to break more.

"I wasn't there, but I was told he lost three patients, one right after another. It broke him. He lost his faith. That's when he sold the house and closed his practice and borrowed money from the bank to buy that little cabin and Poor Man's Dream." Tears shimmered in her eyes, reflecting the flames of the fire. "He couldn't save those people and he blamed himself. Oh, he blamed God, too, but he blamed himself so much more. I took care of him more than he took care of me, but that was all right. I didn't mind."

"What will you do when you find him? Logan, I mean."

"Take his life like he took my father's," she responded in her matter-of-fact manner, her voice strong and commitment-filled as she rose to her feet and put the brush away. Brock winced. He thought he'd made her understand his purpose in finding Logan and it wasn't to kill him. He needed to be brought to trial and let the law decide his fate. It wasn't up to Brock, though he longed to see the man swing from a rope. He wasn't judge and jury. Neither was she. He'd have to remind her once again, make his intentions clear, but now wasn't the time. He doubted she would listen. Or even hear him. Too much hatred filled her heart.

Brock held a match to the bowl of his pipe and puffed it alight, but his eyes were on her as she removed her boots and slid between the blankets. She nodded once in his direction and said good night, her voice tight with suppressed emotion.

Firelight reflected on the top of her head, shimmering in her honey gold locks as she turned on her side, her back to them.

"Did I tell you I brought in Slim Garner? Found him in San Antonio, of all places," Sam said, drawing his attention. "Sumbitch nearly killed me, but I got the drop on him."

Brock gave a noncommittal grunt and let the man talk, but he wasn't listening. He watched the rise and fall of Stevie Rae's even breathing and wondered how he'd be able to keep her from killing a man who deserved to die.

Chapter 11

Stevie Rae wiggled the fingers of her right hand, trying to relieve the numbness. She'd been gripping Willow's reins so tight, she'd lost feeling in both hands. Pins and needles flared beneath her skin as the numbness began to disappear. She repeated the process with her left hand before she glanced over at Brock riding beside her. He sat tall in the saddle, his body stiff. He hadn't spoken much since they packed up their camp earlier this morning. She supposed he was all talked out, having stayed up with Sam after she had turned in the night before.

Sam, though, hadn't stopped talking since he'd woken up that morning and she wondered if he spoke when no one was around to hear him except himself. She glanced in his direction. He grinned and kept up his recitation of criminals he'd brought to justice. The list never seemed to end and for a moment, she wished he'd be quiet—which struck her as odd considering it wasn't too long ago she'd hungered for the sound of another person's voice.

They'd been following the railroad tracks that led straight into Española almost as soon as they started riding earlier, passing small farms and ranches along the way. The Denver and Rio Grande Western Railroad had done some good here in town. The streets bustled with pedestrians. A sign hung over the window of a store, announcing the grand opening. New buildings constructed of lumber were interspersed between old buildings made of adobe. Several people waved in greeting as they strolled, and yet, she took no pleasure from the friendly gesture. In truth, apprehension filled her, growing steadily from the moment Brock had told her about the murder in this town. She had no way of knowing if Logan had committed the crime, but she was almost afraid to find out.

A wooden placard with the simple word "Sheriff" painted in bold black letters hung from metal hooks screwed into the roof of the covered walkway. A slight breeze pushed the sign, producing a squealing sound as metal rubbed against metal. The sound went right through her, ratcheting up her anxiety. She took several deep breaths in an effort to will the unease away but it didn't help.

With Brock in the lead, they rode up to the sheriff's office.

"I'll just wait here," Sam said as he peered through the window, still in the saddle. He made no move to dismount. "No sense all of us crowding into that office."

Stevie Rae slid from Willow's back as Brock did the same and glanced through the window. The office was very small. Two desks were crammed into the space with a narrow walkway between them, and a single unoccupied jail cell with a bunk bed ran the width of building toward the back. A small Ben Franklin stove, its smoke pipe rising up to the ceiling, sat in a corner.

A young man sat at one of the desks, his feet up on the desktop, a magazine open on his lap. He brought a cup to his lips and drank deeply. She assumed by the level of comfort he exuded, he must be a deputy. She would have been surprised if he was the sheriff. He seemed too young.

"We're looking for Sheriff Newbold," Brock announced as they entered the office, his boot heels loud on the bare wooden floor. The deputy's badge winked in the sunlight streaming in through the open door.

The young man jumped up from his seat, startled. The magazine dropped to the floor. Liquid sloshed out of the cup in his hand, but she doubted it was coffee as there was no coffeepot in sight. Redness stained his face, almost matching the shock of thick, wavy hair on his head.

"What do you need him for?" The question wasn't asked with any amount of courtesy. In fact, the tone was downright rude. Stevie Rae glanced at Brock. His jaw tightened and she wondered, however briefly, if he would give the young man the comeuppance he deserved.

He did not. Though his hands were clenched at his sides and the muscle in his jaw jumped, he took a deep breath and remained calm. His voice low and menacing, he said, "My name is Brock MacDermott. Sheriff Newbold sent for me."

The boy swallowed hard, his Adam's apple bobbing. If possible, the redness on his face grew deeper. Tiny beads of sweat popped out on his forehead. "My...my apologies, Mr. MacDermott." Again, he swallowed, then reached down to pick up the fallen magazine. "The sheriff ain't here. He's out at the Weston place."

"And how would I find the Weston place?"

"It's just outside town. Take a right at the rail station and keep riding. Can't miss it. It's the only one out there."

Brock gave a slight nod and left the room without a word. Stevie Rae followed, just as silent.

"Where we headed?" Sam asked as he lightly jerked the reins in his hands. His horse, a beautiful black and white mare with the unlikely name of Daisy, moved slightly and snorted.

"The Weston place," Brock answered as he unwrapped Resolute's reins from the post in front of the office.

As she climbed into Willow's saddle, Stevie Rae glanced through the window and grinned when she saw the deputy sink into his chair and wipe the sweat from his brow. MacDermott sometimes had that effect on people.

It wasn't hard to find the Weston place. The house wasn't quite finished yet. It needed a coat of paint, but that was all. The barn, however, was completed and a bright red color. There were horses in the corral, and Stevie Rae heard the plaintive lowing of a milk cow as they cantered into the homestead. Chickens clucked and pecked at the feed on the ground while a rooster strutted in front of them, fanning his feathers and crowing. A small vegetable garden, its rows freshly tilled, already had sprouts of green.

A man walked out of the freshly painted barn leading a horse by the reins and pulled the brim of his hat lower to shade his eyes.

He stopped and wrapped the leather straps around the top rail of the corral, a warm, sad smile creasing his face. "Brock," he said with a nod, his voice low and gravelly. "Glad my telegram found you. Knew you'd want to see this."

"Paul." Brock dismounted and moved toward the man, his hand extended in greeting. They shook, then, as old friends do, grabbed each other in a bear hug.

Stevie Rae watched as the men broke apart. For a man as quiet and stoic as Brock MacDermott, he sure had a lot of friends and acquaintances, but then, maybe he was only silent around her.

"Who's riding with you?" Paul asked as they approached.

Brock completed the introductions, then nodded toward the house. "Who were they?"

"The Westons? Easterners. From Connecticut." Paul removed his hat and wiped his brow before fitting the headgear back on his head. "Jared Weston was a nice enough fellow and Mrs. Weston— Clara—was a real sweetheart, though a little sickly. Gave up his law practice and came out here for her health, or so he told me when I first met him." Sadness reflected on his face, and his voice held a poignancy that was hard to bear. "Clara and my wife took to each other like ducks to water. Broke my heart to have to tell Sarah about this. She hasn't stopped crying since."

Stevie could imagine how difficult it had been for the man to tell his wife about their friends. Clearly, the Newbolds had been fond of the Westons and vice versa. Sorrow gleamed from his eyes before he blinked and his jaw set, replacing the sadness. "I ain't sayin' Logan was the one who did this, but it sure seems to fit everything I've heard about him."

Brock didn't speak much, but his eyes took in everything as he helped her from the saddle. "Who found them?" he asked over his shoulder.

"I did. Sarah wanted them to come to dinner. Knew something was wrong the minute I rode up." He drew in a breath in an attempt to keep the reins on his emotions tight, though it didn't seem to help. Stevie Rae understood. Those same emotions attacked her on a daily basis, making it difficult sometimes to hold on to the desire for something besides vengeance.

"Come into the house. Gotta warn ya, though, it ain't pretty." Paul Newbold led the way toward the house like a man going to the gallows. Stevie Rae had noticed when she first met him that his actions were well thought out, his movements full of purpose, but right now, he walked across the dirt yard as though lead weights were tied to his ankles. He stepped on the front porch and reached for the door, then stopped, his hand resting on the doorknob.

Brock stepped up behind him and rested his hand on the sheriff's shoulder. "You don't have to do this, Paul. I can take a look by myself."

The man visibly relaxed, his breath blowing out between his lips in a relieved huff as he stepped away from the door. "Thanks. I've seen a lot in my fifteen years as sheriff, but this was…different. The brutality. The senselessness of it all. The Westons were good people." He turned and looked at Brock before his watery gaze traveled to her. "There are no words."

Tears smarted Stevie Rae's eyes, and her throat constricted. If a lawman as tough and experienced as Paul Newbold had a hard time going into a house where a murder had been committed, how would she feel? Her thoughts traveled back to the little ramshackle lean-to they'd found in the Sangre de Cristos and the sure knowledge that Zeb Logan had been there to mete out his particular brand of cruelty. His evilness seemed to live and breathe and haunt the places where he committed his horrible acts. She'd felt that in her own home after Logan had killed her father.

Would she experience the same feelings here?

Her stomach clenched and her hands began to shake, but she steeled herself for what she was about to see.

Brock opened the door and stopped on the threshold, effectively blocking her passage, his body stiff, tension thrumming through every tendon and sinew, but he couldn't stop the odor from wafting out the door. The pungent odor of death and misery and heartache—even though she stood behind him—hit her immediately. Stevie slapped her hand over her mouth and nose in a vain attempt to keep from breathing it in, but it didn't work. The smell was too strong, the misery too new.

He turned toward her. "You should stay outside." Concern for her well-being reflected in his clear gray eyes, but she couldn't wait outside. She had to see for herself.

"I'll be all right." She removed her hat and held it in her hands, her fingers worrying the brim as she slipped past Brock and stepped into the main room of the little house. The icy bite of evil struck her immediately, like a blow to the belly, making her heart thunder in her chest.

Brock stepped behind her and laid a comforting hand on her shoulder. "Stevie Rae?"

She couldn't speak. As Sheriff Newbold had stated, there were no words to describe what she saw. She nodded, but didn't turn to look at him, afraid of what she might see on his face.

Sam touched her hand, offering comfort, as he, too, just stopped in the middle of the parlor.

Jared and Clara Weston were no longer here—Sheriff Newbold must have taken care of them—but the evidence of what had happened to them remained. Dark crimson stained the wooden planks of the floor as well as a small rag rug crumpled in the corner of the room. Splatters of the same color marked the walls and freshly painted ceiling. Even the settee pushed against the wall beneath the window had not been spared—splotches of blood marred the pale blue fabric.

Someone—Mr. Weston, perhaps—had fought back against the assault. Splinters and larger pieces of what remained of a kitchen chair littered the floor. The chair, which should have been around the table with its mates, had been shattered, perhaps over someone's head or across someone's back. Shards of what once were plates with a pretty rose pattern were scattered throughout the tiny kitchen. Blood stained the pristine porcelain of the sink and the lacy curtains hanging over the window above the basin.

She didn't need to be shown where Mr. and Mrs. Weston had lain after they'd been killed. The dark stains on the floor told the tale without words.

And there, on the freshly painted cabinet door, a bloody handprint. Left hand. Missing little finger.

Stevie Rae closed her eyes against the sight of so much mayhem, but that was a mistake. With her eyes shut, her other senses heightened and she could almost hear the screams in her ears, smell the Westons' fear. Her eyes flew open. Nausea coiled her stomach and bile rose, scalding the back of her throat. Logan had been here. He had hurt these people. His malevolence lingered, leaving her cold and angry and so utterly sad. She shivered despite the heat of the day and blinked back the tears blurring her vision.

What made a man be so vicious? What drove someone to kill without remorse? Without censure? What had the Westons ever done to him to make him behave in so deadly a fashion? The questions running through her head had no answers and were useless to even ask. Zeb Logan didn't need a reason to hurt anyone. He might actually enjoy it. She remembered seeing him through the slats of the root cellar's trapdoor and the deadly smile that crossed his face when he shot her father. And then his laughter, as if the blood seeping from her father's mortal wound amused him.

Some people—men and women both—were that way— exerting their power, their strength. Some did it like Logan. Viciously. Brutally. In plain view. Others were a bit more devious, hiding their nasty deeds and malicious intent behind dazzling smiles and soft-spoken words.

She ran outside and stood at the end of the porch, her hands gripping the railing, gulping in air in an effort to tamp down the rising nausea. She shook, so violently she thought her bones would rattle loose beneath her skin and leave her a quivering mess with the consistency of pudding.

Brock approached her, his footfalls heavy on the wooden planks. She turned toward him and drew in a ragged breath, then another and another until she could control the urge to cry and scream and rail at the heavens for what had been done to these decent people. She almost lost what little control she had gained when she looked into his eyes. Concern for her had softened his features and she didn't think twice when he opened his arms. She stepped into his embrace and clung to him, gathering strength from his solid body. His heart pounded in a steady rhythm beneath her ear as she laid her head against his chest.

"Are you all right?" His voice, low and tight with suppressed emotion, cut through the chaos of her thoughts.

Stevie Rae nodded against him and she took that moment in his arms to try to erase the images burned in her brain, but it did little good. She cleared her throat, then pulled away from him to stare into his eyes.

"It was Logan, wasn't it?" he asked before she could say a word. "I saw the handprint this time. Couldn't *not* see it."

She nodded, uncertain of her voice, still fighting the nausea twisting her stomach, but absolutely certain Logan had done the killing.

Paul and Sam approached as well, but it was the sheriff who spoke. "I'm sorry you had to see that, miss."

Beside the sheriff, Sam had finally run out of words, probably for the first time in his life, but sympathy and pain radiated from his dark eyes. He shifted his weight from one leg to the other, clearly uncomfortable, his muscles poised to flee at the first opportunity. A peculiar expression settled on his face, and

Stevie wondered if perhaps his stomach protested at the amount of violence Logan had left behind. Though a bounty hunter of some fame, it all seemed to be too much for him at the moment.

She didn't dare look at Brock again as she pulled herself together and scrubbed her hands over her face to remove the wetness from her cheeks, unaware until this moment she had shed tears for the Westons. She reached out and laid her hand lightly on the sheriff's arm, offering what little reassurance she could. "It's all right. I had to know."

The man nodded and turned away, his hands resting on the porch railing as he studied the flowers blooming in the small garden below him. He took a deep breath and let it out slowly. "He took everything of value he could find. Jared's gold watch. The string of pearls Clara always wore. The money from the little glass jar next to the coffee canister where Clara kept it. Some food. He even took their Bible, the bastard."

"When did this happen?" Brock asked Paul, though his eyes darted to her continually and worry left its indelible mark on his face.

Paul took off his hat and wiped the sweat from his brow before finally turning to face them. Stevie Rae felt his loss as keenly as she felt her own. The Westons might not have been related by blood, but sometimes friends were closer than family.

"Can't be sure, but I'd say three days ago at the most. The last time I saw Jared was Saturday, when he picked up supplies at Kirby's General Store." Paul's voice grew hoarse and he swallowed several times. When he spoke again, his words were clipped and terse. "I found them the day before yesterday, which was what? Tuesday? I took care of them. Sent you that wire and sent one to Jared's son in Connecticut. Took out a posse, but it was too late. Logan was long gone. Son of a bitch didn't even leave a broken branch in his wake. At least, not that we found."

He stepped off the porch, his movements stiff, his expression a strange combination of disgust and heartache. "I'm heading back into town. Nothing more I can do here except arrange for someone to come out and take care of the livestock until Jared's son arrives." He hitched up his trousers, then adjusted the gun belt around his hips. "You're welcome to stay with Sarah and me at the house, if you're of a mind to stay in Española."

Brock looked at her and tilted his head to the side. "Stevie, do you want to stay?"

She shook her head, deciding in an instant that staying with Paul and Sarah would be a bad idea. Not only would Logan get farther away, free to roam the country and commit more acts as heinous as the ones he'd already committed, but she just didn't think she could bear to stay with people who were grieving. Their sadness would be contagious and she already had buckets of her own grief to deal with. Sharing sympathy with Paul and Sarah would be her undoing. She needed to stay angry and determined in order to keep on the trail of a madman. "Thank you, no. I think we should ride out. It may not be too late to pick up his trail."

"Sam? What about you?" Newbold asked as he turned toward the bounty hunter.

Sam declined the kind offer with a quick shake of his head. Sheriff Newbold gave a slight nod, then almost staggered to his horse, a weary, heartsick man who'd seen too much. He climbed into the saddle, touched the brim of his hat, and rode off.

Stevie Rae watched him go, her heart hurting for him, then turned toward Sam, a question on her lips, but she never had the chance to ask as Brock studied the man. "You all right, Sam? Never known you to be this quiet."

Sam blushed and opened his mouth several times, but no words poured forth. He removed his hat and fingered the brim while he rocked on his heels until finally, he found his voice. "Ain't nothin' to say," he murmured, then jammed his hat back on his head. His eyes held a gleam of sorrow. "Been nice riding with you two, but I think this is where we'll part ways." He scratched his chin beneath the scraggly beard covering it. "The bounty on Logan would be welcome in my bank account, but truth to tell, I ain't got the stomach for chasing him down. Give me a straightforward bank robber or cattle rustler, and I'll follow him to the ends of the earth, but this is too much."

He held out his hand toward Brock. "Godspeed, MacDermott. I hope you catch that bastard."

"Thank you, Sam."

"If you need me, I'll be in El Paso. Got me a girl who wants to settle down and I'm thinking now might be the time to make an honest woman out of her."

Stevie Rae watched the display. There was genuine fondness between the two men and the embarrassment that sometimes accompanied it. Redness colored Sam's face as he stepped away from Brock, then moved toward her, his mustache stretching across his upper lip when he gave her a somewhat shy smile. She was unprepared for the bear hug he wrapped her in.

"And you." He sighed as he hugged her tighter. "It's been my pleasure to meet you."

Her throat constricted and she swallowed hard as she nodded against his chest. "You as well, Sam."

"You keep safe and keep MacDermott safe, too. And don't let him rile you."

Stevie Rae almost lost her balance when he let her go.

He touched the brim of his hat and winked. "Keep your pistol holstered, sweetheart."

Before she could offer a wisecrack in response, he took the porch steps in his loose-hipped swagger, sauntered across the yard, and climbed into the saddle. One last time, he nodded in their direction, then dug his heels into Daisy's sides and rode off, leaving a plume of dust.

Chapter 12

"If I was Logan, where would I go? He seems to have no fear of being caught." Stevie Rae took a sip of her coffee and settled herself on her bedroll with a sigh. Exhausted and heartsore didn't begin to define what she felt. After Sam left the Westons' ranch, she and Brock stayed around for a little while, looking for anything that might tell them in which direction Logan had gone, but the man was careful. He'd left no clues. At least, none that they could find.

They'd headed west, away from Española, but hadn't traveled very far when Brock stopped their progress, saying it didn't feel right. They turned north, but still were unable to pick up Logan's trail. Hours later, hot, sweaty, and with the sun beginning to sink into the horizon, he finally suggested they camp early and start again in the morning.

They'd found a homestead...or what was left of one. Several planks of rotted wood, ready to disintegrate with the slightest of breezes, was all that remained of the barn. The house was in equally bad shape—roofless, defined only by crumbling adobe walls that defied gravity and the elements, but cool water still filled the well dug deep into the ground near the front of the house.

Stevie Rae stared at the wild profusion of roses twisting and turning around the well, then focused on Brock. He sat against a wall, removed his hat, and put it to the side, then pulled pipe and tobacco from his shirt pocket. He went through his ritual of preparing his pipe, which usually relaxed him. It did not this time.

"It's more than a lack of fear, Stevie." Brock clamped the pipe between his teeth and spoke around the stem as he tucked the pouch of tobacco back in his pocket. "I think he enjoys the chase. It's doing something to him, making him braver. More diabolical. Look at what he did to the Westons." Sadness crept into his eyes as his jaw tightened. The pipe rose under the pressure and she winced, afraid he'd snap the stem between his teeth, then she relaxed a bit when he removed the pipe from his mouth and gestured with it. "Since I've been after him, his violence and the senseless killings have increased…almost like…"

"He's showing off for you. Taunting you. Rubbing your nose in the fact he's still committing crimes…and you haven't stopped him."

Brock sat straighter against the wall he'd been resting against, his muscles tensing. A frown pulled down the corners of his mouth and created furrows between his eyes. "He *is* taunting me." His shoulders slumped as if beneath the weight of Logan's horrible actions…and his own part in the commission of those crimes.

Stevie Rae's heart went out to him. "It isn't your fault, Brock."

He glanced at her, his eyes dark like storm clouds, then slowly rose to his feet and walked away from the camp.

She watched him disappear behind what was left of the barn, noticing how stiffly he walked, like an old man hunched with age and brittle bones…and regret. After a moment, she rose to her feet as well and followed him. He stood with his hands on his hips, the pipe clenched between his teeth, though still unlit, the muscle in his jaw twitching.

"Maybe it is my fault." He removed the pipe from his mouth and jammed it his pocket, mindlessly spilling tobacco down the front of his shirt. His eyes were focused on the horizon and the last rays of the setting sun. "If I weren't chasing him, maybe he wouldn't take so much pleasure in killing. Maybe I should—"

"Logan would be killing people even if you weren't after him." She refused to listen to the words uttered by this brave, honest man, nor could she tolerate the doubt she heard in his voice. Tears pricked her eyes, and her throat tightened. She laid her fingers on his arm, feeling the steel-hard muscles beneath his shirt. He didn't pull away from her. "That's who he is. What he does. He's been killing for years, Brock, long before what happened in Paradise Falls and your vow to stop him. His behavior has nothing to do with you. Or me."

Brock turned and finally looked at her and Stevie Rae sucked in her breath. Such pain radiated from his eyes, from his entire face. It was all she could do to hold his gaze as she repeated the words in her heart. "It's not your fault. None of it, Brock." Instinctively, she wrapped her arms around him and held tight, offering what little comfort she could give. He stiffened within her embrace.

Stevie Rae rested her head on the hard planes of his chest and tightened her arms around him until he accepted her gift for what it was. The tension in him started to abate and his muscles relaxed. After a long time, he rested his chin on the top of her head, then wrapped his arms around her and pulled her against him even closer.

How long they stood in the dying rays of the sun, holding each other, Stevie Rae didn't know. What's more, she didn't care. Peace stole into her, a feeling of comfort that warred with the turmoil she'd felt since seeing the devastation at the Westons' ranch. Surprisingly, the horrible visions in her head started to fade. Not forgotten—never forgotten—but somehow, within his embrace, not nearly as vivid as they'd been earlier. The sadness in her heart eased enough so she could draw in her breath without pain.

The urge to rail at the heavens for what had been done to good, innocent people receded and a new emotion took hold.

She raised her head from Brock's chest and studied his face. The pain was still there and uncertainty glittered in the clear gray of his eyes, but at least his features were no longer carved in stone. She loosened her hold on him and rose up on her toes, following through on a newly awakened yearning for an affirmation of life. Gently, she touched her lips to his.

Brock stiffened before running his fingers through her hair and lowering his mouth to slide over hers with a desperate hunger that made her blood sizzle through her veins.

His stomach rumbled.

Startled by the sound, she broke the kiss, realizing neither one of them had eaten since breakfast. "Are you hungry?"

"No."

"You say 'no' but your stomach says otherwise. You must eat. Even if it's just a little. I can make some of those biscuits you like."

Without waiting for him to respond, Stevie Rae broke their embrace and walked back to their camp. She heard Brock follow, but at a much slower pace, as if the mental ache in his mind had become physical. She headed straight for the sacks of supplies tied to Whiskey Pete's back and found everything she needed to make the simple fare. Brock settled himself once more on his bedroll, his back against the wall. He pulled the pipe from his pocket, filled it again with tobacco, and clamped it between his teeth. Moments later, he struck a match against the bottom of his boot and brought the flame to the pipe. Smoke wreathed his head as he puffed it alight, and the aroma of fine tobacco filled the air to compete with the scent of roses growing wild and untended around the water well.

As she prepared the biscuits, she kept watching him, her eyes darting from the skillet to his face, worried about him and the way he felt at this moment. Would he stop pursuing a man who was as difficult to capture as quicksilver? Would he just give up?

She prayed he wouldn't. She didn't want to do this alone, but she would if she must.

Stevie Rae put the lid on the skillet, slipped it under the coals in the fire, and...didn't quite know what to do with herself. The inclination to hold him, to touch him, still lived within her and yet, she couldn't bring herself to approach him again. The expression on his face left no doubt that he wished to be left alone.

To wallow in his own doubts?

To accept blame for the actions of another?

It wouldn't do. She knew all too well what happened to a person's mind—and their heart—when one allowed guilt to corrode one's sense of worth. She'd seen it with her own father. The guilt of not being able to save either his wife twelve years earlier or his patients two years ago had eaten at him, changed him from a brilliant doctor who treated everyone regardless of their ability to pay to a man who was afraid of everything.

She didn't want that to happen to Brock. He was an honorable man with a good heart, much like her father had been.

Brock needed a distraction from his self-torture. "It's still light enough. You could give me another shooting lesson." She willed him to say yes, but he just shook his head, his eyes focused on the horizon, the pipe stem clamped between his teeth.

Stevie Rae let out a long sigh, slid the skillet out from the coals, removed the lid, and poked her finger against the biscuits to test for doneness, then used her pocket knife and lifted the edges. Golden brown on both sides, they were perfect.

"They're ready."

Brock didn't move, didn't even acknowledge she had spoken. She moved several biscuits to a tin plate and handed them to him. He nodded his thanks, but that was all.

Stevie Rae let out another sigh. It was going to be a long, silent night, even more silent than usual.

• • •

Morning did not bring an improvement to Brock's mood. He'd spent a sleepless night, haunted by nightmares of the bloodstains on the floor of the Westons' little house. What horror they had gone through. He awoke feeling, deep in his bones, that Logan's increased terrorism was his fault. Stevie Rae didn't believe that, but he did. If he weren't hell-bent on bringing the man in, would

Logan simply quit his murderous spree across northern New Mexico?

The answer was simple. Logan would never stop. Stevie Rae knew it. He knew it. Killing was in Logan's blood. He enjoyed it.

Logan had changed, though, leaving Lily alive to witness his act of terror.

Another part of his game? To what purpose?

Brock froze, his breath seizing in his lung. *Shit! Logan left Lily alive so I would find her and see what he's capable of.*

He shook himself, but the thought remained in his head. He tried to ignore it as he filled their canteens from the water well, his gaze resting on Stevie Rae. Worry ate at him, especially knowing what Logan had done to Patrice.

Could he protect Stevie Rae? Keep her safe?

He hadn't been able to keep Kieran safe, nor Mary or Matthew.

Stevie Rae smiled at him as she adjusted the cinches on Willow's saddle, then plopped her battered hat on her head. She adjusted the collar of her duster and pulled on her gloves, then, grabbing the pommel, slipped her foot into the stirrup and climbed into the saddle. With a few clicks of her tongue and a gentle tug on the reins, she neatly turned Willow and walked up beside him and Resolute, Whiskey Pete following behind her, but not happy about it. His loud *hee-haws* disturbed the peace of the morning as he tugged against the reins. "I'm ready."

Brock nodded once, then handed her one of the canteens. She looped the long strap around the pommel, a gentle smile curving her lips.

He led the way, heading north once more. Rolling hills, dotted with yucca, juniper, and creosote, spread out before them. Dew sparkled in the morning sun, making those plants and trees shimmer. In the distance, a coyote gave chase to a hare while an eagle soared high above, its wingspan nothing less than astonishing.

Brock tugged lightly on the reins and slowed Resolute's pace, allowing Stevie Rae to catch up to him. He glanced at her and admiration filled him. The woman handled her mount well. She sat tall in the saddle, her long honey-colored hair spreading out from beneath her hat to curl down her back. He swallowed over the dryness in his throat. "About last night…"

"What about it?"

He opened his mouth, but the words seemed stuck in his throat. He swallowed hard and tried again. "I'm sorry."

"For what?"

For letting you come with me. For letting you see things no woman—or man for that matter—should see. For putting you in danger. For so many things. Though the words popped into his brain, he didn't say any of them. He couldn't, not beneath the steady gaze of her warm blue eyes. "For taking advantage—"

"You didn't take advantage, Brock. I kissed you."

He nodded once, accepting the truth, though the truth didn't lessen his guilt. He had liked the feel of her lips against his, and God help him, he wanted to kiss her again. He wanted to run his fingers through her gloriously thick hair and feel her body pressed against his until he just couldn't think.

But he couldn't allow that to happen again. Not now. Perhaps not ever again. Three times had been tempting fate. A fourth time, well…he had a mission. Two of them, if he were honest: find Logan and keep Miss Stevie Rae Buchanan safe and untouched. He couldn't do either of those things if all he thought about was holding her in his arms and caressing her soft skin.

He filled his lungs with sweet morning air, nodded once more, and trained his eyes on the horizon. The steady *clip-clop* of Resolute's hooves against hard ground echoed in his ears and became a refrain in his head. *Keep her safe.*

Brock glanced in her direction, but her eyes, too, were on the horizon, her back straight, hands loosely holding the reins.

She squinted beneath the shadow of her hat before she tilted her head, her attention drawn to something in the near distance. "What is that?"

"What is what?"

"There's something glistening in the sun. Do you see it?" Stevie Rae pointed to a spot where several creosote bushes shaded the earth, then she nudged Willow's sides and trotted ahead, Whiskey Pete following behind, braying for all he was worth.

"Wait!"

But she didn't wait. She never did. Headstrong and sometimes foolhardy, she rushed in without thought to the consequences, whatever they might be.

Brock drew in a deep breath and lightly kicked Resolute's sides. He caught up with her as she slid from the saddle and picked up a string of pearls, holding them outstretched in her hand. "These must be Clara's. Remember, Paul said Logan had taken them from her."

Brock dismounted, but he didn't take the pearls from her hand. Instead, he hunkered down so he could study the ground. The dirt had been disturbed by hoofprints, clods of earth kicked up as if Logan had struggled to control his horse…and failed. "Looks like his ride reared and Logan fell. Dropped the pearls without realizing it." He rose to his full height and finally took the necklace from her hand. Bile burned the back of his throat as the memory of the chaos in the Weston house flitted through his mind. A slight breeze ruffled the edges of his duster, and a chill chased up his spine that had nothing to do with the weather and everything to do with his pursuit of a madman.

"We're on the right track then." Stevie Rae took the pearls from his hand and stuffed them into the pocket of her duster. "Embudo isn't too far from here. Maybe he's headed there."

"Maybe. Or maybe he doubled back and is on his way somewhere else, one step ahead of me." The futility of his task settled deep in his bones. How long would he search for a man who didn't want to be caught before he realized it was pointless? Bringing Logan to justice wouldn't bring Kieran or Mary back. Seeing a noose around Logan's neck wouldn't reverse time and allow Matthew to grow into the man he had been destined to become.

The doubts that plagued him yesterday and this morning revisited him in full force. Feelings of incompetence and inadequacy afflicted him, and the hopelessness of his mission turned sour in his stomach. And yet...he couldn't allow himself to give up the search, couldn't allow Logan to win.

He looked at Stevie. She hadn't moved but she watched him, weariness shadowing her brilliant eyes, her mouth set in a grim line of determination. She wouldn't allow Logan to win either. That was plainly clear.

"He won't always be one step ahead, Brock. We *will* find him. We have to." She hooked her foot into the stirrup, hoisted herself into Willow's saddle, then picked up the reins, all without taking her gaze from his. "I'm heading to Embudo. What about you?"

He gave a slight nod, then climbed into Resolute's saddle and lightly nudged his sides. They rode side by side, neither one speaking until they reached the small town nestled in a sweet spot where the Embudo River flowed into the Rio Grande, aware of her intense stare as if she knew of the uncertainty drifting through his mind and tried to enforce her determination and stubbornness on him with nothing more than the warmth of her gaze.

Like Española, Embudo showed a surge in population with the building of the train station. People meandered along the raised wooden sidewalk, shopping at new stores as well as old, but even with the growth, it hadn't changed much in the year since he last visited.

He stopped in front of the sheriff's office and dismounted, then turned to Stevie Rae. She looked tired, shadows framing her beautiful eyes, but her lips were still pressed together in grim resolve. "You all right?" he asked as he helped her from the saddle.

She nodded once, but he knew she lied. She wasn't all right. Chasing after Logan had taken a toll on her, just as it had him, no matter how determined they both were. Did she harbor the same doubts he had? If she did, she never expressed those misgivings aloud. He drew in a deep breath and pushed all thoughts from his head then stepped onto the raised wooden sidewalk.

A small chalkboard had been nailed into the wood beside the door frame. "Back in fifteen" had been written in white against the black slate. Brock tried the doorknob anyway, but found it locked.

"Sonny isn't in." He glanced in Stevie Rae's direction. She had removed her hat, placing it on the pommel of Willow's saddle, and quickly pulled her shining hair into a ponytail at the back of her head.

"If it's all right with you, we'll wait." He shrugged. "Unless you'd rather find lodgings for the night."

She shook her head as she stepped up on the sidewalk beside him and leaned against the building. "We can wait."

They hadn't waited long when a young man approached from the south, a small canister in his hands, the Silver Star pinned to his vest gleaming in the sunlight. "Can I help you?" he asked as he stepped up to the sidewalk beside them.

"We'd like to see Sheriff MacLeish."

"Sonny? He's not sheriff anymore. He retired." He pulled a ring of keys from his trouser pocket, unlocked the door, and swung it open. "I'm Will Rafferty," he said with a wide grin. "Elected sheriff by a landslide vote eight months ago. Come on in."

"Brock MacDermott. This is Miss Buchanan." They shook hands in the doorway. "We're on Zeb Logan's trail. Thought he might have passed through Embudo within the last couple of days. Have you seen him?"

Rafferty led the way into the office and placed the small canister on a table next to a potbelly stove. "Logan? No, I haven't. If he's been here, I highly doubt he'd make his presence known with me." He spoke over his shoulder as he unscrewed the tin's cap and proceeded to make a pot of coffee. "Never seen him except for that poster on the wall. In truth, I don't really want to. I know what he's done."

The news wasn't what Brock wanted to hear. He glanced at Stevie Rae, but she wasn't looking at him. Instead, her eyes were on the Wanted poster and Zeb Logan's brutish face. She shivered, her entire body quaking despite the duster she wore, and when she turned to face him, he saw the disappointment and raw anger in her features, but no fear gleamed from her eyes. He swallowed hard and turned back to Rafferty. The man stood with his hands on his hips, his fingertips brushing the top of his gun belt, his eyes, filled with curiosity, darting from him to Stevie and back.

"Anything unusual happen lately?"

Rafferty shrugged. "A few drunken rowdies lookin' for a fight, but nothin' unusual in that."

Another dead end. Brock couldn't help the long sigh that escaped him or the frustration that built within him.

"Is MacLeish still in town?"

The sheriff shook his head. "Nah, he moved in with his daughter and her family. They have a ranch outside Santa Fe. Heard from him a couple of times since he retired. He seems happy to be chasin' grandchildren instead of criminals."

Brock took in the information and a small smile tugged at the corner of his mouth. Yes, he could see MacLeish trying to keep up with a passel of young ones. The vision in his head grew for a moment then disappeared, sobering him instantly. "Any place I can send a few telegrams?"

"Sure. Bud Hollings at the depot can help you. Just tell him I sent you."

Brock nodded. "Thanks for your time, Sheriff. Come on, Stevie, let's go."

She tipped her hat to the sheriff, then stepped outside. "Where to now?" she asked as she stopped on the raised sidewalk and glanced at him. Weariness made her voice huskier than usual, but it was the sadness lurking in her eyes that struck him the hardest.

"The train station."

They walked the horses to the depot, as it wasn't far. "Do you want to come in with me? It shouldn't take long."

"I'll just wait here."

He handed her Resolute's reins, then went inside. As was his habit whenever he rode into a new town, Brock sent out his telegrams. There were a dozen in all, lawmen throughout New Mexico and Colorado whom he'd become friends with and knew of his search for Logan, but at the moment, he had little hope they would pan out. Logan was smart. And getting smarter. More cunning. He might have come to Embudo, but he hadn't stayed long enough to cause mayhem or perhaps, he hadn't come to town at all, had just made them *think* he'd come here. The pearls could have been dropped on purpose—to draw them here while Logan went in the opposite direction, getting farther and farther away.

As he handed several crisp bills to Mr. Hollings, Brock turned his head and caught a glimpse of Stevie Rae. She had moved from where he'd left her and now leaned against a split-rail fence just outside the train depot, hat tipped back, face turned toward the sun, her duster tossed over Willow's saddle. For a moment, all he could do was stare at her loveliness. As his gaze traveled her lithe form and delicate face, he wished things could be different, a desire that had come to him more than once and seemed to be growing.

Time seemed to have stopped, and for a moment, there was no one but him and her—no passengers buying tickets, no small children bickering as they sat beside their parents, waiting for the train, no young lovers sitting side by side, their hands clasped together—

Mr. Hollings cleared his throat and extended his hand through the small space between the counter and the bottom of the grill he sat behind, the coins shining dully in his palm. "Your change, sir."

Reality rushed back with brutal clarity and he clenched his jaw. He'd never have a moment's peace until Zeb Logan was no longer a menace.

He studied the money in the man's slender hand. "Mr. Hollings, if you wouldn't mind, I'd like to send one more telegram."

"Of course." The man nodded, then drew back his hand and dropped the coins in a drawer to his side. He grabbed the short stub of a pencil and half a sheet of clean paper. "Whenever you're ready."

Brock dictated the note, thanked Mr. Hollings, and left the building.

Stevie Rae tilted her head and squinted up at him as she watched him cross the street. "All done?"

He didn't answer her question. Instead, he asked, "How's your backside?"

Startled, her eyes opened wide, then narrowed against the bright sunlight streaming over the peaked roof of the train station. "My what?"

"Your backside."

Suspicion pulled down the corners of her mouth. "Why do you want to know?"

Brock shrugged. "Just trying to determine if you're ready to get back on your horse right now or wait until tomorrow."

"That depends. Where are we going?"

"Santa Fe."

"Why?"

"To see Sonny. He's the only man I know who came close to capturing Logan and probably would have except Logan got the drop on him and shot him in the back." He took Resolute's reins from her grasp and started walking back toward the main street. Stevie fell into step beside him and he glanced in her direction. "Took a long time for Sonny to heal after the surgeon removed the bullet and I don't think he was ever the same after that, which is probably why he retired." He paused where the fence ended. Stevie stopped as well, giving him her full attention, her eyes bright despite the brim of her hat shading her face. "I think we should go see him. Maybe he can tell me what I'm missing."

She nodded before she hoisted herself into Willow's saddle. "My backside is fine. Let's go." The lie flowed from her lips, like he knew it would.

Brock climbed into Resolute's saddle but didn't nudge the horse's side. Instead, he just sat there, looking at Stevie Rae until she flashed him that soul-catching grin and urged Willow forward. Caught off guard, he couldn't help the chuckle that escaped him. She made him want to pull her from her horse's back and kiss her in the middle of the street. In the shadows or in the sunlight, it didn't matter, he wanted to feel the touch of her lips beneath his own. She did that to him. When he hit his lowest and didn't think he could take another step in any direction, she managed to make him believe he could.

"Are we just gonna stand here all day, or did you want to go to Santa Fe?"

Chapter 13

Four days later, they rode into Santa Fe. Banners hung across the streets, inviting one and all to a rodeo event, and the streets bustled with people as Brock and Stevie Rae maneuvered through the throng toward a hotel. Tired, dirty, hungry, her resolve starting to slip, Stevie Rae ignored it all as she glanced at Brock. If he felt those same things, he didn't share, but she could see the exhaustion on his face. He hadn't smiled since they'd left Embudo, although she had tried to get him to.

"I'll see if there are rooms available here." Brock swung down from the saddle and wrapped his horse's reins around the post in front of the building before he climbed the steps and disappeared inside.

She slid from Willow's back and stretched the kinks from her shoulders and back. Sitting so long in the saddle had made her muscles ache more than she would have expected. Or perhaps, it was sleeping on the hard ground. Oh, it would be lovely to sleep in a real bed on a thick mattress and soak in a hot bath.

The hotel's door opened a few moments later, and Stevie glanced up, expecting Brock to usher her inside. But it wasn't Brock who stood in the doorway. It was the last person she expected to see—Lucas Boyle, doctor of medicine—and her former fiancé.

Stevie stiffened as memories flooded her. She didn't want to see him, or talk to him, and the inclination to walk away before he noticed her became too strong to ignore. She turned, ready to make her escape.

"Stephanie?"

Too late.

Stevie closed her eyes and resisted the urge to grind her teeth. He was the only one who insisted on using her proper name, no matter how much she disliked it.

He stepped into the street and strutted toward her, his long-legged stride still full of purpose, his smile just a touch condescending, like it had always been. And why had she never noticed that his smile never reached his eyes, as if he held something back?

It had been months since she'd seen him, and just as long since she'd thought about how he'd broken their engagement and the terrible words he had thrown at her. She had been devastated and angry then, but time had lessened the hurt. She thought of him fleetingly, those moments never lasting long, but seeing him again, she thought she'd feel something—a pang of regret or a flutter in her belly like when she looked at Brock. But she didn't feel much at all. The sight of him didn't reduce her to tears, nor did she have the desire to slap him across the face, like she had at one time.

Stevie straightened and allowed her shoulders to relax. She even managed to smile at him. "Hello, Lucas."

He grabbed her hands, then bent over to kiss her, but at the last moment, she turned her head and his lips landed on her cheek.

"What are you doing here?" he asked as he released her, then took a step back. His gaze swept her from head to toe and back and it didn't take more than two seconds, perhaps, for his mouth to settle into a disapproving line. She'd seen that before—too many times to count. "Oh, I see. You're still chasing after that outlaw, aren't you? Determined to do a man's job. As stubborn as always and hell-bent on doing things your own way." He shook his head. "I thought you'd come to your senses these past few months, but I see you haven't."

Stevie Rae opened her mouth but never had a chance to respond as her attention was drawn to the hotel's porch and Brock leaning against the door frame. Jaw clenched, eyes narrowed and glinting like granite, he stared at Lucas, a stranger to him. "You all right, Stevie Rae? He bothering you?"

Every muscle in her body tensed as his gaze met hers and held. How much had he heard? "No, he isn't bothering me. I'm all right." She took a step back and gave a slight nod of her head. "If you'll just give me a moment…" She didn't finish the sentence, but hoped he would understand.

He did, though reluctantly, if the muscle jumping in his jaw and the rigid set of his shoulders was any indication. He moved away from the door and sank into one of the rocking chairs on the porch, affording a little bit of privacy but close enough to intervene if need be. She glanced in his direction and tried to smile, then focused her attention back on Lucas.

"Is that who you're with now, Stephanie? Some lowlife cowpoke with nothing to his name? Is he better than me? Can he offer you more than I can?" He sneered then, not even bothering to hide his disdain. "Have you taken him to your bed, too?"

Time apart had not changed him. Not his blond hair, which lay over his forehead in a thick sheaf, nor his dark green eyes or his self-satisfied smirk. If anything, he seemed even more arrogant. Why hadn't she seen that before? Could love truly be that blind?

Yes, she supposed it could, but then, maybe it hadn't been love. And maybe the problem didn't lie with him at all, but with her. If she had truly loved him, wouldn't she have missed him these many months? Thought of him every day instead of every now and then?

She hadn't. Absence had not made her heart grow fonder.

She studied him now, her gaze resting on his handsome face, and came to the startling conclusion that it didn't matter. None of it. Her life had changed in ways he'd never comprehend and never approve of. And he had no part in it.

"Thank you for your concern," she said and took a few steps away, "but if you'll remember, it was you who left me. As of that moment, you lost whatever say you *thought* you had in what I can and cannot do. For your information, that man is Brock

MacDermott. He's a bounty hunter and he's helping me to do what you refused to—find my father's killer."

He moved so quickly, Stevie Rae didn't have a chance to react. He grabbed her by her upper arms, his fingers squeezing into her soft skin. From the corner of her eye, she saw Brock shoot out of the rocking chair, vault over the porch railing, and jump to the street. The expression on his face bespoke of murderous intent, the tension in his muscles proof of his ability to follow through on that threat.

"Mister, I don't know who you think you are, but if you don't let that lady go, you'll be answering to me."

Lucas glanced at him, a sneer twisting his lips before dismissing him. "This is a private conversation between the lady and me."

"Doesn't look like a conversation from where I'm standing." Brock tipped his hat back, revealing his whole face and the smile that didn't quite reach his eyes. "Looks like you're manhandling her and she doesn't like it."

Stevie Rae drew in her breath. She'd seen that look before, had been on the receiving end of it several times. His expression harbored nothing good, but before she could speak, Brock took a step closer and his voice softened—another warning Lucas wouldn't be aware of. "Now if I were you, I'd take my hands off the lady and I'd do it quickly."

Something flickered in Lucas's wide eyes—self-preservation, perhaps? He released her and took several steps back.

"Nice seeing you, Stephanie." Lucas touched the brim of his hat, then walked away quickly, his movements stiff. Stevie watched him cross the street then disappear around the side of a building. Her breath released in a rush and she rubbed her arms where he had pressed his fingers so cruelly into her skin.

"You all right?"

Stevie Rae nodded, unable to speak. The worry in Brock's voice was enough to make tears sting her eyes, and his kindness brought a lump in her throat. She swallowed hard. "Thank you."

He touched her, lifting her chin with gentle fingers. "Who was that man?"

She let her gaze roam over Brock's face. His normally clear gray eyes were now as dark as thunderclouds. "Doctor Lucas Boyle. Up until a few months ago, we were engaged to be married."

"Engaged?"

"Yes."

"But not anymore. What happened?"

Stevie dropped her gaze and stared at the tips of her boots for a moment before she glanced at him again. "He broke our engagement and left town when I told him of my intentions to find Logan."

Understanding dawned, and his eyes changed from that polished pewter of a thundercloud to the clear gray she knew so well. "He didn't approve, did he?"

"No, he didn't approve...of many things, which I'm just beginning to realize." She took a deep breath and willed herself to remain calm. "But I didn't let him stop me." She drew herself up to her full height, her gaze meeting his. "I won't let you stop me, either."

They stood in the middle of the street, nearly toe to toe, but Stevie Rae wasn't about to back down or let him try to change her mind. He'd already tried on numerous occasions...and lost, but he surprised her by smiling and touching the brim of his hat with his fingers in a mock salute. "I wouldn't dream of trying to stop you, Stevie. It wouldn't do me any good. I know that. I can admit defeat when it's staring me in the face." The smile faded, concern once again claiming his expression. "You sure you're all right?"

"I'm tougher than I look, Brock."

He watched her for a moment, his beautiful eyes warming her from the inside out, before his lips twitched into a smile once again. "I know. And you're a lot more stubborn, too." There was humor in his voice now, which was unexpected, but very much appreciated.

Stevie Rae let out a chuckle. "You're teasing me."

"I would never tease you, Stevie. I will always tell you the plain, unvarnished truth. And the truth is, you're as stubborn as Whiskey Pete over there." He fished a key out of one pocket and four gold coins out of another. "I was able to get us rooms." He handed her the items. "You're in room seven. I'm right next door in six. Top of the stairs and to the left. There's a stable around back and a boy named Jackson. He'll take care of your horse as well as Whiskey Pete. One of those coins is for him. The other three are for Barry, Simon, and Maris." He unwrapped Resolute's reins from around the post and hoisted himself into the saddle, but didn't explain who any of those people were. "I'll be back in a bit."

"Where are you going?"

He grinned and tipped his hat as he looked down at her, the warmth of his gaze sending a shiver along her spine. "To send my telegrams, see Marshal Dameron, and get a message to Sonny." He nudged Resolute, then changed his mind and lightly pulled on the reins, stopping the horse's progress. Once more, his silvery gaze met and held hers and something in the depths of her belly fluttered. "Meet me for dinner at seven."

"All right. Where?"

"The hotel's dining room."

She nodded as he saluted one more time then set Resolute into a slow walk with his knees. Stevie Rae watched him as if she were in a dream until he disappeared around a corner. Mentally shaking herself, she brought Willow and Whiskey Pete to the back of the hotel, where the boy named Jackson relieved her of her burdens. Grabbing her saddlebags and the cloth valise from the mule's back, she headed into the hotel, sailed past the registration desk with a slight nod to the man who stood behind it, and climbed the flight of stairs carpeted in a muted rose. Her room was down the hall, as Brock had said it would be.

Stevie slipped the key into the lock and swung the door open. She caught her breath as she glanced around. Room number seven of the Old Square Hotel was nothing less than charming. Pleasantly surprised, she entered and dropped her bags and valise on a rocking chair. She moved to the window and flung open the draperies to admire the view, then turned her attention to the four-poster bed in the middle of the room. She lifted a corner of the quilt and marveled at the height of the mattress then tested the firmness, and grinned—not nearly as hard as the ground she'd been sleeping on. She sat on the edge of the bed, the softness of the mattress easing some of the discomfort of her tired, sore behind, and she let out a long sigh before she lay back.

I'll just close my eyes for a moment.

A knock startled her, waking her from the unintentional nap. Stevie sat up and rubbed her eyes, then glanced at the clock ticking merrily on the bureau. She'd slept for less than five minutes. She looked toward the door, which she had forgotten to close, to see a young woman, a tray balanced in her hands. She gave a shy smile and a quick bob of her head. "Miss Buchanan?"

"Yes?" Stevie rose to her feet.

"My name is Maris. Mr. MacDermott asked that I bring this to you." She entered the room and carefully placed the tray on a small round table, the silverware clinking together as she did so. Stevie stepped closer and inhaled the steam rising from the bowl of *sopa de albondigas* in the middle of the tray. Her mouth watered. Corn tortillas peeked out from a cloth napkin and her stomach growled—she knew they'd be warm and soft to the touch. And delicious. A small pot of coffee and a piece of chocolate cake completed the meal.

"If you would like your clothes cleaned, I'll take them when I pick up the tray later."

"Thank you. That would be lovely." She fished one of the gold coins from her pocket and handed it to the girl.

Maris clutched the coin in her hand, dropped a quick curtsey, and left the room, closing the door behind her.

Stevie Rae's stomach growled again, fighting with her desire to sleep longer than five minutes. She gave in to the hunger. A nap would have to wait. She made herself comfortable at the table, dipped her spoon into the soup, and tasted the concoction. A groan of pleasure burst from her. "Heaven."

She'd almost finished the soup and the tortillas when she heard a noise—a screeching, squealing cacophony that set her teeth on edge—and she stepped into the hallway to investigate. A young man, one who looked so much like Jackson, the stable boy, he could have been his twin, pulled on a rope. With each tug, another squeal rent the air as a dumbwaiter came into view. He removed two buckets from the dumbwaiter as another boy, who also looked remarkably like Jackson, came up the stairs, carefully carrying two more buckets. Water sloshed but didn't spill from any of the pails as they padded down the hall.

"Afternoon, ma'am." The first boy nodded as he sailed past her and entered her room.

"I didn't order a bath."

"Mr. MacDermott did." The boy spoke over his shoulder as he put the buckets down, moved aside the draperies hanging from a long table pushed against the wall, then pulled a small brass bath from its hiding place and began filling it. He nodded again as he walked past her, swinging the now empty buckets. "We'll be back."

The other boy followed without a word, but a dimple appeared in his cheek as he grinned, bobbed his head, and disappeared down the hall. Both boys returned three more times, the water in the bathtub rising with each successive trip. Steam rose, lending a heated dampness to the room, and her anticipation grew.

"Is there anything else you need, ma'am?"

Stevie Rae gave them the last of the coins Brock had given her. "No, thank you."

The first boy gently tested the coin between his teeth and grinned before the money disappeared into his pocket. He gave a quick nod then gestured for his brother, nearly pushing him out the door before closing it behind them. Stevie quickly locked the door. She pulled a small paper-wrapped package from the saddlebag and peeled the paper back to reveal the last precious sliver of scented soap. She held it to her nose and inhaled before dropping it into the steaming water. A shiver of delight passed through her as she shed her dirty clothes and kicked them into a pile near the door, then sank into the depths of the bath.

A warmth settled over her that had nothing to do with the heat enveloping her and everything to do with the kindness Brock had shown her.

• • •

Brock dismounted in front of the marshal's office and flipped the reins around a post. He stepped onto the raised wooden sidewalk and stopped with his hand on the doorknob.

A smile spread his lips beneath the mustache that had been growing since leaving Taos as a vivid image stole into his mind. He could see Stevie Rae undressing, removing one article of clothing at a time to reveal what he could only imagine was beneath, her muscles flexing as she twisted her long, honey blond hair into a knot. How he wanted to kiss that sweet spot at the back of her neck...and everywhere else.

His body reacted, blood sizzling through his veins, heating him from the inside out as the vision expanded. She'd unwrap the scented soap, humming as she did so, and drop it into the water, a scene he'd never admit he'd accidentally witnessed on the trail before he turned away and left her to her privacy. The subtle fragrance of honeysuckle filled his nose, even though she was nowhere near him. It didn't matter. He'd associate that sweet perfume with her for the rest of his life, the scent having settled into his heart over the past few weeks.

"You coming in? Or you just going to stand there, grinning like an idiot?"

Startled by the masculine voice coming from an open window, so at odds with the sultry voice he heard in his head, Brock turned the knob. The vision clouding his mind disappeared, but the scent of honeysuckle remained as he let himself into Marshal Dameron's office.

"Been a long time." The marshal held out his hand as Brock closed the door.

"Yes, it has, Alden." Brock shook, then pulled him into a bear hug. "Good to see you."

"You as well." They broke apart and Alden offered him a seat as he walked behind the desk to his own chair. "Coffee? Whiskey?"

"Neither," he said as he slumped into his chair and placed his hat on the corner of the desk, exhaustion and frustration overwhelming him for a moment. "I can't stay long."

"I suspect I know what brings you to Santa Fe."

Brock smirked. It was no secret to anyone he chased Zeb Logan, nor did anyone doubt that eventually, he'd bring the man in. "I don't suppose you've seen him."

"No, I haven't, and truth be told, I have no desire to." Alden pulled a bottle and two glasses from the cabinet behind him. He gestured with the bottle, offering one more time, but Brock just shook his head and watched as the man poured himself a drink. He took a long swallow and let out a sigh, then wiped his mouth with the back of his hand. "He has no good reason to be here and if he was here, it would just be trouble. I know what he did in Paradise Falls, to your family, and I know what he did before—and after. Frankly, I don't want that in my town."

"I don't blame you, Alden." He stood, unable to remain seated, and started to pace the confines of the marshal's office from door to jail cell and back. "I wish I could figure out where he's going and get there before he does. I'm tired of always being one step behind him."

"You won't always be. One of these days, you'll be—"

"But can I wait? And can I find him before he murders someone else?" He stopped pacing and slumped into his chair once more. "You know, I think I will take that drink."

Without a word, Alden poured and slid the glass across the desk. Brock picked it up and cradled the glass in his hand before he took a breath and brought the whiskey to his lips, swallowing the contents in one gulp. The liquor warmed him right down to the pit of his stomach, where, instead of soothing him, it curdled. He put the empty glass on the desk. "You know Sonny MacLeish?"

"Sure do. He and I have spent many an hour bending our elbows at the Rusted Spur and talking about the men we've put away." He sobered, the grin disappearing as he held the glass with the tips of his fingers and twirled it back and forth, the whiskey catching the light coming in from the window and changing color from darkest honey to lightest amber. "And the ones we didn't." He grew quiet, then let out a long sigh and placed the glass on his desk. It wasn't empty, but he poured in a little more whiskey, adding to the liquor already there. "Damn shame about him. He was a good lawman, the kind I'd want watching my back. Logan's bullet nearly killed him, but that's not what pisses him off the most. It's the fact that he had that bastard in his hands and lost him."

"I know how he feels."

The marshal nodded. "Yes, you do. There have only been a handful of men who had Logan that close. You were one of them."

The whiskey in his belly curdled a little more as memories better left forgotten flooded him. Kieran. Mary. Little Matthew. Once more, he saw their faces and the blood flowing from their mortal wounds, heard their startled cries.

Mentally, he shook himself, forcing the visions in his mind to disappear. "Know where I can find Sonny?"

"Sure. Small farm just north of town. He's staying with his daughter and her family. I can send my deputy out there, give him a message that you'd like to see him."

Brock rose from his seat and reached across the desk, grasping the man's hand in his own. "Thanks. I'm staying at the Old Square Hotel. Not sure where I'm headed next, but I'll keep in touch."

Alden rose and grinned. "Ah, the famous telegrams. I always look forward to receiving them." His grin grew and his eyes twinkled as he finally let go of Brock's hand. "Come for dinner. Jennifer would love to see you."

"That would be nice. I'd love to see her as well. Tomorrow perhaps, or the next day, but not tonight. I have plans."

"Plans, huh?" One eyebrow rose over a dark brown eye. "Do they involve that pretty girl I saw you ride into town with?"

Heat flushed his body, but Brock didn't say a word as he grabbed his hat and strode out the door.

"We'll expect you tomorrow night at eight." Alden spoke through the open window as Brock unwrapped Resolute's reins from the post in front of the office and climbed into the saddle. "Bring the girl."

Brock gave a slight nod. "Eight o'clock," he repeated, then lightly nudged Resolute's sides and headed toward the telegrapher's office a couple streets over.

He caught the time as he dictated his last telegram and paid the man behind the counter. He had another stop to make before he was to meet Stevie Rae in the dining room of the hotel.

An hour later, anticipation making him grin like the idiot Alden proclaimed him to be once more, he handed Resolute's reins to Jackson in the stable, grabbed his saddlebags and paper-wrapped packages, and headed into the hotel.

"Mr. MacDermott, wait, please." Maris hailed him as soon as he walked through the lobby. "You have a message."

She reached into the key box behind her and retrieved an envelope, which she slid across the desk. Brock approached, placed his paper-wrapped packages on the smooth surface of the counter, and grabbed the envelope. He ripped it open and read the words written on stationery emblazoned with a fancy *M* at the top of the page. Sonny would meet him tomorrow afternoon at one at the farm. Directions were included on the note along with instructions to bring his appetite.

"Thank you." Brock smiled at the girl and started for the stairs, then stopped and turned around to face her once more. "Is there still a bathhouse on Saguaro Street?"

"No, Mr. MacDermott, that closed a few weeks ago, but I can arrange to have bathwater brought to your room." She grinned, showing a full complement of pearly white teeth. "Or you can use the new rain shower we installed. It's at the end of the hall on the second floor, just past room number eight. Everything you need—towels and such—are there."

Brock pulled out his pocket watch and checked the time. He had just enough time to make himself presentable before he met Stevie Rae in the dining room. "Thank you. I think I'll try that." He slung his saddlebags over his shoulder, grabbed his packages, and trudged up the stairs to his room. He stopped at his door, key in hand, and looked farther down the hall. The door to Stevie's room was closed and no sounds came from within. He moved a little closer and pressed his ear to the portal. He still heard nothing—no splashing in the bathtub—but then, even the most devout bather would not stay in a bath that was no longer hot, and he had been gone for more than two hours.

Did she sleep now, resting before they met for dinner? He could picture her burrowed beneath the quilt with nothing showing except her wealth of honey blond hair. Better yet, he saw her stretched out atop the quilt on the bed, her arm resting across her face, covering her eyes, her long legs crossed at the ankles, dressed in nothing but a chemise, drawers, and stockings. He grinned, liking the image in his mind, but resisted the urge to knock. She needed this respite. Though she never said a word, he knew how exhausted she'd been since Española and the nightmare of what they'd seen there. He would be able to tell her soon enough about visiting Sonny MacLeish.

He stepped away from the door, his footsteps quiet on the carpet, and sauntered down the hallway, past room number eight, and found another door. No number adorned this portal. Instead, a wooden plaque hung from a nail in the wood with the simple words "Rain Shower" stenciled on it. A smile crossed his lips as he swung the door open.

Chapter 14

Brock had loved the rain shower, the hot water flowing over him from above, washing away the dirt as well as some of his exhaustion. He now sat in the dining room on the other side of the hotel, revitalized, clean shaven, except for the mustache, which he decided made him look distinguished, and dressed in the new suit he'd bought himself after leaving the telegrapher's office.

He checked his pocket watch for the fourth time and noted that the clock hand had only moved a fraction. It was still not quite seven o'clock. He had been early, eager to be in Stevie Rae's company, which surprised him, yet didn't. He glanced around the dining room, noting the number of finely dressed people occupying the tables. The wait staff, male and female alike, dressed in black and white, took orders or delivered meals. A violinist stood on a dais in the corner of the room near the stairs, his bow gliding over the strings of his violin to produce the most amazing sound Brock had ever heard. Though the music was soothing, he was becoming more and more anxious.

Where is she?

He glanced at his menu in an effort to resist checking his watch one more time when he became aware something in the atmosphere had changed. The din in the dining room—the clatter of cutlery, the hum of conversation, the sweet strains of violin music—died, leaving a stunned silence. Brock looked up from his menu, his gaze darting this way and that, taking in the other diners and the wait staff and realized they all, every single one of them, stared at the staircase. His gaze drifted that way, too, and in an instant, he knew why every last soul in the dining room had stopped to stare, why the room had silenced. His breath seized in his lungs.

A vision of loveliness glided down the rose-carpeted stairs, her white gloved hand resting on the polished mahogany banister. Honey blond curls bounced as she took each step. The blue velvet of her gown reflected in her eyes and somehow, made them sparkle more than usual.

Those eyes widened as they came to rest on him, and her smile—the one he'd pay his last dollar to see—spread her full, utterly kissable lips. A becoming blush rose to color her cheeks.

After weeks of riding side by side, never once seeing her without her reliable trousers or the split skirt she'd purchased in Taos, this was a side to Stevie Rae she'd kept hidden. She was beautiful then, but now? She was quite possibly the most beautiful woman he'd ever seen. And the other diners seemed to think so as well.

Caught in a spell he didn't know he could succumb to, Brock dropped the menu on the table and rose from his seat.

He opened his mouth, several times, but the words were stuck in his throat as she drew closer to him, weaving between the other tables like an angel floating between clouds. If he had been a poet, he would have penned sonnets to the loveliness she portrayed. An artist? He would have painted her as she looked at this moment. A musician and he would have written melodies that could never compare to the vision he saw before him.

"Good evening, Brock."

Brock opened his mouth one more time and uttered, "You clean up real nice."

Tears sprang to her eyes in an instant, making them luminous, and her smile faded as her tall, lithe form stiffened. The blush staining her cheeks deepened with embarrassment.

He wanted to shoot himself. What woman wanted to hear that? Apparently, not Stevie Rae. For all her dogged determination, for all her bravery and uncomplaining silence as they slept in bedrolls on the ground and ate tinned beans while they searched for Zeb Logan, underneath it all, she wanted to hear what every other young woman wanted to hear—that her beauty was beyond compare and took his breath away.

So what, in God's name, possessed him to say that?

Her chin trembled and her lips tightened before she drew in a deep breath, then turned and ran back up the stairs, her back ramrod stiff, her head held high.

Brock watched her go, as did every other diner in the dining room. As soon as she reached the top of the stairs, all eyes turned to him, the reproach unmistakable.

"You'd better go after her, son," the man sitting at the table behind him said. When Brock turned his head, he met dark green eyes full of censure and something else. Sympathy, perhaps. "If you don't, I will."

He nodded once to the gentleman, grabbed his hat, and made his way between the tables to the stairs. He didn't pause as he took the risers two at a time—to the applause of everyone in the room.

Her door was closed, but not locked. He swung it open and paused in the doorway, unable to take another step. Stevie Rae sat at the dressing table, her hair already unpinned and flowing over her shoulders and down her back, though the curls still remained. She pulled a brush through the silken strands with angry, scalp-scratching jerks. Her gaze caught his in the mirror's reflection.

"Get out!"

"No."

"I don't want to talk to you or see you or even…" The words died in her throat and she turned away, drawing the brush through her hair once more.

He worried the brim of his hat between his fingers as he took another step into the room. "I'm sorry."

"You should be." She tossed the brush on the dressing table, then stood, her hands on her hips, and mimicked his words. "'You clean up real nice'? What was that?" She began to pace, the bell of her long skirts swishing around her legs and stocking-clad feet.

"Am I so ugly that you cannot bear to look at me? So unattractive I scare small children? Good God, Brock, should I never be seen in public without a flour sack over my head?"

"I…I didn't…that's not what I… Aw hell, Stevie, I didn't know what to say. You stunned me. Took the words right out of my mouth. Hell, took them right out of my head!"

He closed the door with a move of his foot and advanced on her. Not only was she angry at him, but she was hurt, too. So hurt, her eyes flashed pure blue fire that seared his heart. He wrapped his arms around her, trying to draw her unwilling body closer to him, but she remained stiff and unyielding—and who could blame her? He had opened his mouth and stuck his foot in it, boot and all, leaving a horrible taste.

He tightened his embrace, despite the tension in her, and his voice lowered. "You are beautiful. Not just now, but always." He ran his fingers through her hair, loving the silkiness between his fingers, then traced her delicate jawbone with his fingertip. "Even with dirt on your face, you are still beautiful. Do you know how hard it's been to keep my distance? To not touch you? I fail more often than I succeed."

A sigh escaped him. How could he be telling her these things? When had these feelings started happening for him?

"Do you know how hard it's been not to kiss you—" He tilted her chin upward, bringing her tempting lips closer to his. Her magnificent eyes glistened. "Like this?" His mouth descended and the touch of her lips was pure heaven to his soul. He wanted more, so much more, not just this, but everything. "And like this?" His lips lowered to hers again and again, his heart thundering in his chest. The fragrance of honeysuckle surrounded him, lifting his spirits higher than he thought possible.

He left her lips to pepper kisses along her jawline and whispered in her ear, "Do you forgive me?"

She didn't answer. At least not with words, but her actions spoke volumes and promised more. She pressed against him, then cupped his cheek, her thumb lightly caressing the mustache he'd become fond of, her eyes sparkling as she brought her mouth to his.

She was perfect. Her long, lithe body fit to his as he pressed her against the wall, her breasts crushed against his hard chest, the restraint he'd maintained gone in an instant as her tongue thrust into his mouth and her fingers delved into his hair, pulling his head closer.

Need surged within him—a need to touch her, become one with her. With one hand, he unbuttoned the row of mother-of-pearl buttons from the neckline of her dress down to below her waist, spreading the edges apart, then pulled away from her for just a moment to push the gown down her body. She stood in front of him in her short chemise embroidered with tiny flowers, plain white corset, drawers edged with lace, and white stockings, held in place with simple silk garters.

Slow down, the words echoed in his head. *Make it good for her, you ass.*

But he couldn't slow down. Neither could Stevie. She helped him unclasp her corset, letting it fall to the floor to join her dress, then pushed his brand-new jacket off his shoulders and onto the polished wooden planks beneath them. The palms of her hands were hot against his chest through his shirt, her kisses wild and untamed and bold. She reached between them and fumbled with the buttons of his trousers.

Brock held his breath. If she kept touching him like that, he just might lose what little control he had, and yet he wanted that with her. Wanted to lose control and forget who and what he was, if only for a moment. His trousers dropped downward, but became stuck on the top of his boots. It didn't matter. He wasn't about to stop, not now, maybe not ever. His arousal surged free.

He leaned into her and backed her against the wall once more as his mouth took possession of hers.

He lifted one of her stocking-clad legs, hooking it around his waist, then the other, leaving her exposed yet hidden and dangerously close as Stevie Rae tightened her grip, pulling herself closer, the heat of her nearly searing his skin and his soul. He found the slit in her drawers and his fingers traced her wet, swollen folds. Stevie Rae let out a strangled cry of pleasure and squeezed her legs tighter around his waist, trapping his hand between them while her arms encircled his head. His fingers continued to stroke her, slow then fast then slow again.

Her hips picked up the rhythm his fingers had set and rocked of their own accord. Her breathing quickened, and she clung to him, her strong legs holding him captive, the bow on one of her garters rubbing against his skin, tickling him.

She was ready. And so close. He knew that from the way she panted and rubbed against him, but that didn't mean she was experienced. He wanted to be inside her—desperately—and feel her body throb around him when she reached her moment, but he didn't want to hurt her. What if she'd never…?

"Stevie?" he whispered as he nuzzled her neck. "I can't wait. I have to be inside you, but…I don't want to hurt you. Have you… done this before?"

She didn't answer his question. Instead, she pulled him closer, her body moving against him and nearly screamed, "Oh God, Brock, don't stop now! Please!"

He needed no more reassurance than her words as he moved his hand from between them and thrust into her tight sheath. He met no resistance as he sank into her depths and found the rhythm she had set.

Stevie let out a long groan of pleasure as her body adjusted to him then and brought her mouth down to meet his, her tongue sliding against his.

Peace. The word skittered through his brain and the feeling flowed through him as her heat surrounded him. He felt her heart beat against his chest or did he just imagine that? Anticipation swept through him. The rush of blood pounding through his veins surged faster and faster as he moved within her. Still, beneath the intense pleasure, the feeling of peace remained, like a soft blanket encircling him.

The cadence of her breathing changed again, her breaths coming in short little gasps. She pulled her mouth from his and leaned her head back against the wall behind her. Brock ground his hips into her, his movements concise and centered until her eyes flew open and a small surprised squeak escaped her. Her body shuddered around him and he knew she had reached her peak. Now he could reach for his own release. He thrust into her over and over, changing the pace, pumping hard then slowing down only to change the tempo again, until Stevie Rae expelled another startled shout and the hot rush of his seed exploded into her, intense, powerful, as if coming from the depths of his soul.

Breathing hard, his knees a bit wobbly, he withdrew from her, and moved away from the wall but Stevie Rae didn't let go. Her cotton-clad legs were still wrapped around him, though not as tight as before, and moist heat radiated from her body.

Brock shuffled toward the bed, which, thankfully, wasn't far, the trousers around his knees and calves preventing him from taking longer steps. Gently, he laid her down on the soft mattress. For a moment, she clung to him, the muscles in her thighs strong from years of riding, her arms wrapped around his neck.

She said nothing as she finally released him. He studied her and smiled. The blush on her face, neck, and chest started to fade, but wonder and curiosity still sparkled in the depths of her eyes. For reasons he couldn't explain—or perhaps didn't want to—that wonder made him want to shout to the rooftops. He knew a satisfied woman when he saw one. Instead, he asked, "Are you all right?"

•••

Stevie Rae nodded as he tenderly caressed her face with the tips of his fingers. Her body still pulsed, but her heartbeat was beginning to return to normal. That didn't last long as Brock leaned down and pressed a kiss to her lips. The swirl of emotion, the taste of him, the thought of what he could make her feel, had her blood surging through her veins in an instant.

He smiled, kissed her again, then rose to his feet and stepped away from the bed. She smoothed a ribbon from her chemise between her fingers, but her gaze remained on him. A satisfied grin spread her lips. If she had been alone, she would have stretched and purred like a kitten. Or maybe giggled. Stevie Rae never giggled, but she felt like it now as a new thought swept into her head.

So that's the "wild ride" Ruby's girls always talked about but very seldom got.

Relegated to the kitchen while her father treated the girls at Ruby Wheeler's house, Stevie Rae had heard the ladies talk. No topic was sacred and the women who lived and worked at Ruby's spoke about everything…from the size of a man to whether or not he could give her a "wild ride." She remembered the girls blushing when they realized she had been within earshot, but at the tender age of twelve, though curious, Stevie had had no idea what any of it meant. And no one bothered to explain it to her. Not Ruby's girls or her mother, whose face flamed with embarrassment and who told her young ladies had no business even asking about such things, or her father, who stammered out a dry lecture and refused to look her in the eye.

Lucas hadn't explained either, nor had he shown her. But now…maybe she did know what those girls had giggled about long ago. And God help her, she wanted to go for a wild ride again. And again.

A sigh of satisfaction slipped from between her lips as Stevie Rae released the ribbon and rolled to her side, propping her head up on her hand. She watched Brock as he shrugged out of his shirt and tossed it toward a nearby chair, then sat on the edge of the same chair, right on top of his shirt, and pulled off his boots and trousers.

His eyes were on her, though, the soft gray seeming so much softer, and then he flashed the smile she adored, the one she had seldom seen before but seemed to be seeing a lot more lately. Anticipation curled low in her belly.

He rose from the chair in all his naked glory and slowly walked toward her. His body was how she'd imagined it would be—perfect—and she let her gaze roam over him. She took in his broad shoulders and muscular arms, the dusting of dark hair covering his chest just begging to be touched. A blush crept up her face and her heartbeat picked up its pace as her gaze dipped lower. Her eyes widened. Earlier, she hadn't seen him, had only felt his hardness with her fingertips as she unbuttoned his trousers.

Now? Now, she got an eyeful of his fully aroused state. It took every ounce of willpower to suppress the giggle building in her throat. Ruby's girls would have been impressed!

And she wanted him, more than ever, but he didn't move. He stood beside the bed and simply looked at her. She felt the warmth of his gaze as it traveled from her legs still clad in stockings to her lace-edged drawers covering her most precious secrets to the chemise that revealed more than it hid. His gaze finally settled on her face and her cheeks heated as a flush rose from her chest upward. The expectation swirling in her belly increased. She licked her suddenly dry lips.

Wasn't he ever going to speak? She'd become comfortable with his long silences while riding through the countryside, but now? She needed to hear his voice, needed to...

She never had a chance to finish her thought as Brock grabbed her leg at the ankle and twisted gently, rolling her onto her back. A squeal of surprise erupted from her.

He didn't release her ankle, but held it in his big hands, his thumb gently caressing her skin. "I think it's unfair you're still dressed," his voice was soft and slow, like warm honey, "while I'm standing here in the altogether." He grinned that wicked grin, then plucked the ribbon of her garter, dropping the pale peach lace and silk band to the floor. He rolled her stocking down her leg, from her thigh to her foot, his fingertips brushing against her skin as he did so. His gaze never left hers and a sweet wonderful ache began to build within her as he repeated his action with her other leg.

He dropped the stocking to the floor and shook his head. "You're still wearing too much." He held out his hand. Stevie slipped her hand in his and warmth surrounded her as he pulled her to a standing position beside the bed, one bare foot on the rug, the other on the cold floor. Brock's arms slid around her and his mouth covered hers in a kiss she felt down to her toes. He stopped kissing her, just long enough to pull the short chemise over her head. Seconds later, her drawers slid down her legs to puddle on the floor.

He took a step back and a lazy smile twitched the mustache covering his upper lip. "That's much better."

Stevie Rae let out a squeak, caught between embarrassment and excitement. She hadn't been naked in front of another person since she'd developed breasts—not even when she'd been with Lucas, and he'd certainly never looked at her as Brock was looking at her now, with desire smoldering in his dark gray eyes. She crossed her arms over her chest, hiding her breasts from him, then realized what she left exposed and lowered her hands to shield the secrets of her womanhood. But it was too late. He'd already seen and touched and loved. "Don't."

"Don't what?" he asked.

His gaze roamed over her, from the tips of her toes to the top of her head and everywhere in between and Stevie Rae trembled, her body shaking on the inside. She felt...feverish and breathless and oh so wanted. "Look at me like that."

"Why not?" He took a step closer, pushed her hands away, and raised her chin with his finger. "You're beautiful. Perfect, in fact." He lowered his lips to hers and kissed her in such a way, she felt as if her bones melted and it was a miracle she could still stand on her own two feet. Her body responded to the sweet onslaught of his mouth, the heat of his arms around her as he pulled her closer, the feel of his steely arousal pressing against her. Blood surged through her veins, thundering in her ears. Moisture gathered between her legs as the folds of her sex swelled and the heady smell of musk filled the air.

Did that make her wanton? Did that make her like the girls in Ruby's house or the other houses they'd seen in Taos? Lucas had always implied...and why was she thinking about Lucas now? She had a handsome man in her arms and he wanted her as much as she wanted him. Pushing all thought from her mind, giving over entirely to emotion and just *feeling*, Stevie Rae drew him down to the bed, every inch of her flesh touching his. And yet, it wasn't enough. She needed to be closer. She brought his lips to hers, kissing him deeply, and felt bereft when his mouth left hers. His tongue and lips seemed to singe her skin as he placed gentle kisses along her jawline, neck, and collarbone on his journey farther south.

Stevie Rae nearly came off the bed as his mouth covered one nipple, suckling gently, his tongue swirling and rasping against one sensitive nub then the other then back, again and again, leaving a trail of wet heat on her skin. When she thought she'd go mad with wanting and couldn't bear much more of his teasing, his mouth descended to hers as his hand trailed over her stomach and hips before blazing a hot trail along the outside of her swollen sex. He parted her flesh and Stevie Rae sucked in her breath and held it as his fingers slid through her curls. She released her held breath in a groan of intense pleasure, then moved her legs, opening herself to him more fully.

"My little wildcat," he whispered in her ear, causing shivers to run up and down her back and her hips to rise off the bed as he slowly caressed the very core of her. And she was close, so close, to the same feeling as before, when the world went dark for a moment then brightened with colors that danced before her eyes, when her body pulsed around him, her mind blanked, and she thought of nothing except how wonderful she felt. Her body seemed to tighten even more, the coiled spring close to shattering from tension and need.

She couldn't help the whimper that escaped her as he stopped caressing her nor the groan that erupted from deep in her throat when he settled between her thighs and pushed into her and began to move. And a new set of sensations surged through her.

Stevie Rae found the rhythm quickly, the same rhythm as before, and moved against him, her legs tight around his hips to pull him closer, her heels digging into his backside.

"Easy," he whispered in her ear as he deliberately slowed his pace, pushing into her then pulling out nearly his entire length before filling her again, leaving her on the brink. "There's no need to hurry." He chuckled, but the sound wasn't mocking in the least. It was happy and filled with joy. "We have all the time in the world."

Though she knew that wasn't true, she didn't care. In the world beyond this bed, danger lurked in the shadows and a madman killed for enjoyment, but here, within these walls, within Brock's arms, she felt safe and cherished. Stevie Rae closed her eyes and gave herself over to those feelings…and so much more. Sounds became more defined as he moved in her…she could hear her own heartbeat, his heavy breath, and the rasp of skin against skin. Sensation became almost unbearable...the crispness of his chest hair teasing her sensitive nipples, the weight of his body rocking against her. Colors danced behind her closed eyelids as anticipation built within, coiling, twisting, spiraling....

She opened her eyes as Brock picked up his pace, moving in her faster and faster, then slowed his rhythm and pressed deeply into her, his body stiffening, his arms locked on either side of her head as he rocked against her. Perspiration made his face shine and his lips twisted into almost a grimace as he spent himself inside her, spinning her out of control until her world darkened. She screamed at her release and clung to him, pulling him closer still as her hips continued to move against him and he pressed tighter, deeper into her. Unbelievable sensations skittered through her as her body pulsed around him and her world brightened once more with vibrant colors.

Brock held her close as he kissed her, then slowly slid from her body and rolled to his side. Stevie Rae let out a sigh as the heat of him left her. She started to rise. He pulled her back and cradled her in his arms. "Where are you going?"

"I thought...you'd want to be alone now."

"Whatever gave you that idea?"

"I...I thought...that's what men wanted. I'd been told—"

"Whoever told you that was an ass! Men—real men—would never treat a woman like that." His arms tightened around her, surrounding her with warmth, so at odds with the anger she heard in his voice.

Breathless, still reeling from the shattering climax that shook her to her very soul, Stevie Rae nestled in Brock's arms. His fingers lazily stroked her shoulder, but in a different way from just a bit ago. This touch was meant to comfort and reduce the frantic beat of her heart...or at least that's what she thought, but she had nothing to compare it to. Lucas had never held her like this after the few times they'd…she wouldn't exactly call it making love. There had been none of the tenderness she'd just experienced. Rather, it was more of Lucas relieving himself within her body when he felt the need and leaving her wanting so much more.

Why am I thinking about him again?

The question rambled through her brain, but she knew the answer. Making love to Brock had opened her eyes in so many ways, made her see how selfish and wrong Lucas had been.

She moved slightly so she could see his face. The smile she so loved seeing had taken up permanent residence on his lips and for reasons she dare not explore or question, seeing that grin made her happier than she'd been in a long time. She nestled a little closer, laid her hand over his heart so she could feel it beat, and closed her eyes.

Chapter 15

Stevie Rae glanced over at Brock and grinned as he laughed at a joke Sonny told. A tingle of pleasure settled in her belly, not only because memories of making love and the things he made her feel were still fresh in her mind, but because he seemed, at the moment, almost carefree. She couldn't remember the last time *she* had laughed like this or felt this free, either.

These emotions running riot within her were because of Brock, but the laughter—the laughter was compliments of Fergus "Sonny" MacLeish, his daughter, Brynna, and her three children. The luncheon Brynna prepared had been wonderful and the former sheriff kept everyone entertained with his brilliant humor. Stevie Rae liked him—from the moment Brock introduced them in the foyer of his daughter's home, she'd felt welcome. He was the male version of Martha Prichard, warm and kind and not afraid to tell the truth, though he used humor to dull the sting, whereas Martha used love.

He wasn't what she expected either. She thought she'd be meeting a much older man, one with a generous helping of white hair and perhaps an abundance of wrinkles on his face. Instead, she met a man only several years older than her own father with a few streaks of white to mar his otherwise wealth of ginger hair. And the wrinkles only appeared when he smiled, like now, as his loving gaze roamed over his three grandchildren.

His smile grew and a look of understanding passed between him and his daughter as Brynna dropped her napkin beside her plate and rose from the dining room table. She came around to her father's chair and rested her hands on his shoulders. "It's a beautiful day, Papa. Why don't you and your guests sit on the patio? I'll bring your tea."

"Excellent idea, Brynna."

She started to help him rise, but Sonny waved her off and placed his hands on the table to push himself into a standing position, his movements stiff and apparently painful. Brynna made a sympathetic noise and attempted to help him again, but he shrugged her away. "I'm all right, Bryn." He grabbed his cane beside the chair. "I just stiffened up from sitting so long. I'll be movin' easier in two shakes of a lamb's tail. Just give me a moment."

Stevie Rae, seeing the expression on Brynna's face and the pain so evident in Sonny's, stepped forward, though Brock shook his head and mouthed the word no. "Perhaps you'd like to escort me to the patio." She casually slipped her hand into the crook of his arm.

"Ach, lass, have ye pity fer this poor mon then?" He lapsed into a bit of brogue, his accent thick, but humor danced in his startling green eyes.

"No, sir, no pity. Respect, certainly." She leaned closer and whispered, "Truthfully, I just wanted to hold your hand."

He laughed, as she hoped he would and allowed him to lead the way through the house at a slow pace. Brock followed, his boot heels loud on the tile floor then muffled as he stepped over carpet. She glanced behind her. He wore a silly grin on his face and the downcast set of his eyes had her believing he stared at her backside as she walked in front of him.

Caught, his gaze lifted to meet hers, the smile she so adored flashed across his lips before he winked.

A flush rose up her face and she nearly stumbled. One didn't have to be a detective to know what thoughts were going through his mind. The flush deepened and spread over her entire body. Desire heated her blood and she couldn't wait to get back to the hotel.

"My daughter has been a godsend," Sonny said with a sigh once they were outside in the sunshine. His pain seemed to have lessened and his movements weren't so rigid. "But she'll only tolerate so much. She doesn't like it when either her husband or I talk *work* in front of the children. My son-in-law, Michael, is a lawyer. As you can imagine, we've had some lively discussions, but Brynna wants no part of it. She said she heard enough when she was young that she doesn't want to hear it anymore, which is why we've been banished outside."

"I grew up listening to my father." She smiled as the memory of him sitting in the rocking chair on the front porch, his pipe clenched between his teeth, became clear. "He was a doctor. A good one. Kind and caring. Like your daughter, my mother forbade him from talking about certain things, but I never minded."

"You're a sweet lass, Stevie Rae. Knew it the minute I laid my eyes on you." He gestured to a table covered with a colorful tablecloth, and several cushioned chairs beneath a ramada. "Sit, please."

Stevie Rae smoothed the fabric of her split skirt and slid into her seat. Brock took the chair to her right, leaned back, and stretched out his legs. He hadn't spoken much during lunch. But then, that wasn't unusual and Sonny seemed to do enough talking and joking for any three people. She forced her gaze away from him and focused her attention on Sonny.

He did not sit at the table with them. Instead, he paced in a slow gait, using his cane, but not as often now. The stiffness seemed to have eased a great deal and a long sigh escaped him. He patted first one pocket of his suit jacket then the other, his smile wide when he found what he wanted. "Do you mind if I smoke?"

"Not at all."

Sonny pulled a thin cigar from his pocket and lit it with a match he struck against the wooden post of the ramada, then finally eased into a chair opposite Stevie Rae and Brock. "So, how is it, lassie, a fine girl such as yourself is looking for a murdering son of a…ah…gun like Logan?"

Stevie opened her mouth, but stopped herself from saying anything as Sonny's eleven-year-old granddaughter, Violet, stepped onto the patio, a heavy tray in her hands. The ginger-colored curls framing her face hardly bounced as she crossed the expanse of flagstone, taking one careful step after another, and the fine china cups didn't rattle at all as she slid the tray onto the table. She grinned at her grandfather, obviously pleased she hadn't spilled or dropped anything. Her eyes, very much like Sonny's, glowed with accomplishment.

And Sonny couldn't have been prouder of his granddaughter, nor could anyone doubt the love he had for this child. His smile brightened his entire face and his bright green eyes twinkled as he kissed the girl on the cheek. "Good job, lass. Thank you. And thank your mother, too. Now, scoot."

The girl skipped away, humming a merry tune before she disappeared into the house. Stevie watched her with a touch of envy. Had she ever been that young and carefree? That lighthearted and untroubled? She remembered taking care of her mother, when her mother allowed her close enough to do so, then taking care of her father after her mother died, but she couldn't remember a time in her life when she didn't have responsibilities, when someone else's need wasn't more important than her own. Martha was fond of telling her she had an old soul, though she never quite understood the comment. Until now.

The light touch of Brock's fingertips against the top of her hand and the rattle of fine china as Sonny slid the tray closer to her snapped her out of her musings. She raised her gaze to the former lawman and smiled.

"Would you do the honors?"

"Of course." She poured tea into one of the rose-patterned cups and passed it to Sonny, then repeated the process, handing the second cup to Brock. His gaze met hers as he accepted the cup and saucer, the look in his eyes warm and inviting, the touch of his hand evoking visions in her mind. For a moment, she couldn't turn away, lost in the memory of what had happened between them last night and again this morning and the way he made her feel...until she remembered where she was and why. With effort, she turned her attention back to Sonny. "You asked why I'm looking for Logan."

Smoke swirled and climbed upward from the glass dish on the table where Sonny laid his cigar while he stirred sugar into his tea. "That I did."

"He killed my father."

The spoon tapped lightly against the rim of the cup as Sonny's gaze rose to hers. Genuine sadness reflected in his eyes. "I'm sorry, lass. Logan doesn't seem to care who he hurts...or kills. Tell me what happened if it'll help."

She opened her mouth, ready to share the events of the night she lost her father when Sonny shifted his weight in his chair and she noticed, again, how the pain transformed his face and caused every muscle in his body to tighten for a fraction of a second.

The words died on her tongue, replaced with concern for Sonny, as Stevie Rae glanced at Brock. His expression mirrored her own. She reached across the table and took Sonny's hand. "Are you all right?"

"Right as rain, lass, don't fret about me. Every once in a while, I am reminded of the bullet Logan put in my back. Doc Hawkins did a fine job of removing it." He winked then and the pain on his face dissipated nearly as fast as it had come. "At least he says he removed it, but sometimes it feels like that piece of lead is still there." He took a long drag on the cigar and exhaled a plume of smoke before he pulled a small flask from the inside pocket of his jacket and poured a little of the contents into his tea. He gestured toward her cup as well as Brock's. "Gets a little worse when there's a storm brewing, and there is a storm coming. Maybe not tonight or tomorrow, but definitely by the end of the week. Hawkins says it's phantom pain. Not really there. Feels real enough to me." He took a healthy swig from his flask, then screwed on the cap and tucked it back in his pocket. After a moment, his color came back to normal. "You were going to tell me what happened to your father."

Stevie Rae shook her head. "I think that can wait for another visit. We—" She turned toward Brock and tilted her head. He gave a slight nod in return. "We don't want to tire you. I feel we have already overstayed our welcome."

"Nonsense, lass. Having you and Brock here has been a bright spot in my day." His grin widened and white teeth flashed. "But I understand. You have a schedule to keep, so to speak. I would imagine you're not planning on staying in Santa Fe for very long, so what can this old lawman tell you about Logan that you don't already know, Brock?"

Brock shrugged and straightened in his chair. His booted foot tapped the flagstones beneath the table. "At this point, anything might be helpful. He knows I'm after him. That's no secret, but he always seems to be one step ahead of me. And the brutality of his crimes is getting worse. He seems to be changing, too."

Brock reached for her hand, almost unconsciously, and curled his fingers around hers so gently, so lovingly, Stevie wanted to weep. Did he draw strength from her through a touch so simple? Or was there another reason he held her hand so tenderly? She glanced at his face, but couldn't glean the answer she sought. She only knew what she felt and at this moment, despite the topic of conversation and the madman they chased across New Mexico, she felt cherished and adored.

"Changing? In what way?" Sonny interrupted her thoughts.

Brock shrugged and took a sip of tea, his Adam's apple bobbing as he swallowed the tasty brew. "Before, he never left anyone alive if he could help it. Now? He's leaving witnesses to his violence. Stevie here he didn't know about—she'd been hiding in the root cellar—but in Taos, he definitely left someone alive. I can't help wondering why. Why change? Is there a purpose?" He let out a long sigh and closed his eyes for a moment. When he opened them, Stevie noticed the change in color—from clear gray to an almost polished pewter and further evidence of his frustration. She squeezed his hand.

He didn't smile at her, but he did squeeze her hand in return. "Stevie thinks he's taunting me every time he hurts or kills someone because I can't stop him."

Sonny's intent stare shifted from Brock to her. Something flickered in his eyes. Admiration? Appreciation? "Well now, not only is Miss Stevie beautiful and charming, she's got a good head on her shoulders. Maybe he is, Brock. God knows, he's a cruel man, but he's smart, too. I knew that the moment he let me get close enough to arrest him. He turned the tables on me so fast, I didn't know if I was coming or going." He shifted his weight again, and leaned forward until his forearms rested on the table, this time without any accompanying pain. "He's baiting you, hoping you'll keep after him until you're so exhausted and frustrated, you'll make a mistake, like I did. You could end up with a bullet in your back, too. Or worse."

Getting killed was a distinct possibility. Stevie Rae knew it. She'd always known it, but it hadn't stopped her. Nor had it stopped Brock.

Brock leaned forward as well, almost mimicking Sonny's position. "What about family? Is there anyone he would go to? A place? Somewhere he'd feel safe?"

Sonny shook his head as he rolled the cigar between his fingers. "There's very few of the Logans left, just Tell and Jeff. As you know, Jeff is in prison. No one knows where Tell is. If we're lucky, he's dead, but I haven't heard. There was a sister, too. Prissy? Patty? Something like that."

"Could it have been Patrice?" Brock asked, his voice low and hoarse.

Stevie stiffened. Taos. The woman who had been beaten to death. Her name had been Patrice. Had she been Logan's sister? She exchanged a quick glance with Brock, then turned her attention to Sonny, waiting for an answer. He leaned back in his chair, one hand resting on the handle of his cane, which Stevie noticed was in the shape of wolf's head. He continued to roll the cigar between his fingers with his other hand. His eyes closed for a moment, as if deep in thought, then opened as he shrugged.

"Might be. I think she took off with a gambling man, but I don't know what became of her. Salome, his mother, passed away not too long ago, but his father died when Zeb was just a boy." The flask came out of his pocket once more. Sonny unscrewed the cap then took a deep swallow. He continued relating Logan's history as he knew it while he put the flask away.

"That's when the Logan boys started their life of crime. It all started innocently enough, I suppose. Ma Logan needed to keep food on the table, and the boys, never ones for farming the land, helped her as best they could. They weren't always killers. They started out small, robbing stagecoaches and rustling cattle, then progressed to bigger things like robbing banks." He paused and sipped from his cup, his lively green eyes a little sad, then took another deep pull on the cigar. The red tip glowed as the tobacco rolled tightly in a tube grew smaller. "As far as I know, Logan's got no place to go and no one to take him in. The little farm outside San Luis, Colorado, where the Logans were raised, is gone, the land taken after Salome Logan died, but I did hear of a hideout up in the Sangre de Cristos. I don't know how true that is."

"Why is he in New Mexico?"

Sonny grinned as he crushed the glowing end of his cigar into the glass dish. "Maybe because too many men are looking for him in Colorado."

"There's just as many here in New Mexico. And Arizona. Texas, too. Maybe even California."

"Son, if I could answer that, I'd probably be a rich man. No one knows what drives Logan or makes him do the things he does."

"Stevie thinks he does it because he likes it."

Sonny nodded as his gaze swung to her and a smile played on his lips. "Well, now, that could be true, darlin'. One never knows what truly drives a man. Or a woman, for that matter. We have choices and free will, so what makes one of us choose a life of crime while another chooses the law? What makes one of us think life would be easy if we stole instead of worked for a living? What makes one think he or she can kill just because they want to?"

A wispy cloud, the only one in sight, rolled across the sky, blocking the sun for a moment as Sonny's words resonated within her. Perhaps there were no easy answers and she'd never know what made Zeb Logan choose to kill her father or Brock's brother or shoot Sonny in the back and leave him for dead. She shivered as a cold chill skittered up her spine, then looked up between the slats of the ramada and watched the cloud dissipate as if it had never been there at all.

"Ach, listen to me! I'm getting maudlin in my old age. Or maybe it's the whiskey talkin'." And with those words, he found his flask, untwisted the cap, and poured a little more of the liquor into his tea. "Will you stay for dinner? As you know, Brynna is an excellent cook. Learned it from her mother, God rest her soul."

"We would love to, but unfortunately, we have another obligation." Brock stood and reached across the table to shake the man's hand. Stevie wondered if he did so because he didn't want Sonny to stand. "Thank you for the invitation, though."

"Yes, thank you." Stevie Rae stood as well and ran her hands along her split skirt though there were no wrinkles that needed smoothing out before she stuck out her hand as Brock had done. "And thank you for seeing us."

The gambit failed as Sonny struggled to his feet, using both his cane and the table to aid him. Again, he waved off any help, though his face turned red then white and beads of sweat dotted his forehead despite the sudden gust of cold wind that swept across the patio. Regardless of his obvious pain, he took her hand and raised it to his lips. "The pleasure has been all mine, lass. Please, come and see me anytime." He kept her hand in his and drew her a little closer. His voice lowered. "He's a good man, MacDermott is. Keep him safe."

"Yes, sir. That is my plan."

"Good lass." He sighed then, but Stevie Rae couldn't be sure if the sigh was because he was in pain or because they were leaving or for some other reason. She decided it was a combination of those things and more as he slumped into his chair and waved them away, as if suddenly exhausted from fighting his constant pain—or perhaps too much whiskey had made him drowsy. "Brynna will show you out."

As good as his word, Brynna waited by the patio door, their hats in her hand. "Thank you so much for coming," she said as she led them toward the gate in the side yard, where a garden filled with herbs scented the air.

"Will he be all right?" Stevie asked, recognizing the melancholy some people experienced. Her mother suffered from it on and off for as long as Stevie could remember. Her father, too, after Raelene had passed away.

Brynna nodded and glanced away, but not before Stevie Rae saw the sheen of tears in her eyes. "Today was a good day. Who knows what tomorrow will bring?" She shrugged then turned toward Brock, the brightness in her eyes now not caused by tears but by simple joy. "You will never know how much he looked forward to your visit. It was all he could talk about from the moment he received the message. I know he would like for you to come back and visit again." She took his hand in hers then bit her lip, as if undecided. After a moment, she drew in her breath and said, "We've only met a few times, Brock, but my father speaks of you often, always with the highest praise, and I feel I must say this to you. Please, do not let your hunt for this man do to you what it has done to my father." She glanced at Stevie, her eyes filled with sadness. "After Mama passed, I'm told, he became reckless and irresponsible. Uncaring. Single-minded to the distraction of everything else in his life, obsessed with finding Logan. Perhaps he became that way from grief. Perhaps it was the bargain he'd made with God when Mama was so ill. I'm not sure, but I am glad my mother did not see the man he'd become. I am glad I did not see him that way either, as I was married by then and living here." The tears were back in her eyes and her voice grew hoarse, as if she fought the urge to cry. "It is only by the grace of God he did not die from Logan's bullet, but I know, there are times when he wishes he had." She let go of Brock's hand and took a deep breath as she opened the garden gate and ushered them through. "I will say no more except to wish you peace."

The gate closed and Brynna disappeared around the corner of the house at a run before Brock could gather his wits. He stood looking at the wooden slats of the gate with his mouth still open, then turned toward her. Clearly confused by Brynna's behavior, he shook his head. "Why did she run off like that?"

"Perhaps she's afraid she said too much." *Or didn't say enough. How much of that was meant for me?*

Brock did not respond, but his eyes closed, as if he considered her words. When he opened them again, he reached for her hand and led her toward the front of the house and the waiting horses. He said not a word about Brynna's message. Instead, as he helped her into Willow's saddle and handed her the reins, he asked, "What did he say to you?"

"Who?"

"You know very well who." He mounted Resolute then clicked his tongue and started the horse on a leisurely walk back to town. "When Sonny was saying good-bye, I saw him lean over and whisper something in your ear."

Determined not to let Brynna's warning ruin a perfectly good afternoon, Stevie Rae shrugged as her gaze met his, then lowered to his kissable mouth, which was parted now in a half smile. Desire swirled low in her belly and a warm tingle raced through her veins. She could have told him the truth, but she couldn't resist teasing him a little. "He said I should have my way with you."

"What?"

The look on his face made her want to laugh. Actually, it made her want to pull him from the saddle, peel off his clothing, and kiss every inch of him right there in the drive. "He said I should have my way with you."

"Sonny said that?" His smile widened, the mustache on his upper lip twitching. Gray eyes darkened with passion as he moved Resolute closer to her.

"He did."

"And?"

"And what?"

"Are you going to take his advice? I can be accommodating."

"Thinking about it." She giggled, which astounded her, then sank her heels into Willow's sides and led the way back to town. And hopefully, to bed.

Chapter 16

Rain from the storm Sonny had predicted dripped from the brim of Brock's hat, saturating his clothes, despite his duster. Streaks of lightning lit up the sky, followed quickly by a crack of thunder so loud, he nearly jumped out of his skin. Brock turned in the saddle and glanced behind him. Stevie Rae was just as soaked as he, her duster as ineffectual as his against the driving rain, which sometimes came straight down, but more often had a tendency to slant sideways.

They had to find shelter to ride out the worst of the storm.

A deep sigh escaped him as he faced forward again. Weariness, not only of the body, but of the mind and heart as well, overwhelmed him. What was he doing? The longer he searched for Logan, the more hardened and embittered he'd become, but something had changed and it surprised him to realize he wanted…more. He wanted to stop chasing a man who didn't want to be caught. He wanted a happy home. A woman who loved him. And children.

Most of all, he wanted peace.

Was it because of Stevie Rae?

Most definitely.

He turned again and searched the landscape around him. If he remembered correctly, they were in the vicinity of a cave he'd found a few months back, but with the rain obscuring his vision, he wasn't quite sure. That first time, he'd been in the same circumstances as now: cold and wet and needing shelter desperately. He'd been back a time or two since that first night. The last time, he'd left it well supplied with wood. Hopefully, no one else had found it. Or if they did, they replaced what they had used.

He pulled his hat lower to keep it from being swept up by the wind, and more water poured from the brim, dripping onto his saddle and anything that wasn't protected by his duster. He studied the terrain to his right, squinting against the driving rain, then turned to his left to get his bearings. If he could figure out exactly where they were, he could direct them to the cave and safety.

He slowed Resolute to a walk and motioned for Stevie Rae to catch up. He shouted against the howling wind when she reached him, "There's shelter not too far from here."

"A house?"

He shook his head. "A cave, but it's dry and big enough for us, the horses, and Whiskey Pete, too."

She tipped her hat, trying to keep the slanting rain from hitting her in the face. "How far?"

"Maybe a mile."

"How far is Mora?"

"Maybe five miles or so." Brock almost smiled as she tugged on her bottom lip with her teeth, which she always did when she considered her options. "Look, the cave isn't much, but it's shelter. The last time I was there, I stocked up on wood, but that was months ago. I can't promise it's still there."

Her lips held a tinge of blue and her teeth chattered as she adjusted the collar of her duster, drawing it closer to her neck. Not only was she wet, she was cold, too. Finally, she shook her head. "If it's all the same to you, we should keep going to Mora. We're already soaked to the bone—and cold. I'd much rather sleep in a warm, dry hotel room than a dark, damp cave." She peered up at him, and despite the water dripping in her face, smiled. Brock's heart rate picked up its pace, and peace, that elusive goal he so wanted, filled him.

"Mora it is. Stay close."

By the time they rode into Mora, Brock was miserable and cursing himself for a fool. He should have insisted they find the cave and stop. True, there might not have been wood for a fire and they might have spent a very uncomfortable cold, damp night, but at the very least, they'd be out of the elements. He'd ridden in foul weather before, but this was different. They were lucky they'd made it. Several times, he doubted they would. Rain like this, in a steady deluge, could be dangerous. Swollen rivers and massive flooding could carry a man—and his horse—to their deaths.

And it hadn't let up at all. In fact, it seemed to come down harder, pounding on them in big, fat, freezing drops or stinging exposed skin like little needles. A full-blown gale gusted first one way then another, stronger than anything Brock could remember, pushing water into his face though he had pulled his hat as low as it could go to shield his eyes, nose, and mouth. Several times, the force of the wind had buffeted him so hard, he'd gone off the trail...or what he thought was the trail. Thunder rumbled and boomed. Lightning lit up the sky, turning night to day and making it easier to see that the road they followed had turned to mud. It sucked at the horses' hooves to make travel much harder than it had to be. An ache settled in his shoulders and back from trying to guide Resolute through one of the most vicious storms he'd ever seen.

And if he was miserable, then Stevie Rae had to be as well. She hadn't said a word though, hadn't complained at all. He glanced at her and the feeling of peace, the one he liked so much and found himself needing more and more, rushed through him. He couldn't help the smile from parting his lips. Despite the water dripping from the brim of her hat, plopping onto her already drenched duster, she was still the most amazing woman he'd ever known.

Brock shook his head as emotions swept through him. As he did so, he spotted a small sign swinging from the post of a porch to his right, just over Stevie Rae's head. He squinted against the darkness and the constant drip of the rain from the brim of his hat to read it, but he couldn't quite make out the words. He thought—hoped—it was a hotel, but at this point, it didn't matter. The building attached to the porch was shelter from the storm.

Soft lantern light spilled into the street through the windows, an invitation to come inside and stay awhile. Hopefully they had rooms available. And if luck was with them, perhaps there would be some hot food to appease the gnawing hunger in his stomach.

He shouted her name over the howling wind, drawing her attention, and pointed toward the newfound safe haven.

She nodded once, then nudged Willow and headed in the direction Brock suggested. Whiskey Pete followed behind, his bellowing *hee-haw* a sign of his displeasure. On the side of the building, the eaves of the roof created an overhang. It wasn't big, but it did stop the rain from hitting them in the face and protected their rides somewhat.

Stevie dismounted and let out a startled squeak as her foot sank several inches into the mud beneath her. Brock caught her before she fell face-first into the thick, sucking mire, then physically lifted her and moved her closer to the side of the building. "Are you all right?"

"I'm just a little stiff." She pushed her hat back a little. In the lamplight spilling through the window he saw her face and sucked in his breath. A weary smile crossed her lips but her eyes glowed warmly. "Would you grab my valise and saddlebags? It'll be nice to change into clean, dry clothes."

"Of course." He released her, then grabbed her saddlebags from Willow's back. He slung them over his shoulder as he untied her valise from Whiskey Pete.

He didn't hold out much hope. What little clothes she'd stuffed in her saddlebag might be dry, but he doubted the same could be said about the items in her valise. The bag felt heavier, the cloth sides just as soaked as everything else. He tied their horses' reins to a hitching post, then grabbing her hand, raced around the building to the front steps and the wide porch. As they climbed the stairs, he noticed a hat stand had been set up beside the front door. Drops of water hit the floor and pooled beneath the garments hanging from the hooks before running in little rivulets to the end of the porch and the muddy road as he helped Stevie with her hat and coat. Her teeth chattered as she shivered. "I'm sorry, Stevie. I should have insisted we find that cave when I thought of it." He removed his hat and shrugged out of his duster, hanging them up to dry, then wrapped his arms around her.

"No need to be sorry. I was the one who thought we should move on to Mora. Who could have predicted we'd be in the middle of Noah's flood?"

He chuckled, despite the fact they were both cold, wet, and exhausted. "Come on, let's get you inside and dry."

Warmth from the flames that crackled and popped in the fireplace hit him as soon as he opened the door and stepped into the lobby of the small, quaint inn. Several towels lay on the bare floor beneath his feet and he took a moment to wipe the mud from his boots as his gaze swept the room. Beside him, Stevie did the same, then edged a little closer to him.

A man mopped excess water from the wood floor near the registration desk, his movements quick and methodical…it was obviously not the first time this night he had done so and it likely wouldn't be the last. Tomorrow, when the rain stopped and guests stopped bringing in water and mud with them, Brock was certain the man would unroll the rug now pushed up against the wall and cover the bare wood.

Brock closed the door, but didn't venture farther into the room. He cleared his throat. When that didn't get the man's attention, he tried again. "Excuse me."

The man stopped swabbing and squinted at them, then moved his spectacles from the top of his bald head down to his nose. "Ah, that's better," he mumbled almost to himself in an accent that was definitely not from this part of the country…and might not have been from this country at all. He stood the mop in its bucket and leaned the long, thick handle against the desk before grabbing a towel from a nearby chair and rushing forward. "Come in, come in. Welcome to Rose Cottage. I'm Milton Winthorpe, proprietor. Mind you don't trip now." He gestured to the towels on the floor, then gave the one he held to Stevie Rae. He smiled and his light brown eyes glowed with sympathy behind the lenses of his glasses. "This night is not fit for man nor beast."

"On that we can agree. We'd like a room."

"Sure. Sure. This storm caught everyone off guard, but you're in luck. I have one room left." He moved away from them and slipped behind the desk, a monstrosity of gilded wood and brass that should have been in a museum or a castle, and pushed the register across its surface along with an inkwell and pen. Brock stepped up to the desk, dropped his saddlebags on the floor, and signed the ledger while Mr. Winthorpe grabbed a key hanging from a small hook behind the desk. "It's my best room. You and your wife will be quite comfortable. Most importantly, you'll be warm and dry."

He handed Brock the key, then rang the bell on the desktop. "Top of the stairs and to your right. Room three."

Brock immediately handed the key to Stevie Rae. "Why don't you head on up?" The key disappeared in her trouser pocket. "I'll join you as soon as I get everything settled." His gaze roamed her face, noticing the circles beneath her eyes and the paleness of her skin. She looked exhausted. And hungry. And still soaked, although her hair had stopped dripping down her back, courtesy of the towel Mr. Winthorpe had given her, which now lay over her shoulders like a mantle.

She gave a quick nod, then headed for the stairs. He watched her take the risers, one hand gripping the banister like it was a lifeline, the other clasped tightly around the handles of her valise. He turned away and spoke to the innkeeper as Stevie stepped onto the landing and walked down the hall.

"Do you have a dining room? Or can you recommend someplace close where we might get a bite to eat?"

Mr. Winthorpe grinned and adjusted his glasses on his nose, which had a tendency to slip downward, and he fixed them by pushing at the nosepiece with his middle finger then swiping his hand across his bald head in one smooth, continuous motion. "Don't have to leave Rose Cottage at all. The dining room is closed for the evening, but the wife is an excellent cook. Best in town, if I do say so myself. I'm certain we can rustle you up something to eat." He glanced at Stevie Rae as she let herself into room three and his grin widened. "I'll have some hot water brought up, too."

"My wife"—lightning didn't zap him for keeping up the assumption the innkeeper had made though he fought the urge to duck—"will appreciate that." He gestured to the front door. "We have horses—"

"And we have a stable. No need to worry—" He peered at the ledger, his finger pushing at the nosepiece of his spectacles once more, followed by the hand swipe over his bald head. "We'll take care of everything, Mr. MacDermott." He looked to his left as a young man entered the lobby, his boots loud on the hardwood floor, a rain slicker slung over one arm. Water dripped from his hair onto the collar of his shirt. Still, he was dryer than Brock. "Ah, there you are, Will. Would you please see to Mr. MacDermott's horses? Then have water for a bath brought up to room three."

"Yes, sir." The boy turned away, and started to go back the way he'd come, but the innkeeper's voice stopped him. "Please ask Martha to see me before you go."

"Yes, sir," he repeated, not even bothering to turn around. He slipped his arms into the rain slicker, then passed through an arched doorway into what Brock assumed was the dining room. Mr. Winthorpe watched the boy, then turned his attention back to Brock. "Give us a few minutes. I'll have a tray brought up as quickly as possible."

"Thank you." He nodded toward the man, hefted his saddlebags over his shoulder, and started to walk away, then changed his mind and came back to the desk. "We'd like to keep the room for a couple of days, perhaps a full week. Is that possible?"

"Oh yes, indeed." The innkeeper's eyes lit up behind the lenses of his spectacles as he quickly made several marks among the pages of his ledger, then closed the book with a snap. "Room three is yours until Friday."

"How much do I owe you?"

He did a quick though silent calculation on his fingers, then came up with a more than fair price. Given that people were desperate to get out of the rain and have accommodations for the night, hotel owners and innkeepers alike could charge whatever they liked…and people would pay or be forced to deal with the storm raging outside. Brock pulled money from his pocket, counted out the appropriate amount for a week, and slid it across the shiny surface of the desk. Mr. Winthorpe slipped the money into the desk drawer without recounting it.

With one final nod, Brock crossed the lobby and climbed the stairs.

He knocked softly on the door to room three, then let himself in, only to stop short in the doorway and suck in his breath. Stevie stood in front of the fireplace, her hands stretched toward the crackling flames. Firelight reflected on her face, giving her a warm glow. The towel Mr. Winthorpe had given her earlier was wrapped around her head in a turban. She had pulled the colorful quilt from the bed and draped it around herself, clutching the material close to her body, her right shoulder exposed and gleaming. Underneath the quilt, he guessed she wore nothing—her clothes, the ones she'd put on this morning, were scattered about the room. Frilly drawers hung from the doorknob of the armoire in the corner, her lace-edged corset was laid flat on the bureau, her split skirt and blouse were spread over chairs so they could dry, her chemise hung from one of the bedposts.

She turned toward him, but didn't move away from the heat of the fire. He noticed a smudge of ash on her cheek, but at least her teeth had stopped chattering. She gestured to her improvised toga and shrugged. If she blushed, he couldn't tell in the meager light cast by the fire and the small lantern on the table. "Everything is wet and if it isn't wet, it's damp and cold so I decided this would be better."

Outside, rain slammed against the window as the wind howled over the rooftop, but inside, flames flickered behind the ornate brass screen, where her thick wool socks hung to dry. Her gaze rose up to meet his. She didn't blink, but she did smile...and what a beautiful smile. Desire swept through him, heating his blood, warming him despite his wet clothes. For a moment, all Brock could do was stare and take in her loveliness.

"Brock?"

"Hmmm?"

"It would help if you closed the door."

"What? Oh. Sorry." Startled, he felt the rush of heat on his face as he took a few more steps into the room and closed the door. His gaze swept over her once more, from the top of her head to her feet, which peeked out from beneath the quilt. She wiggled her toes, again startling him. Unexpected laughter burst from him as he crossed the room and wrapped her in his arms. She squealed as his wet clothes touched her but didn't move away from him.

"Mr. Winthorpe is sending up some soup." He let her go, then reached out to caress the side of her face with his thumb. "I'm so sorry, Stevie. We should have stopped earlier."

"No, this is much better than a cave. It's a cozy room, don't you think?"

"It's quite cozy," he agreed, but he wasn't interested in the furnishings. Well, that wasn't quite true. The huge four-poster bed certainly had his attention and he could think of nothing he'd like better than to lay her down on the thick mattress and make mad, sweet, passionate love to her. With that thought in mind, he nuzzled that sweet spot between her ear and collarbone while he pulled off the turban around her head. Mostly dry now, her hair tumbled down her back in wild curls. He tangled his fingers into those silken strands and inhaled her honeysuckle scent as he started walking her backward toward the bed.

"You're still wet," she chuckled against his chest, then moved her head and gazed up into his face. Brock needed no more invitation than that. His mouth descended to hers in a deep, rousing kiss, his fingers still tangled in her hair.

A brisk knock on the door interrupted his intentions. Brock groaned and pulled away from her. He gestured to the quilt, which had slipped a little, exposing more of her than anyone other than himself should see, and motioned for her to move out of sight. Once Stevie Rae did so, he opened the door a crack.

A girl, caught in that awkward stage between adorable child and stunning young woman, dark brown hair in braids hanging behind each ear, stood on the other side of the door, a wheeled cart in front of her. "Father asked me to bring this up for you." Mr. Winthorpe had outdone himself. Or rather, his wife had. Several covered dishes adorned the cart's surface along with silverware and a small pot of coffee. Silver candlesticks held long, slim tapers, and a beautiful red rose in a crystal vase completed the arrangement.

His stomach growled, but instead of letting her into the room, Brock opened the door a little wider. "Thank you. I'll take it from here." He reached into his pocket for a coin, which he gave the girl.

"But sir, I'm supposed to—"

"That won't be necessary."

The girl nodded, though it was clear she wasn't happy, and walked away, stopping once on the landing to look at him, tilt her head in curiosity, then shrug and skip down the stairs, flipping the gold coin she'd been given.

Brock brought the cart into the room and closed the door behind him with his foot, then rolled it forward, placing it beside the table between the fireplace and one of the windows.

Stevie Rae wasted no time transferring everything to the table. He was unable to take his eyes from her as she moved with infinite grace, the quilt flaring open just enough to reveal a long shapely leg. She sighed with obvious pleasure as she started removing the silver covers to reveal a feast for the eyes as well as the stomach.

Cold chicken breast lay spread out on one plate, the edges of each slice topped by a strip of golden brown, and steam rose from a small tureen of soup. A loaf of dark bread with a bowl of soft, creamy butter beside it lent the heavenly scent of rosemary to the air. Sliced apples and pears alternated between equally thick slices of cheese on another plate. A bottle of wine as well as a small pot of coffee completed the meal.

He glanced up from the table to find her steady gaze on him as she padded toward the bed in her bare feet. Her toes peeked out from beneath the quilt, and again, he saw a flash of shapely calf as she pulled another blanket from the mattress.

She handed him the blanket, then sauntered over to the fireplace where she moved the screen aside and grabbed a piece of kindling from the fire. Brock stood in the middle of the room, blanket over his arm, unable to move. He hoped to see more of her, another flash of her creamy skin, as she lit the candles on the table with the flaming end of the stick, then tossed it back into the fire and adjusted the ornate screen.

She pulled out one of the chairs and sat. The quilt parted, revealing her knees, calves, and feet but nothing else. "Are you going to stay in your wet clothes?" Her voice, soft and sultry, echoed in his ears, and heat surged through him as did that feeling of peace he liked so much.

"Hmmm?"

The tip of her tongue swiped against her bottom lip, making it shine, before the corners of her mouth lifted up in a smile. "You should change."

It took more willpower than he thought he possessed, but finally, he was able to tear his gaze away from the temptation that was Stevie Rae. "Yes. I should." Brock sat on the edge of the room's blue-striped camelback settee and pulled off his boots. He wiggled his toes in his wet wool socks, amazed that his socks could become so wet *inside* his boots. He shook his head, peeled the socks off his feet, padded barefoot to the fireplace, and hung them over the ornate screen, next to Stevie's. He placed his boots beside hers, too, then started to unbutton his shirt.

• • •

Stevie Rae sat at the table and admired the view as Brock shrugged out of his shirt. Firelight reflected off the perfection of his bare back, muscles moving beneath taut skin as he tossed his shirt across the back of the sofa. He turned to face her and grinned. The world as Stevie knew it turned on its axis and spun in the opposite direction, leaving her a bit woozy as desire for this man surged through her.

His grin remained in place and she thought he might be teasing her as he slowly unbuckled the gun belt slung low around his slim hips and put it aside, but still within easy reach. She let out her breath in a rush as his hands slipped down to the waistband of his trousers and watched, unembarrassed, as he unbuttoned his pants and slid them down to the floor. He wore no drawers beneath his trousers, and she caught an eyeful of his perfect backside as he sauntered over to the fireplace and slung the trousers over the screen next to his socks.

Her face grew hot, but her mouth dried as her eyes rose up to his face. There was a promise in his eyes, which roamed over her, leaving her warm and feeling oh-so-wanted. His gaze drifted toward the big four-poster bed, the mattress now missing blanket and quilt, then back to her. Moisture gathered between her thighs.

He wrapped the blanket around himself much the way she had done, hiding that hard, muscled body from sight, and slipped into the seat beside her.

"You didn't eat anything."

"I waited for you."

They ate in silence with just the hiss and snap of the fire and the rain pattering against the window for accompaniment. Though her body craved the food so thoughtfully prepared, she craved his touch so much more. She popped a piece of succulent chicken into her mouth and chewed, though she hardly tasted it. Warm and dry now, expectation settled in her belly as his gaze swept over her, his eyes a dark, smoldering gray in the candlelight. Their plates were almost empty, the bread nearly gone. Her hand shook just a bit as she reached for the crystal glass and finished the last of the hearty red wine in one swallow. As she did so, her eyes drifted toward the bed again. The craving to feel the heat of his body pressing against her became a physical need. She wanted him. Now.

Beneath the table, she moved his blanket aside with her foot, then caressed his leg, her toes sliding up to his knee then back down. Brock grinned and raised an eyebrow, then opened his legs a little wider.

Knuckles rapped against their door, interrupting her play.

"Ah, that must be the hot water for the bath."

"A bath? You ordered one for me?"

He said nothing, but a crooked smile tilted the corners of his mouth. This wasn't the first time he'd thought of her, and the sweetness of his gesture made her heart beat a little faster.

Brock put his napkin aside, rose from his chair, and adjusted his blanket before padding across the floor. He opened the door a crack and peered through. Stevie heard a low-voiced conversation, then the door opened wider and a young man entered the room carrying buckets. He nodded once toward her as he tromped across the floor and stopped before a section of the wall to the right of the fireplace. Stevie Rae watched him, curious as to why he stopped where he did. There was no door she could see. He placed one of the buckets on the floor and pressed against the panel with his hand. Stevie Rae heard a distinct *click* before the panel moved. The boy slid the panel along the wall to reveal a small hidden alcove with a brass bathtub big enough for two.

Another boy followed, bringing more water. They made several trips between them to fill the tub a little more than halfway. Finished, and several coins richer, they closed the door to their room softly behind them.

After the boys left, Brock made himself comfortable at the table and picked at the last of the apples and pears. He poured another glass of wine, leaned back in his chair, took a sip, and watched her, a smile playing on his lips. Mischief twinkled in his eyes and the heat of his stare warmed her from head to toe and every place in between. He nodded toward the bathtub in the small alcove. "You shouldn't let the water get cold."

Self-conscious beneath the directness of his gaze, Stevie rose from her seat and pulled her quilt closer around her body. She moved toward the tub and tested the water. It was perfect. But he hadn't taken his eyes off her. She could close the panel, she supposed, but that would leave her in total darkness. There were no wall sconces, no shelves to place a candle.

"Are you just going to sit there and watch me?"

"Yes." His voice seemed tight, as if he struggled with the one word.

He had seen her naked before, but for reasons she couldn't explain, his intent gaze made her a bit nervous. Perhaps it was the raw desire she saw gleaming in the depths of his eyes. Or perhaps it was the anticipation surging through her in an uncontrollable tide. Whatever the reason, she hesitated then drew a deep breath and dropped the quilt on the floor. She sank into the hot water, the last vestiges of coldness leaving her, and let out a long sigh as she leaned her head back on the rim of the tub. Closing her eyes, she let the heat of the water soothe her. "Oh, this is heaven."

She heard him grunt and the sound seemed a little closer than before, but she didn't think anything of it, nor did it disturb her when she heard him rummage around in his saddlebags or when his bare feet padded across the floor.

"Stevie." His voice was much closer now. Her lips twitched into a smile before a soft *plink* and the sudden splash of water on her face made her open her eyes wide. "You forgot your soap."

She'd been right. He was much closer—standing beside her in all his naked glory, a devil-may-care grin spreading his lips beneath his mustache, his blanket puddled on the floor. She could have reached out and caressed his thigh or better yet, his fully engorged manhood. She could move her head a little and probably slip him into her mouth.

Her eyes opened wider, startled and surprised by her own thoughts, and the rush of anticipation surging through her left her feeling weak, yet empowered. Could she? Did she dare? She'd never…but…

She didn't have time to decide or even act on the impulse. Brock leaned forward, his hands resting on the rim of the tub, and captured her mouth beneath his. Stevie Rae rose up to deepen the kiss, her body thrumming with expectation, but she didn't have the chance to do anything else except stifle a startled gasp as he pulled away, then slid into the tub behind her. Water sloshed against the sides of the bath, splashing over the rim to splatter on the floor. "Brock!"

He settled behind her and wrapped his arms around her, pulling her closer so she leaned against him, her back to his chest, her hips between his thighs, his full arousal hard against her lower back.

"Now, where is that soap?"

Stevie Rae stifled a giggle as he searched the bath for the sliver of soap he'd dropped into the water. His hand encountered her thigh, leading to a long caress that left her anticipating more. He did not disappoint—his fingertips traveled upward and just grazed the curls at the juncture between her thighs, enough to make her gasp with pleasure.

"Got it." The teasing quality of his voice made her heart thump as did the sight of him rubbing the soap between his big hands. Foamy lather bubbled over his skin before he allowed the slim sliver to drop back into the water. She held her breath, waiting for his touch, and sighed when he smoothed the lather over her stomach and upward to cup her breasts, his thumbs sliding over her nipples. Instantly, the dusty rosebuds hardened. She closed her eyes and reveled in his caress, not daring to move lest he stop the sweet torture.

"Do you like that?" he whispered in her ear, producing goose bumps over her entire body, and she shivered when his teeth grazed her earlobe.

"Hmmmm" was all she could manage as his hands moved over her, caressing her breasts before moving lower, smoothing over her belly once more, then lower still. He didn't touch her where she wanted to be touched the most, though she thrust her hips upward. Instead, his fingers just grazed the place that yearned for his caress while he planted kisses on the back of her neck.

Her breath quickened, her blood surging through her veins to her center. Unable to tolerate his teasing glances against her swollen folds for a moment longer, she grabbed his hand and trapped it between her thighs, then drew her legs together.

"So that's what you want." He chuckled, sending another shiver down her spine and more heat racing through her. "Happy to comply." His fingers delved between her swollen folds, finding the very core of her. Of their own accord, her legs parted and her hips rocked, trying to set a pace that would ease the pressure building within her, but he seemed to have his own rhythm and her actions brought no relief. Her body was tightening, coiling, ready to explode in pure pleasure, and yet, he wouldn't give her what she wanted, what she needed. He seemed to enjoy building the tension within her. She whimpered as he rubbed the soapy fingers of one hand around and around her erect nipple while he kept up a slow, steady cadence over the nub between her folds with the other.

Desperate, she groaned, "Now, Brock! Now!"

Once again, he complied and pressed hard against her with his fingers. Her release rippled through her immediately, making her shudder with its power. Stevie couldn't help the deep moan that escaped her as her body pulsed beneath his hand.

She turned in his arms, splashing water over the sides of the bath, and sprawled atop him, her spine arched, her breasts crushed against his chest, his arousal hard against her belly. She touched her lips to his and kissed him deeply, the place between her thighs still throbbing from the force of her climax.

"Maybe we should move to the bed," she whispered when she broke the kiss.

"Maybe we should." He touched her lips with his, then grinned. "Or maybe we can stay right here." He took possession of her mouth, his tongue sweeping the warm recesses as he reached between them, his hand snaking along her belly and lower, to once more delve into her springy curls. Stevie Rae sucked in her breath as his fingers unerringly found the key to her release and started slowly caressing her. She couldn't help herself. She moved against his hand, her back arching even more, then rose to her knees, her legs wide as she straddled his thighs, his hand still between hers, caressing her lightly. A soft whimper escaped her as Brock lifted her breast closer, then drew her nipple into his mouth, swirling his tongue around the pointed crest.

She was so close, on the edge of another shattering climax, her body tightening, building toward release. The whimpers easing from her throat deepened, becoming more of a groan as she moved against his hand. And then he stopped caressing her, his fingers no longer between her aching folds.

Stevie Rae sucked in her breath and opened her eyes, but before she could beg him to continue, Brock grabbed her hips in his big hands, and guided her until she hovered just over him, barely touching him. He moved his hips to slide his fully engorged shaft against her wet folds, seeking and finding her entrance. He thrust upward at the same time his hands at her hips pulled her down. Stevie Rae let out a groan as he filled her completely.

"Don't move. Let me," he whispered before he took possession of her mouth.

Slowly, he started moving against her, flesh against flesh, heat against heat. Water sloshed out of the tub, but Stevie Rae didn't care as new sensations whipped through her. There were no deep thrusts into her body, but a steady movement of his hips against her, his hard shaft filling her, which was just as powerful. Again, her body prepared—tensing, coiling, so very close to that moment she sought. Her breaths came in short gasps even as her lips met his and her tongue plundered his mouth.

"We should move to the bed," he whispered in her ear when she broke the kiss, his body no longer moving against her, but now utterly still. She had been so close. Stevie Rae gasped as her eyes flew open to see his smile. Was he purposely bringing her to the very brink of release then not following through? Building the torment as well as the pleasure?

"What?"

"We should move to the bed."

"I don't think I can. I…"

"But I can. Hold on."

Stevie Rae wrapped her arms around his neck as Brock sat up, then wrapped her legs around his hips as he instructed. Still joined together, he used the sides of the tub for leverage, then lifted them both out of the water. The floor around the bathtub was a sudsy mess, but neither of them cared.

He brought her to the edge of the bed, which was the perfect height, and rested her backside on the mattress. "Lie back," he whispered as he nuzzled her neck. Feeling as if she would fall off the bed at any moment, Stevie Rae lay back as he'd asked. He brought first one of her legs up to his shoulder, her ankle caressing his ear, then the other, and with a wicked grin, began to thrust into her while his hands held her hips steady.

Stevie Rae sucked in her breath. This was new and different, and she didn't know what to do except experience the flood of sensation. Her hands caressed his chest, the crisp dark hair tickling her palms, but even that became too much. She felt weightless as if she could have floated to the ceiling and beyond. And boneless. He could flip her around like a rag doll and she wouldn't care…as long as he didn't stop!

Brock lowered his chest closer to hers but didn't rest on her, his arms taking all his weight, muscles bulging. Her legs, still over his shoulders, began to tremble as he pressed his hips tighter between her thighs, slowing his movement so that he was no longer thrusting into her, but rather moved against her as he'd done in the bathtub.

The mounting pressure and the heat consuming her was all too much and yet, not enough. She wanted more, wanted him closer still, wanted relief from the physical ache within her. "Don't stop!" she yelled as she grabbed his hips, pulling him deeper within her, rocking against him, beyond desperate, no longer thinking, just feeling.

Close. So close.

With a deep cry from the depths of her soul, Stevie Rae reached her peak. The pleasure was so intense, tears blurred her vision. Her world darkened even more than it had in the past, but when the darkness fled, no vibrant colors swirled through her brain. Instead, a soft radiant light seemed to warm her with its golden touch until he pulled all the way out of her. Disappointment raced through her. She wanted more. So much more.

She opened her eyes to see that wicked grin stretching his lips and squealed when he kissed her feet and slowly lowered her legs from his shoulders. He scooped her up and began nuzzling her neck. "Brock!" she giggled as he gently laid her in the middle of the bed. "What are you—?"

She never had the chance to ask her question as he crawled onto the mattress, settled between her thighs, and plunged into her, filling her completely. "Oh!" Her legs wrapped around his hips, pulling him closer, deeper.

A moment passed, then two, before he started to move, his body pressed tightly to hers, his gaze never leaving her face, and then he dipped his head and took possession of her mouth, his tongue sweeping against hers. Excitement zinged through her veins as she caught his rhythm, her hips moving in time with his. Her body tightened around him, her insides coiling, like a spring twisted too tight, and that moment—that utterly wonderful, breathtaking moment—burst upon her, leaving her dazed and filled with awe.

Brock chuckled, the sound vibrating in his chest as his rhythm changed, becoming faster and harder. His breathing quickened and his arms began to quiver as he thrust into her—long, deep strokes she felt to her very core—before a groan ripped from his throat and he plunged into her one last time. He shuddered, his shaft pulsing deep within as the heat of his seed filled her.

He withdrew from her gently and gathered her in his arms, his heavy breath in her ear, his chest rising and falling quickly. Exhausted, her body still pulsating with the force of her release, Stevie Rae laid her head on his chest and listened to the sound of his heartbeat slowly return to normal. Rain slashed against the windows and the wind howled beyond the glass, but here, with Brock holding her close, all was right with the world. Stevie Rae smiled and closed her eyes as sleep overtook her.

Chapter 17

"Hello, Joe."

Marshal Joe Bennett looked up from the papers on his desk and grinned. "Brock. Glad you could come." He rose from his seat a second later, walked around the desk in a stiff-legged gait, and held out his hand. Brock took the hand offered him and pulled the man in for a generous hug.

When they broke apart, Brock continued to study him. Joe looked…tired. And so much older than he had on their last visit a few months ago. Wrinkles—or lifelines, as Brock's mother had called them, evidence of a life well-lived—bracketed his mouth and fanned out from his eyes and more gray streaked his dark hair. Deep circles seemed to bruise the skin beneath Joe's light brown eyes, as if something kept him up at night, unable to rest and draw strength from a good night's sleep…exactly how Brock used to feel, until Stevie came into his life. "Your telegram said it was urgent."

"I think it is." The man sighed, then perked up a bit when his gaze drifted toward Stevie Rae standing in the doorway, and a smile broke out on his face, effectively erasing that tired look as if it hadn't been there at all.

Brock smirked—it was no secret Joe loved the ladies and couldn't resist a little harmless flirtation now and then. The flirting *was* harmless. Joe was completely and utterly devoted to his wife, Cora. Brock performed introductions with a shake of his head. "I'd like you to meet Miss Buchanan. Stevie Rae, this is Joe Bennett, marshal here in Mora for what? Six years?"

"Eight years now. And married for seven. Can you believe that?" He took Stevie's hand and brought it to his lips, his mouth curving into a smile. "A pleasure to meet you, Miss Buchanan."

"Nice to meet you as well. Please call me Stevie."

He gave a quick nod as he drew her toward a chair, then released her hand as she sat. He leaned against his desk, addressing both of them when he spoke, but looking at neither. Instead, his gaze focused on the view outside the window. "I've seen a lot in my eight years as marshal, but nothing like this. It's most unusual. Not sure if anyone else has ever run into this."

"Into what?" Stevie asked, drawing his attention.

A look passed over Joe's face, an expression Brock knew too well. Sorrow. Loss. Regret for the things that should have been said but never were. Anger. The same emotions Brock lived with day in and day out. He understood. He glanced at Stevie. She understood as well.

Brock said nothing as he gave the marshal a moment to collect his thoughts. Several minutes dragged by, long minutes during which the only sound in the room was a cricket chirping in one of the jail cells.

"Has someone..." He didn't want to be indelicate, nor did he want to blurt out questions, but he needed to know why Joe had summoned him. The only reason he could think of was that Logan had passed through here and left death and destruction in his wake. As much as he wanted to know, he also didn't. Things had changed for him. "Did someone die? Was it Logan?"

"What?" Joe's brow wrinkled as he shook his head. "No, no one is dead. At least not that I'm aware of."

"Then why did you send for me?"

"There's something you need to see." The marshal moved away from his desk, grabbed his hat from the hat rack, then led the way outside into the sun-filled day. The only evidence of yesterday's torrential downpour, which had soaked everything, was a few puddles in the middle of the road and the mud, which seemed to be everywhere. Joe closed the door, then quickly wrote a note on the small blackboard that he'd be back soon. He put the chalk back on the little shelf beneath it, turned toward Brock, and smirked. "I think you got someone riled up, my friend."

"Riled up? What are you talking about?"

"You'll see." He sauntered down the few steps to the muddy street, untied his horse's reins from the post, and climbed into the saddle.

"Where are we going?"

"Out to the Garcias' ranch after a couple other stops. I'll explain along the way, although once you see why I asked you to come here, everything will be clear."

As Brock helped Stevie Rae into Willow's saddle, trepidation skittered up his spine. Why was Joe being so odd? Why didn't the man just come out and tell him what had happened, instead of being so mysterious? It was unsettling to his already raw nerves.

"Brock?" Stevie asked.

"Hmmmm?" he responded as he tightened the cinch on Willow's saddle, then rested his hand on Stevie's leg.

"Are you—?"

He sighed as he reached for her hand, effectively cutting off her question midstream. He already knew what she was about to ask just by the tone of her voice and the expression on her face. He could have told her the truth—he was not all right and wondered if he'd ever be again—but he lied instead. "I'm fine."

He mounted Resolute, then tugged lightly on the reins and brought him alongside Stevie Rae.

Joe led the way down the street, heading north, but he didn't go very far. He turned the corner at Wheeler's Saloon and stopped. When Brock pulled up beside him, he nodded toward the white clapboard wall of the building. "This is why I sent you the telegram."

Stevie Rae gasped as both she and Brock turned toward the structure. Stunned and disconcerted, he swore before he could stop himself. "What the hell?"

Written on the side of the building were the words *Give up, McDermit*. Faded and dulled by the recent rain, the shaky rust-colored letters were still easily discerned. His stomach lurched and he tasted bile in the back of his throat. His eyes immediately swung toward Stevie Rae. Her face, so rosy after their lovemaking this morning, had lost all color, and when she met his glance, there were tears in her eyes. And there was nothing he could do. He had no words to set her mind at ease. Hell, there was nothing he could tell himself that would erase the warning written on the side of the building nor cease the anxiety building inside him.

It was a warning. He had no doubt of who had left it, either. The muscles in his stomach tightened even more as he tore his gaze away from Stevie and turned toward Joe. "There's no chance you have a family named MacDermott living here in town, is there?"

Joe shook his head, and Brock caught the sadness in his eyes before the shadow of his hat brim hid it.

"Is it paint?"

"No, sir. Not paint." Joe moved his horse closer to the wall and reached out to touch the *T*. "When I found it a couple of days ago, it was still relatively fresh. You can see where I tried to wipe it off. It's blood. Whose I don't know. No one is missing. No one has died. No crimes at all have been reported, not even drunkenness." He took a deep breath and wiped his finger against his trousers, though there was nothing to wipe off. "I wouldn't let Wheeler Telford—he owns the place—clean it off until you could see it."

Brock said nothing. His gaze once more shifted to Stevie. She hadn't moved. Tears still shimmered in her eyes, but her lips were pressed together. He recognized her expression—he'd seen it enough and he wondered how she was able, time after time, to draw strength and determination from her soul when there was none to be had.

Joe gestured to the wall again, drawing Brock's attention. "I've seen two other warnings, but there may be more that I haven't.

Like I said, you got someone riled up. I'm thinking you know who it is."

Of course he did. There was only one man Brock pursued, only one man audacious and insane enough to do this.

"Aren't you going to say anything?" Joe asked after a long, drawn-out silence.

Brock shrugged and struggled to keep his voice calm despite the fear rampaging through him. "What's there to say?" He glanced at Stevie Rae once again. She still hadn't moved. In fact, she sat absolutely motionless atop Willow's back, her hands clutching the reins in a grip so tight, he was surprised her fingers didn't break from the pressure. She didn't even blink, but he suspected she held on to her emotions the same way he held on to his. He drew in a deep breath. "You said there's more?"

Joe gave a slight nod, then nudged his horse and led the way north, away from town. They picked up a deeply rutted road, one of three choices. Water filled the grooves, producing a viscous mud that seemed to suck at the horses' hooves. He didn't speak, which was more than fine with Brock. Stevie Rae didn't speak either, which was both welcome and frightening. He couldn't help asking himself what was going through her mind. He couldn't tell from her expression. Eyes narrowed, lips pressed together, she might have been angry…or upset. It was possible she was both at the same time.

Twenty silent, tense minutes later, the trio turned down a smaller road to a tiny farm that reminded Brock immediately of the Westons'. Memories assailed him. It was hard to forget the bloodstains on the floor and the pervasive smell of death. His hands gripped Resolute's reins tighter in preparation for what he was about to see, even though Joe had said no one had died.

He needn't have worried. The farm had that desolate look of abandonment. Glass missing from windows, front door wide open and held in place by one hinge, paint chipped, peeling and faded.

"This farm belonged to the Merriweathers, but they haven't lived here in years." Joe tugged on the reins and brought his horse to a stop, then gestured to the barn to his left.

Brock had been concentrating on the farmhouse, and trying to push the memories away. He had not looked at the barn until Joe drew his attention to it but wondered how he could have missed it. The barn was big and painted white, though bare spots showed plain wood where the color had worn away. The faded rust-brown words written on the side were easily seen from the road…if he'd been paying attention.

I'm comin' fer ya, McDermit.

Brock sucked in his breath and tamped down the uncertainty twisting his bowels. It was one thing to chase a man. It was another thing entirely for that man to turn the tables and do the chasing. The moment Logan made that decision, he became more dangerous and unpredictable than he already was. Turning in his saddle, Brock scanned the horizon, waiting for his nemesis to pop out from behind a rock or the abandoned farmhouse and shoot him dead. Would he be brave enough to do it? Was he even still in Mora, waiting for the perfect opportunity?

Stevie.

His gaze focused on her and he exhaled the breath he'd been holding, not only at a loss for words, but filled with an anxiety and a fear he could not express even if he tried. His mouth dried as his heart began to thunder in his chest. Every muscle in his body tightened as nausea settled in his stomach.

What if she was caught in the crossfire? Concern for her outweighed any apprehension he had for himself. He could handle this—being threatened by criminals was part of the job description for lawmen—but he could handle it much better if Stevie wasn't with him.

Her gaze met his. She pushed her hat back on her head and leaned forward in the saddle, her wrists crossed and resting on the pommel. One eyebrow rose higher than the other as if she knew where his thoughts had strayed. She spoke for the first time, her voice tight, "Don't even think it, MacDermott."

It took effort, but Brock finally managed to tear his gaze away from her and get himself under control. He licked his lips and found moisture in his dry mouth, though his heart did not stop its erratic beat. He could only guess what other warning was written at the Garcias'. "Take us to the Garcias'."

The marshal nodded and, without a word, led the way.

A short time later, Joe brought his mount to a stop on a small rise above a verdant valley. Stevie Rae stopped as well. Brock did the same, then took a deep breath as he unclenched his hands and released the reins he'd been gripping tightly. Despite the shade of his hat, he squinted while he took in the view.

From this point, one could see forever…or so it seemed. It was a beautiful vista, but Brock didn't really appreciate it nor did he waste time studying the heavily forested mountains on the horizon. He was more interested in the sprawling ranch house shimmering in the afternoon sun in the valley below, protected by a long, winding rock wall that disappeared into the distance. Smaller buildings dotted the landscape, popping up behind and to the east and west of the main house. Even squinting, Brock couldn't make out the sign over the entrance, but he could see a fountain splashing in the courtyard beyond the fence.

"Paradise," Joe announced. "The Garcias have been here for a long time. Good people." He nudged his horse's side and cantered down the gentle slope, picking one of the two ruts that wagon wheels had cut into the earth over the decades.

As they rode closer, Brock noticed a man pacing in front of the break in the rock wall, his steps measured and unhurried as he passed a closed split-rail fence that offered only the illusion of safety. Another man leaned against the same wall, knee bent, one foot planted firmly on the wall. The second man tilted his head and brought his hand up to his face. Smoke billowed from beneath his hat, then dissipated in the air.

Brock wasn't fooled. The smoking cowboy may appear to be relaxed, but he wasn't. Neither was the other man, though his pace hadn't changed. Both sported gun belts, the holsters tied low around their thighs in the fashion of a gunfighter. Both also carried rifles. Family members? Guards? Professional gunmen? Brock didn't know, but his anxiety rose another notch, especially when the smoking cowboy raised his head and peered directly at him. He made no other move, but that didn't bring any comfort.

Brock turned his head, his eyes seeking out Stevie Rae, and let out his breath, relieved she was still beside him, yet concerned at the same time. She was afraid of this new game Logan seemed to be playing. He could see that plainly in the way she looked at him, and he wouldn't blame her if she headed back to town. Or better yet, back home. In fact, that might be the best thing for her. Logan wasn't after her—didn't even know she existed. She could go back to Little River, meet a nice man, and marry. Have children. Grow old with someone else.

As soon as the thought popped in his head, he stiffened in his saddle and a jolt of pain settled in his chest. *She deserves to have a good life. A safe life. She deserves to grow old with someone who loves her. Why should that bother me?*

The pain in his chest increased and his jaw tightened, his teeth grinding together as he answered his own question. It wasn't *him* she was growing old with. The vision in his head did not include him and truthfully, it couldn't, not with this new threat hanging over his head. She deserved so much better…and he couldn't give it to her.

He shook his head, hoping to stop the whirlwind of his own thoughts and doubts, and he forced himself to unclench his jaw. He also tore his gaze from Stevie, as hard as that was, and concentrated on the cowboys protecting Paradise. "They gonna let us get close enough to see who we are before they shoot us?"

"Maybe." Joe shrugged and grinned. He pointed to the man leaning against the wall. "That's Natanil, Antonio's oldest boy. A little hotheaded, like his father. He's faster than a rattlesnake and just as deadly." He gestured to the man who paced back and forth in front of the gate. "That's Rafael. You don't have to worry about him."

"So Rafael isn't a good shot?"

"I didn't say that." Joe's grin widened, the creases bracketing his mouth deepening. "He's a damn excellent shot. I just said you didn't have to worry about him. He tends to think before he acts, whereas Natanil just shoots and thinks about asking questions later…if at all."

"Great." He couldn't help the sarcasm that slipped into his voice "Stevie, I want you to stay behind me, all right?"

She didn't say a word. In fact, she didn't argue at all, just flicked the reins in her hands and Willow fell into step behind Resolute. They rode closer, close enough to see that the rifle resting in Natanil's hand was a Henry Repeating Rifle, close enough to see the fancy stitching on the shirt of the shorter man. Apprehension whipped through him. Despite the fact Joe seemed to know these young men and didn't appear concerned, Brock knew how quickly something could change, especially with a hothead like Natanil. All it would take would be one wrong word, a wrong look, a misunderstood movement, and the shooting would start.

He took his eyes off the boys for a moment and glanced around, unease crawling up his spine. Was Logan here? Was he watching? Was he inside the ranch house, just waiting for him to walk straight into his trap and bring Stevie with him?

Joe brought his mount to a halt in front of the gate. Brock and Stevie did as well. He nodded to Natanil, who did not return the greeting. Instead, the young man dropped his cigarillo and crushed it beneath the heel of his boot, then walked away, the rifle still clutched in his hand.

"Don't mind him, Marshal." Rafael pushed the brim of his hat back on his forehead as he approached them. "He's just upset Father is making him stand guard." He grinned, showing straight, white teeth and dimples in his cheeks, then turned his attention to Brock and Stevie. "Welcome to Paradise." He gave an exaggerated bow, then opened the gate, allowing all three of them to enter the yard.

The fountain Brock had seen from the distance was more impressive close up. Water shimmered and sparkled as it streamed into the air from the four mermaids surrounding a reflecting pool. The effect seemed to ease some of his tension…not all, but a little.

Joe dismounted and tied the reins to his horse around a thick post. Brock followed suit, slipping from the saddle easily even though every muscle in his body thrummed, every nerve ending screamed. He glanced to his right. Stevie hadn't moved, though Willow stood quietly by the rail.

"Stevie?"

She jumped, startled, then climbed from the saddle, her movements stiff. She stumbled a bit as her feet met the flagstone, but Brock caught her arm in one hand so she wouldn't fall while he grabbed the reins with his other. "You all right?"

She didn't answer, just nodded, but her eyes were dark, almost slate blue, and huge in her pale face. She was afraid—he felt the slight tremor beneath his hand, and for a moment, he thought he could hear her heart pounding in her chest, but perhaps it was only his own.

He didn't know what to say—or do—to put her at ease. *Hell, man, you can't even put yourself at ease.* As he searched for words of comfort that couldn't be found, he reached up to cup her chin in his palm, his thumb caressing the soft skin of her cheek.

It was enough. Color seeped back into her face and she exhaled, though her eyes remained dark. She gave a slight nod, then taking his hand in hers, stepped up to the intricately carved door.

Joe used the knocker on the big, heavy portal of the sprawling ranch house, the deep sound echoing in the courtyard. Brock shivered despite the warmth of Stevie Rae's hand in his. The banging sounded like a death knell in his head. Stevie squeezed lightly. He glanced at her, studied her as she stood beside him, both grateful she was here yet afraid at the same time. Her hat now lay against her back, suspended by the corded string around her neck. Her hair, tied back in a ponytail, reflected the sunlight and gleamed in every color from pale wheat to rich honey gold. A hank of that hair slipped from the leather thong she used to tie it back and fell forward to curl near her cheek. He reached out and tucked it behind her ear, then jumped and stiffened when a small covered square in the middle of the door popped open and a man who looked remarkably like Rafael peeked through. His face was set in stern lines until he recognized Joe, then his features softened a bit. "Marshal." The little door closed. The big door swung open a moment later. "Please, please, come in."

Brock stood back and let Stevie Rae enter first. He hid his smirk when she wiped her boots on the woven straw mat, then stepped over the threshold. He followed, stepping into a wonderfully warm receiving room.

The marshal performed the introductions. "Antonio, I'd like you to meet Miss Buchanan and Mr. MacDermott."

There were no handshakes, no exchange of pleasantries. Antonio Garcia's entire body stiffened. "So, you are MacDermott. Please, follow me." It wasn't disrespect Brock detected in his voice, but rather anger. And fear. The man said nothing more as he led the way down a hallway toward the back of the house, his footsteps loud on the Mexican tile when they weren't muffled by several thick throw rugs. A maid dropped a curtsey, then quickly scurried out of the way.

He stopped before a set of French doors and fished a key out of his pocket. "I've kept this room locked ever since…" He did not finish his sentence as he fitted the key into the lock. Instead, his face flushed with anger as he pushed the doors open and invited them inside. "This is our formal parlor. We never use it except on very rare and special occasions; however, it is cleaned once a week." His voice trembled slightly as he pointed toward a wall and the message written there, once again in blood.

Yer a ded man, McDermit. The girl to.

Brock heard Stevie Rae gasp, but it hardly registered over the buzzing in his ears as he read the words, blinked, then read them again. The humming grew louder, interspersed with the sound of his heart thundering in his chest.

Antonio's voice came from a distance although the man stood beside him. "This is what Anjanette saw when she came in here to clean. Poor girl screamed then fainted. My wife came running when she heard the screams. Neither one of them will come in this room again." His voice grew louder, his statement punctuated with the staccato slap of his fist hitting his palm. "Someone was in *my* house and did this horrible thing *while we were home!*"

"He's long gone, Antonio. Logan doesn't stay anywhere too long," Joe said as he worried the brim of his hat between his fingers and looked the older man right in the eye, but his expression of confidence fell a bit short and Antonio was not at all appeased.

The rancher's body stiffened. "I don't care that you're certain he's gone. The point is—" He punctuated his words with his fist in his palm once again, as if trying to make others understand the importance. "*He came into my house!* My wife—or one of my children, God forbid—could have stumbled on him in the act, and then what?" He took a deep breath and wiped the sweat from his forehead. "I am sorry. I should not take my frustration out on you, Marshal." He took another breath, then slumped into a chair, his fingers drumming on the arm. "Believe it or not, I am much calmer now than when I first saw this." He gestured to the warning on the wall then turned away from the bloody words.

"You have a right to be angry, Mr. Garcia. I would be. I am." Brock approached the man slowly, his footsteps muffled by the thick carpet on the floor. "But he's not after you or your family. Why he chose your home to vandalize, I can only assume it's because he saw an opportunity and he took it." He didn't say that if Logan wanted the Garcias dead, they would be. The man was upset enough and didn't need to know that.

"What is he doing?" Stevie Rae asked, her voice hoarse and filled with fear.

He turned toward her and tried to swallow the dryness in his throat. One thing and one thing only made itself clear to him. Logan might not know who she was, but he sure as hell knew Stevie Rae traveled with him. Heat rushed to his face and his muscles grew taut as nausea roiled in his gut. "Trying to scare me. Intimidate me."

"This is a game?" Antonio sputtered, unable to control his temper, and jumped from his chair.

"Yes." Brock didn't look at the man when he answered. Instead, he studied Stevie Rae's face—the hollows beneath her cheekbones, the plumpness of her lips, her impossibly blue eyes, all of which had become so dear to him—and in that moment, the shadows disappeared, leaving a startlingly clear light, and the truth struck him to his very soul.

I'm in love with her.

The knowledge came not only with the feeling of peace he associated with her, but also with a pervasive fear that settled in his bones.

When, precisely, had he lost his heart to her? Was it when she stood up to him and demanded, more or less, to join him in his search for Logan? Or when she walked into a saloon full of outlaws and kept her wits about her even though she'd been terrified? Or when she let down her defenses and cried in his arms?

He couldn't pinpoint the moment exactly, but it didn't matter. The fact remained—he was in love with her.

Stevie Rae Buchanan was, by turns, frustrating and comforting, too stubborn for her own good, and yet kind to a fault. She had been good company, reminding him that it wasn't wise to be alone so much, and he'd found himself telling her much more than he'd ever told anyone, and wanting to share even more. Over the miles they'd traveled together, he'd come to admire her, then actually like her, but when had that turned into love? And why did he feel as if his heart was breaking now?

Logan.

He would—and could—come after Stevie just to hurt him.

As he stood looking down into her beautiful face, his love for her filling him, Brock came to a decision she might hate. In fact, he knew she'd hate it. And she'd probably hate him, too, which was just as well.

Stevie Rae Buchanan was going home.

Chapter 18

Yer a ded man, McDermit. The girl to!

Two days later, Brock could still see the words painted in blood as he and Stevie Rae rode north beside the Mora River in one of the canyons the river had cut through the landscape. Mora was behind them by about two hours or so, Little River hours ahead, but time had not lessened the devastation of seeing the warning sprawled across the wall of the Garcia home, the blood having dried to a dark brown against the bright white of the paint.

Fear rode with him. Not for himself, but for Stevie Rae. The decision to take her back to Little River had come without discussion because she didn't know the plan. He hadn't told her. He'd simply made up his mind as he read the words written on the wall when the threat to her life had become more than clear. Because he loved her, there was no other alternative. For her own safety and for his peace of mind, Stevie Rae had to go home.

Brock almost grinned, but stopped himself. She had no idea that was why they were heading north again.

"MacDermott!"

The voice echoed and bounced off the canyon walls, making it impossible to know exactly where it came from—behind them? In front of them? The only two things Brock knew for certain was that it came from above, somewhere along the rim—but which rim, east or west?—and that it belonged to Zeb Logan. He'd know that gruff, deep voice anywhere—

"You'll never take me alive."

"Where is he?" Stevie whispered as she pulled on the reins and brought Willow to a halt. She tipped her hat back as she scanned the rim of the canyon, much the same as he did.

"I don't know." His mouth went dry and his hands fisted around Resolute's reins. He'd made a mistake. Several of them. The first was leaving Mora. The second? He should never have taken the trail down to the river a few miles back, but he had done so because he'd felt so exposed on the ridge. Now they were caught with nowhere to go. To the left was the steep canyon wall rising skyward. To the right, the Mora River, still swollen from the recent rains. Brock glanced at the water flowing swiftly beside them. He had no idea how deep it was or how fast the current, but if they tried to cross here, they'd be out in the open, a clear shot if Logan decided to take it. Chances were good he'd hit one of them. Or both of them. If the current didn't take them first.

How long had Logan been following them, waiting for such a perfect opportunity? And it was perfect. The way he saw it, he and Stevie had no choices at all. Try to get out of the canyon and get shot. Or stay here and get shot. Either way, someone would end up dead. He'd rather it wasn't Stevie Rae. Or himself.

"Don't let him rattle you," Stevie hissed as she and Willow sidled up beside him, Whiskey Pete following behind, but not happily, his braying echoing off the sides of the canyon. She gestured to an outcropping of rock, a shelf of sorts protruding from the cliff face that might offer a little protection. Brock nodded and motioned for her to head that way. He didn't follow, but rather rode by her side, careful to keep her as protected as possible.

"If ye quit doggin' me, I'll stop killin'."

Brock stiffened in his saddle. It was quite an offer, even if untrue, and others, he knew, might consider it, but he couldn't. Wouldn't. Logan would never keep his word. The killing would continue simply because Logan was an evil man. He enjoyed it. The warnings he painted in blood made it quite clear who was next on his list, and to prove his intentions, a shot rang out, echoing against the canyon walls, followed quickly by another.

"Stevie!" Brock vaulted out of the saddle and pulled Stevie Rae down to the ground just as a third and fourth shot were fired in quick succession. Resolute and Willow, startled not only by the bullets slamming into the canyon wall, but by his own scared leap from the saddle, raced farther down the canyon. Whiskey Pete no longer trailed behind but was almost in the lead, the mule's braying mingling with the crazed laughter floating down from the rim of the canyon. He sent a silent prayer heavenward for their safety and cussed, almost within the same breath. His rifle, as well as Stevie's shotgun, was now heading south beside the Mora. All he and Stevie Rae had were their pistols, which would do little good from this distance.

"Get off me!" Beneath him, Stevie squirmed and struggled. Brock simply tightened his embrace as more shots pinged into the dirt and rock beside him, and he silently counted. Five. Six. Seven. Logan's choice of weapon was a good one, if it was a Henry Repeating Rifle…and Brock thought it might be. He knew exactly how many bullets the rifle could hold—seventeen, if one loaded the chamber—and Logan would be a man to load the chamber. How many would he fire to keep them pinned to the ground? All of them? How long would it take him to reload?

He didn't have time to learn the answer as another shot rang out. Pain seared his thigh as the bullet found its mark and he couldn't help the groan rising up from his throat.

"Son of a bitch shot me!"

Another bullet slammed into the ground beside him. Bits of rock, as sharp as needles, flew into his face. Brock turned his head, grateful this bullet had not slammed into him—one bullet wound was enough, thank you—and tried to shield Stevie Rae as best he could, though she continued to squirm beneath him. "Stay still, Stevie," he whispered.

"I'm not going to let him take me lying down, Brock," she hissed back and tried to buck him off of her.

"He's not going to take anyone."

"How do you know that?" Her breath fanned the dirt in front of her. "Just let me reach my pistol."

"Why? So you can shoot me again? I don't think so." He tightened his grip on her, enfolding her in his arms.

The fight left her and she no longer struggled to get out from beneath him. "At least let me turn over. I have rocks digging into my stomach, not to mention my face and...everything else. And I can't breathe."

Without a word, Brock loosened his embrace. Not a lot, but enough to allow her to turn in his arms, her back now in the dirt, her breasts crushing against his chest. He would have smiled if his leg didn't hurt so much. Hell, he would be laughing and kissing her right now if circumstances were different. Her mouth was so close, her lips so tempting. For a brief moment of insanity, he thought if he was going to die anyway, he wanted one last taste of her.

Brock lowered his head, his lips touching hers tenderly...

Pain blossomed in his side, sharp as a knife blade and hotter than the flames of Hades. Blood wet his shirt, first hot then cold. "Damn!"

"Brock? Did he hit you again?"

He didn't answer her. He couldn't. He fought against the pain, which seemed to be spreading, the burning, stinging sensation settling deep within. His concern wasn't for himself. He'd been shot before—he was shot now. He had survived, but she—

"I'm not hurt." She shook her head, her gaze roaming his face, her hands coming up to smooth the fine lines on his forehead. "What about you?"

"I'm good."

"Liar."

He shook his head and grinned, despite the pain. He should have known better than to try to lie to her. "Bastard shot me again."

She stiffened beneath him, her bright blue eyes wide and filled with so many emotions, he couldn't define them all. "Where?"

"Left side, just above my waist," he panted. "Upper thigh."

"Let me up, Brock. Let me at least look at you."

"You're not going anywhere until he's gone or I'm—"

Another shot rang out, followed by two more, all three slamming into the ground on either side of them. Brock held her tighter, shielding her face, covering her body as best he could.

"Don't you dare say it, Brock MacDermott. Don't you—" She began to wriggle beneath him, which just made him pull her closer, despite the waves of dizziness sweeping through him. Loss of blood could do that, and he had lost some blood. His leg and side were wet with it, his leg throbbing with every beat of his heart. He couldn't even begin to describe the pain in his side except that it was cold yet hot and burned with an intensity that made holding on to a coherent thought difficult. He tried. He shook his head to clear it and forced himself to listen. New sounds intruded into the slight buzz filling his ears.

The pounding of hooves raced across the top of the canyon, followed by more gunshots, but these were different in pitch… higher, faster…and none of them were coming his way. "Someone's chasing him off."

It grew quiet. The crazed laughter and the bullets whistling past his head stopped, but the pain remained as he rolled onto his back, allowing her to scramble out from beneath him, then quickly rolled back to his stomach to keep dirt from getting into the wound. He pulled air into his lungs and concentrated on fighting the dizziness.

• • •

Stevie Rae shot to her feet, her attention immediately on Brock. Her gaze roamed over his body, assessing his injuries. Blood seeped from his wounds—one in his thigh, the other in his side—soaking his shirt and trouser leg. Her stomach lurched to see him hurt, but she forced the nausea away. She was her father's daughter—he had taught her well—as had the instructors at medical school. She had seen worse than this, but that was in a different time and place. She kept her tone light. "It's not too bad."

"That's easy for you to say." He grunted and spoke into the ground beneath him. "You're not the one who's been shot."

"No, I wasn't, thanks to you." *But I could have been.* The thought brought her up short. He had done this for her, had saved her life. At the cost of his own? She shook her head, determined his sacrifice would not be in vain. "Don't worry. We'll get you fixed up."

Again, he grunted and turned his head to look at her. "Now who's the liar?"

She didn't answer the question. Instead, she crouched beside him. "I'm sorry. This is going to hurt." She tugged at his shirt, pulling the tails from the waistband of his trousers. Brock didn't move or say a word, though he gasped loudly and his muscles stiffened. Her stomach tightened from the pain she caused him.

Lifting his shirt away from his skin, she examined the bloody crease along his side. The bullet had grazed him, leaving a deep groove that welled with blood, but it wasn't life-threatening. At least, she didn't think so. She pulled a handkerchief from her pocket—the one he'd given her so long ago—and pressed the square of cotton to his bloody side. It turned crimson in an instant. Fear trickled through her, leaving the taste of metal in her mouth, as she pressed the bloody handkerchief to the wound.

He needed a doctor. Now. But how? What choices did she have?

Not many. At least the shooting had stopped, but the horses were gone, as was her stubborn mule, which meant that they were stranded here with no supplies at all, not even her father's old black medical bag.

She needed to stop his bleeding before she did anything else, wrap up his wounds as best she could with whatever was at hand—in this case, his clothing and hers. There was nothing else. Even bandaged, he could still lose enough blood to…she refused to finish that thought.

"We can't stay here, Stevie. We have to go." Brock struggled to his hands and knees, his breath wheezing in and out of his lungs. Fresh blood flowed from both wounds—dripping from his already sodden shirt and pant leg. Sweat beaded on his forehead, and his skin took on a waxy sheen beneath his tan but somehow, he managed to get to his feet.

"We have to go," he repeated as he slung his arm around her shoulders.

Her heart pounded as she staggered under his weight. If he fell, she would never be able to help him back up. "Go where, Brock?"

"Out of this canyon." His breath hissed through his teeth as he put all his weight on his injured leg and would have collapsed if he hadn't had his arm around her shoulder.

Stevie stifled the panic rising in her and kept him on his feet by sheer force of will. "How do you suppose we do that? In case you haven't noticed, the horses are gone and you've been shot."

"No choice but to walk."

"And you're in fine condition to do that." Exasperation and worry made her tone sharper than she intended. The blood seeping through the handkerchief as well as her fingers didn't help, either. "At least let me look at your wounds. Bandage them up. See if I can find something we can use as a crutch."

"We don't have time. Logan—"

"Forget about Logan. Besides, how can you chase him now? You can't even stand up straight."

"Not chase." His eyes rolled back in his head, and he started to slip back toward the ground. "Not chase. Need someplace safe."

She stumbled as she took more of his weight on her. "Don't pass out on me now, Brock." She took a deep breath, more to calm her nerves than anything else. If he fell... "We're going to walk slowly. One step at a time. Can you do that?"

He nodded, but did not speak. It was just as well. He needed to conserve his energy so they could make it out of the sun.

Spurred on by the fear rippling up and down her spine, Stevie Rae helped him to the shade of the overhang and steadied him as he lowered himself to the ground, once again on his stomach.

"I think the bullet is still in your leg. I didn't see any blood on your trousers in the front, only the back."

"Do what you have to do."

Stevie nodded, then ripped the leg of his trousers where the bullet had made a hole. Brock's breath whistled between his teeth as he sucked in his breath, but he didn't move.

Again, her stomach lurched as she blotted the blood away with the already drenched handkerchief, which wasn't much help. "Give me your flask."

He twisted to the side and dug the silver container out of his pocket. He unscrewed the cap with his teeth and took a drink before handing it to her.

"This is going to sting." Pulling the handkerchief away, she poured the whiskey he liked so much over her fingers as well as his wound.

Brock cursed, a word that normally would have made Stevie blush, but under the circumstances, she didn't blame him for saying it. She might have said the same. She glanced at his face and wondered how he held on to consciousness. This would be so much easier if he simply passed out. Then she wouldn't be afraid of hurting him more than he already was.

"Are you ready?"

"Yes." He closed his eyes and breathed deeply but stiffened and suppressed a groan when she used her finger to follow the path the bullet had made and tried to locate the brass slug. As she suspected, it was lodged deep in his thigh.

She ripped the sleeves off her blouse, wadded one, and pressed it over the wound, then tried to bandage his leg with the other. It wasn't nearly long enough—the edges met but there was no way to tie them together. His thigh was too thick with muscle. Frustration made tears well in her eyes and blurred her vision. "Think, Stevie. Think. What would Papa do?"

"About what?"

"My sleeve isn't long enough to bandage your thigh. I…" She didn't finish the sentence. Instead, she took a deep breath and closed her eyes. Memories of assisting her father as he treated his patients flowed through her mind, but it didn't help. He'd always had his medical bag, the sturdy leather case a treasure trove of everything a doctor would need. She had no such bag of tricks, just her own common sense, which told her she needed to stop his bleeding by whatever means necessary, be it right or wrong.

Pulling her knife from her pocket, she cut a slit at the top of the sleeve where it would meet the shirt's shoulder and ripped down to the cuff. She made another slit at the seam and ripped that side as well, leaving the cuff intact. Now long enough, she tied the two ends together, keeping the other wadded-up sleeve in place. She glanced at his face. He wasn't smiling, but pride seemed to radiate from his pain-glossy eyes.

"That's my girl. I knew you'd figure it out. Now finish. Quickly, if you can."

Stevie nodded, then pulled up the tail of his shirt and turned her attention to the bloody gash in his side. If she had needle and thread, she could have sewn the edges together, but she had neither. What remained of her blouse would never reach around him to make a bandage. She studied the legs of her split skirt—they fell in graceful folds over her boots. Were they wide enough? Would the soft suede be suitable to absorb the flow of blood if it were wide enough to fit around him? She didn't think so, which left her with one choice…really, no choice at all. She'd have to use his clothing, too.

"I need to use the sleeves of your shirt as bandages."

He didn't speak as he rolled to his back and sat up against the rocks, then held his arms straight out. Taking her knife, she cut his sleeves from his shirt, then tied them together at the cuffs and wrapped everything around his waist, tying off the ends. Finished, she leaned back against the rock.

Brock reached out and caressed the side of her face, then wiped the tears from beneath her eyes with his thumb. "Thank you."

She nodded, unable to speak over the lump in her throat, then jumped up, collected her hat where it had fallen, and ran down to the water's edge, ever mindful that Logan might still be around. She washed her hands and rinsed the blood from the handkerchief, then scooped cold water into the crown of the hat before heading back to the overhang.

Despite the shade of the rock shelf above them, the temperature was rising and sweat made her chemise stick to her skin. Pain and the heat made Brock's face shine with perspiration. She dipped the handkerchief into the water and swiped the cloth on his cheek and forehead.

"Hey," he whispered and grabbed her hand. "Are you all right?"

She bit her lip and nodded, trying hard to keep her emotions in check. Falling apart now wouldn't help either one of them. She pulled her hand free of his, dipped the handkerchief into the water, and dabbed at his face again.

"I know what you're thinking." He reached for her hand once more, forced her to drop the handkerchief, and brought her fingers to his lips.

Stevie was about to ask him what he knew when a noise off in the distance drew her attention. She jumped, startled.

"Stevie? What is it?"

"Shhhh! Listen."

The steady *clip-clop* of horses' hooves against hard rock met her ears. The clatter came from the north. Or maybe from the south. It was impossible to tell—sound echoed and bounced off the canyon walls. Stevie Rae swallowed hard and whispered, "Horses. Coming closer."

Was this their salvation? Or their doom? Was Logan making his way to where they were to kill them? Would their bodies be found months or years from now? Or never? Would anyone mourn their passing?

"Can you see who it is?"

She shook her head and slowly rose to her feet, then pulled her pistol from its holster, cocking the hammer. If she was going to be killed, it would be while standing her ground and protecting her man.

My man? She pushed the thought away for a more convenient time, if there would be such a thing, and scanned the horizon. She saw nothing except rock wall, cloudless, blue sky, and a hawk catching the thermals caused by the rising heat. Her focus shifted to her left. Only the meandering Mora and a path leading north met her intense focus. Beyond that, dense trees clung to the banks of the river, making it impossible to see anything more. To the south, much the same view.

The sound drew closer, and panic made her stomach clench. She raised the pistol, using both hands the way Brock had shown her, and waited, hardly daring to draw breath. Moments later, the plaintive braying of the world's most unhappy mule echoed off the canyon walls, and relief surged through her, leaving her weak-kneed. A silent prayer of thanks skittered through her mind when Joe Bennett rode into view from the north, leading their horses as well as Whiskey Pete, who was carrying her medical bag.

She uncocked the pistol and slid it back into the holster, then turned toward Brock. He, too, had drawn his gun. "It's Joe."

He nodded once, then released the hammer and let the pistol fall to his lap, his energy expended. Blood from the wound in his leg dripped to the dirt beneath him.

"Brock. Stevie." Joe touched the brim of his hat with his gloved fingertips, then dismounted with ease a few moments later. "Glad to see you're both still alive. Wasn't sure I'd be in time."

"It would take more than a few bullets to kill me," Brock said.

Stevie bit her tongue, knowing that sometimes it only took one well-aimed bullet to take someone's life. He'd been lucky. So had she. She took the reins from Joe's hand and led the horses as well as Whiskey Pete closer to the water's edge, where they could drink their fill. She scratched the mule between his ears, then rejoined the men in the shade.

"Not that I'm not grateful, Joe, but what are you doing here?" Brock's voice was tight but filled with appreciation.

"As soon as you left town, I got this feeling something just wasn't right." Joe hunkered down beside Brock and removed his hat. "Why would Logan leave messages specifically for you, then disappear? He had to know I'd get in touch with you and that you'd come to see what he'd done. And then it occurred to me: What better way to finish what he started in Paradise Falls than to lie in wait for you somewhere along the trail?" He shrugged and stood, nearly hitting his head on the rock overhang. "I grabbed some men and rode out to find you. Saw someone sitting on his horse and shooting into the canyon. Figured it was Logan and he had you pinned. Hopefully, Sylvester and Pecos Bill will catch him." He shrugged again, and his face took on a slight flush. "Guess I wasn't in time, though. He got you."

"But I ain't dead yet."

"No, you're not." He turned and mumbled something about being tired of losing friends, then approached Stevie Rae. He gestured toward Brock with his thumb. "Can he ride?"

Stevie Rae shook her head. "I'm sure he could, but I don't think he should. One of the bullets grazed his side. I bet it hurts like the dickens, but it's not life-threatening. I am worried about the bullet lodged in his thigh, though. It's pretty deep. I can remove it, but no, he won't be able to ride after that."

Joe nodded and pulled a long, wicked Bowie knife from its sheath and tested the sharpness of the blade. "I can build a travois to bring him back to town."

"I'd rather ride." Brock's mouth turned down in displeasure, an expression Stevie had seen more than once and usually directed at her, as it was now. "Wouldn't be caught dead being dragged behind a horse on one of those things."

"Logan almost took care of that for you, and if you don't shut up, I may finish what he started," Joe told him with equal parts sarcasm and affection, then ignored the colorful cuss words Brock threw his way.

Under normal circumstances, Stevie Rae would have smiled. Perhaps even laughed. She liked the way these two men interacted with each other, but these were hardly normal circumstances and she had no time for shenanigans. She shot them both a look, hoping to stop their nonsense, but it had the opposite effect. Instead of becoming contrite, they both grinned at her like little boys who'd been caught raiding the cookie jar, ones who would do it again as soon as her back was turned.

An admonishment for their behavior was on the tip of her tongue, but before she could utter one word, Joe took her hand and squeezed gently. "What would you like me to do?"

"Help me remove that bullet and stitch him up."

He gave a slight nod. "Yes, ma'am."

After giving him instructions about heating some water, Joe went off to start a fire. Stevie Rae walked down to the water's edge and moved their rides closer to where Brock rested, then untied her bedroll from the supplies Whiskey Pete carried on his back.

Brock's gaze followed her every move as she spread one of the old quilts on the ground. "What are you doing?"

"I'm going to remove that bullet from your leg."

An eyebrow rose, but confidence shined from his eyes. "Have you done that before?"

She didn't answer his question directly. Instead, she said, "Once upon a time, a very long time ago, I wanted to be a doctor, like my father. It was the next natural step for me, I suppose." She untied the much-worn bag from Whiskey Pete's back, the supple leather wrinkled and creased in a few places. She placed the bag on the quilt beside him, then sank to her knees and twisted the clasp to pull the satchel open. The smell of leather rose upward, filling her nose, bringing with it happy memories as well as a feeling of confidence. "There are four children running around Little River that I delivered when my father…couldn't. Two of them are named after me."

"Why didn't you? Become a doctor, I mean."

"Has it somehow escaped your notice that I'm a woman?"

"No, it hasn't escaped my notice." He grinned, and mischief lurked in his soft gray eyes. "You have all the right parts, but what does that have to do with it?"

"Have you ever seen a woman doctor?" From her father's medical bag, now hers, she pulled a square of white, cotton cloth and spread it out over the blanket, then brought out a silver container. It looked like a chafing dish but was much, much smaller. She lifted the lid. All the instruments she thought she'd need to remove the bullet from Brock's thigh were contained within. She knew how to use them, too.

He thought for a moment then shook his head. "Can't say that I have seen a woman doctor. Why is that?"

"It's very difficult for a woman to become a doctor. There are only a handful of schools willing to accept female students. And, of course, there is prejudice. People are unwilling to believe that a woman has the stamina to treat patients." She stopped herself from going into a familiar tirade and instead, concentrated on the task at hand. A hank of hair escaped the ponytail at the back of her head and she tucked it behind her ear before reaching into the bag again and drawing out a leather case with various needles and several spools of thick black thread. "I applied anyway and I was accepted."

Brock's eyes widened in surprise. "You went? To medical school?"

"Yes, but I never finished."

"Why?"

A long sigh escaped her. "Things happened while I was in Boston."

"What things?"

She didn't want to talk about this, didn't want to bring up old, painful memories, but they were coming anyway, filling her mind.

"Martha wrote me about my father." Tears stung her eyes and she blinked quickly, focusing on the medical bag opened before her. "The plan was for me to graduate, then join my father in his practice. I think I told you he'd lost three patients, one right after the other, and it...broke him. I came home to find the house where I grew up sold, his practice closed, and him, sunk so far into despair I was afraid he'd never come out."

"What did you do?"

She shrugged. "I did what I could. I took care of him and he was getting better, becoming more like his old self again. We talked about me going back to Boston and finishing school, but I—"

"It was him, wasn't it? That ass we met in Santa Fe. The one you were going to marry. He convinced you somehow that you couldn't be a doctor. Or shouldn't be one. He changed your mind about finishing school." His tone was harsh as was the scowl on his face, which somehow lifted her heart. He had confidence in her, believed in her. That much was clear just by his expression and the warm gleam in his eyes. "I should have punched him in the mouth when I had the chance."

"And I would have paid good money to see that." She smiled then continued rummaging in the bag, setting out rolls of dressing on the blanket before peering into the valise one more time. "Ah, there it is."

She pulled a tinted bottle from the depths of the satchel. Laudanum. He'd need that to dull the pain, maybe even make him sleep, so she could do what she needed to without fear of hurting him more.

He eyed the bottle with suspicion. "Is that what I think it is?"

"What do you think it is?"

"Laudanum. I've had it before. I didn't like it or the way it made me feel." Brock folded his arms across his chest and winced when he hit his side. "I don't want it."

Stevie raised an eyebrow and smiled. "But you'll take it. For me." She removed the stopper and handed him the bottle.

Several long, tense moments passed as their gazes met and held, a silent battle of wills, until Brock let out a long sigh, then tipped the bottle to his mouth. He took a big swig, his Adam's apple bobbing as he swallowed. When he was done, he handed the bottle back to Stevie Rae and shuddered, his mouth skewed from the bitter medicine. "Still tastes like shit."

"But it'll help." She smiled as she put the stopper back in the bottle and dropped it in the bag. "Can you lie on your side on the quilt?"

Once Brock rolled to his right side, facing away from her, Stevie Rae finished preparing her makeshift surgery, something else she'd helped her father with a hundred times. Steven Buchanan could use anything as his operating room—a kitchen table, a bed, the cold, hard ground. She kept up a steady stream of chatter, talking about anything and everything, and listened to his responses become slower, his words slurring as the laudanum started to take effect.

"I sure am tired of getting shot at," he murmured. His breathing deepened and his body relaxed as his pain eased, but she didn't think he slept or lost consciousness.

She resisted the urge to call his name, but she couldn't stop herself from peeking over his still form to study his face. His eyes were closed, his impossibly thick black lashes resting on his cheek. She drew in a deep breath, then stood and strode toward Willow to retrieve the brand-new bar of soap she had purchased just yesterday.

As she walked back to Brock, she unwrapped the soap. The scent of honeysuckle assailed her and brought with it vivid memories of her and Brock in the bath together at the Rose Cottage, then making love while the wind gusted over the roof and the rain slashed against the windows. A flush heated her that had nothing to do with the warmth of the sun.

She shook the image from her mind, knelt beside Brock, and whispered a silent prayer before making quick work of removing the makeshift bandage from around his waist. The deep groove in his skin started bleeding again, but not nearly as much as before.

"That looks bad," Joe said as he approached, his body blocking the sun's hot rays as she blotted at the blood. "Water's heating like you asked. Should be ready in a few more minutes."

"Thank you." She turned her head and glanced at him. Concern shadowed his features. "He'll be fine."

"I know." He squeezed her shoulder, then moved away. The heat of the sun struck her back and shoulders once more. Her gaze slid over Brock as her fingers smoothed the curls brushing up against his collar. In an instant, a rush of emotion swirled through her and would have brought her to her knees if she hadn't already been kneeling.

I love him.

Somewhere along the trail, in the middle of chasing a madman across New Mexico, she had lost her heart to Brock MacDermott. She felt like she'd been hit with a…she didn't quite know what she'd been struck with, but she'd been struck. Hard. She loved him, for everything he was—honorable and principled, though a bit stubborn—and for everything he wasn't. He never patronized her, nor doubted her, and he made her believe not only in him but in herself.

Her heart swelled, and joy, an emotion she hadn't felt in quite some time, filled her soul.

"It's ready."

Stevie Rae jumped, startled. Joe stood beside her, coffeepot in one hand, skillet in the other. He set the skillet on the blanket and gave her one of those quizzical looks men sometimes gave women when they didn't quite understand.

"What do you want me to do?"

She picked up the soap, then held her hands out over the skillet. "Pour a little water over my hands." As he complied, she washed beneath the steady trickle of hot water, then washed Brock's wound as well, using one of several cloths she'd found in her father's bag.

With a steady hand, Stevie Rae threaded one of the needles from the case with a length of black thread, took a deep breath, and started stitching the bloody gash, pulling the edges together to close the wound and keep it closed although the very act of doing so made her stomach twist. Thankfully, Brock didn't seem to feel it. He didn't move or speak or show any evidence of pain and for that, she was grateful.

"Have you done this before?" A touch of awe filled Joe's voice.

Stevie Rae nodded as she knotted the thick black thread, then cut it with a small pair of scissors. "Too many times to count." She washed the blood from Brock's side once more, then wrapped a clean dressing around his waist. She leaned back on her heels and studied her handiwork. There would be a scar on his side, but that just added to the mystery that was Brock.

She took a deep breath and moved on to the bullet in his thigh.

Chapter 19

Stevie Rae watched as Doc Capshaw, an older man with wire-rimmed spectacles perched on his nose, inspected the stitches closing the wound in Brock's leg. He said not a word, though he did *hmmm* a lot as he removed the makeshift bandage from around Brock's waist and scrutinized the thick black sutures there as well. Brock sucked in his breath and winced. His lips, those kissable lips, were now pressed together in a thin line, though she could see only part of his face as he lay on his stomach. The laudanum he had taken earlier had worn off. Stevie Rae flinched as he gasped again—she felt his pain as keenly as if it were her own.

Knowing that she loved him, knowing he'd been shot to protect her, left her feeling…

Stevie Rae didn't know what she felt—her emotions were still in turmoil. A queasiness settled in her belly and she held her breath as the doctor leaned down and smelled the injury. She knew exactly what he was looking for—the putrid smell of infection, although it would have been too soon for that. It had only been half a day since Brock had been shot. In many ways, that seemed like a lifetime ago. She didn't think her heart had beat properly since.

"Looks good." He paused in his examination and glanced at her. "I understand you did this—removed the bullet from his leg and cleaned him up." His bushy mustache twitched as he rewrapped both wounds with clean dressing, then looked at Stevie Rae and winked. "Good job, young lady. Mighty fine stitchin', too. Couldn't have done it better myself." His lips spread in a gentle, understanding smile as he moved a little closer to her and took her hand in his. "You can breathe now, my dear."

She complied, her breath leaving her lungs in a rush.

"Good, good," Doc Capshaw muttered. He patted her hand once more, then turned back to his patient.

"As for you, young man, you need some rest." He stepped away from the bed. Stevie Rae took that moment to help Brock turn over on his back, then tuck another pillow under his knee to keep any pressure off his thigh before she pulled up the sheet from the bottom of the bed, hiding his bare chest and muscular thighs from view.

"No unnecessary moving around," Doc Capshaw continued, though she could feel his gaze sweep over her a time or two as she adjusted the sheet. "We don't want those stitches to rip. In fact, I recommend you stay in this bed for at least a week." He pulled a bottle from his bag along with an odd-shaped spoon, then closed the bag with a definite snap. "Give him a spoonful of this every couple of hours for the pain."

Stevie Rae took the bottle as well as the spoon.

"Again with the laudanum?" Brock asked from the bed, his gaze on the bottle and her. Suspicion and pain glazed his clear gray eyes, turning them darker, like rain clouds on the horizon.

"Yes," Stevie Rae answered.

He shook his head and crossed his arms over this chest. "No thanks. Once was enough for me. Still can't get the taste out of my mouth or the fuzziness from my head from the first time."

"I'm not going to argue with you," she shot back at him, her patience at an end. The past few hours had taken their toll on her. Her nerves were raw. If Logan's aim had been truer, if Brock hadn't launched out of the saddle and tackled her to the ground when he had, she wouldn't be here. She'd be at the undertaker's arranging Brock's burial. Or he'd be arranging hers. It didn't help her nerves that Sylvester and Pecos Bill hadn't come back with Logan, either. The man was long gone. Or was he? "You don't have to like it, but you will take it."

Doc Capshaw chuckled. "Looks like you don't have a choice, son. Just take it and let yourself rest."

Her hands shook as she poured the laudanum into the bowl of a spoon and carefully brought the medication to his mouth.

Mischief sparkled in his eyes as his lips tightened. He shook his head, like a little boy then reached up to grab at her hand. To lighten the mood, perhaps?

Whatever his intention, Stevie wasn't having any of it. She pulled away, just out of his reach, almost spilling the liquid.

"Don't," she warned, her voice low but strong, her frustration showing as she set the bottle on the bedside table. She mentally counted to ten, which didn't help. Tears pricked her eyes. She blinked rapidly in an effort to hold those tears at bay, though the truth was, she wanted to cry. She had wanted to cry from the moment he'd been shot. "I will get this down your throat if I have to sit on you to do it."

"That could be fun," he teased, then laughed. Stevie Rae shoved the spoon at his mouth while it was open. Surprised, Brock coughed and sputtered but swallowed the medicine, which brought another chuckle from Doc Capshaw.

"I would do exactly as she told me, if I were you." He patted Brock on the shoulder. "I'll stop by tomorrow." The doctor grabbed his bag and faced her. "If you need anything, anything at all, just send Joe. He knows where to find me day or night."

"Thank you," she managed over the lump in her throat.

He gave a slight nod, then let himself out of the room and closed the door. Stevie Rae allowed her shoulders to slump with fatigue. A slight rustling from the bed caught her attention, and she turned quickly to see Brock struggling to free himself of the sheet covering his body.

"What are you doing?"

"I'm all right, Stevie. I've been shot before." He tried to rise from the bed, nearly knocking over the bedside table as he grabbed for it but missed.

She lunged for him, fighting with him for control of the sheet, trying to keep him covered and in bed. "Didn't Doc Capshaw say he wanted you to rest?"

"I don't have time to rest," he insisted, though his words were already starting to slur and his movements grew clumsy.

"I'm not going to fight with you, Brock. I am telling you that you are going to stay in that bed and rest if I have to—oh!" Brock grabbed her hands and pulled her on top of him, trapping her hands against his body and her hips between his thighs. His mouth sought and found hers with unerring accuracy, his lips fastening to hers in an unexpected, utterly arousing kiss. He released his firm grip on her hands as the kiss deepened and his hands slid over her backside, pulling her closer. She felt his hardness against her belly and the sudden rush of moistness between her thighs.

Appalled and stunned by his behavior and her own response, and afraid she had hurt him when she fell on him, Stevie Rae broke the kiss and scrambled off the bed. Her breath wheezed from her lungs. She hadn't hurt him. In fact, he seemed to have enjoyed their little tussle, if the grin parting his lips was any indication. She yanked on her shirt, adjusting the garment back into place when what she really wanted to do was slap the silly grin from his face. "That wasn't funny, Brock!"

"Sure, it was." His grin widened as he patted the bed beside him, then moved the sheet aside.

Before she could reprimand him or tell him what she thought of him, the door opened behind her and she whirled around, still breathing hard. Joe stepped into the room with a tray balanced on one hand. His sharp eyes went from Stevie Rae to Brock then back again, and a dark eyebrow lifted in question. "Everything all right in here?"

"Yes, everything is fine," she huffed, her face burning with embarrassment as she turned away to face her patient, who returned her glare with an expression of innocence, his leg bent at the knee, effectively hiding anything he didn't wish to be seen. "He just thought he could get out of bed."

"That sounds like something Brock would try." Joe grinned as he edged farther into the room and placed the tray on a small table beside the window. "Cora thought you might want something to eat."

Steam rose from a big mug on the tray, and the smell of coffee filled the room. Stevie Rae sniffed, inviting the fragrant aroma into her nostrils. Beside the cups, yeast rolls adorned a plate along with thick slices of ham and cheese. Though her stomach still churned with anxiety, it also grumbled with hunger—she hadn't eaten or drunk anything since early that morning.

"Thank her for me."

He nodded then gestured toward Brock. "Other than him trying to get out of bed, how is he?"

"Stubborn. Irritating. Smug. Defiant."

In the bed, Brock smiled broadly and nodded with every word she said, although his eyes seemed to be unfocused and hazy. They fluttered shut, then opened again, and finally closed one last time. The laudanum must be taking effect and for that, she was grateful. She didn't think she could fight with him again.

"So, all in all, himself."

"Unfortunately, yes." Though exasperated with him, she couldn't help smiling as a slight snore slipped through his lips.

Smothering a chuckle, Joe strutted to the door. He paused with his hand on the knob. "If you need anything, just let me know. He's a stubborn cuss but a good man."

"Thank you, Joe. For everything."

He nodded once more, then closed the door softly.

Stevie Rae stood in the middle of the room for several moments, allowing her heart to slow its rapid pace, allowing herself to breathe deeply. She heard Joe and Cora put their three-month-old son down for the night, then turn in themselves. Silence crept through the house except for Brock's light snore. Through the open window, she heard the caterwauling of a cat prowling the neighborhood, the howl of coyotes off in the distance, and the faint plunking of a piano from the saloon down the street.

The energy that had kept her upright and moving from the moment Brock had been shot vanished, and she wearily pulled the rocking chair between the bed and the table and slumped into it, drained of everything except the tears that blurred her vision. Scrubbing her face with her hands, she wiped away the offending moisture and studied him, her gaze touching every part of him in a mental inventory.

Exhaustion, not only of the body but of her spirit as well, overwhelmed her and she inhaled deeply as she broke apart one of the yeast rolls and shoved a small piece in her mouth. She barely tasted it, but she had to eat. She felt dizzy, as if she'd spun in circles with her arms outstretched for far too long. If she could just finish this roll then close her eyes for a moment, she could get her strength back.

• • •

Stevie woke to the dim light of the lantern on the bureau, moonlight seeping in through the space where the heavy draperies covering the window didn't quite meet, and part of a yeast roll still in her hand. Her gaze took in the unfamiliar room, then finally fell on Brock. His eyes were open…and on her.

"Are you all right? Do you need anything?"

"I'm finished, Stevie."

"Finished?" She dropped the roll on the plate, then rose from the chair and stretched the kinks from her shoulders and back before she adjusted the light sheet over him. She sat on the edge of the bed, her heart rate already picking up its pace. "What do you mean 'finished'?"

He drew in a deep breath and opened his mouth, but no words emerged. Instead, he simply stared at her. After a moment, he reached for her hand, curling his long fingers around her slender ones. "I'm sorry, but I just can't do this anymore. Today..." He took a deep breath and brought her fingers to his lips, kissing the tips lightly. "You could have been killed, Stevie Rae. Any one of those bullets could have hit you and taken your life. If something had happened to you because of me, I...I..."

Her heart began to thunder in her chest. Tears smarted her eyes as she gazed into his. "But you protected me. You took those bullets yourself. You..." She snatched her hand away. Her fingernails dug into the soft skin of her palm, leaving indentations in the shape of half moons, as the enormity of his words struck her. "Are you saying you're giving up?"

He nodded slowly and tried to reach for her again, but she shot to her feet and stepped away. His eyes radiated pain, perhaps mental as well as physical, the color now the soft gray of early morning. "Don't be angry."

"Angry?" she shouted, then remembered where she was and lowered her voice to a harsh whisper, her voice shaking in an effort to keep it level. "You promised me we'd bring Logan in together, Brock. You said—"

"I know what I said. I know...what I promised. I..." He struggled with the words, probably because of the laudanum. "I've been thinking...for a long time, and I just...we have to stop, Stevie. I want peace. I want—"

She couldn't believe what he was saying. Her body trembled— so much so, she thought she would simply break apart. And the tears, the ones she fought against shedding earlier, burned her eyes once more. "You can't mean this, Brock. It's the pain talking."

"No, Stevie." He took a deep breath, his eyelids fluttering, dark lashes sweeping against his pale cheek. When he opened them again, his eyes were clear, but only for a moment before becoming unfocused once more. His voice grew softer. "I do mean it. I won't...chase him anymore." He tried reaching for her again, but his aim fell short and his hand flopped to the mattress. "And neither...will you. It's over, Stevie. Go home. You—"

He lost the battle with the laudanum and drifted to sleep once more, the words dying in his throat.

Stunned, Stevie Rae sank into the rocking chair and stared at him as the full implication of his words filtered into her mind. He meant them.

He's giving up. Logan's won.

Her throat constricted as she tried to pull air into her lungs and gasped as pain seized her chest. "*Go home, Stevie*" echoed in her head, as if he continued to repeat the words over and over, his voice soft.

He doesn't want me. After everything, he doesn't want me.

Tears fell unheeded down her cheeks. She didn't even bother to wipe them away. What would be the point? Only more would come, her broken heart feeding the supply of hot regret- and anger-filled tears.

How long she cried, she didn't know, but eventually, her tears lessened then were gone. There was nothing left except a grittiness in her eyes and an emptiness in her heart.

She watched him sleep, his features full of the peace he wanted. She rose from her chair and laid her palm across his forehead to look for signs of fever, then adjusted the sheet over him before she started pacing the floor. She'd only traversed the room once when she remembered the Bennett family still slept. Weary and heartsick, Stevie moved to the window and pushed the draperies aside to watch the glow of dawn lighten the sky.

Brock mumbled in his sleep, the tone urgent. He dreamed, of what she could only guess, but the panicked, horror-filled way in which he said her name told her whatever visions he saw terrified him.

Stevie Rae rushed to the bed and touched the side of his face. "Shhh. It's all right, Brock. I'm here."

He quieted immediately beneath her caress, and she continued to stroke his whisker-laden cheek, then went further and ran her fingers through his thick, dark hair. The gray at his temples seemed more pronounced in the glow of the lamplight. He whispered her name in his sleep and this time, there was no fear or panic in his tone, just a sweet caress.

In that moment, she understood why he uttered those terrible words to go home. He wasn't giving up the search for Logan for himself, though he said he wanted peace. He was giving up out of concern for her. Logan had warned them he would kill them and, at least once so far, he'd tried to make good on his threat. Brock didn't want her to go home because he didn't want her. He wanted her to go home because he thought she'd be safe there.

"I understand, my love," she whispered, "but I can't—I won't— give up looking for Logan." She took a deep breath and let it out slowly through her parted lips as she brushed the hair off his brow with her fingertips. He smiled and sighed in his sleep, and the resolve she'd always counted on came back to her, strengthening her will. She drew another deep, cleansing breath into her lungs. "I will find him and kill him. For both of us."

Chapter 20

Sunlight filtered through a crack where the draperies didn't quite meet, shining in Brock's face, forcing him awake. He turned his head on the pillow, expecting to see Stevie Rae in the rocking chair beside the bed, where she'd been every other time he'd opened his eyes.

Disappointment rippled through him. He turned his head the other way. Still no Stevie, but the comforting sounds of dishes being washed and low-voiced conversation punctuated by Joe Junior's gurgling met his ears. A slow smile curved Brock's mouth as he closed his eyes. Stevie would be back. He could wait.

Brock opened his eyes and drew in his breath as he looked around the room. The sun was higher in the sky, but still coming in through the gap in the draperies. He'd fallen asleep again, and his thoughts were fuzzy and incomplete.

"Good. You're awake." Joe pushed against the door with his hip and entered the room, a tray in his hands. "Cora thought you'd be ready for something a bit more solid than broth." He placed the tray on a table and looked at him, hands on his hips.

"And good morning to you, too, Joe."

Joe cocked an eyebrow. "It's afternoon, pal."

"Afternoon?" His brain was still foggy, making it hard to think, and his mouth felt like he'd tried eating his boot. He moved his tongue around his mouth, trying to find some moisture.

"Yup. You've been sleeping on and off since we brought you here."

"And when was that?"

"Four days ago. Doc Capshaw said he thinks you can try sitting up today. Want to try?"

Without a word and without waiting to be helped, Brock struggled into a sitting position and paid the price. Pain shot through him and a cold sweat broke out over his entire body. His head, feeling like it was filled with tons of wet cotton, could have fallen off his neck and rolled across the floor by itself. Joe *tsk*ed as he tucked pillows behind his back, propping him up then adjusted the sheet over him. He saw a pitcher of water on the bedside table, along with a half-filled glass…and the little tinted bottle of laudanum, which was almost gone.

"When was Capshaw here?" He fumbled for the glass, almost knocking it off the table then wiggled his fingers, which weren't working the way they were supposed to. "Shit."

"Earlier this morning," Joe answered as he grabbed the glass before it crashed to the floor and placed it in his hands. Brock drank deeply, finishing the water, letting the coolness of the liquid slide down his throat to ease his thirst.

"You slept right through his visit."

"I did?" All he remembered were bits and pieces, a kaleidoscope of images and visions. Sunlight streaming in through the gap in the draperies, like now, replaced the next moment by moonlight. Cora or Joe coming into the room, carrying on low-voiced conversations with Stevie. The taste of chicken broth on his tongue. The sound of a baby crying from far away mingled with the tinny *plink-plink* of an out-of-tune piano. The loud, rhythmic ticking of a clock. And Stevie.

Always Stevie.

Whenever he opened his eyes, she'd been there—sitting in the rocking chair, her hair falling in her face as she read a book. Several times, he caught her sleeping, her hands folded over her stomach, head tilted to the side. In those moments, she looked so young and carefree, without the weight of the world on her shoulders. Once, he woke to find her holding Joe's three-month-old son and the look on her face was one of pure bliss. How beautiful she had looked, peaceful and happy, the shadows beneath her eyes curiously absent as she rocked Joe Junior, sending him off to dreamland.

As Joe flung the heavy draperies open, flooding the room with light, Brock winced. He glanced at the hated bottle of laudanum on the bedside table, and laid blame for his scattered, incomplete memories and sensitivity to light on the opiate mixture.

And where was Stevie?

Before he could ask or speak at all, Joe handed him the tray. "Eat."

Brock settled it across his legs. The aroma of beef stew rose from the steaming bowl and his stomach gurgled. He'd been living on broth, Stevie Rae making him drink the savory stock from a cup every time he woke. He dipped his spoon into the thick gravy, capturing chunks of beef, potatoes, and vegetables, and brought it to his lips, his mouth watering. Cora Bennett was a good cook and he finished every last bit of the hearty meal. Neither he nor Joe spoke as he ate—the only sound in the room, aside from the constant ticking of the clock, was the scrape of his spoon against the bottom of the bowl. He grabbed a thick slice of bread, spread soft butter on it, then used it to sop up the last of the gravy.

Belly full, he wiped his mouth on a napkin and let out a long sigh. "Give Cora my regards. That was the best stew I've had in a long time."

Joe took the tray and started to leave the room.

"Will you ask Stevie to come in?"

Joe stopped at the door but didn't turn around. His body stiffened, though. That didn't bode well.

"Joe?"

When the marshal finally faced him, Brock not only saw his anger, but he felt it as well…it was like stepping too close to a blast furnace. He should have burned to a crisp just by the fire in Joe's golden brown eyes.

"She's gone, as if you didn't know."

"Gone?" Brock sat up straighter, ignoring the pull of his stitches in his side. "Where?"

"She didn't say exactly, but if I were a bettin' man, she—" His eyes narrowed and his lips tightened before he demanded, "What the hell did you say to her anyway?"

Jolted by the accusatory tone in his voice, Brock turned his focus on Joe. "What are you talking about?"

Joe put the tray on the table once more and stood beside the bed, his arms folded across his chest, his expression dark. "I wasn't going to say anything. It isn't my business how you handle your affairs, but I like Stevie and don't want to see her hurt."

Brock shook his head, trying to clear the cobwebs and produce a coherent thought or a full memory. Just one would be enough, but nothing became clear. He just saw more jumbled visions in his mind, though something niggled at the back of his brain.

Something important.

He remembered talking to Stevie, remembered the touch of her warm hand on his brow and the tears in her eyes, but nothing cohesive. There was no order to his mishmash of memories.

He brought his attention back to Joe, who hadn't stopped speaking, which was unusual—he being a man who believed actions were louder than words. "I don't know what happened between you two, but something got her all upset. I'm thinkin' it was something you said...you can be meaner than a grouchy bear sometimes. She'd been crying. More than once. I saw that plain enough, and it wasn't because you were hurt. Well, maybe that was part of it. Cora saw it, too, but Stevie didn't say a word. Just told us she had to go as soon as Doc Capshaw could assure her you would recover completely from your injuries. That was the only thing she was waiting for." He shrugged his broad shoulders and some of his anger dissipated. "After Doc Capshaw left this morning, Stevie packed her saddlebags and was just saying her good-byes when the telegram came."

Brock had listened without interrupting nor had he moved a muscle when Joe put Stevie's leaving directly on his shoulders, but now his muscles grew taut, his entire body tensing. "Telegram? What telegram?"

"The one that arrived early this morning just as Stevie was leaving." Exasperation colored his voice. "It was addressed to you, but she read it then took off outta here like her feet were on fire. Didn't even take that ornery mule of hers." He shook his head. "Never saw a person turn that pale before and still keep standing."

"Show me."

Joe drew in a deep breath as he straightened to his full height but he hesitated, his eyes darting all over the room just to avoid looking directly at Brock.

"Show me," Brock demanded, more forcefully this time. After a moment, Joe pulled the paper from his pocket and shoved it at him. Brock studied his face, aware and clearheaded for the first time in days, as if the fuzziness of the laudanum had finally worn off. He unfolded the missive.

There were only four words on the telegram, but those four small words were enough to make Brock suck in his breath. *Dan shot. Come now.*

Dan probably had Martha Prichard send it and could only mean one thing. Logan had shot Little River's sheriff. No wonder Stevie Rae had lit out of here like her feet were on fire.

Angry, not only at himself for still being laid up, but with Joe for not showing him the missive immediately and at Stevie Rae for taking matters into her own hands, he crumpled the telegram in his hand. "Damn fool woman! She went after Logan herself!" He cursed then glared at Joe. Fear and frustration made his belly clench, and the beef stew, which had been so good a moment ago, now felt like a rock in the pit of his stomach.

"How do you know she went after Logan?" Joe asked. "The telegram doesn't mention anyone other than Dan."

Brock didn't answer the question. Instead, he glared at Joe, his heart thundering in his chest, his mouth dry with anxiety. "Why did you let her go?"

The marshal took a step back, his brow lowering in anger. "I'm not taking the blame for this, pal. It was all you. Something *you* said or did. *You* made her want to leave." He took deep breaths and struggled with his temper. When he spoke again, it was with a much calmer tone, his anger gone as quickly as it came. "To answer your question, Stevie wasn't a prisoner here. Short of tying her to a chair or throwing her in jail, there was no stopping her. Cora and I both tried to make her see reason but you know her."

He ran his fingers through his hair and blew out his breath. "You're right. It is my fault," he admitted. "I must have said or done something. It's there. Niggling at the back of my brain, but I can't...shit." He flung the sheet off and swung his legs over the side of the bed. A wave of dizziness made the room spin around him, but he made it to his feet and remained standing. A cold sweat broke out on his forehead as the stitches in his side and his leg pulled taut and more pain rushed up to greet him. He gasped, finally drawing in breath.

"Brock!" Joe reached out and grabbed him, holding him upright so he wouldn't fall. "Where do you think you're going?"

"After her. Someone has to stop her from trying to get herself killed."

"You can't go after her like this. You've been shot and lying in this bed for four days, which means you have no strength."

"You don't understand. I have to do this." Despite feeling weak, his words were strong.

Joe gave a slight nod, then let him go, though he hovered close just in case. His eyes, though, never left him. Brock squirmed beneath the scrutiny of his friend's continuous stare and turned away, but it was too late.

"I'll be damned." Joe grinned. "You're in love with her."

He stopped moving long enough to shoot Joe a look, the denial on the tip of his tongue, but what was the point in lying? The truth always came out in the end anyway. And he didn't want to deny what he'd been feeling for a long time. Stevie deserved that much. "Yes, I'm in love with her." He smirked, then gave a small chuckle. "Never thought it would happen for me, did you, Joe?"

"The truth? I never had any doubts. Just knew it would take someone special." He slipped a shirt, freshly laundered and smelling of sunlight, from a hanger in the armoire and held it up.

Moving slowly, grasping one of the bed's four posts for steadiness, Brock slid his arms into the shirt, then buttoned it up. Despite his worry, a small smile curved his lips as he looked down and noticed the simple, white cotton drawers he sported. Both legs had been cut high above his knees and loosely sewn so they didn't touch the bandage around his thigh. He looked up and met Joe's amused smile.

"You kept kicking the sheet off. Stevie thought it would be best if you were 'covered.' She said Cora didn't need to see…everything." He pulled a pair of trousers from the armoire. "Frankly, I didn't need to see everything either."

Brock said nothing, just reached for the trousers Joe held out. He dropped to the edge of the bed and started pulling his pants on. The stitches pulled and sharp, shooting pain made him gasp, but it was tolerable and seemed to be less than before. One thing was for certain—no matter how bad the pain got, he wasn't ever going to take laudanum again. He much preferred to be clearheaded and in control of all his faculties.

He reached for his boots and slid them on, sucking in his breath as he did so.

Fighting another wave of dizziness, Brock rose to his feet and reached for the gun belt Joe now held in his hands, the pearl handles of his pistols glowing dully in the sunlight coming into the room. Brock buckled his gun belt around his hips, then pulled one of the pistols from its holster. He flipped open the cylinder and counted six bullets. Satisfied, he snapped the cylinder back in place and slipped the gun into the holster, then repeated the process with the other revolver.

"I'm coming with you."

Brock shook his head. A thousand excuses for why Joe should not join him flitted through his mind. "I appreciate the offer, but it's best if you didn't." Emotion made his voice tight as his throat constricted. "We both know what Logan is capable of. Cora needs her husband, and I'd like for Joe Junior to grow up with a father."

Joe's scowl proved he wasn't happy, but he didn't argue. "If that's what you want."

"It is."

In short order, Brock said good-bye to Cora and Joe Junior, giving them both kisses on the cheek, accepted a burlap sack filled with food Cora thought might be easy to carry, and climbed into Resolute's saddle, albeit slowly and gingerly. It didn't matter how carefully he eased himself onto the leather, it still hurt like a son of a gun. Though the wound in his thigh had been stitched and bandaged and begun to heal, sitting on Resolute brought a new definition to the word pain.

He needed another day in bed. Maybe two. But he didn't have a choice. Stevie Rae had more than half a day's lead on him. He couldn't afford to lose any more time. Though only sixty or so miles separated Mora and Little River, some of the terrain he'd have to travel was difficult—rivers to cross, canyons to navigate, mountains to climb. If he hadn't been hurt, if he'd left earlier, he could have ridden hard and made it before nightfall, but as it stood at this moment, he'd have to stop at some point. He still had a few hours of daylight left. He'd have to make the best time he could and to hell with the pain.

He adjusted the reins in his hand, then looked at Joe. Emotion once again tightened his throat. "Thank you. For everything."

"You'd do the same for me," he said and flashed a grin. "You be careful now. Stay out of canyons."

Brock tugged on the reins and turned a corner, but still heard Joe's shout, "I expect a wedding invitation."

In a matter of moments, he picked up the trail beside the Mora River and rode along the river's edge. He prayed he wouldn't be too late. Stevie *was* reckless and headstrong, but she was smart and she'd learned a few things from him over the last couple months. She could shoot now and hit the target nine times out of ten, but a motionless target was different from a flesh-and-blood man. She'd wanted to be a doctor—could she kill instead of heal? Would she be able to pull the trigger if Logan stood in front of her?

A shiver ran through him as coldness seeped into his bones, not from the weather, but from his own fear. No matter how good a shot Stevie Rae was now, there was still the element of surprise.

Logan had taught him that on a dark day in Paradise Falls. He gripped the reins tightly in his hands as his brother's face swam before his eyes. With effort, he forced the image away. He didn't need a reminder of what could happen, but he was hell-bent on making sure it didn't.

I failed once to keep someone I loved safe. I will not fail again.

Brock swiped at his face, surprised to find it wet, then dug his heels into Resolute's sides and pushed the horse faster. "Not this time."

• • •

Covered with sweat, Willow's sides heaved as Stevie Rae brought her to a stop behind Martha Prichard's boardinghouse. She'd ridden hard, pushing the horse when the terrain permitted, and taking it a bit easier only when circumstances demanded. She rode into Little River just as the clock on the town hall chimed ten times.

Lamplight spilled through the kitchen window as well as several other windows on the first floor of the house. It struck her as odd. Why would there be so much light at this time of night? Panic seized her. Her mouth dried and her body began to shake. *Am I too late? Is Dan...gone? Is this his wake?*

Stevie Rae jumped from the saddle and flung the reins over the porch rail. She should take the time to brush the horse down, walk her a little bit, but fear made Stevie race up the steps, her heart thundering in her chest. She tugged off her gloves and tossed them on the chair beside the door, then let herself into the kitchen, barely remembering to wipe her feet on the woven mat in front of the door.

The room was empty, but she smelled fresh coffee and glanced toward the stove. Steam rose from the coffeepot's spout, but the sink overflowed with coffee cups, dishes, and silverware, so unlike Martha.

She stumbled down the long hall, remembering how many times she'd done so in the past. The familiarity brought a sense of comfort, but the fear in her heart forced her to push away that feeling.

She stopped at the doorway to the parlor, then stepped inside. All the wall sconces were lit and more lamps were spread out on lace-covered tables, shedding soft light to touch on the small bookshelf in the corner as well as vases of fresh-cut flowers. The chairs and the camelback sofa had been moved into a semicircle in the middle of the big room, as if several people had recently gathered, but no one was there now.

Relief slammed through her with such power, she nearly dropped to her knees. Dan Hardy was not laid out in the middle of the room; there was no vigil or wake for those to pay their last respects, but that didn't necessarily mean it hadn't happened. She might still be too late. People had been here. A lot of people.

She turned, Martha's name on her lips, but she did not have the chance to speak as the woman eased from a bedroom, and quietly closed the door. She still wore a starched white apron over a pretty blue gown with darker blue flowers, despite the late hour.

"Martha."

The woman jumped, startled, her hand flying up to press against her chest, a coffee mug falling from her fingers to roll back and forth on a thick rag rug. "Land sake's, Stevie Rae, you just scared ten years off my life!"

"I'm sorry. I didn't mean to scare you." She moved out of the parlor, searching for the courage to ask what she needed so desperately to know. "Where's Dan? Is he...did he...?"

Martha stooped to pick up the mug, her movements slow, as if her back had stiffened and hurt with her actions. "What, child? Spit it out."

"Is Dan...dead?"

"Oh, heavens no." She straightened to her full height, the skin around her eyes crinkled with worry and exhaustion. "He'll be just fine in a couple of days."

"Oh, thank God!" Stevie Rae almost laughed, her relief was so profound. Her knees had not stopped shaking, though. "I got your telegram, then I saw all the lamps lit and thought... Why *is* the house lit up like there's been a party here?"

"Deputy Parker and the rest of his posse left just a little bit ago." Martha peeked over her shoulder into the parlor, her eyes scanning the entire room then turned toward the kitchen. "Is Mr. MacDermott with you?"

Stevie Rae shook her head.

"Is he behind you?"

She shook her head again and glanced down at her dust-covered boots. "He's...he's still in Mora." She touched Martha's arm and wished the woman would pull her into her warm embrace and tell her everything would be all right as she'd done so often in the past. Martha made no such move. "I came as soon as I got your telegraph. Was it Logan?"

Martha studied her, the expression on her face one Stevie Rae knew well. She flinched beneath the inquisitive stare. She knew what she looked like—sweaty from her mad ride from Mora to Little River with barely a stop and dirty from the fall she'd taken when she urged Willow through a place she shouldn't have earlier in the day. But those were physical things. It was the emotional things she wasn't quite ready to share, but the way Martha scrutinized her, Stevie Rae was certain no secret would remain a secret for very long.

Can she tell by looking in my eyes that I fell in love with him? Does she know, just by looking at me, that Brock and I were…intimate?

Martha didn't comment on Stevie Rae's appearance or what secrets her silent perusal had exposed. No judgment colored her voice when she finally answered the question. "Dan says it was Logan, but I'll let him tell you."

"Can I see him?"

She hesitated, her brow wrinkling, then nodded toward the room she had just exited. "But not too long. He needs to rest." Again, that look came over her face and her nose scrunched a bit, as if she smelled something horrible. "Take your hat off before you go in there."

Obeying her as she'd done most of her life, Stevie Rae swiped her battered hat from her head and ran her fingers through the wildly curling mass. Several leaves fluttered to the floor. Martha *tsk*ed and shook her head. "If your mother could see you now." An exasperated *harrumph* escaped her as she turned and walked down the hall to the kitchen. Over her shoulder, she said, "Put your hat back on. No sense scaring the man."

"Yes, ma'am." A flush of embarrassment swept through her, heating her face as well as the rest of her body. She donned the hat, fitting it tightly to her head, took a deep breath, and let herself into the room.

Dan lay in bed, propped up by several pillows, wire-rimmed glasses low on his nose. He had a bandage swaddling his chest and shoulder, which she glimpsed beneath the unbuttoned shirt he wore, and another on his left hand. He didn't look up from the paper in his hand. "For cryin' in a bucket, Martha, leave me be."

Hearing the annoyed tone of his voice, Stevie Rae smiled for the first time since getting Martha's telegraph. She could just imagine how Martha had fussed over him, reprimanding him one moment then letting him know how much she loved him the next, but never with actual words. She was that way with everyone she loved.

"It's not Martha."

Dan's gaze rose from the paper in his lap, his eyes widening, a warm smile lighting his whiskered face. "Hello, chickadee."

Stevie Rae's breath hitched in her chest at the use of his nickname for her, and the tears she'd tried so hard to hold at bay began to flow even though she didn't think she had any left.

"Aw, come on now." He held out his bandaged hand, beckoning her to come closer. "It's not as bad as it looks. I'll be good as new in a few days. Martha's been taking good care of me."

She sniffed and swiped at her face, then walked across the room and settled herself in the chair beside the bed.

"You look like hell, Stevie Rae."

"I was so worried about you."

"Shouldna been. I'm tougher than I look, as you well know. Both you and your father patched me up more than once." He grinned again and time seemed to stop for a moment. Yes, she remembered those times when Sheriff Hardy had staggered into her father's office, bleeding from a gunshot wound or stab from a knife, but those weren't the only memories she had of this man. There had been many nights when he and her father played chess into the wee hours of the morning, sometimes talking as if neither one of them would run out of words, sometimes so silent, the only sound was an occasional *humph* as the chess pieces moved across the board. He'd been a part of her life for as long as he'd been sheriff, and she had no doubts he loved her like her father had.

"MacDermott with you?" he asked, interrupting her thoughts.

Stevie Rae swallowed over the lump in her throat and shook her head.

"Hmmmm. Heard you were riding together."

Stevie Rae didn't acknowledge his statement, nor did she look at him. Instead, her eyes roamed to the paper spread out on his lap. She recognized the map. For many years, it hung over his desk in his office. "Tell me what happened. Was it Logan?"

"It was. Never saw him before, but I got to tell you, he's uglier in person than he is in his Wanted poster." He rolled the paper in his hand into a tube and slid a circlet made of string over it, placed it on the bedside table, and pushed his glasses to the top of his head. "I didn't see him ride into town, but I heard from a couple of people how bold he was. Heard his horse was almost dead, too, sweat glistening on his sides, blowing steam." He scrubbed at his face with his bandaged hand, then winced when the action caused pain.

"I was sitting in Nate's barber chair, soap all over my face, when I heard a shot. Jumped outta that chair as quick as you please and went racing outta there to see him—Logan—stealing Johnny Rhodes's horse, Johnny dead in the street. I tried to draw, but I was wearin' that stupid cape thing Nate puts on you when you're gettin' a shave and haircut and the wind was blowin' like it does and I couldn't get to my gun. Bastard was laughin' when he shot me, then sank spur and hightailed it outta town. Parker and a bunch of men rode out soon as they could after Parker brought me to Martha's, but Logan hasn't been seen since." He drew in his breath after speaking for so long and let it whistle through his lips with his exhale. "Coulda been worse, though. He coulda shot up the town like he's done other places."

Her eyes drifted to the map on the bedside table. "How far into the mountains did the posse go?"

Dan squinted, scrutinizing her face, then pulled his glasses down to his nose to get a better look. He grabbed her hand and squeezed lightly. "What are you planning to do, Stevie Rae?"

When she said nothing, he warned, "Now don't you be goin' after that man, not without MacDermott. You promise me."

How well he knew her. She couldn't promise him, though, couldn't force the words from her throat. She'd never lied to Dan. She didn't intend to start now. She studied his face and the concern shining from his eyes and finally nodded. Appeased, Dan released her hand and she rose from her seat. "I should let you rest. I'll see you tomorrow." She slipped out the door, already making plans Dan wouldn't be happy about.

Martha was up to her elbows in soapsuds when Stevie Rae entered the kitchen, half the dishes that had been in the sink now on the sideboard, draining on a towel. "He tell you what happened?" she asked without turning her head.

"Yes." Stevie Rae dropped her hat on the spindle of a chair, then picked up a towel and a coffee mug and started to dry it.

"Oh no!" Martha grabbed the towel and mug from her hands and put both down. "As dirty as you are, I don't want you touching my clean dishes." She started nudging her toward the hallway and the bathroom. "Why don't you go take a bath? I still have some of your clothes upstairs."

Stevie Rae scooted out of the way. "I have to see to Willow. I worked her hard today."

"Already took care of her. Had Annie bring her down to Wilson's Livery." She pushed hair out of Stevie Rae's face and tucked it behind her ear, her touch gentle and so comforting, it nearly brought her to tears. "Thanks for sending her, by the way.

She's a good girl and she's been a godsend these past couple of days." Her quizzical gaze went from Stevie Rae's head to her feet. She *tsk*ed again. Several times. A sound all too familiar. "All skin and bones. You eat today?"

"Yes."

An eyebrow rose and lips tightened until she asked, "You lying to me, Stephanie Raelene?"

Stevie Rae had no choice but to smile. The tone, the use of her full name, the familiar expression on Martha's face—all made her feel loved. Impulsively, she wrapped her arms around the older woman and squeezed. "I love you, Martha!"

"Aw, get on with you." Voice gruff and tight with emotion, Martha pulled out of Stevie Rae's embrace. "Gettin' me all dirty." She dabbed at her eyes with the corner of her apron, but it was there, a certain look that couldn't be denied: the love was reciprocated, though Martha would never admit it, nor would she probably ever say the words aloud. She showed her feelings with food, comfort, and kindness, with some hard truths thrown in, which, in itself, brought more comfort. One always knew where one stood with Martha.

She grabbed Stevie Rae by the shoulders and spun her around until she faced the doorway and the long hall. "By the time you're done with your bath, I'll have a nice hot meal waiting for you. Everything will be better after your bath." She gave a slight push and Stevie Rae found herself propelled down the hall. "And while you're eating, you can tell me all about Mr. MacDermott. Know you been ridin' together."

Chapter 21

Exhausted, frustrated, and hurting, Brock rode into Little River much later than he wanted. It was late morning, the sun just reaching its zenith. He had ridden as far as he could the night before, stopping only when he could no longer see in the darkness and the pain, in both his body and his heart, had become more than he could bear.

Tipping back his hat, he wiped the sweat from his forehead with his sleeve. His stomach growled, reminding him he hadn't eaten anything since finishing off the jerky Cora had packed for him yesterday.

He rode by the sheriff's office without stopping and continued up Main Street, turning the corner at Nate's Barbershop. Martha Prichard's boardinghouse loomed up ahead, the biggest house on the street, and he headed that way. He didn't know Martha but Stevie Rae had talked about her all the time, and Dan had spoken of her often as well. Both had nothing but good things to say about the woman.

He dismounted and nearly fell to the ground, his leg giving out on him. "Shit!" He grabbed Resolute's pommel to keep himself steady, then forced his body up the steps, grasping the railing as if it were a lifeline. When he reached the top of the porch stairs, he paused to catch his breath then twisted the bellpull.

The door opened and a woman who reminded him very much of his mother stood in the doorway, dish towel in hand. Flour dusted the apron over her floral print gown and the smell of freshly baked bread wafted through the open portal. Her gaze held that weariness of someone who had seen too much—life hadn't always been easy—but was still warm and welcoming. She studied him as he studied her, then her eyes opened wide as she drew in her breath.

"Miz Prichard?"

She gave a slight nod.

"We've never met. I'm Brock MacDermott." He swallowed against the dryness in his throat. His tongue cleaved to the roof of his mouth.

"I know who you are," she said, which surprised him though it shouldn't have. He was certain either Dan or Stevie Rae—or both—had talked about him just as they had talked about her.

"I'm looking for Sheriff Hardy."

She finished drying her hands, then slung the dish towel over her shoulder. "Dan?"

"Yes, ma'am."

Her eyes narrowed, the warmth in them a few moments ago, gone, replaced with what? Suspicion? Annoyance? Anger? He couldn't quite tell, but he found himself backing up a step just the same.

"Are you sure you're not looking for Stevie Rae?"

"Yes, ma'am. I mean, no, ma'am."

"Which is it? Dan or Stevie Rae?"

Flustered and embarrassed, not quite sure what to make of this woman…or her attitude, he said, "Well, both, ma'am."

"You might as well come in." The woman heaved a sigh and opened the door a bit wider, allowing him to enter. Brock stepped over the threshold and stood in the foyer, hat in hand, as the door closed behind him and Martha moved down the hallway. "Well, don't just stand there," she said over her shoulder.

Brock followed and entered the kitchen just a few steps behind her. His stomach rumbled when he noticed two loaves of bread cooling on a windowsill as well as two bowls, each filled with dough, on the table. Martha poured him a cup of coffee and handed it to him, then washed her hands, pulled a white blob from one of the bowls, and started kneading. Though she gestured to a chair, Brock didn't sit, afraid he wouldn't be able to rise again if he did. Instead, he leaned against the door frame, sipped at the fragrant brew, and concentrated on ignoring the constant throb in his thigh.

"Is she here?"

The woman shook her head as she kneaded the dough, punching the mass with surprising strength.

He didn't have time for this. He needed answers and he needed them now. "Where did she go?" Impatience made his tone sharper than he intended.

He realized his mistake as Martha looked up and rubbed her nose with her forearm. Her eyes narrowed as she looked him up and down, then settled on his face. "Why should I tell you?"

Brock didn't think twice. The words were out of his mouth before he could draw a breath. "Because I'm in love with her."

If she was surprised, she hid it well. The only evidence he had that she'd heard him was the raising of one eyebrow as she shaped the dough into a loaf, slipped it into a metal pan, then pushed the pan to the end of the table. Her gaze never left his face, though, and Brock squirmed a bit under the scrutiny, until a slight smile twitched the corners of her mouth. "You're in love with her," she repeated, her eyebrow rising a little higher, if that was possible. "Did you ever tell her that?"

His face burning, Brock shook his head. "No, but I should have." He shifted his weight from one leg to the other, then shifted back quickly. The pain in his leg was nothing compared to the pain in his heart. He needed to be out there, looking for Stevie, not inside Martha's overly warm kitchen, sipping her excellent coffee. "Where did she go, Miz Prichard?"

"She didn't tell me—didn't even say good-bye—but I know her as well as I know myself." A mixture of pride and fear gleamed from her eyes, which glimmered with tears he suspected she would never shed in his presence. "I'm thinking she went up to the mountains to look for Logan."

"When did she leave?"

"This morning." She picked up both pans and slid them into the oven, then cleaned the table of flour and bits of dough. Once finished, she moved to the icebox. "She was already gone when I got up." She removed several items from the shelves and placed them on the now clean table. "Are you hungry? Can I make you something to eat before you head out again?"

Stevie Rae had left already, probably before dawn, and was well on her way deep into the mountains. How would he ever find her? Urgency to leave now and look for her filled him, shrieked through his mind like a train's whistle, but he couldn't deny his hunger. It wouldn't do well for him to ride off, already hungry and in pain. If he lost consciousness on the trail, who knew how much time he'd lose? His stomach rumbled even louder than before as his gaze went from Martha at the stove to the assortment of foods on the table—cooked ham, some cheese, a bowl of what looked like mashed potatoes, half a cherry pie, the cherries oozing from the crust.

"Won't take a minute to heat something up for you." Without waiting for an answer, she pulled a large cast-iron skillet from a cabinet.

"Son, do you know you're bleeding?" He recognized Dan's voice, but jumped anyway, startled, even as relief rushed through him. He turned quickly, ready to embrace Dan Hardy, but stopped himself when he saw the bandages visible beneath the light cotton robe the man wore.

"Bleeding?" Martha exclaimed. "You've been standing here for the past ten minutes bleeding all over my clean floor!" She threw up her hands in exasperation, the items on the stovetop forgotten, and rushed toward him as she whipped the dish towel from the top of her shoulder, already wadding it up to staunch the flow of blood. "Just as bad as her! Neither one of you has the sense God gave a turnip, but at least she wasn't bleeding!"

"Martha." Dan said her name in a calm, even tone, drawing her attention as he grabbed the towel from her hand. "I'll take care of it. Just keep doing what you're doing."

The fight went out of her as quickly as it came, leaving her features a pasty white, and her lips pressed together in a thin line. Her gaze went from him to Dan, then back to him before she gave a quick nod and returned to her skillets.

"Come with me."

Brock followed as Dan led the way down the hall to a bedroom on the first floor. He opened the door and gestured toward the bed. "Drop your pants and let me take a look."

"I don't have time for this. I need—"

"How far do you think you'll get, bleeding all over the place?" Hands on his hips, the sheriff glared at him. "Besides, if you think I'm going back out to that kitchen and face Martha without fixing you up, you're mistaken, son. She'll have both our hides and I kinda like mine." Ignoring the bed, Brock grabbed the chair beside it, turned it around, then unbuttoned his trousers and slid them down his legs just far enough so Dan could take a look. He rested one forearm on the chair's back and held his pants in place with his other hand.

The sheriff made quick work of unwrapping the bandage, but Brock was unprepared for the rush of pain that made him clench his jaw as the man dabbed at the fresh blood with the bandage he'd just removed. "Looks like you ripped a few stitches. I can try to fix it, but Martha is better at it than I am."

Frustrated with the loss of time, and angry at Stevie Rae for taking off after Logan alone and at Dan and Martha for letting her go and at himself for getting shot in the first place, he growled, "Just do it. I don't care how it looks."

"Mighty prickly, ain't ya?" Dan remarked as he gathered everything he'd need—Martha's sewing basket as well as clean bandages—and brought them closer to hand.

Brock turned away as the man pulled a wicked-looking needle from the basket and threaded it with thick black thread.

"How'd you get shot anyway?" Brock asked, more so he could take his mind off what the man was doing than anything else, but it didn't help much and he clenched his jaw at the first stab of the needle. "Was it Logan?"

"It was," Dan answered and began talking as he worked. By the time he tied the knot of a fresh bandage to protect his handiwork, Brock knew everything. Fear, his constant companion of late, made his belly roil even more than the pain had.

"You're done. You can pull up your pants now." Dan wiped his hands, then tossed the bloody bandage into the trash basket in the corner. "What are you going to do now?"

Brock glared at him as if it were the stupidest question ever asked as he pulled his trousers over his hips and worked the buttons. "Find them. What did you think I'd say?"

The sheriff didn't take offense. In fact, he grinned. "Figured you say that." He patted Brock on the back and said, "Wish I could go with you, but Martha would...well, let's not say what Martha would do. She's after me to retire as it is." He chuckled. "Won't marry me until I do." He opened the door to the bedroom and led the way down the hall to the kitchen.

Martha leaned against the sink, arms folded across her chest, dish towel slung over her shoulder. She didn't ask about his injury, but her gaze inspected him thoroughly before she pointed at the food on the table and ordered, "Eat."

Brock recognized the tone. It was the same one his mother had used on all four of her boys. Dutifully, though he didn't think his stomach could handle it, he grabbed a plate and ate—standing up—while Dan filled him in on what he remembered from the map Stevie Rae had taken. When he was done, his mind filled with information and his stomach no longer empty, he handed Martha the plate. She gave him a tremulous smile, tears glimmering in her eyes. Then, to his surprise, she kissed his cheek and shoved a burlap sack into his hands. "Now you go find my girl and bring her home."

"Yes, ma'am."

It was a promise he intended to keep. Brock left the house and stood motionless on the front porch, his hands on his hips. He glanced to the north and the high mountains, then toward the south. Stevie Rae had a good six hours on him.

Which way would she have gone?

Dan opened the door and joined him on the porch. "You ain't gonna get far on Resolute." He eyed the horse waiting patiently, his reins looped around a post. "He looks done in. Take Samson. He's at Wilson's Livery. Tell Conrad I sent you."

"Thank you." He turned and shook the man's hand, then limped down the porch steps and untied Resolute's reins. He didn't mount up. Instead, leading his horse, he headed toward Wilson's Livery at the end of the street, his mind a whirlwind. If he was to find Stevie Rae, he'd have to figure out where Logan would go.

Where would a man such as he feel safe?

"You kill that outlaw, you hear?" Dan yelled after him.

Brock nodded, letting the man know he'd heard, but didn't stop his progress. Didn't even turn around, but something stuck in his brain. A word. One single word that kept repeating in head.

Outlaw.

The word grew louder, until it was the only thing he heard.

Outlaw.

He almost stumbled from the force of it in his mind, and when the word turned into an image, he did stagger.

Of course. Where else would an outlaw lie low but a place filled with other outlaws?

Brock picked up his pace, the extra padding covering his wound making his trouser leg ride up. He tugged on his pants as he entered the livery. The smell of fresh hay and the sound of horses moving about their stalls, chuffing into the air, greeted him. A man sat on a small stool near the back of the building, speaking softly to the horse whose hoof he held in his hand. Brock moved forward. "Excuse me."

The man looked up.

"Are you Conrad?"

"Yes, sir." He released the horse's hoof and rose from the stool. "Can I help you?"

"Dan sent me to get Samson."

"Of course. How is the sheriff?"

"Healing," he said as Conrad brought Dan's big, black mount from one of the stalls. As he did so, Brock led Resolute farther into the big stable. They met in the middle and exchanged reins. "This is Resolute. He needs a good rubdown. And a bucket of oats. He deserves them." He removed the saddle and placed it on Samson's back, then tightened the cinches.

"Anything you say." Conrad walked Resolute to the stall Samson had just vacated.

"Thank you." Brock knotted the bag of food Martha had given him around the pommel, then climbed into the saddle, gritting his teeth against the pain, and rode out of the livery. He passed Dan, still standing on Martha's porch. "I'm heading to that outlaw stronghold. You know the one I'm talking about. If Stevie—and Logan—are anywhere, it's there."

"I'll have the posse head up that way. Good luck, son."

"I don't need luck. What I need are wings on this horse to get there before Stevie Rae does," Brock called over his shoulder, then kneed Samson's sides. The horse responded with a burst of speed, his hooves pounding the dirt beneath him as they left Little River behind.

• • •

Weary and heartsore, her backside numb from sitting in the saddle so long, hunger cramping her belly, Stevie Rae nudged Willow's sides and urged her down the mountainside as the outlaw stronghold came into view between the trees. It hadn't taken her long to figure out where Logan would want to go to ground and hide until the posse grew tired of looking for him. He'd hole up in a place where no one cared how many people he'd killed.

A place where his deeds might even be applauded.

A place where she might meet her end.

She took a deep breath, then another and another to clear her mind, to grab hold of the fear shimmering through her and use it to her advantage. She needed her wits about her, needed to stay sharp, not dwell on the possibility she could lose her life today.

She could turn around right now and no one would be the wiser. She couldn't. Wouldn't. She'd come too far. Lost too much.

Her father's face flashed in her mind. A man devoted to healing, he would not condone her desire to see Logan dead, no matter what he'd done. She thought of her mother before she became ill, singing in the kitchen as she cooked while Stevie Rae studied at the kitchen table. Raelene Buchanan would not be happy with the path Stevie Rae had chosen, as Martha had told her so many times before. Martha. Dear, sweet Martha, hiding her gentle heart beneath her no-nonsense, tough-as-nails bluster, showing her love rather than just saying the words.

And Brock.

Her heart ached for him. She missed the way he'd flash that smile at her, the one that sent butterflies whirling in her belly. And she longed for his touch, his hands caressing her skin to make her body come alive, her thoughts reeling in a thousand different directions...if she had a thought at all.

She should have said good-bye to him, held him in her arms one last time and told him that she loved him…more than she ever thought possible. She wanted to be able to tell Brock that his nightmare—and hers—was over, then make a life with him, if he'd have her…if he loved her as much as she loved him.

No, this has to end now. For him. For us.

Tears smarted her eyes and she blinked quickly to remove the moisture, then shook her head to clear it. She dug deep into her soul to find the determination that had stood her in good stead for so long and firmly pushed all thoughts of Brock and everyone else from her mind.

Her mouth set in a grim line, courage once more racing through her brain side by side with her fear, she kneed Willow's sides and urged the horse forward at a slow pace until she was almost upon the small collection of buildings. Still hidden within the woods thick with evergreen and aspen trees, her gaze swept the mostly abandoned town. A buckboard rolled to a halt in front of the Silver Spur, loaded down with crates. The driver jumped from his seat and entered the saloon. A moment later, he returned, the bartender with him, and the two of them started to unload the wagon, bringing the crates inside the saloon. Other than those two, the street remained empty. Her eyes darted toward the left, and settled on the corral beside Bill Ransom's old stagecoach station. Her heart thundered in her chest as she recognized one of the horses in the corral. It belonged to Johnny Rhodes, the man Logan shot in Little River before he shot Dan.

Logan's here, but where? He could be in any one of these houses, sleeping off a drunk. Or waiting for the posse, his pistols cocked.

Stevie Rae tugged lightly on Willow's reins, bringing her to a halt, and slipped from the saddle. "This is as far as you go." She let the horse's reins dangle on the ground, then scratched Willow between her ears. "If I don't come back, you find your way home." The horse chuffed and nuzzled her face, as if she understood.

Stevie Rae traveled the rest of the way on foot, staying within the shelter of the trees, moving as cautiously and as silently as she could. The outlaws might have gotten smart since the last time she and Brock were here and posted guards to warn the patrons of the Silver Spur Saloon that a stranger—or worse, a posse—was riding into town.

She met no one, but that didn't stop her mouth from going dry. Keeping to the shadows behind the ramshackle buildings, she made her way to the back of the Silver Spur. A shiver snaked down her spine as she pressed herself against the wall beneath a set of stairs leading to the second story veranda and waited, willing her heart to cease its frantic pace. After a moment, still hugging the wall, Stevie Rae edged her way to the side of the saloon and peered into the building's window. The years of accumulated dirt and grime allowed her to see little more than the glow of lantern light and shadows. There were people in the saloon, but who they were could not be discerned.

She took stock of her situation. Yes, she had surprise on her side, but she just couldn't go rushing inside without knowing what criminals were there. She had done that once before and nearly gotten both Brock and herself killed. She'd learned her lesson.

No, this time, she would be smart.

Stevie Rae glanced toward the second story verandah. Her lips clamped together in grim determination as she sidled along the building, back the way she'd come, and studied the staircase as well as the yard behind the saloon. She took a deep breath, and silently climbed the steps. No one stopped her progress or sounded an alarm as she stepped on the verandah and let herself into the saloon through an empty bedroom window on the second floor. On tiptoe, she made her way across the room and opened the door a crack to peer into the main room.

She couldn't see directly below—the balcony railing was in her way—but what she could see struck terror in her heart. She recognized Hal and Tom Beech from the last time she was here, but there were three others she didn't know, one of whom leaned against the bar, his hands dangling near the guns in his holster as he joked with the barmaid. The other two played cards at one of the tables, intent on their game and nothing else, not even the deliveryman who bumped into one of their chairs as he brought another case of whiskey into the backroom. Her gaze shifted to the other side of the saloon and her breath seized in her lungs.

Logan sat at a table in the corner.

He picked up the bottle of whiskey, tipped it toward his mouth, and drank the rotgut, intent, from what she could see, on getting drunk and getting there quickly.

Looking at him, all Stevie Rae could see was a hazy red before her eyes as rage swept through her, making her shake and tremble like a leaf clinging to a branch in a windstorm. How dare he sit there like he hadn't a care in the world? How dare he still breathe, still live, after what he'd done to her father? And Brock? And countless others? Her hand dropped to the pistol in its holster, her fingers curling around handle. She started to pull the gun free of the leather then stopped herself.

If she shot him right now, as he deserved, she'd never make it out of the saloon. She'd be dead as every other outlaw in the room turned their guns toward her. She didn't want that. She wanted to live—and love—with Brock.

There had to be a better way.

She eased her grip on the revolver and closed the door, leaning against the sturdy wood to regain her balance before tiptoeing back the way she'd come and slipping out the same window she'd used to enter the building.

Her hands gripped the railing of the verandah, knuckles white, her entire body violently shaking, as she drew much-needed air into her lungs and tried to calm herself.

Think, Stevie. What would Brock do? What would Dan do?

From her vantage point on the verandah, she studied the horizon and the trees rising up toward the peak of one of the mountains that surrounded this little valley, willing her mind to come up with a solution. Her gaze lowered and she spotted the outhouse. A door slammed and she jumped then quickly dropped to her haunches behind the porch railing as the bartender appeared below and headed into the little wooden structure with a half moon carved out of the door. Stevie Rae sucked in her breath as he fumbled with his trousers and entered the privy, slamming the rickety door behind him. He came out a short time later, adjusted himself, and went back inside the saloon.

Not once did he look up.

Relief rushed through her, making her light-headed. At the same time, an idea came to her.

Eventually, Logan, too, would avail himself of the outhouse.

She could wait.

• • •

Brock took his first real breath in hours as he spotted Willow in the trees surrounding the settlement, her reins dangling on the ground while she munched sweet grass. He slowed Samson to a walk as he approached her, then slid from the saddle. As his feet hit the ground, pain shot through his leg and side and he gritted his teeth against it, though by now, he should have been accustomed to the burning, stabbing ache. "Where is she, Willow?"

The horse didn't answer. Brock didn't expect her to, but still, it felt good to ask. Hands on his hips, he turned in a slow circle, his eyes shaded against the bright sunlight by the brim of his hat, but he didn't see her. He could see the town and watched as a buckboard headed north, dust from the dirt road rising upward. Other than that lone person, the streets were deserted, as they had been the last time he was here.

Where are you, Stevie? Please, please, don't do anything stupid. If the situation weren't so serious, he would have chuckled. *What am I thinking? She's already done something stupid. She's gone after a killer alone.*

Limping, his lips pressed together, Brock took off on foot toward the saloon standing sentinel at the edge of town, determined to protect Stevie Rae from herself.

Sweat trickled down his back, wetting his shirt as he stumbled and staggered down the mountainside at a pace he shouldn't have tried to maintain, but he couldn't stop himself from running full-out, hoping with each step he wasn't too late.

Movement and a flash of color captured his attention and he stopped beside a tree, resting his hand against the rough bark, panting from his efforts and the knife-sharp pull of skin against the stitches Dan had so recently repaired. He squinted, focusing on the spot where he'd caught a glimpse of white against the green of the pine trees, then slowly shifted his gaze to the right and sucked in his breath.

Stevie.

Her stride was long, filled with purpose, the edges of her split skirt swirling around the tops of her boots.

What is she doing?

He focused harder and moved a little closer, creeping from one tree to another to remain hidden.

Is someone behind her, forcing her to march up the mountainside?

His eyes scanned the mountainside behind her, but he saw no one, and his gaze shifted back to her. He lowered his hat to shade his eyes, then drew in his breath sharply as sunlight glinted off the barrel of her father's Colt. She held it in her hands the way he had shown her.

He moved closer still, carefully choosing his steps, and then he knew all he needed to know as Zeb Logan came into his field of vision. The outlaw marched ahead of her, one hand bunching the waistband of his trousers, the other waving madly as he tried to keep his balance on the rough terrain as Stevie Rae urged him higher up the slope.

He resisted the urge to call her name. It would be fatal to startle her and give Logan a chance to turn the tables. Instead, he started to run, his feet pounding the soft dirt beneath him. Pain blossomed…in his leg, in his heart, but he kept going until he was several yards behind them.

"That's far enough," he heard her tell Logan, her voice shaking, when they reached a small clearing. The man stopped, both hands now clutching the waistband of his trousers. "Turn around. I want to see your face when I put a bullet through your heart."

Slowly, the outlaw turned around…and grinned. "You ain't gonna shoot me, or you woulda done it when you surprised me in the shitter." He spit and took two steps toward her, then hesitated and took two more.

Brock knew what Logan was trying to do—make her angry so she'd lose her focus, but Stevie Rae held her ground, her legs spread slightly for balance as he'd shown her so long ago, her features a tight mask of concentration. She didn't rise to the bait, nor did she respond to him. She simply held the pistol straight out and pulled back the hammer. The loud *click* sounded like a thunderbolt in the stillness.

And then she did the oddest thing. She smiled at him, as if daring him to take another step toward her, and started to speak, so softly, he strained to hear. "Don't you want to know why I want you dead?"

Logan shrugged and spit on the ground again. "Don't care."

Stevie Rae gave a slight nod. "I'll tell you anyway because I think you should know. My father was a doctor. Steven Buchanan, but you probably don't remember him. He removed a bullet from your leg and one from your shoulder, and for his trouble, you killed him. Shot him through the heart. So that's what I'm going to do to you. Shoot you in your black heart and watch you die."

Logan laughed. "Hell, girl, I thought this was about MacDermott. 'Cause I shot him."

It was the wrong thing to say. Stevie Rae's entire body stiffened. Redness colored her cheeks, and for a moment, the gun barrel shook in her hand.

Brock stepped out of the shadows, her name frozen on his tongue as her finger squeezed the trigger, the loud report of the pistol firing echoing against the mountainside. Smoke curled from the barrel of the Colt as Zeb Logan fell to the ground, blood seeping from the wound in his chest, just above his heart. He didn't move, didn't speak, but he still breathed, his chest rising and falling in a shaky rhythm.

"Stevie Rae!"

She gave a startled cry and whirled to face him, the revolver still in her shaking hands, and now aiming straight at him. He ignored the gun and concentrated on her face, his eyes boring into hers as his long legs ate up the distance between them. He recognized shock when he saw it, and it was there on her pale features and in her trembling body.

"Give me the gun."

She raised weary eyes to him, tears spiking her impossibly dark lashes, and handed him the pistol without a word. She melted against him, her hat slipping off her head as she did so. Brock stuck the pistol in his belt behind his back, the muzzle still warm, and wrapped his arms around her, squeezing tight, promising himself he'd never let go. And it was a promise he intended to keep.

"Are you all right?" He raised her chin and looked deeply into her eyes.

"Yes," she said, but her voice was tight and hoarse and the tears shimmering on her lashes fell to her cheeks before she rested her head on his chest again. His brave girl wasn't nearly as brave as she pretended to be, but he knew that, had known it all along.

"You don't know what hell I've been through these past few days, Stevie. Waking up in Mora to find you gone, knowing you'd gone after Logan yourself. Not knowing if I'd find you in time. Afraid I'd never see you again. Or hold you. Or make love to you. Promise me you'll never do that to me again." He felt her nod against his chest and drew in his breath. "I love you, Stevie Rae."

She raised her head and looked at him, her tear-filled eyes the bluest he'd ever seen them. "You love me?"

"Yes," he whispered, though he felt like shouting. "I love you with everything I am and ever hope to be." He lowered his head and captured her lips with his. "Tell me you love me, Stevie Rae. Say you'll marry me and make me the happiest man who ever walked the earth."

"Yes, Brock, I do love you. And yes, I'll marry you." She touched her lips to his, sealing her promise with a kiss, then laid her head back on his chest with a sigh. "What do we do about Logan?" she asked, her voice muffled in his shirt.

He kissed the top of her head. "The posse is a couple of hours behind me. They can take him in." He held her, his heart still thundering, though not as hard as before. "We have a future to plan. You're a good doctor. I see you finishing medical school, Stevie, and I'll be right there beside you, helping you, supporting you. But first, I want you to come to Paradise Falls with me. Meet my brother and tell him that Zeb Logan will be paying for his crimes. A telegram won't do this time. I think he should hear that news in person."

"You've been thinking about this, haven't you?" Stevie Rae asked as she raised her head and gazed into his eyes, the smile on her face the most beautiful thing he'd ever seen.

Brock chuckled. He couldn't help himself. He'd never been so damn happy in his life. "I've had nothing else to think about since

I woke up in Mora and learned you were gone. I promised myself that when—not if—I found you, I'd hold on to you and never let you—"

Movement in his peripheral vision drew his attention and took the words from his mouth. He turned quickly in time to see Zeb throw a knife, the sharp point glinting in the sunlight, coming straight for Stevie's face. He didn't even think, his reaction second nature as he pushed Stevie away, pulled his pistol from its holster, and fired. The knife flew past them and sank harmlessly into the ground, but Brock's aim had been true. This time Logan took the bullet in the heart. A bloom of bright-red blood stained his dirty shirt as the life slipped away from him.

Zeb Logan would never hurt anyone again. He and Stevie Rae were free, but the danger wasn't over. The gunshots had echoed against the mountain, possibly alerting the outlaws drinking in the saloon even though they were some distance from town. No sense taking any chances. "We gotta go, Stevie."

"What about him?"

"Leave him. The posse will be here soon. They'll take him."

Epilogue

What is he up to?

Stevie Rae felt the warmth of her husband's steady gaze and turned away from the view outside the stagecoach window. He smiled, that same smile she'd fallen in love with so long ago, and a certain look came into his soft gray eyes. After almost four years of marriage, she recognized that look and immediately, a rush of heat warmed her from the inside out. Tonight, once they were settled, there would be long, slow kisses and hot, feverish caresses and so much more.

Making love was not the only thing he had in mind. She could tell just by the way he acted. He was up to something else.

He'd hardly said a word since Santa Fe, not even when they realized they were the only two making this last leg of the journey. They could have spread out on the seats of the top of the line stagecoach and yet, here they sat, side by side, touching…but not talking, which was all right. Brock had never been much of a talker anyway. Her gaze drifted over his face now, memorizing every detail and her heart swelled with love for this man.

He'd made sacrifices for her while she attended school and worked at the hospital in Boston, for which she remained so grateful. She couldn't have finished her studies nor worked the long hours treating patients if she hadn't had his support…and his love.

Though he liked Boston, Brock had never felt at home there. The city was too big, too cosmopolitan. Yes, there were museums and restaurants and the opera, and he enjoyed all that, but there was something missing. He hadn't liked being a police officer either, but he had walked the streets in a uniform and shoes that pinched his feet to pay the bills so she could pursue her dream. And though he never complained, she knew he missed his well-worn boots, missed the wide open spaces and slow pace of a small town, where everyone knew everyone and cared about each other. She had missed those things, too.

"It'll be good to see Martha again." Stevie Rae slipped her hand into his, her thumb caressing the plain gold band on his ring finger. "I can't believe she and Dan are finally getting married."

"I can't believe he's retiring," Brock responded then lapsed into silence once more though the warmth of his gaze never left her and neither did the silly little grin on his face. He looked like a man who had a secret, one he was hard-pressed to keep. Or perhaps, behind that adorable grin, he hid the fact he wasn't happy they hadn't headed straight to Paradise Falls. He would do that on occasion—hide the truth so she wouldn't worry.

Surely, he wouldn't want to miss Dan and Martha's wedding. Though the plan was for her to open her practice in Paradise Falls and for him to join Teague as a deputy—for months, she'd been acquiring supplies for her office and having Brock ship them to his brother—a few more days' delay shouldn't be too difficult. Or was it?

She studied her husband and still couldn't tell. He turned to face her and her heart picked up an extra beat. His eyes were a soft gray that reminded her of smoke rising from a fire, but there was no worry in them, only love shining brightly within their depths. Still, she had to ask, "Is it all right we're stopping in Little River?"

"Of course it is. I wouldn't miss this wedding for anything. Why?"

"You've hardly said a word since we left Santa Fe."

"I'm just thinking," he said with a shrug.

"About what?"

"You, mostly. How proud I am of you and what you've accomplished." He squeezed her hand. "You found your dream and you pursued it"—he chuckled and the sound went straight to her heart—"with the same dogged determination and perseverance you used to hunt down Zeb Logan. When other women were dropping out of the program because the curriculum was too hard, you rose to the challenge." His voice lowered, becoming a deep rumble that made every nerve in her body come alive. "I was remembering the first time we met." He pointed to the sheriff's office that came into view through the window. "I saw that same stubbornness when you offered to ride with me. Nothing has changed since that moment." His grin widened. "Have I told you today how much I love you?"

She stared into his eyes and let out a breath of anticipation. "Only once."

He brought her lips to his and slowly, with a passion that still stunned her, slid his mouth over hers. "Then I'm not doing my job," he said when they broke apart. "I promised when we married that I would tell you I loved you at least ten times a day." He traced her bottom lip with his thumb. "I do, you know. I love you with everything I am. You saved me. Made me see the sunlight beyond the shadow."

Heat flooded her, rising up from the depths of her soul to touch every part of her. "We saved each other."

The stagecoach rolled to a rattling, creaking halt in front of Hagan's Saloon. Brock pushed open the door and stepped out, stretching the kinks from stiff muscles while she gathered the few belongings she'd brought inside the stagecoach and stuffed them in the trusty leather medical bag that had once been her father's. Her door opened and Brock's hand stretched toward her, and in that moment, Stevie Rae couldn't stop herself from grinning like an idiot. She was the luckiest woman in the world to have the love of such a man.

As the stagecoach driver handed their trunks down to the man who had ridden shotgun, Brock took her hand and helped her from the coach.

"Ah, there's Dan." He pulled his watch from his pocket and grinned as the sheriff came into view, perched on the seat of a buckboard that looked like it wouldn't last another day. "Right on time."

"Have you ever known him to be late?"

"Never."

The man in question saluted them smartly, then tugged lightly on the reins and brought the rattletrap wagon to a stop not three feet away. He jumped from his seat and swept Stevie Rae into a bruising hug, nearly knocking her hat—not her treasured cowboy hat, but a fashionable thing with feathers that matched her traveling ensemble—from her head. "Chickadee, you're a sight for sore eyes."

"Oh Dan, I'm so happy for you!"

When he released her, she saw that his eyes were shiny and filled with moisture. It didn't surprise her when he gave Brock the same welcome.

"Where's Martha?"

"I'm making her rest," he said, a touch of smugness in his voice. "And she finally listened to me. She's been running around these past few days, worried that you and Brock wouldn't arrive in time, worried that the flowers for her bouquet would be wilted by the time she and I walked down the aisle tomorrow. She's even worried the preacher will forget the words." He chuckled but there was affection in his voice. "Let's get you all settled."

They piled their luggage in the back of the wagon and climbed into the seat. "Martha will be so happy to see you," Dan said as he flicked the reins with a well-practiced turn of the wrist.

They passed the dress shop, the one where Stevie Rae had once admired a dress in the window, and Garrity's General Store. There was a new café and a hotel on the main street and several new homes higher up on the mountainside, but not much else had changed here since Brock had slipped the plain gold band on her finger in front of Dan and Martha and they'd begun their new adventure as a married couple.

They turned the corner at Nate's Barbershop. The barber stopped sweeping the raised sidewalk outside his store and waved as they drove by.

Stevie Rae waved in return, then faced forward. Martha's house stood at the end of the street, the two-storied structure picturesque against the mountainside background, but they didn't make it to Martha's house. Instead, Dan lightly tugged on the reins and brought the dilapidated buckboard to a halt…in front of the house Stevie Rae had grown up in.

"Why are we stopping here?"

"There's someone you need to see." With those cryptic words, Brock climbed down from the seat, then helped her down as well. He placed her hand in the crook of his arm, opened the gate in the fence that surrounded the front yard, and led them through. Flowers bloomed beside the walkway, and she noticed the fence and the deep front porch had a fresh coat of paint. The porch swing, the one she'd spent hours in when she was younger, swayed with the breeze and lacy curtains fluttered in the open windows on the first floor.

Stevie Rae stopped before reaching the steps of the wide front porch, nearly yanking him from his feet. "We can't just go barging in on people, Brock. It isn't right."

"I promise you, the people who live here now won't mind a bit." He slipped his hand into hers and gently led her up the porch steps. "Come on. It'll be all right. I promise."

The front door opened, and a very beautiful young woman stood in the entrance, her face wreathed in a smile that made her velvety brown eyes twinkle.

Stevie Rae stared at the woman, then blinked. "Annie?"

The woman gave a slight nod.

Tears instantly stung Stevie Rae's eyes as memories flooded her. The last time she'd seen Annie was when the woman had served her whiskey at the outlaw saloon so long ago. She'd given her money and sent her to Martha, who took Annie in and gave her what she needed. A home. Respect. Good food and Martha's particular brand of tough love. And Annie had thrived, though in the beginning, she'd been shy and reserved and hid from everyone, including Stevie. Not now, though. Now, she seemed like a totally different woman. Confident. Realizing her own worth. Happy. "I almost didn't recognize you."

"Hello, Miss Stevie." She opened the door wider and pulled Stevie Rae into a warm embrace, then stepped back, embarrassment coloring her face. "I've wanted to thank you for so long. If it wasn't for you, I'd probably be…dead." She acknowledged Brock with a big smile. "Mr. MacDermott."

He tipped his hat in return.

"You live here now?"

"Oh no, Miss Stevie, I'm just getting things ready for the new owner." She stuffed a dust rag into the pocket of her apron, then took another step back. "Conrad and I have been staying here until he finished building our home."

"You're married?" Martha hadn't told her, but then, Martha had been busy planning her own wedding.

The woman nodded and again, her smile dazzled. "Please, come in. I'll be back in a moment." Annie ran down the hall as Stevie Rae stepped farther into the parlor. Her eyes opened wide and her heart pounded fiercely in her chest. Nothing had changed in this house where she'd grown up. The parlor looked almost exactly as it had before her father had sold the house, right down to the flowered wallpaper. She spun around in a slow circle, her gaze landing on familiar objects, memories bringing tears to her eyes. She reached out to slide her hand over the back of a rocking chair. "This was my mother's." She pointed to a desk in the corner and the big leather chair behind it. "And that's my father's desk." She glanced down the hallway and saw the kitchen table she'd shared with her parents when her mother had been well enough to cook, and beyond that, the window in front of the sink where she had dreamed of her future while she washed the supper dishes. She turned toward her husband, her vision blurred by tears. "I don't understand."

"You will." Brock tilted his head and grinned. "Come, I want to show you something else." He reached out and grabbed her hand, pulling her back toward the front door then along the porch to the side of the house. "Close your eyes."

Excitement rippled through her, but as much as she wanted to see, she kept her eyes closed. For him. Because he seemed so excited. She heard whispering, but she didn't peek although curiosity swelled within her.

"You can look now." His voice hovered near her ear. Goose bumps broke out on her flesh as she opened her eyes. The first thing she saw was her husband, grinning like a fool. And Annie, her eyes shining. The second thing she saw was the plaque hanging beside the door. It read *Dr. S. MacDermott* in fancy script. Below the sign was another plaque that read *The Doctor Is In*.

"Go on. Take a look," Brock encouraged her, but she couldn't even draw breath, let alone move a muscle.

"I hope I did everything right," Annie said as she grabbed her hand and led her into the room, which looked no different than when her father had his practice here. Her feet sank into the thick rug on the floor and for a moment, she felt as if she'd stepped into one of her own memories. Several comfortable chairs lined the wall. There were even magazines on the tables between the chairs and through another door, the examination room, just as her father had set it up so long ago. Glass-fronted cabinets held bandages and medicines—all the supplies she'd had Brock send to Paradise Falls. "I'll be your first patient."

Startled, her heart racing, hardly able to believe what her eyes were seeing, Stevie Rae turned toward her. "What?"

"I'll be your first patient," Annie repeated. "Conrad and I are having a baby."

"A baby?" God, she felt stupid repeating everything, but she couldn't help herself. It was all happening so fast.

The woman nodded, her face aglow, then slowly drew her farther into the room and moved off to the side.

Stunned, unable to take it all in, Stevie Rae stood still and looked around with the eyes of the child she had been and the adult she had become. Her breath hitched in her chest. It was all too much. So unexpected and so...just like Brock to surprise her like this. Their marriage had been full of surprises—unexpected flowers or candy when she'd had a particularly trying time in school, hot baths waiting for her when she came home from a long day at the hospital—but nothing like this. Now she knew why he'd been so quiet and why he couldn't stop smiling. Tears gathered in her eyes, and she swallowed hard against the lump in her throat as she faced her husband in the doorway. "How?"

"Martha, mostly. Believe it or not, your father had given her much of the furniture when he sold the house. She kept those pieces, hoping someday to give them back to you." He glanced at Annie, his smile deepening, warmth and affection in his voice—and in his beautiful, soft gray eyes. "Dan and Annie helped me, too. All those supplies you had me send to my brother? I sent them here instead and Annie set everything up."

"But..." She couldn't find the words, though they filled her heart. "You did this for me?"

"I thought about this for a long time, Stevie Rae, and when your old house came up for sale, I... It just felt right." He entered the room, his long legs eating up the short distance between them. "Can you imagine how hard that's been to keep a secret? I wanted to tell you so many times, but couldn't." He gathered her in his arms, his finger tracing her cheek. "We don't belong in Paradise Falls. Or Boston, kid. We belong here in Little River. This is where I want to raise our family. In this house. In this town. Where you grew up."

Once again, he had sacrificed his own happiness for her, and that alone nearly brought her to her knees. "What about you?"

His chest puffed out with pride and the smile she'd fallen in love with so long ago stretched his lips. "You're looking at the new sheriff of Little River. Dan brought my name up to the town council. I was voted in unanimously. So you see, all the pieces have fallen into place." He pulled her into his arms and held tight, his voice in her ear making shivers race up and down her spine. "I love you, kid—or should I say Doctor MacDermott? Welcome home."

Author Bio

Marie Patrick has always had a love affair with words and books, but it wasn't until a trip to Arizona, where she now makes her home with her husband and her furry, four-legged "girls," that she became inspired to write about the sometimes desolate, yet beautiful landscape. Her inspiration doesn't just come from the Wild West, though. It comes from history itself. She is fascinated with pirates and men in uniform and lawmen with shiny badges. When not writing or researching her favorite topics, she can usually be found curled up with a good book. Marie loves to hear from her readers. Drop her a note at Akamariep@aol.com or visit her website at www.mariepatrick.com.

More from This Author
Mischief and Magnolias Marie Patrick

Natchez, Mississippi
September 1863

Shaelyn Cavanaugh leaned against the railing of the second-floor gallery of her home and focused on the two men coming up the road, their blue uniforms unmistakable. They rode at a swift pace, a trail of dust behind them.

Since Natchez, Mississippi, surrendered to the Union forces, it wasn't unusual to see blue uniforms, especially since they'd made Rosalie, the home next door, their headquarters. But the two men didn't turn into Rosalie's drive as she expected.

Her breath caught in her throat when she glimpsed light auburn hair, much like her brother's, gleaming in the sunlight. "Ian!"

His companion had raven-black hair, though it too reflected the sun's light. Traveling with Ian, he could be only one man—the one she had promised to wait for. "James." Her hand gripped the wrought-iron railing, her knuckles white. Tears blurred her vision. Her heart beat a frantic rhythm in her chest as excitement surged through her veins.

"They're home!" she cried. "Mama!"

She lifted her skirts and ran for the outside staircase at the back of the house. "They're home!"

She jumped, missing the last few stairs, and hit the veranda at a run, her skirts held high as she ran into the house through the French doors in the small sun parlor.

"Mama!" Shaelyn darted into the central hallway, her footsteps clicking on the marble tiles as she ran to the front door, flung it open, and rushed headlong into a pair of strong arms. She rested her head against a firm, hard chest, and squeezed tight. A button pressed into her cheek, but she didn't care. They were home. "Thank God," she whispered into the uniform.

"Well, that's quite a greeting," a deep, rich voice as smooth as drizzling molasses responded. Laughter rumbled in his chest. "Not expected, but certainly welcomed."

"Hmm. Where's mine?" his companion asked in the clipped tones of New England.

Shaelyn recognized neither voice nor accent and turned her head to glance at the auburn-haired man. Ian Cavanaugh did not look back at her, which meant she did not have her arms around James Brooks.

Her face hot with embarrassment, Shaelyn pulled away from the man. She drew in a shaky breath and stared. The most beautiful pair of soft blue-gray eyes she'd ever seen stared back. "Forgive me. I thought you were someone else."

"Obviously," the man replied. "Perhaps introductions are in order, although after your greeting, it may be too late." Amusement gleamed from his eyes as a wide grin showed off his white teeth in a charming smile. She wanted to touch the dimple that appeared in his cheek. "Major Remington Harte." He gestured to the man beside him. "This is my second in command, Captain Vincent Davenport."

"Miss." Captain Davenport bowed from the waist.

Shaelyn nodded in his general direction, but her focus remained on the major. She'd never seen hair so black or so thick. An insane impulse overwhelmed her—she wanted to run her fingers through that mass of thick, shiny hair and feel its silkiness. Struck by her own inappropriate thoughts, she stilled. He wasn't James. She shouldn't want to run her fingers through his hair.

"Are you Brenna Cavanaugh?"

"What?" Startled, Shaelyn shook her head. "No, I'm her daughter, Shaelyn."

Footsteps rang out down the hallway. Shaelyn dragged her gaze away from the man in uniform for just a moment as her mother joined them at the door. "I am Brenna Cavanaugh." A sweet smile accompanied the hand she offered the major. "May I help you?"

Introductions were quickly made, and Shaelyn watched the exchange of pleasantries, but her gaze was drawn back to the major. He looked dashing in his uniform. The dark blue complimented his eyes quite nicely. The material molded to his body, emphasizing his broad shoulders, lean waist, and slim hips. He stood tall, well over six feet she guessed, as her gaze swept the length of his body with admiration. She noticed a silver-tipped cane in his hand, which he leaned on. He must have been injured in battle.

She had always loved seeing a man in uniform. They stood differently: straighter, taller. Proud. They acted differently, too, as if wearing a uniform had something to do with how the world perceived them.

Her gaze met his and she felt the warmth of a blush creep up from her chest. A smile parted his full lips and her face grew hotter. She'd been staring at him and he knew it.

"Is this about Ian, my son?" Hope colored her mother's tone, a hope she had tended carefully, like one tends a garden.

"Or James Brooks?" Shaelyn added.

"May we go inside?" Major Harte gestured toward the open door.

"Where are my manners?" Brenna smiled. "Of course." She turned to Shaelyn. "Please show our guests into the sun parlor, dear. I just finished making tea."

With effort, Shaelyn dragged her gaze away from the major and the pulse throbbing in his neck, above the collar of his uniform, which had mesmerized her. "Please follow me."

Major Harte's uneven footsteps echoed in the hallway and the tip of his cane tapped on the marble tiles as Shaelyn showed them into a small, comfortable, sun-filled room at the back of the house, while Brenna pushed through the swinging door to the kitchen. "Please, make yourselves comfortable."

"Thank you." The major moved to the fireplace and rested his arm on the mantle while Captain Davenport sat on a rattan love seat.

Shaelyn sank into a chair across from the captain, her fingers settling into one of the rattan grooves, and let out a slow breath—anything to still the anxiety plucking at her spine with its icy fingers and chilling her from the inside out. After a moment, the heat of the major's gaze rested on her, negating that chill. He didn't speak as she turned to face him, nor did he smile, but the warmth in his slate-colored eyes captured and held hers.

She opened her mouth, but no words issued forth. She didn't know what to say. Or do. She'd never had to entertain Union officers, although her brother had marched off to war wearing blue. In all truth, she hadn't entertained in a very long time, and the lessons her mother had taught her about proper decorum and genteel manners simply escaped her.

Captain Davenport didn't speak either, and a heavy stillness filled the room, the only sound the rhythmic ticking of the grandfather clock in the corner. An ominous sense of foreboding stole through Shaelyn with each passing minute. Her heart pounded, not with excitement now, but with dread. A lump rose to her throat. She knew, deep down, whatever the reason for these men to be here, no good would come of it.

Brenna entered the parlor and broke the silence. "Shaelyn, would you please pour?" Her mother placed a silver tea service on the table in front of the divan and took a seat in her favorite wicker chair.

Shaelyn rose from her seat, though her entire body trembled. With shaking hands, she lifted the teapot and started to pour. A few drops of the dark brew spilled onto a linen napkin on the tray and stained it brown.

She glanced up and caught the major's wince before he addressed his second in command. "Captain, would you be so kind?"

"Of course." Captain Davenport leaned forward and took the pot from her hands.

Shaelyn gave him a tremulous smile. Every muscle and sinew in her body tensed with apprehension as she moved behind the settee, her hand resting on her mother's shoulder.

Captain Davenport handed Brenna her teacup and attempted to give one to Shaelyn as well, but she declined without a word, afraid her voice wouldn't work over the lump constricting her throat.

Major Harte straightened and limped over to the chair opposite the divan, a grimace tightening his features. Shaelyn watched his painful progress and a surge of sympathy rippled through her.

"Now, Major, please tell us why you're here. If it's bad news, don't make us wait, I beg you." Brenna's voice shook as she said the words. She grabbed Shaelyn's hand and squeezed.

He hesitated. Shaelyn wanted to drag the words from his mouth. Whatever he needed to say, she just wished he'd do it. He took a deep breath. She prepared herself, swallowing hard against the bile burning the back of her throat.

"Mrs. Cavanaugh, are you the owner of Cavanaugh Shipping and the steamboats the *Brenna Rose*, the *Lady Shae*, and the *Sweet Sassy*?"

"Since my husband passed away," Brenna replied. "Yes, I am, but Shaelyn runs the business. She's quite good at it, despite this terrible war."

"And are you the owner of record for this home, Magnolia House, and the warehouse and shipping office located in Natchez-Under-the-Hill?"

"What is this all about, Major?" Shaelyn asked. She didn't like the expression on the major's face at all. He seemed sad almost, as if he didn't relish what he needed to do, and her dread intensified, those icy fingers no longer plucking at her spine, but squeezing her heart. She stiffened against the blow that was sure to come.

He removed a document from his uniform pocket, slowly unfolded it, and began to read. "By the order of the government of the United States, for the duration of this war or until they are no longer needed," he said softly, "you are hereby commanded to relinquish your home, steamboats, warehouse, and shipping office to the Union Army. Specifically, me." He glanced at Shaelyn, an apology in his eyes.

"What!" Shaelyn let go of her mother's hand and came around the sofa on legs that felt like wooden stumps instead of flesh and bone. "You can't do that. They belong to us."

She stopped in front of Major Harte and stared at him. The brief moment of sympathy she'd had for him vanished, and her face burned with anger. Indeed, her entire body felt as if fire consumed her. She grabbed the document from him, but her hands shook so badly, she couldn't read the paper in front of her.

"Indeed, I can, Miss Cavanaugh," he said, his voice no longer soft, but commanding and strong. "I have my orders." The expression in his eyes hadn't changed, though. They were still apologetic.

She knew the army, on both sides, frequently took homes and other possessions, but it didn't assuage her anger one bit. "Why my steamers? And my home?"

"The Union Army has need of your boats to transport men and supplies and your home, being in such close proximity to Rosalie, is perfect to quarter my men."

"What are we supposed to do? How will I support us if you take my steamboats? Where are we to live?" Incredulity made Shaelyn's voice sharper than normal. Although she was usually unflappable, even in the most dire of circumstances, this whole tableau had her feeling like she was someone else, someone she didn't even recognize. "What if I refuse, Major? What will you do then?"

A muscle jumped in the major's cheek as he stood to tower over her. "You have no choice in this matter, Miss Cavanaugh." His voice remained strong, but the warmth of his eyes conveyed another message. "It's nothing personal. Consider this your contribution to the war effort."

The lump constricting her throat threatened to suffocate her. She took a deep breath and swallowed hard.

"My my mother and I have already contributed far more to this blasted war than you could ever imagine." Her voice barely above a whisper, she almost choked on the words. "My father suffered a stroke when war was declared. I watched him struggle for life for two months before he succumbed." She blinked against the tears filling her eyes. "I have heard nothing from my brother or my intended in over a year. I can only hope they are still alive and were not at Gettysburg. I have lost two riverboats to shell fire. They lay at the bottom of the Mississippi, along with the people who were aboard."

She drew in her breath, tried to control her shaking body, and tried but failed to control her temper. "Now you will take my home and my business, and I am to give it to you graciously? I don't believe I can, Major."

A strong desire to do him bodily harm made her clench her fists as he stood before her, his expression impassive.

"I am sorry for your losses, Miss Cavanaugh, but we have all made sacrifices," he replied softly. His gaze held hers and he shifted his weight to his other leg, as if mentioning the word *sacrifices* made him remember his own. "Some more than others. It is the way of war."

"Your war, not mine!" The words exploded from her, despite the constriction in her throat. How much more would this blasted war take? How much more could she give? Had she brought this on herself by applying for a government contract? She'd been denied, of course, and immediately tried again and again. Had she drawn attention to Cavanaugh Shipping by her sheer persistence? Instead of getting the contract she so hoped for, she had her possessions taken.

A small sound drew her attention. Shaelyn tore her gaze away from the major and glanced at her mother. Brenna had not moved, had not uttered a sound except for a small whimper, but her face had lost all color. Her chin trembled and tears shimmered on her lashes. Pain and confusion flashed in her eyes. Shaelyn's heart came close to shattering.

She had promised her father she would always take care of her mother, a privilege she gladly accepted. She wouldn't break her promise now. She took a deep breath and managed to smile at her mother to let her know it would be all right.

"I'm certain you are a reasonable man, Major." She forced her gaze away from Brenna and faced the man who stood to take everything from her. "We have nowhere to go, sir. No family left, no friends able to take us in. The war has seen to that." She took a deep breath and tried to keep her anger under control. "Perhaps we can strike a bargain?"

• • •

Intrigued, Remy cocked a dark eyebrow. He hadn't missed the look she'd given her mother, nor could he mistake the devastation on the older woman's face and his part in putting the desolation there. He hadn't had this issue with the other homes where some of his men were now staying. "A bargain, Miss Cavanaugh? What did you have in mind?"

"Perhaps we can discuss this privately," Shaelyn suggested, and nodded toward Brenna.

"Of course," he conceded, and followed her from the parlor. They stepped across the hall, toward the front of the house, and into a well-appointed study. Remy limped to the desk and leaned against it, taking the pressure off his leg in an effort to alleviate the pain, which never seemed to abate.

Shaelyn shut the pocket doors then moved to the center of the room. A ray of sunlight fell on her, and Remy sucked in his breath.

Heaven help me, she is a beauty. Damn Jock MacPhee!

Her light auburn hair, twisted haphazardly into a loose knot atop her head, left wispy tendrils to frame a lovely, heart-shaped, and at the moment, angry face. Bright patches of color stained her cheeks. Dark brows arched over smoldering eyes the color of cobalt. Her pert nose turned up slightly at the tip. He had no doubt her mouth, now compressed in annoyance, broke hearts when she smiled.

She had spirit. He'd give her that. Her rage was tangible; he felt the heat radiate from her from across the room. Her eyes never left him. They sparkled with dangerous intent.

"You have my undivided attention." He hid a smile as she stomped toward the desk, the lace at the hem of her dark plum skirt swishing like ocean foam. He wondered briefly if the skirt had had lace originally or if she had used it to hide a badly frayed hem like so many other young ladies did during these difficult times. She wore no hoops or crinolines beneath her skirt, but he did glimpse pristine white petticoats and the tips of her worn, scuffed shoes.

Shaelyn said nothing. The expression on her face spoke for her. Remy kept his gaze steady on hers, frankly admiring her blushing cheeks and flashing eyes.

"You're staring daggers at me, Miss Cavanaugh. Does the color of my uniform offend you?" he asked, unable to resist.

"The color of your uniform makes no difference to me, sir." Her eyes narrowed as she spoke, yet still glittered like rare dark sapphires. "What offends me is the color of the blood that runs so freely because of this war. What offends me is the way you all do whatever you all damn well please, without thought for the consequences of your actions. What offends me, at the moment, is you!"

"I'm sorry you feel that way, Miss Cavanaugh." He'd always admired a woman with strength and courage, with character, with what his mother called fortitude. Shaelyn Cavanaugh seemed to have all that and more, and he rather enjoyed this confrontation, despite the circumstances, despite how her attitude had changed. It made him feel alive in a way he hadn't felt in quite some time. "Regardless of your feelings, this is the way it is. You must accept it as fact."

He straightened and took a step toward her. Before they'd left the parlor, she'd been willing to swallow her anger and strike a bargain. Now, however, she didn't seem so willing. "I find it remarkable how much your manner has changed since we left the parlor."

She glared at him, her head tilting back on her slim neck, but she didn't move, didn't back down.

His attitude softened as she stood in front of him, defiant and bold. He expected her wrath, even her resentment. Almost welcomed it. He would have been in full fury if his home and business were taken away. "You wished to strike an agreement?" he reminded her.

"My mother is an excellent cook. She will prepare meals for you and your men and I will clean, do your laundry—" she paused and licked her lips "—and anything else you need to have done if you will allow us to stay in our home."

Her words finally penetrated his brain. No wonder she looked at him as if she would happily stab him through the heart. His blood ran cold as he realized she assumed by confiscating her home, he'd be asking—no, telling—them to leave, throwing them into the street. He'd seen it happen before. No doubt they had, too. Truthfully, he *had* planned to ask them to leave, though Jock had asked him to allow Shaelyn and her mother to stay. He hadn't quite made up his mind....not until he met her and then everything changed in a split second.

He should disabuse her of her misinterpretation at once but just...didn't want to. No one had dared to stand up to him such as she had in a very long time, and the longer they stood staring at each other, the more fascinated he became. She drew in her breath, the flesh above the décolletage of her white blouse turning red. A vein throbbed along the side of her neck, drawing his attention to the soft column of her throat. His gaze rose higher and he watched the subtle shading of her eyes darken to almost violet.

He hid the smile that threatened to turn up the corners of his mouth. "You and your mother may stay with conditions."

"And what would those conditions be?"

"You will treat my men with respect, regardless of the color of their uniform or the reasons they are here."

"I would have it no other way," she told him, her mouth set. "By the same token, I will have the same from you. My mother is a kind, gentle woman, Major, and naive in many ways. I will not have her abused or mistreated, by either you or your men. If we must treat you and yours with respect, then I demand you treat my mother that way as well."

"You aren't in any position to make demands, Miss Cavanaugh."

"I understand. I still ask you to honor my request."

Remy's heart skipped a beat as he gazed into her flashing eyes. They didn't merely sparkle; they danced in her lovely face. He detected no fear in those glimmering orbs of blue, just fury. What would she look like with her temper—or her passion—unleashed?

"It will be as you wish, Miss Cavanaugh," Remy conceded. "My men will show your mother the respect she deserves." He took another step forward and smelled the warm, inviting fragrance of her perfume. The alluring scent conjured images in his mind, images better left alone. He wanted to touch her, to kiss the spot on her neck where her pulse throbbed, to rub his thumb against her lips and feel them soften. "And what of you? Do you not deserve the respect of my men as well?"

"I expect nothing less."

Intoxicated. That's what he felt. As if he'd drunk all the whiskey his father distilled. Her scent wafted gently to his nose and a vivid vision filled his mind. He saw her in his arms, saw them making love until they were both breathless, moonlight glowing on her bare skin, passion flushing her lovely face—

She's taken, promised to another.

The reminder did little to stop the kaleidoscope of visions cascading through his mind. With a bit of disappointment, Remy mentally shook himself and moved away from her, more to save himself from her sensual, alluring fragrance and the images in his mind than anything else.

"I realize this is an inconvenience for you, Miss Cavanaugh, but I will try to make it as pleasant as possible." He gazed into her eyes. The most peculiar sensation settled in his chest, one he could not define, but which made his heart a little lighter. "I suggest we both make the best of a bad situation. I am willing to allow you and your mother to stay. Do we have an agreement?"

Slowly, she let out her pent-up breath and stuck out her hand. He grasped it firmly and a jolt of desire slammed into him. He wanted to pull her into his arms and kiss her tempting lips. Now. If she felt it too, she gave no sign.

He pulled his hand away quickly and cleared his throat. "Please show me the rest of the house."

"As you wish." She led him out of the study, her hands balled into fists at her side, and into the central hallway. Remy followed, admiring the subtle sway of her hips beneath the plum skirt, the long line of her back, the wispy tendrils curling at the back of her neck, begging for his touch.

From the study, they took the marble-tiled corridor toward the rear of the house. She poked her head into the sun parlor, where Brenna held Captain Davenport in subdued conversation. Her mother looked up. Shaelyn said not a word, but the expression of relief on the older woman's face could not be denied.

Shaelyn opened the swinging door to the kitchen a moment later and stood aside. She said nothing as he inspected the room, but her anger smoldered. The heat he'd felt earlier shimmered around her. He couldn't concentrate on the room's appointments. Instead, he felt the intensity of her stare and turned to face her.

A blush spread across her face, but her eyes never left his.

Is that a challenge I see?

He tore his gaze away from her and walked around the kitchen, opening all the cabinets and drawers, inspecting their contents, satisfied his stay at Magnolia House would be a comfortable one.

He finished looking into the cabinets and moved to a door to his left. His hand rested on the knob. "Where does this lead?"

"The cellar, backyard, and a small room where one can remove muddy boots." Her answer was clipped, bordering on rude. "Also the servants' stairway."

Remy ignored her tone as he nodded and limped to another set of doors. "And these?"

"Servants' quarters."

He opened the door to the first room, noticed it was clean, the small bed made, but vacant, as if no one had resided there in a long time. "Where are they now? Your servants, I mean."

"Gone. I couldn't afford to pay them anymore."

He closed the door and walked around the butcher-block counter in the middle of the room. A set of carving knives sat on the surface, and he wondered if he should remove them before they became an enticement for her.

Another swinging door led to the dining room. Shaelyn pushed through it a few steps before him and let it swing back. He drew in a deep breath and stopped the door from hitting him in the face with his hand.

This is going to be more difficult—and more entertaining—than I thought.

He didn't take more than a moment to glance around, but in that time he saw all he needed to see. The dining room table, covered in a lace cloth, seated twelve comfortably. Extra chairs lined one wall and a long sideboard sat across from it against another. The hutch stood empty—perhaps the fine china had been sold to put food on the table.

Shaelyn left and waited in the hall. Impatient, her foot tapped a beat on the marble floor. Remy grinned and slowed his pace to annoy her a bit more.

The ground floor of Magnolia House held a myriad of surprises, not the least of which was a billiard table in the game room and a fine piano in the music room. No artwork adorned the walls, but he noticed bright squares on the wallpaper where pictures had once hung. No carpets covered the floor, either, and the rhythmic tap of his cane seemed very loud, especially in the room he suspected was the formal parlor, which contained not a stick of furniture, not even a plant. Perhaps the furniture and paintings had been sold as well. Or bartered.

"This is a lovely home, Miss Cavanaugh."

"Yes, and I'd like to keep it that way, Major. I would appreciate it if you and your men leave it exactly as you find it." She led the way upstairs to the bedrooms at a quick step. Remy followed slowly,

310

using his cane and the carved banister for support. After so many hours on horseback, his leg felt like a foreign appendage made of lead as he placed one foot in front of the other on the treads. Each time he put pressure on his leg, a fresh wave of pain shot through him. Sweat beaded on his forehead. Still, he endured, welcoming the burning rush. His circumstances, like so many others, could have been much worse and he could have died, several times, since the day he'd been shot.

Shaelyn waited at the top of the stairs, her fingers gripping the banister, knuckles white. He looked at her for a moment, saw how stiffly she stood, and forced himself to move faster. He had too much pride to show her his weakness.

When he reached the landing, he took a deep breath. He didn't apologize, nor did he acknowledge her as his gaze swept the upstairs hallway.

There were six bedrooms in all on the second floor, some with adjoining sitting rooms, some without. All led out to the gallery, which encircled Magnolia House. He inspected each bedroom, mentally naming who would occupy which.

The manse more than met his expectations. His officers, those who had elected to stay with him and not somewhere else in Natchez, including the apartments over the Cavanaugh warehouse, would be quite comfortable here for the duration of their stay. The proximity to Union headquarters at Rosalie was perfect.

Between the last two bedrooms stood a closed door. Thinking it held linens and such, Remy opened it. A smile curved his lips.

"The bathroom," Shaelyn said from behind him.

The small room contained a commode, a sink with brass spigots, and a large clawfoot bathtub. "Indoor plumbing," he remarked with pleasure. He entered the room and faced the sink, then turned the tap and waved his finger beneath the flowing water. Steam rose to coat the mirror and he wondered if there was, perhaps, a copper tank somewhere in the house that kept water heated. It didn't surprise him. Sean Cavanaugh owned steamboats. Surely he could devise something…or pay someone to devise something. Remy didn't ask though. Instead, he wiped the steam away and caught his grinning reflection. And something else—a tile-floored structure in the corner of the room. "What is this?"

"We call it a rain bath." Shaelyn moved into the room, opened the wooden door, and pulled the lever connected to the pipe leading up to a wide, round brass…thing. Water flowed onto the tile floor, like it sprinkled from the sky during a rainstorm, before she turned it off. "Instead of taking a bath, you can stand in here and let the water flow over you to get clean."

He'd heard about them, but had never seen one. And couldn't wait to try it. The structure gave a completely new way to keep clean, and after what he'd been through, cleanliness was something he valued. He said nothing more as she moved past him and stood by the door to the last room, her arms folded against her chest as she waited for him.

Remy poked his head through the doorway. He liked the stark simplicity of this room. The walls were papered in a soft white with sprigs of purple violets and green leaves. The draperies repeated the pattern. An intricately carved four-poster bed took up space between the French doors leading to the gallery. The bed looked inviting with its plump pillows slanting against the headboard.

"This will be my room."

"But…but this is mine," Shaelyn sputtered.

"No longer," he said as he made his way down the hallway. "Have your possessions removed before dinner. Your mother's also."

"And where am I supposed to sleep?"

He turned and grinned at her, couldn't help it. "You could stay with me."

Her eyes widened and color stained her cheeks. She drew in her breath sharply. "How dare you even…suggest…such a thing!"

Remy shrugged. "It's your choice." The idea of her warming his bed brought a vivid image to his mind.

"I am not that sort of woman!" Her eyes flashed with pride.

He took pity on her and relented. She didn't know him, didn't know his sense of humor. She couldn't have known he wasn't like most men, who would have taken advantage of this kind of situation. "You may move into the servants' quarters for the duration," he said over his shoulder as he continued down the hall.

"I thought we had an agreement, Major. You said you'd try to make your stay as pleasant as possible." She caught up with him and grabbed his arm, stopping his progress. Her eyes narrowed. "You said—"

"I know what I said, Miss Cavanaugh." He looked at her small white hand on his arm and felt an infusion of warmth seep through his sleeve. Her touch ignited a fierce yearning in him. In another time and place—he didn't allow himself to finish the thought. "I am allowing you and your mother to remain here, but make no mistake. I am in command. My orders will not be questioned. I don't accept it from my men and I won't accept it from you. Do I make myself clear?"

Shaelyn nodded and stepped back, releasing her grip on his arm.

"I'm glad we understand each other. We are in the middle of a war. We all must make sacrifices."

"Yes, Major, we are in the middle of a war," Shaelyn said, her voice strong with defiance, her body stiff and unyielding. "But your battle has just begun."

She spun on her heel and sashayed down the stairs. Remy watched her, fascinated. "If it's a battle you want, Miss Cavanaugh, it's a battle you shall have."

Praise for *Mischief and Magnolias*:

"Plenty of intrigue, romance, and an unforeseen plot twist will captivate the audience of this spirited tale; enthusiastically recommended."—*Library Journal* (starred review)

For more from Marie Patrick, also check out
A Treasure Worth Keeping.

In the mood for more Crimson Romance?
Check out *A Widow's Salvation by Becky Lower* at
CrimsonRomance.com.

Printed in the United States
By Bookmasters